M000209279

The Sagittarius

Book Three in the Arrow of Artemis series

K. Aten

Yellow Rose Books
by Regal Crest

Copyright © 2018 by K. Aten

All rights reserved. No part of this publication may be reproduced, transmitted in any form or by any means, electronic or mechanical, including photocopy, recording, or any information storage and retrieval system, without permission in writing from the publisher. The characters, incidents and dialogue herein are fictional and any resemblance to actual events or persons, living or dead, is purely coincidental.

ISBN 978-1-61929-386-1

First Edition 2018

9 8 7 6 5 4 3 2 1

Cover design by AcornGraphics

Published by:

Regal Crest Enterprises

Find us on the World Wide Web at
http://www.regalcrest.biz

Published in the United States of America

Acknowledgments

Unlike a few other publishers, Regal Crest Enterprises took a chance on me and wanted to publish this series. My publisher, Cathy, and Author Liaison, Patty, have taught me so much about the entire crazy process of seeing a work in print from start to finish. Besides those two, Micheala has done a phenomenal job editing through all three books and is a master at cutting the fat and streamlining my prose. To all three of you I say thank you from the bottom of my heart. Kyri has always been alive to me, but with your help she has come alive for others as well.

Dedication

Oh, what do I even say about this book? First and foremost it is the completion of Kyri's tale and emotional to me for that alone. So much of my heart and soul went into this particular series and I received the most love and support in regards to my fans. It started on a fiction site and the more emails I received from people telling me how much they loved the tale, the more impetus I had to find a publisher. And while people think that I purposely ended the second book on a cliff-hanger, I can assure you that I was just as unhappy with it as you were. As a matter of fact, the very afternoon that I finished The Archer, I began writing the third book. I couldn't leave it like that. I simply HAD to know what was to happen to her. And as you can see from this book, the last part of the saga is big. There was a lot to cover and it took many words to do it. I'm afraid there was just no way that I could've compiled books 2 and 3 together, hence the sad and anxiety-inducing ending in the second. With this completion though, I sincerely hope you'll forgive me.

As for publishing, the greatest push to see my novels in print came from one person. My beta reader, Ted, is a wonderful soul with thousands of lesbian fiction books and reviews under his belt. I've learned that he knows quality when he sees it and I've come to trust his opinion. He came into my life after I'd already begun writing *The Sagittarius* and I warned him ahead of time about the ending of book 2. He was the one who really convinced me that Kyri's story was good enough to share with everyone, and that I shouldn't give up on finding a publisher. Of course he was extremely unhappy with me when he reached the end of *The Archer* but quickly forgave when a week later *The Sagittarius* was complete. So thank you Ted, and thank you everyone for sticking with me through the end of this series. This one is for all of you.

The Sagittarius (Arrow of Artemis book 3) Cast

Telequire Tribe

Kyri/Kyrius - Fourth Scout Leader/ Gladiatrix/Consort
Orianna - Queen
Iva Biros - Second to Queen's Left Hand
Basha - Regent
Margoli - Queen's Right Hand
Steffi - Queen's Left Hand
Glyphera - Priestess
Kylani - Training Master
Shana - Ambassador
Coryn - First Scout Leader
Thera - First Level Healer
Certig - Fourth Scout Leader
Pocori Zevasdater - Junior Scout (Deceased)
Theodosia - Mother to Pocori
Panphilla Zevasdater - Sister to Pocori
Saba - Scout
Trina - Scout
Maeza - Fourth Scout
Geeta - Fourth Scout
Shelti - Fourth Scout
Malva - Fourth Scout Veteran
Milani - Second to Queen's Right Hand
Cyerma - Second to the Training Master
Deima - Second to Fourth Scout Leader
Semina - Second Level Healer
Degali - Fourth Scout
Taren - Scout
Kerdina - Master Carver
Filipina - Hostler
Gata Anatoli - Leopard raised by Kyri

Romans

Caius Caecilius Claudius Isidorus – Freedman and Slave Owner
Allectus (Allecte) – Son of Isidorus
Aureolus (Aureole) – Captain/ Doctore/ Slave Trainer
Gaius Claudius Marcellus – Slave Owner
Calcineus - Slave Overseer
Aelia – Slave Gladiator Attendant
Cassia – Slave Gladiator Attendant
Drusus – Whip man on the slave ship
Aethon - Sagittarius Mount
Achillia - Gladiatrix
Gaius Octavius/ Caesar Augustus - First Emperor of Rome or Princeps Civitatis

Centaurs

Risiki - Queen Orianna's sister
Gostig Stonehoof - Risiki's husband

Ujanik Tribe

Bikala - Northern War Amazon Slave
Deesha - Dohre's sister, Scout leader
Dohre - Northern War Amazon Slave
Bagheela - Queen

Kombetar Tribe

Agafya - Queen
Kynthia - Priestess
Ritsa - Queen's Right Hand

Tanta Tribe

Myra - Queen
Deata - Training Master
Baeza - Scout Leader

Shimax Tribe

Alala - Queen
Alcina - Princess
Megara - First Royal Guard of Princess Alcina

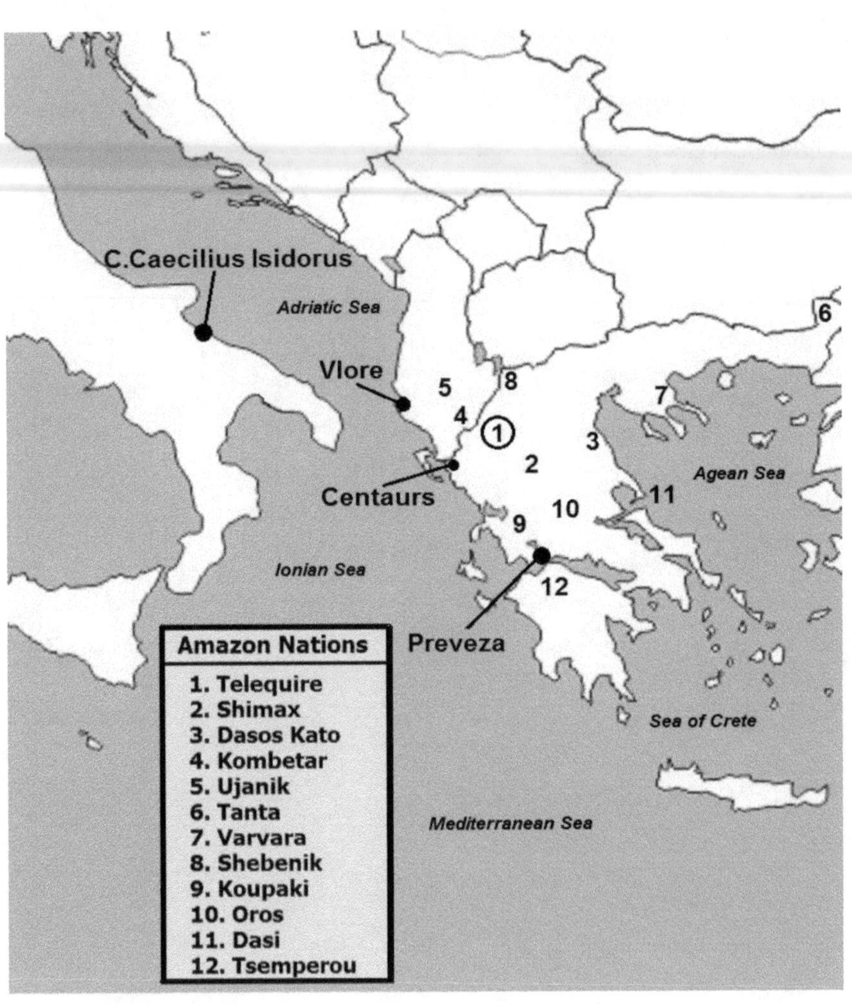
C.Caecilius Isidorus
Adriatic Sea
Vlore
5
4
8
1
2
3
7
6
Centaurs
Agean Sea
11
10
9
Ionian Sea
Preveza
12
Sea of Crete
Mediterranean Sea
Amazon Nations
1. Telequire
2. Shimax
3. Dasos Kato
4. Kombetar
5. Ujanik
6. Tanta
7. Varvara
8. Shebenik
9. Koupaki
10. Oros
11. Dasi
12. Tsemperou

Chapter One

Spoils of War

THE LEAVES WERE a blur of green as they passed quickly by my head. For the first time in what felt like ages, I was free. Great gasping breaths brought clean air in and out of my lungs. Missing was the stench of steel and boiled leather. Gone was the ring of swords and the rippling muscles of Aethon between my legs. I felt my black oak bow against my back and reveled in its comfort and familiarity.

As I approached the village, I grabbed a nearby rope and swung down from the high canopy. The feel of soft loam beneath my feet made me smile. I was home. A sound startled me out of my introspection and I looked up into the eyes that had haunted my dreams for more than six moons. The queen was resplendent in ceremonial leathers and her Monarch Mask. In my excitement I rushed to her, giving no real thought to the fact that she took a step back. In the face of her beauty and my remembered love, I dropped to a knee at Ori's feet. "My queen, I have returned just as I promised." My voice was sore from disuse. Her mood finally registered to me when she took another step back.

"Who are you and how did you make it past the scouts? We do not allow strangers into the village."

Fear clawed at my throat as I looked up to see a Roman's eyes, and I knew him from the slave ship. Green irises turned dark brown as Drusus started laughing. "Hello little slave, so good to see you again. Would you like another taste of my whip, or would you prefer something a little thicker?" He grabbed his crotch and licked thick chapped lips. Rather than answer I launched myself at him and my hands closed tightly around his neck.

"I will kill you, Roman pig!"

I choked him with all my strength and would have continued until he lay dead at my feet save for one small thing. "Kyri." Faint as the wind through the trees, my name shifted by me. White-knuckled hands loosened as I heard it again. "Ky—Kyri!" Dismayed at the familiarity of the voice I looked down. My hands were circled firmly around Ori's neck. Her eyes were open and lips turned blue.

"Goddess!" I released her then and threw myself backward, striking the wall behind me. It was dark save for the moon shining between the slats of the shuttered window. Iva lay on the floor gasping for breath as my heart pounded staccato in my chest. My voice was rough when I could finally manage words that had been spoken too many times before. "Are you okay?"

Iva sat upright rubbing her bruised throat. "Yes." I pulled my legs up trying to be as small as possible on the pallet we shared. She sat next to me and put a tentative hand on my knee. "You were having another nightmare. They're getting more frequent, Kyri."

I closed my eyes to the name and anger took me back to the place of blood and chanting. "Do not call me that."

Risking my volatile wrath, Iva's hand squeezed tighter. "I will call you by your true name, the name of the woman who became a Telequire Amazon and fights daily for our freedom! I will never call you that which the Roman pigs chant after you've danced to their pleasure!"

Sorrow burrowed into the hole created by her words. My eyes shut tighter to the memories of who I once was, and to the deeper thoughts of all I had lost. The barest of whispers passed through my lips as I shook my head in denial. "No, that woman is dead. There is only Kyrius the gladiatrix now. Kyrius the *sagittarius*. Until we have our freedom, it is who I must be." When I opened my eyes again, Iva's grief was laid bare.

"He promised that you'd be made *stipator*. He said that he'd only fight you occasionally. You've nearly made us enough silver to buy our way back home. How do you know he's not going to change his mind about our freedom when the time comes? Romans are greedy and he makes more money with you here than with you gone!"

I shook my head. "I do not know anything but what our master tells me." A glimmering of insight took me then. "Is that why you pray to Artemis every night?"

She looked at me brokenly and my already fractured soul lost another piece. "Is that why you don't?" I sighed but did not answer her question of a question. Few knew of my lack of faith and I preferred to keep it that way. I crawled around her and walked over to the other pallet in the room. We started sharing pallet and blankets when it turned cold since even my status as gladiatrix did not allow me any more for warmth. They wanted us healthy and tough, not coddled.

I sat on the rough-made bed near the window. "You can stay

there with the blankets. It is not long to sunrise. I will rest over here until then."

"Kyri."

I shook my head at her, knowing she would protest my sacrifice. "It is fine. You are safer over there without me." I rolled away from her then and curled into a ball to stay warm. The sun would shine soon enough.

IVA AND I had grown very close in the moons after we became slaves. We rarely saw each other except in the evenings. While she was better off than the slaves working in Isidorus's fields, she still suffered more than I did from the daily degradations of slavery. As a sagittarius, I received plenty of fruit and vegetables because that was necessary for my health. Because I took it as my duty to make sure my sister was just as healthy, I brought extra food back for Iva whenever I was able to hide it away. My trainer knew but never once reprimanded me.

The days blurred together in an endless stream of training and the only pleasure left to me was in the late evening when we would talk. Iva told me of her life as Steffi's second and about her friends and family. I told her about my mam and da, and about the things I missed. Though as time went on I spoke less and less about the loss I felt and more about the rage that grew inside each day. Sometimes I would cry. I would breakdown into what felt like a lifetime's worth of tears and she would hold me close, whispering words of reassurance and hope. Unfortunately hope was a commodity I could ill afford when every day was a battle for survival.

The other light I found in my monotonous gladiatorial existence was actually the son of the *dominus* himself. Allectus was a smart young man and he would ask endless questions as I did my physical conditioning. Whenever I would be forced to eat my noon meal, he would sit with me and ask to hear tales of my life with the Amazons. He would tell me about his mother and the subjects he learned from his teachers. He seemed the sensitive sort and I felt protective of him, but I also thought he needed more friends than just me. It was still nice talking to someone who did not share in my misery or did not have expectations beyond the bounds of friendship. I knew I would miss him once we had gone and I often wondered if he would miss me if I died.

AETHON'S MUSCLES BUNCHED beneath me as we rode around the temporary arena. Six men lay dead, scattered from one end of competition space to the other. Each time I fought they sent more than the previous time. There was a horse cantering around, set free when I shot the sagittarius from his back. Another sagittarius remained under cover behind some trees. All who fought me were afraid of my bow. All were afraid of my reputation. The crowd chanted around me and my blood pumped steady with the familiar rhythm. "Ky-ri-us, Ky-ri-us!" They never seemed to tire, even when my body shook with exhaustion and blood ran freely over the whorls and callouses of my hands.

Two more men approached warily. One was a *dimachaerus* with a curved sword in each hand. He wore light armor and a visored helmet so I was unable to see what thoughts or fears might reflect in his eyes. He was exceptionally fast and had knocked half a dozen of my arrows away since we entered the arena. His speed and style reminded me of my past and I swallowed down the bile that rose on the back of such painful memories. The other man was an *eques*. He was on horseback and carried both a gladius and a *verutum*. The sword and short spear were being held in check by my two remaining arrows and his mount looked to be just as tired as my own. The entire time I watched the two approaching men, I remained cognizant of the other sagittarius. Two arrows for three men. Two horses to my one.

Green eyes and sweet laughter echoed through the back of my mind. How could I possibly win? If I did not win, who would see Iva home? I pushed down the thoughts of loss and self-doubt because neither would serve me in my bid for the gold laurel. Instead I let the chants fill me, bloat me with anger and bravado. The spectators' voices were like fire and fueled me into a barely banked rage. The men of Rome stank of latrine and watered wine and I hated every one of them. The citizens and senators, patricians and plebs, all came to watch the *Amazonae*. All came to bathe their souls in the sweat and stink of death.

I raised my bow and for the first time my arms shook. Exhaustion had near done me in. The gladiators were far enough away that my compromised bow skills gave them the courage to approach closer yet. With a deep breath in and another out, I raised my bow before they could react. The eques fell to the ground below and another horse was set free. I was left with one arrow and two men. The other sagittarius was now out from behind his tree and the dimachaerus grinned at my dilemma. I tried to think, tried to plan for the situation. Who should I save my arrow for? Of the two, the man with the swords was the more dangerous. But he was also the one most likely to avoid my last arrow. The other horseman cantered closer, knowing I was torn.

Another memory surfaced, one from my early training with the Tanta weapons master. I smiled and surprised both men by putting my arrow back into the quiver. Both men reacted immediately. The sagittarius shot at me first. I caught and fired his arrow back at him right before my saddle girth was sliced through by one of the dimachaerus's swords. I threw myself away from Aethon as I felt the saddle go and ended up in a roll. The horse took off and I was left to stare at the madly grinning swordsman. My bow had tangled with the pommel and was ripped from my hand as I jumped free. Despite the fact that I still wore a *pugio* on each hip, to the gladiator I was unarmed. After all, I was a sagittarius and everyone knew that a sagittarius was a good as dead on the ground. I was not just a sagittarius though, I was first and foremost an Amazon.

His voice sounded rough as he struggled to be heard over the screaming crowd. "What's the matter, Amazonae? Perhaps you are not so tough without your bow and mount, hmm?"

I took in the condition of my own body, crouched low in the dirt. I drew my pugiones and stared through the gladiator. With eight men dead and stinking under the hot sun, I was still fairly well off. I had a bruised shoulder, a puncture wound in my left calf, and a sluggishly bleeding slice on my right side. I sized him up and knew he could take my life. What would the man do to finish me? Would he come at me with flashing, spinning blades? Would he drag out my death for the sake of glory and notoriety? I had made a name for myself in the gladiator community of our region, and as a woman, the gladiators did not like it.

I did not answer his taunting questions nor did I acknowledge the pains and worries that coursed through my body. I let the crowd wash over me. "Ky-ri-us, Ky-ri-us!" What would he expect me to do? I spared a glance for the man who watched me intently from the stands, Caius Caecilius Claudius Isidorus. My dominus was resplendent in a formal toga and his son, Allectus, sat to his right. I could not see the boy's face but I knew it would be awash with worry and fear. The dominus was waiting for a show and I knew that failure was not an option. Decision made, I startled the swordsman when I turned and sprinted toward the wall directly below Isidorus.

I was not particularly fast with my wounds and the dimachaerus rapidly gained ground. I continued running at full speed even as the wall loomed large in front of us. I could hear the gladiator's heavy breathing behind me and I knew he would strike in the next heartbeat. Perhaps he thought I was trying to escape, or maybe he hoped to pin me to the wall. He yelled in triumph as I hit the wall with both feet still running. My three steps up reminded me of tree climbing and I launched myself into a flip up and over the top of his head. When I landed behind him my blades were a blur as I came around each side of his neck. The cuts were so deep that by the time his body fell his head was only held on by a bit of skin and bone. The crowd swelled into a deafening chorus and my senses were awash with the metallic stench of hot blood. Like waves of the sea, rage crashed over me and I could not stop my actions. I picked up the man's sword and finished the work my pugiones had started. With a hand tangled in blood-soaked hair, I held aloft my grisly spoil of war. The match was mine.

I WAS ALWAYS given time to recover after fighting. Days after my bloody match with the dimachaerus, I found myself limping through the courtyard. I was tired and jumpy most of the time, never seeming to get enough sleep. Nightmares were certainly the worst cause, but many times I simply could not turn off my mind. It was a candle mark after last meal and I knew that Iva would probably be on her way back to the cell we shared. I nearly jumped out of my skin as I rounded the corner of the latrines and heard the crack of a whip. A familiar voice cried out in pain and I found one of the overseers, a fellow slave, with whip raised high. Before I could overthink my actions I rushed between them, using my body to shield Iva's. His rough voice was loud in the courtyard. "Get out of the way *serva,* this one gets what she deserves."

I refused to move as my Amazon sister cowered in the dirt at my feet. "What could she have possibly done wrong? She follows all the rules here and does her work with no complaint!"

"She had stolen fruit and she must be punished! Now move or you will both get double!"

Iva and I were dressed the same, just as any mid-level slave would be dressed. He had no way of knowing that I was a gladiatrix. My feet never left their place as I spoke the words with anger tensing my muscles. "That fruit was mine. If anyone is to be punished then let it be me!" To raise your hand to a whip man was death but I had raised no hand. I merely practiced the art of passive resistance. For Iva's sake I hoped that he would beat me and let her go. My hopes were not well founded.

"By Mars, you would stand and resist me? I'll beat you both like the Greek *concubinae* that you are!" He raised his whip toward Iva first and I had no choice but to throw my body over hers and take the blows. I felt the remembered pain as the skin split and agony seared my back. While I was harder and stronger than the last time I took a beating, it still hurt. His blows rained down until voices cried out through the courtyard. Then just as abruptly as it began, the whipping stopped.

"What is the meaning of this?" Aureolus's voice thundered through the open area. I was able to turn my head enough to witness the overseer groveling at his feet.

"My apologies Captain, but one was a thief with stolen fruit and the other lied for her. They must be punished." Despite the pain in my back, my body began to shake with impotent rage. I wanted to kill the man, I wanted to whip him until his skin flayed completely from his bones. Iva must have felt me tense for she wrapped a firm hand around my wrist. When I shot her a glance she gave me the most imperceptible shake of her head. She was right, anger would cost me everything. It would cost us both everything.

As it stood I did not have to seek my own retribution because Aureolus did it for me. "They are neither liars nor are they thieves! You are a fool Calcineus for you have beaten your *erus's* prize sagittarius! Gladiators get fruit and whatever other food they need and the other shares her bed." He strode toward the slave with his hand held out. "Give me that whip, *serve*!"

"Please Captain, I did not know."

Aureolus took the whip and pushed the slave to the ground. "You should have known. It's your job as overseer to be aware of what is going on around here. Since you seem to have no sense I will beat it into you!" He struck the man over and over again, until the slave broke down sobbing and eventually passed out. In my moons of training with the captain, I had never seen him lose his temper. Not once. Afterward he called for more slaves to take Calcineus away and to take us to our cell. Iva only suffered one lash so she remained standing while I was laid carefully on my pallet with my back to the air. I had been stripped to the waist while we waited for the healer to arrive. Aureolus paced in the small space, his frustration evident with every step. "What were you thinking, serva? Isidorus is going to be furious at this setback!"

I gritted through the pain and answered his question. "I was protecting my sister. And there will be no setback. I am still on my rest time from the previous match. I heal fast, Captain."

Aureolus abruptly stopped and turned to me with a frustrated look on his face. "But you will not be able to train at all until that back heals. Why are you still here, serva? Surely the amount of gold laurels you've won has more than paid your debt." Before I could answer, the dominus strode through the doorway of my small room. He cast one glance at my back then turned his furious gaze back to Aureolus.

"What is the meaning of this? Tell me what has happened immediately!"

The captain sighed and scrubbed a hand through his short-cropped hair. "One of the slave overseers falsely accused the two Amazonae of being liars and thieves. Your sagittarius sought to protect the other from his whip and took the blows onto herself."

A strange look came over the erus's face. "Is he dead?" Something in his eyes told me that he knew exactly how close I had come to losing myself to the rage. He surprised me with his insight.

Aureolus shook his head. "No, though not for lack of trying on my part. I beat him soundly and sent him off to his cell."

"Well then everything is under control here. How soon before she can fight again?"

My captain gave him a significant look. "She shouldn't." When the dominus looked confused, Aureolus waved his hand vaguely toward me. "Look at her, Isidorus! She's not sleeping, and she's barely eating enough to sustain herself in the ring. That last match nearly finished her."

Anger tinged the erus's words. "That last match was her most magnificent and won almost double the usual purse!"

My *doctore,* my trainer, and the most loyal captain of Isidorus's guards did not answer right away. Finally, he waved Isidorus from the room. Iva gave me a look and I feared that I knew its meaning. Despite the fact that the two men took privacy around the corner their voices were still quite clear. "If you fight her again like that she will not survive. Being a fighter is not truly in her soul."

"No, she is my property, which means she is whoever I say she is! And if I say she is a gladiatrix then she will remain a gladiatrix until she dies or I change my mind!"

"And what of your bargain?"

"She doesn't seem too concerned. The bookkeeper tracks her

earnings and they both must know she has the money to be free by now."

"The money does no good if she is dead. Perhaps you should ask her why she has not spent it."

One of the men gave a great sigh that was followed by a candle drop of silence. Iva had just taken a seat on the other pallet when the two men walked back in. Straight to the point, Isidorus spoke. "Why have you not bought your freedom and concluded our bargain, serva?"

I spared a quick glance for Iva and thought about how to answer. I had not even told my Amazon sister why I was still fighting. "Because I need more silver, ere."

"Why?"

I sighed and hoped that he would understand my motivation. I hoped they all would. "Because I would like to buy some slaves. That is allowed, yes?" I heard others talk about the rules for all the various types of ownership. Some of the gladiators had purchased their own slaves. A slave of another slave was called a *vicarius*. My words brought forth a gasp from Iva just as shock appeared clearly on the two freedmen's faces. Finally I gave him a name and hoped he would understand. "Gaius Claudius Marcellus."

Aureolus continued to look confused but the dominus's head went back and his lips parted slightly. "You wish to buy his Amazonae!"

I nodded. "Yes, ere."

He rubbed his chin in thought while the rest of us waited. Another great sigh preceded his words. "If what Severus said was true, they are merely field labor and should cost very little. I'll make inquiries on one condition. Call it another bargain, if you will."

I nodded, only a little painfully. "And your bargain?"

"You give me one more fight as a gladiatrix."

Aureolus interrupted then. "Not sagittarius? That is not where her strength lies! If you take the bow out of her hands it will be nothing more than suicide!"

Isidorus turned to the other man and gave him the coldest look I had seen since coming to the Roman lands. "You forget your place, Captain. I do not need your permission in any of this. If she wins, the purse should more than cover the purchase of a dozen broken Amazonae and I'll set up the sale. She can always say no and simply complete her bargain now." He turned to me then. "Is that what you wish, serva?"

I shut my eyes to the thought of fighting again. "No, ere. I need to bring them home."

Iva stood then, unable to keep silent any longer. "Why, Kyri? We are so close to our freedom, why would you risk it all?"

Guilt settled over my shoulders like a cloak and it took everything I had to hold back the sorrow that threatened my very sanity. "Because our other sister is lost forever. Pocori will never go home. I failed her and I will not fail the others!"

Her eyes told me more than any words that she understood. Iva was someone who had always been outside my circle. We were not close in age and, until we were taken as slaves, we had been nothing more than strangers. We were acquaintances thrown together by fate and circumstance. But since we had been sharing space, she had come to understand me. More than the captain and more than our master, she knew the tenderhearted girl I had been. And she also felt pain for the death of Pocori, our most junior scout and sister Amazon. Barely sixteen summers, Pocori had killed herself rather than become a slave to the carnal pleasures of Romans. I knew her death would haunt me for the rest of my days.

The dominus gave me one more significant look before nodding at my answer. Perhaps he knew me as well. "I'll inquire about purchase, or possible trade. His villa is about a day and a half ride to the south. I'll send a messenger out tonight and let you know when I receive his answer. If he agrees to the sale, we will expand our bargain. The new bargain being that if you win one final match, I will let you pay double for you and the other serva's purchase fee, and single what I pay for the other Amazonae. After that I'll give you manumission papers for all and see you to the nearest port. Do you concur?"

I thought for a heartbeat and went out on a limb. "You can pit me against whomever you like, but if I die please uphold my bargain with Iva. Let them free in my stead."

Iva drew in a breath and I could see tears shining in her eyes. A candle drop went by and then another while Isidorus thought about my words. Finally gave another nod. "You have shown me and my house nothing but honor, so I will agree to your condition. Now you will rest. There is to be a grand celebration in a month's time and I need you healed and in top shape by then. I'll let you know as soon as I hear from Marcellus."

The men left our room and silence covered us like a pall. Iva stared at me with an emotion I had never seen on her face and I looked placidly back. "Are you angry with me?" I watched as her bottom lip began to quiver. Before I could register what was happening she threw herself onto the floor next to my pallet and clutched my arm as her composure broke. Great wracking sobs filled the room as Iva's hot tears coated my skin. She finally quieted long after darkness fell in our cell. I knew her leg would be stiff from sitting so long so I urged her up to lie next to me on the pallet. She turned to her side so she could fully look at me while I remained on my stomach to preserve my tattered back.

"You expect to die, don't you?" Her words were true and I could not deny them. I swallowed and nodded. I had no words of my own to defend my actions, or even to care. I shut my eyes and was startled a heartbeat later when fingertips came up to gently stroke my brow. When I dared to look at her again I saw such deep and abiding sadness. "Please don't die, Kyri. I don't think I could bear it if you did. I—I love you." Shock and understanding rode tandem on a horse of awareness but I had no time to process her words or meanings. As soon as the admission passed her lips, she leaned over and sealed her mouth to mine.

All the emotion, all her passion, passed across that small expanse and I felt myself start to respond. Then as quickly as the fire rose within me, it was doused by a pair of green eyes. A cry escaped my lips as I turned my face away. "I—I cannot. I am sorry, Iva, but my heart will always belong to Ori. Even if she does not want me after all I have done."

The other woman gave me a watery smile but nodded her head anyways. "I understand. I just had to get it out. But you need to be aware that going home will mean nothing to me if you are dead."

Her words prompted the memory of Aureolus's words from before my first gladiator match. They seemed fitting. "Well then, I will not be dead." She sighed at my blithe manner and eventually turned away from me. Long after her breathing softened into sleep I continued to stare at the back of her head. I had no idea that she cared for me so deeply. While I hated hurting her, she had to know that another held my soul tightly within her grasp. At least I hoped she still did. There was no Artemis for me, there were no gods. But I still held another prayer deep within my heart. "Please Ori, do not let me go."

Chapter Two

Oath-breaker

JUST AS I predicted, my back healed fast. Within a fortnight I was training for my final match. The dominus was successful in purchasing the Amazons from Marcellus and assigned them to work in his own fields until our bargain was concluded. Aureolus had me drilling with two swords but he had no idea what or whom my match would be against. The dominus wanted a show and that was as much as either of us knew. To be safe, we also continued to place significant emphasis on my unarmed combat training and my work with the pugiones. Each day I threw myself wholeheartedly into my training and each night I pretended to sleep while Iva wept beside me. Many times I would wake to feel her touching my face and I was surprised that it caused no reaction in my sleep. While my nightmares came and went, there were no more incidents of physical violence toward my bedmate.

Through it all, I continued to battle with my episodes of rage. The worst led me to break the shield arm of a practice opponent. The first few days of the new sun-cycle were cold and each sword blow was felt all the way up my arms. Eventually my hands would go numb and the captain would call a break. He said I had to be able to fight in the cold because my last battle was fast approaching. As it turned out, my final match as a gladiatrix would take me all the way to Rome. There was to be a coronation for the first emperor of Rome, Gaius Octavius. Apparently he had been adopted by his great-uncle and changed his name to Caesar Augustus to honor the man. Aureolus said that it was common knowledge that the powerful Roman had rejected monarchical titles and asked to be called Princeps Civitatis instead. First Citizen of the State still seemed a bit egotistical to me but I was no Roman to judge their governing practices. I was merely a slave providing entertainment.

We traveled for ten days, staying in *manciones* each night. The staying places were frequently overrun by concubinae and thieves but Isidorus seemed unconcerned. Of course we also had a score of guards, Aureolus, two other gladiators, and eight domestic slaves with us. We came into the city late on the tenth night, which was a lucky thing since wagons were not allowed in during the day. One of the other gladiators said it was because they made too much noise. We stayed at our master's *domus* near the city center. With only the light of torches, I could barely make out the inlaid marble paneling and frescos that adorned the great entryway and walls. I was given the honor of having a guest room and two slaves to assist me, both of them familiar. Since my first fight as a sagittarius, Aelia and Cassia had attended me numerous times and I thought it strangely fitting that they would attend me for my last.

I found the city of Rome itself to be a marvel. Roads were paved in stone and buildings were of stone as well. We followed the aqueducts into the city and I got a much better view of them from my balcony the next morning. The sun rose to a clear but cold sky, though I was lucky enough to have a cloak for the trip. The gladiators had to attend the public functions each day that we did not compete. The dominus always requested that I wear the blue tunics to such events and I had to admit they suited me well.

Because we arrived a few days before the ides of *Januarius*, we had plenty of time to train with Aureolus during the day and for the dominus to show us off each night. The evening before the gladiatorial matches was much the same as all the others. The only difference being that Isidorus hosted a *convivium* in his great dining room instead of having us go to another villa. Music played while the slaves served the wandering Roman patricians. Copious amounts of watered wine flowed freely from their cups though none of us gladiators partook. That evening, after the feast and revelry were concluded, I was once again attended to in the baths by Aelia and Cassia. They fulfilled their duty though I was hard pressed to endure their touch. Sleep was a surprising bliss when it found me shortly after.

I HAD NEVER fought in such a grand place as the forum in Rome. Even as we approached the space, the sound of the crowds of people was deafening. I still had no clue what the dominus had planned for me. One thing that caught my attention at the beginning of the trip was that he purposely left Allectus at the villa. I thought maybe he considered it too dangerous since I had saved the boy already once. Or perhaps he was planning for my death and did not want to hurt the boy. He knew that Allectus and I had become friends of a sort. It was a strange occurrence between the young son of a slave owner and a slave. I did not think my erus completely approved of the days his son spent watching my training after his own lessons were complete. But the dominus had plenty of opportunities to interrupt us as I told Allectus stories about my life as a fletcher, the leopard I had befriended back home, and of my time spent with the Amazons. Isidorus never said a word. Allectus was a quiet young man but good company nonetheless. My time with him was a necessary reminder of all I fought for each time I donned the sagittarius armor and mounted Aethon.

After the opening celebration I found myself armored but wore no helm, as was the practice for female gladiators. Aureolus warned me that not only would I be fighting another gladiatrix, but there was to be a surprise opponent as well. While he checked the edge on my swords, a little ball of dread formed in my gut. I did not like surprises, especially ones in the arena. Every time something new was added I was forced to delve further into the persona of Kyrius and I lost a little more of who I had been.

One of the thoughts that kept me up most nights was whether or not I would have anything to come back to in the event I was no longer a gladiatrix. Before I could become distracted further down a path of self-doubt and worry, Aureolus spun me around to face him. "Serva, listen to me well!" He caught my attention immediately with the low urgency in his voice. "You cannot go in there expecting to die. While I do not know what Isidorus has planned for you, I know that he is expecting a show, a grand finale from you. This will be your hardest match yet and you must win that laurel! If you need incentive to fight then think of that mate you left back home. Think of your fellow Amazonae who are expecting you to lead them back to their families and friends." Then, with an unexpected insight to my deepest feelings and thoughts, he gave the last of his advice. "Be Kyrius if you must, but do not let go of Kyri. Neither one must die in that arena, do you understand? Kyrius will win the battle for you, but Kyri will be the one going home to Greece."

I cast my eyes to the ground, nearly undone by the way his words stoked the fears inside me. "But what if they are one and the same? Or what if Kyri is already dead?"

He shook his head and gave me a sad smile. "I know Kyri is not dead because she is the tenderhearted woman who wears the sacrificial whip scars on her back. She is the one who sneaks food to the other slaves and gives Allectus lessons in private. No, Kyri is not dead. She is merely waiting for her sun to shine again." He stepped back suddenly and I knew it was time.

I listened as the other gladiatrix was announced first, along with her sponsoring patrician. The gladiator with the most wins was always announced first as a sign of respect and honor. When my name was announced, there were not so many cheers. I assumed it was because my face and reputation were new to the city of Rome. When I entered, the other gladiatrix, Achillia, was at the opposite end of the arena. I was dismayed to see she carried a short Roman bow with a full quiver, as well as a gladius and pugio. Immediately prompted into action by her first shot, I caught her bolt and threw it to the ground. Then I drew only one of my swords and kept my left hand free as a defense against more of her arrows. Being the only one shooting, I was confident that she would not hit me. I started to advance but was brought up short by what sounded like wood being cut with a copper-bladed saw.

Both of us looked around and did not see anything until I heard the sound again. It was familiar. My gaze was drawn to movement at an adjacent side of the walled-in forum. A door opened and the familiarity was explained when two leopards came through. They were beautiful creatures, clearly a few sun-cycles older than Gata. A trickle of sweat started down my temple at the thought of having to face such beasts with nothing more than my swords. It would be suicide to let either cat close to me. As I warily watched them stalk around and growl, tingling marched up my spine. I caught the arrow before it could hit me and threw it away. I needed the bow that the other gladiatrix had in her hand. I also needed to avoid the teeth and claws of our new adversaries. It was not going to be an easy task because the two leopards looked half-starved and the other gladiatrix would not want to be their meal.

I made my way slowly around the opposite wall of the temporary arena. Having spent so many moons watching Gata grow I knew that it would only attract their attention if I tried to run. Despite Achillia's greater record she clearly knew nothing about the large cats. Seeing me come closer with every step, she darted toward a wagon, perhaps hoping to use it for cover. From what I was not sure since she was the only one with a bow. She fired one more shot at me then turned and fired an arrow at the nearest cat. Unfortunately it leaped forward at the last possible heartbeat and the arrow stuck in the meaty muscle of its hindquarters. The growling let us know that it was injured, but also angry.

Because of her frantic run to the wagon, and my slow movements, she garnered all the attention from the beasts, a fact that relieved me immensely. In my head I was counting her arrows. If she were not careful, she would use them all up before they could take care of the great cats. Seeing that she missed a killing blow on her first shot at the leopard, Achillia began to panic. She shot two more arrows at me and another at the cats that had backed out of range. I tucked the last arrow she shot at me into the empty gladius sheath on my back, for safekeeping. I could see that her quiver was nearly empty and neither cat had sustained more injury. They were wary, as was I.

My slow movement had finally brought me around behind the gladiatrix just as the injured cat charged her. Her aim was better the second time and she successfully put an arrow through the wounded leopard's chest. That was one opponent down and two more to go. While she was momentarily distracted I came at her from behind. She quickly dropped the bow and drew her gladius, bringing the blade around just in time to deflect mine. We traded blows for candle drops, wearing ourselves out without making much headway, all while keeping an eye on the circling cat. Unfortunately, she was the better swordswoman and eventually I lost my blade to her. I dove to the side and drew my pugiones but when I came back up my attention was split. An idea formed and I called out to Achillia. "Gladiatrix, we can defeat the beast together then continue to fight for the Roman pigs. What say you?"

In that moment I wished that the gladiatrices wore helms to cover their faces. It was then that I saw clearly the person I had become. Sure as we both stood there with blades in hands, rage washed over her and through her. Her face became that of Kyrius, and dozens of other gladiators that I had seen since becoming a sagittarius. She screamed at me with her anger burning so bright. "I am Rome! The only one who will be defeated this day is you, Amazonae!"

She ran toward me then with her sword held in the air and I dropped into a defensive crouch with my two blades. Seeing her prey fleeing, the great leopard chose that moment to attack. I called out a warning to Achillia but it was too late. The great cat leaped onto her from behind and fastened its powerful jaws to the back of her neck. She struggled even as the leopard's claws tore her skin to shreds. The gladiatrix screamed as the beast broke her neck and spilled hot blood to the paving stones at our feet. I glanced around, desperately searching for the bow that was dropped. Not finding it, I quickly re-sheathed one pugio and drew my other sword. I would need the longer reach if I hoped to survive against one so magnificent.

Heartbeats went by before the cat released Achillia and turned its piercing golden-green eyes toward me. The sound of the crowd soared to greater heights and I began to make out small pockets of that familiar chant. Though I supposed the Romans were a fickle bunch and if they had known the great cat's name, they may well have chanted that too. I circled to my right and the cat mirrored my actions. The Telequire solstice ceremony came back to me as each foot followed the other. The priestess's words sounded clear in my head despite the outside cacophony. I repeated them to the best of my memory as I circled across the dirt and stone.

"Hail to our goddess Artemis. She who is the hunter, she who is hunted." I struggled to remember other lines in the chant, trying to remember all that she stood for and defended. "Lady of silver moonlight, dark goddess rising over the trees of the forest. Lady of the deep forest pools that sustain the hidden life of the darkness." I could see the cat getting restless and knew it would not wait much longer to come at me. Still the words spilled forth from my mouth. "We ask you, goddess of the forest waters where all wild things slake their thirst, to show us our own secret pools of wisdom. Give us your blessing that we may send our wildest parts to drink in safety from all that would harm them. And let us accept those parts of us and find comfort in their continued freedom." I stopped circling and let the chanting wash over me. I let the focus take me and released my rage into the words of my prayer. "In this nation, followers of the goddess of the hunt, we revere women and wild things and we honor the life giving forest."

I swore an oath when I became an Amazon and part of my pledge came back to me with the force of a hammer blow. "By leaf and by arrow, my creed and my heart, I promise to maintain the balance, and for everything I take from this world I will return something of equal value." What had I done since coming to Roman soil? I watched a sister die rather than be touched by the hands of Roman filth. I allowed another woman to be killed without defending her. I had witnessed one of Artemis's own wild creatures die by the very arrows that I seemed to live by, and I did not intervene. And to return to my family, my friends, and my love, I would have to send the Goddess another one of her creatures. I had become an oath-breaker.

I straightened in that moment of horrific self-discovery and the crowd swelled, sensing I was on the verge of imminent action.

"Ky-ri-us, Ky-ri-us." They continued on and on until I could not take it anymore. Rage returned. I screamed in fury at the animal and that was all it took. With two great strides the cat leaped into the air at me. It was as if everything slowed down. The tingling marched up my spine and I reacted by dodging to the side. A claw raked across one thigh where it was bare below the armor as I continued my spin in a full circle. Sword in motion, I brought it down onto the back of the leopard as her momentum carried her by me. She dropped like a stone into the dirt and I dropped with her, my leg throbbing fiercely and bleeding out my life's blood.

I looked sadly at such a beautiful creature brought low by the blow to her back. I crawled to her then as she panted in the dirt and I mourned at how much she looked like my Gata. And in a way it was my friend next to me in pain. I dropped my blades and ran both hands through her fur, remembering where I came from. She could not stop me nor could the intense pain radiating from the claw wounds in my leg. I knew that I had to finish things and let her go back to Artemis in peace. Tears mingled with the sweat and dirt on my face as I reached back to pick up my gladius. Once the gladius was in hand, I placed the tip to the leopard's chest and said one last prayer. "I am so sorry, my beautiful girl. Artemis forgive me." The blade slid home and then she was no more. I could not stop the sob from escaping but I quickly buried my sorrow when the crowd broke through into awareness. I had to hold on for just a little while longer.

The far door opened and two more gladiators entered. Cursing Isidorus, I ripped the bottom of my tunic and quickly tied it around the leg that sluggishly pumped blood. Then with the help of my gladius I stood to look around for anything that could help with the next fight. Triumph washed over me as I spied exactly what I would need. I tested my leg and knew it would be a hindrance should I try to run. Unfortunately I had to make it to the dropped bow before they drew close enough to do me damage. The gladiators began running toward me and I bolted toward Achillia's body. I picked up the bow when they were twenty paces away and grabbed a nearby arrow when they were at fifteen paces.

The first man went down to an arrow in the throat and the second gave a victorious yell at seeing my only arrow gone. I knew I would not be able to take him with my injury so grave. It was then when I thought all would surely be lost that I remembered the arrow in my sheath. I reached back and smiled as the familiar nock end fit easily between my fingertips. As quick as a man set on murder could be, his fifteen paces turned to ten and less. Just as he drew his sword back to strike, I nocked my final arrow and shot him right in the eye. His sword fell from lifeless fingers as death brought him his last sleep. I held my breath and looked around for another challenger but none appeared.

As the crowd continued to chant, I searched and collected both my swords and then made my way to the center of the temporary arena. Pain and exhaustion robbed my steps of surety but I still found myself standing in front of the Roman who would be emperor. While I hated who I had become and all those that died by my hands, I was grateful for the opportunity to see myself free. Caesar Augustus acknowledged me as I bowed deeply and kissed bloody blades. The crowd continued to chant for Kyrius, but I knew she was dead. I felt myself smiling even as I collapsed to my knees on the ground, my blood soaking the dry earth like a sacrifice.

I WOKE IN my room at Isidorus's domus and could see that night had fallen full. I had been stripped and had my wounds bandaged. There was a light cover over my body and I shivered at the chill of so little protecting my skin. Aelia sat on a pallet nearby, seemingly lost in thought. I took stock of my injuries and was reassured that while I hurt, it seemed distant. I felt drowsy but euphoric and I suspected that whomever had treated me had given me a dose of opium poppy to remove me from the pain. It was a common remedy in Roman lands and for gladiators specifically. I had received it more than once, always with strange reactions. She noticed me then and gave me the oddest of smiles. "Good evening, Kyrius. It is good to see you awake again."

I mentally cringed as she graced me with a name I no longer knew. I searched around for a pitcher so that I could quench my thirst. Anticipating my need, she was up and across the room to bring me a pewter cup of water. After I had my fill, she set the cup next to the oil lamp at my bedside and I gave her a grateful smile. "Thank you, Aelia. What time is it? How long have I been asleep?"

"It's the witching hour now and you've been sleeping since they pulled you from the forum yesterday. You woke a few times but not in such a way you'd remember." I could not believe that I had slept so long! I tensed my leg only to feel the pain and pull of bad injury and worry crept in. Though I remained silent she read my look with ease. "It's not that bad. The healer said it probably wasn't much worse than the one you had on your other thigh." I could not stop the sigh from escaping. It was a strange thing to realize that leopards had marked my skin nearly as much as being a slave had marked my heart. But it was over at last. I had fulfilled my bargain with Isidorus and won our freedom, all of our freedoms.

My breath hitched in my chest as emotion overwhelmed me. It was too much to take for one so battered in body and soul. My precious control came unraveled when relief and sorrow crashed over me like the waves of a vicious sea. I covered my face as the first sob escaped, hoping to hide as the last of my broken pieces fell. In that moment, I realized that sure as anything I had ever known, Kyrius had died in that arena paying court to the lust of the Roman people. But I also knew that the tenderhearted girl, Kyri Fletcher, had died with the gladiatrix. I had no idea who I was anymore or what I had become.

A gentle weight settled on the bed and soft hands wrapped around my bare shoulders to rock me as I cried. My face turned toward the delicate skin of her neck and my sobbing grew louder as I became filled with loss and longing. I wanted to let go of it all. I wanted to feel like me again. Kyrius was a slave to Roman pleasure and Kyri had become an oath-breaker. What queen could possibly want that? Who would understand how empty I had become? Through my breakdown, Aelia stroked my skin and whispered tender words of reassurance. "It is okay, Kyrius. You will be okay. The erus signed your papers yesterday. He said he would wait until you returned to the villa to sign papers on the rest, but you are free now. There is no reason to cry."

My tears slowed then and guilt took the place of self-pity. "What about you? You are not free, and none of the other slaves in Rome are free. What right do I have to this freedom over the rest of you?"

Narrow fingertips tilted my head so I could look at her. For the first time, I noticed eyes of startling green. How had I never seen before? "Freedom can come to a slave in many ways. For me, it is about getting that which I most desire."

My heart sounded loud in my ears as stuttering breath caught in my throat. "And, and what is it you desire? Love?"

She smiled back at me. "Definitely not love. Love is disastrous and full of danger." Her lips were soft on mine as she traced fingers across my jaw and down my neck. I struggled not to respond but I remained frozen in her gaze. Her hands grew bolder and I finally shut my eyes to hers. My breath came in great heaving gasps as I pleaded with her. "Please Aelia, I cannot." But she did not withdraw her hands or lips, and with my wounds I rapidly lost the strength to push her away. Before all was lost, I tried one last time. "My heart loves another!"

She pulled back then and placed a delicate finger over my swollen lips. "If love is what you need then let me be her, if only for the night. Please, Kyri." I thought of who I had been and all that was lost to me with the death of the sagittarius. My limbs were heavy and immovable. When her kiss came again, poppy euphoria and exhaustion robbed my will and resistance slipped away to join with my distant pain.

MORNING TOOK ME by surprise and I woke abruptly. I remembered the vivid dream from the night before and parts of me twitched in the new day. When I glanced over to the pallet, it was empty but my lips felt bruised and my eyes were swollen and gritty from tears. What was dream and what was reality? Had I been unfaithful to Ori or was my mind playing tricks on me? My dreams had not been trustworthy since coming to Rome. Before I could take stock any further, Cassia entered my room with Aureolus fast on her heels. She carried a tray full of food fit for any Roman patrician and my stomach growled to fill the room. The captain laughed at the sound. "Well, it's a good thing indeed that you have an appetite. I've seen how fast you can heal so I have all confidence that we'll be able to leave this place within the next two days. How are you feeling?"

"I am feeling well all things considered. The injuries, while painful, are all familiar to me." I cast my eyes around hoping for more water before I ate my morning meal. Cassia immediately jumped up to pour me a mug.

"Here you are, Kyrius. I put a fresh pitcher out for you so it should still have some chill to it."

I was relieved to see that neither the pitcher nor the mug were the same as the ones from my early morning memory. Perhaps my actions from the witching time were nothing more than visions sent by Morpheus after all. I started eating while Aureolus filled me in on the other gladiator wins of the previous day. My mind wandered quite a bit when he started speaking of various Roman nobles but was pulled up short again when he asked me a question. "How does your first day of freedom taste after so many days without?" I looked at him in confusion and he elaborated. "Isidorus signed your papers yesterday. He said he'd sign the rest when we return to the villa." The memory from my dream came unbidden and goose bumps chased their way down my arms. Oath-breaker. I pushed my tray away as my stomach twisted with nausea. How would she ever forgive me? The captain looked at me with concern. "Kyrius?"

The anger was instantaneous and I flung the tray from my bed. "That is not my name! My name is Kyri Fletcher. I am a—" I stumbled briefly on the words but managed to continue. "I am an Amazon with the Telequire tribe. I am a fletcher, an archer, and the perimeter scout leader. I was the queen's lover and now—now I am free." With eyes shut, I bent forward and cried over my wounded leg. I wept for the friends and family I had lost, and I wept for what I knew I was yet to lose.

Their voices were low in my room but I could hear something in the way they interacted. Some part of me wondered through my grief if there was more to Aureolus and Cassia's relationship than that of a master and slave. Her voice came soft. "She is broken."

His was just as soft but just a little bit louder. "She will heal."

Chapter Three

The Silent Savior

OTHER THAN THANKING Isidorus for my freedom I could barely bring myself to speak after leaving Rome. I avoided company as much as possible for the entire trip home. I especially avoided being alone with Aelia just in case she came to me again. While I was unable to reject her the first time, I was afraid that I would not reject her the second. I felt hollow, empty of emotion and intent. My soul had poured out into the sand of the forum as much as my blood. I still needed to see my Amazons home but after that I had no clue where I would go. I could no longer imagine a future for me, let alone a life in the trees. Iva worried about my silence but I refused to speak of my actions in that last match. Words would not come at all beyond the barest of communication and I knew that it hurt her.

After a fortnight of healing at the villa, I told Aureolus I wanted to leave. With the size of the purse I had won in the last fight, Isidorus let me keep my bow and quiver of arrows along with the pugiones I wore on each hip. While I was sad to say goodbye to Allectus and my beloved Aethon, I felt numb to the rest. My former dominus made good on his promise to pay for our trip back across the sea and for that I was relieved. I was also grateful for the fact that I had enough silver left to purchase supplies and colder weather gear for myself and Iva, as well as the twelve other Amazons that I had purchased.

The town of Brundisium was a day away with the help of a few wagons. From there, it was another day of travel across the Adriatic Sea to the port town of Vlore. We arrived back in Epirus a moon before spring equinox and all but one of us rejoiced. I did not have silver enough to buy weapons but Amazons were famous for making their own. Once we got out of Vlore, we used a hand ax to cut staves for everyone and chobos for a few more that wanted them. They were not the best weapons if we came upon brigands with swords, but I still had my bow and arrows so I did not worry about the dark men of the land. Our first night as freedwomen on Greek soil began quietly. Dinner consisted of a roe deer I brought down and roasted roots dug up from the woods. Despite the cold temperature, the fire kept us plenty warm. As we sat around that flickering light, someone began tapping a rhythm with two chobos on a staff. The singing started quiet and picked up as more and more voices joined in.

"As long as you live, shine. Let nothing grieve you beyond measure. For your life is short, and time will claim its toll." They sang it as a round, then a few voices started to harmonize until the tune was made new again. The song was one that I had heard often, even before coming to the Amazons. Eventually sleep claimed us all as freedom lulled us into dreams of a new day.

While not the best nourished, all the Amazons were fit enough to make good time to the first village of our trip. The one who had it hardest was Iva. I decided it was best to make a litter for her since her leg would not let her walk more than a few candle marks a day and we had many leagues to go before everyone could see their homes and families. Bikala was one of the women from Ujanik that had made the trip to Vlore many times before she was taken as a slave. She assured us it would not take more than five days to get there. She also said it was another two and a half days south from Ujanik to Kombetar. The group consisted of four women from Ujanik, eight from Kombetar, and just the two of us from Telequire.

Over the course of our five day trip, all the women took turns telling their story and I let Iva tell ours. They were sorrowed to hear of our young scout, Pocori, and their sympathy brought my own grief back to the forefront. Every step that brought us closer to the Amazon nations and our home, brought me more fear. How could I face my nation with so bitter of failure coating my tongue? How could I face my queen? I could not voice all the thoughts that crowded my head. As with all the other days since returning from Rome, I kept my own counsel. But at night when all sat by the fire and spoke quietly, I would leave the camp and rage. While they reveled in the freedom they thought was gone forever, I furiously trained and ran the trees around us, trying to remember what the rough bark felt like beneath my palms. More nights than not I ended up on my knees with fingers delving deep into the forest loam. I would return to the camp sweaty and wild, with dirt caked under my nails and dead leaves in my hair. Iva would raise an eyebrow at me but did not ask questions that she knew I would never answer. However, on the night before we were to arrive in Ujanik, she pulled me aside before I could leave the camp. Her words were to the point and I could see deep emotion shimmering in her gaze. "What are you doing?"

I had to turn away from her eyes, knowing they asked for

more than I could promise to anyone again. I felt guilty for my weakness with Aelia because of my betrayal to the queen. But I also felt guilty because the betrayal was not even with another Amazon, with someone who professed their love to me. I had not told Iva all that had transpired the night I won my freedom, nor would I ever. Instead, I gave her an answer she might accept. "I am training. I have been out of practice for nearly a sun cycle and the feel of the trees below my feet is a forgotten memory. I have to stay in top condition to protect everyone, to make sure everyone gets home. Do not worry about me."

I was forced to turn anguished eyes back her way when she gripped my wrist firmly. "I do worry about you!"

"Why, Iva? I am telling you that I am not worth your worry!"

She shook her head and gave me one of the saddest looks I had seen from her. "You know why, don't make me twist the blade in my heart by saying it over again. I know that you'll never return how I feel but I cannot help the worry. Why do you run from your daemons each night?"

I could not help laughing at her statement, and it came out as the torture it was, rather than mirthful. "You have no idea! I do not run from my daemons each night, I have become my daemons. Bow and fletch! It is better my rage meets with the trees surrounding us than with the sisters who depend on me each day. And it is only my exhausted sleep that allows me to forgo the dreams."

Her indrawn breath of surprise was expected but pulling me into her arms was not. "Oh, Kyri, I'm so sorry for all that has happened to you, for all that you sacrificed to bring us home." I accepted the embrace until her words prompted that familiar burn of anger. "But you have to let someone inside to help you or your rage will eat you alive."

I stepped back abruptly, nearly causing her to stumble. "I do nothing that I have no wish to do. I am no one's slave now. I will never be a slave again!" In that moment of fear and anger, I fell back on what was familiar to that broken girl inside. I ran.

After a night spent in the trees, I woke to cold-stiffened muscles and a growling belly. Iva did not say anything when I returned and ate with the group before we broke camp. It was midafternoon when we reached the boundary of Ujanik lands, and shortly after we received a challenge by their perimeter scouts. I made out the approaching troop easily with barely any leaf cover in the canopy, and I stopped to raise my clasped hands over my head. The rest of our group did the same. I had my bow in hand since it was not long enough to wear across my shoulders like my old one. A masked scout made her way to the ground before giving her warning. "You are trespassing on the lands of the Ujanik Amazons. State your business or go back the way you came."

"Deesha?" One of the women, Dohre, in our group stepped forward. She was younger than the rest and had it particularly rough as a slave, but she always maintained a brave face. Dohre had mentioned many times how much she missed her older sister and could not wait to get back home.

The lead scout raised her mask then and we all saw the tears tracking down her cheeks. "Dohre!" She ran to our young friend with a joy-filled heart and spun her around. "Sister, we thought you were dead or enslaved! How did you return?" The other scouts quickly came down out of the trees and greeted the other three Ujanik Amazons. While I was touched to see their reunion, I kept off to the side. Their greeting was not for me. Their joy was not mine.

When the lead perimeter scout set her sister to the ground, Dohre wasted no time in pointing me out. "It was Kyri. She bought us and brought us home. She and Iva were taken from the market at Preveza a few moons after the Western War."

Deesha looked at me then, taking in my hardness and scars. After a heartbeat she held out her arm with a warrior's intention. When I took it, her eyes became serious and even more filled with emotion. "Thank you, Kyri. Our mother died in the Western War and Dohre was all that I had left. When she was taken—" She shook her head to clear away the worst of the memories. "They had to stop me from leaving to find her. I can never repay you for bringing her home."

I shook my head, wanting everyone's curious gaze to move elsewhere. "You owe me nothing. She is a fellow Amazon, a sister. It is my duty and sworn vow to Artemis to safeguard our people."

With just a solemn nod of her head, the lead scout released my forearm and stepped back. After that there was a lot of chatter and catching up until Deesha called for quiet. "I'm going to take this group into the village proper. I want all my scouts to continue with their duty." The perimeter scouts scrambled back into the trees and continued on their way.

Ujanik was very small compared to Telequire and it was only a little over a quarter candle mark before we made it to the village. We had dismantled the litter at the outskirts of Ujanik territory because Iva was determined to walk in on her own two feet. I planned on asking if the tribe could spare a mount for her before we continued our trip south.

After meeting with Queen Bagheela, the Ujanik women were reunited with their families and the rest of us were shown to guest huts. Since there were still ten of us remaining, we had to double up for them to accommodate us all. Iva and I shared a hut and I dreaded the thought of her prodding the tender skin of my anger later.

That evening there was a great feast to welcome their stolen sisters' home, and the rest of us were rejoiced as well. On the second evening there was another feast, except that one started with a ceremony to honor all the Amazons who were enslaved, including those of us from other nations. All fourteen of us received the eagle feather honor from Queen Bagheela. Iva had tears in her eyes when she looked at me, and I felt my stomach turn as the bile rose in my throat. I did not deserve such honor because I was nothing more than an oath-breaker. I had strayed from the path too many times to find my way safely back to the light. I was broken and not worthy of their praise.

Despite my internal emotions, the Ujanik queen tied the new feather into my hair, next to the one that Iva made for me. Her words were quiet on the dais, perhaps because she sensed that I was on the very edge of my sanity and patience. "Thank you, Kyri. Your sacrifice will never be forgotten in Ujanik." I nodded but did not reply.

Perhaps sensing my fragility, Iva did not engage in serious conversation that night and early the next morning saw an emotional leave. The queen had gifted Iva with a mount for our trip south. Being such a small village, she did not have enough for everyone but the rest of us were content to walk. While I missed the feel of Aethon's power between my legs, I was afraid to ride a horse again. I was afraid I would be taken back to my time as a sagittarius and those moments of chanting and blood. I did not voice my concerns. There was no one I could speak with who would truly understand. And all of my fellow former slaves had been through their own ordeals. They did not need me adding to their burden.

OUR ARRIVAL AT Kombetar was nearly identical to the one at Ujanik. Queen Agafya welcomed our group with open arms, especially the eight women who had been taken during the Western War. We stayed another two nights there and received honors again for all that we had gone through. After the first night, Iva and I sported two eagle feathers of bravery in our hair, but we were both sorely missing our rite of caste feathers that had been forever lost to the greed of men. While I cherished the feather Iva had given me as a slave, it was not the same as the original. And it could never replace Ori's caste feather that I had lost.

On the morning of the second day in Kombetar I was summoned by the queen. Iva asked the messenger if she were supposed to come too and the woman said no, just me. My heart raced with trepidation as I followed the runner to what I assumed would be their council chamber. Instead I was led to a hut only a little larger than the guest hut Iva and I stayed in. When she knocked on the door, the queen herself answered. "Hello, Kyri. Come in and have a seat with us."

I followed her into the living space as the runner turned and left. Inside a fire was burning warmly and there were a few low cushions on the floor near the fireplace. A curtain separated the main room from where I assumed her bed would be. My nose caught the scent of something familiar in the air as she led me to a cushion. Two of the cushions were already taken by the Kombetar priestess, Kynthia, and by the queen's Right Hand, Ritsa. They both smiled in greeting as the queen waved me to sit down. "Come over and have a seat. Would you care for some chava? I just put a fresh kettle on the fire a little while ago, it's great for these cold days." Ah, chava was the smell that tickled the edges of my memory. Da loved drinking chava any time of the suncycle. I had not had it since I left home and I smiled at her offer.

"Yes, please. It has been quite a while since I had chava. I was unaware that anyone this far west drank it."

The queen chuckled and poured some of the fragrant spiced tea into a worn wood mug. "Well, I'm from over near Tanta tribe, myself." At my curious look she elaborated. "Much the way you traveled across the land to Telequire to become an Amazon, I did the same in my youth. As for the tea, I was lucky enough to find some reliable traders that started coming through ten seasons ago and they keep me pretty well stocked." I smiled in agreement and sipped from my mug. The liquid warmed me from the inside out and muscles I did not know were tense began to loosen. Nearly a candle drop went by before she spoke again. "You're probably wondering why I asked you to meet with us."

I set the mug down as some of the tension started to creep back in. "Yes, my queen."

She gave another casual wave of her hand. "Please, right here, right now, it's just Agafya. And you've already met our priestess and my right hand, Ritsa."

I nodded. "Yes, Agafya."

She continued. "We asked you to join us this morning because we want to hear your story. Kynthia would like to put the full tale into a scroll for our archives."

Tell my story. She wanted me to tell about all the things that had been done to us. The things that we had done to get back to our current place in time. I could not do it, I could not relive it all for her and the priestess's scroll. My voice was quiet when I finally answered, more of a whimper. I had to first swallow thickly before words would pass my lips and even then I stumbled. "Please, no. Iva can tell you, can give you the story you need. I—I do not have the words." Their faces looked at me curiously and with concern, which caused the nausea in my belly to grow. The room grew too warm and I started to sweat. "Please, do not make me tell." When things began to spin I knew I had to get away, to escape. I stood abruptly and knocked someone's mug of tea over with my foot, perhaps mine. "I have to go."

I turned to flee toward the door and was pulled to a stop by a strong hand on my shoulder. My gladiator training kicked in and I spun in place and took Ritsa's wrist into my own iron grip. I spun her arm behind her back into a painful lock that Aureolus had taught me and quickly pressed my drawn pugio to her throat. The blood pounded in my head and all I could hear were the chants of my slavery. I could smell the sweat and stink of frenzied Romans and I panted as if I had run a race. The woman in my arms did not move, neither did I finish her as I had been taught how to do. We were both frozen in the nightmare of my making. There was a roaring in my ears and all sound was lost as I relived my moments of victory. A voice finally came through, though very faint.

"My queen, no!"

A gentle hand caressed my cheek and the scene disappeared as if it were no more than a bubble of soap popping in the breeze. When I became truly aware again, I was dismayed to see exactly what I had done. My voice was a whisper to the three women in the room with me. "I am sorry." There was a tremor to my hands as I released Ritsa's arm and withdrew the knife from her throat. "I am sorry—I am so sorry." The pugio dropped from my grip then and I quickly followed it to the floor. Pain, grief, and guilt drove me into the ground, threatened to split me apart. Without thinking, I wrapped my arms around myself and rocked in place. I had hurt so many and I knew without a doubt that it had broken something important inside me. All that was left was a woman who was lost and would continue to hurt those around her. I felt as though every day that went by did so with me staring intently toward the past.

The look on their faces became too much so I closed my eyes to the world and attempted to hold back the wracking sobs. When the gentle hands of the priestess settled on my shoulders, holding back was no longer an option. "I am sorry—s—so very sorry. I am sorry." My words repeated as a mantra of pain. I was vaguely aware of someone settling next to me, of arms coming around me with long missed affection. I cried until my nose ran and my breath came in great hiccupping gasps. The tears fell until there were no tears left and I felt hollow inside. I do not know how much time passed. It could have been candle drops or days. When I was able to open my hot and gritty eyes again, the priestess held me firmly in the cradle of her arms, and the queen and Ritsa sat a pace in front of us on the bare floor. The priestess's voice was lower than I expected and had a pleasant burr to it.

"Okay now?"

I nodded and pulled back from her embrace. Embarrassed heat crawled up my neck and face and my ears warmed. I started to apologize again but was interrupted by the queen. "No, Kyri. You owe us no apologies. Instead, I'd like to tell you a short story." I looked at her curiously, wondering how her story would relate to my situation. Finally I nodded and waited. "I was betrothed to a pig farmer twice my age when I was only fourteen summers old. My father had too many mouths to feed and he simply wanted to see me married off and out from under his roof. Despite all my pleading and begging that I had no interest in being a farmer's wife, despite me telling him that I wished to travel and see the land, he gave the man a bride price of twenty piglets and six silver coins. When I threatened to stop eating, he told me that if I didn't eat, none of my brothers and sisters would eat either. Not wanting to see my siblings starve, I tried a different tactic. I told him that I would run away rather than marry a man that had a reputation for lechery with young girls. In response he beat me with his belt until I bled, then he locked me in the storage shed."

She paused and I remembered my own whipping. What must she have felt receiving such from someone who was family, from a man she grew up with and loved? I shivered and she continued after taking a drink from her mug. "Understanding that nothing was going to dissuade him, I became desperate to get away. I eventually worked a board loose and barely squeezed myself through the gap. I ended up deepening the bleeding wounds on my back for my efforts, but I was free. All I had were the clothes I was wearing and my own two feet when I left my homestead. I barely survived on berries, nuts, and fruits as I traveled on foot through the region, heading south.

"Since the time I first heard a bard tell tales of the sea, I'd always wanted to go and see the blue expanse for myself. Unfortunately, my wound became inflamed and tender by the second day. Seeing the state of my clothes and person, many asked if I needed help as I traveled but I always declined. I thought they would judge me for running away from my family, certain they would take me back to my father for costing him a bride price without providing a bride. So I stayed silent and continued along. I could not see the wound on my back, I just knew it was sore and assumed I'd be fine." She paused to stare intently for a breath or two.

"Halfway through the fourth day I was fevered and hallucinating, barely putting one foot in front of the other. I collapsed at the feet of the first woman I ever saw carrying weapons. Her name was Taqueri and she spent a seven-day nursing me back to health. She told me later that my death was such a near thing that she had no idea how I survived its call." After fresh mugs of chava all around, the queen resumed her tale. "As it turned out, Taqueri was a member of the Varvara tribe and together we traveled to her home where I became an Amazon initiate. I even got to see the blue waters of the Aegean before settling in with them. I was with the Varvara nation many sun cycles before wanderlust took me across the whole of Greece and I found myself here in Kombetar." She stopped speaking and I got the sense that she was expecting a response from me. I remembered the distance between Tanta and Telequire and realized exactly how far she had come.

"That is an amazing story. You have come a long way both in distance and in spirit since your betrothal to that pig farmer. Thank you for sharing it."

She shook her head and I grew confused. "I didn't share the story so you could see where I came from. I shared the story to make a point."

I cocked my head at her. "What point is that, my queen?"

"The point that I am making, the moral to my story is, that

sometimes we suffer wounds that we cannot see. And if those wounds remain unchecked, they can and will surely kill us from the inside out. My other point is that more often than not, we need help in treating those wounds."

I sat up straighter, understanding that she had many layers of meaning within her words. Unfortunately I was not able to decipher those meanings. "My queen, please, what has this to do with me?"

She leaned forward and took both my hands in hers. "Kyri, have you never known someone to remain injured at heart long after they've healed in body?" Realization washed over me and I could not help thinking of all that my truest Amazon sister, Shana, had gone through. I remembered the fact that we both suffered nightmares from her attack, though mine paled in comparison. She told me once that she was only able to get over the worst of it when she started spending time with the priestess, talking about all her feelings and fears. I really did not think much of her explanations at the time, I was just happy that she had grown strong in body and soul again. "I—I have. My good friend and sister in Telequire, the one who brought me to them. She was attacked and viciously beaten by soldiers near my homestead. It was the first time I had ever taken a man's life."

I shook my head in denial between our situations. "That was different though, she was brutalized by those men. Despite all I have been through as a slave, I was fairly lucky. I never suffered the aggressive whims of another save in combat, nor was I taken against my will..." I trailed off, remembering the hazy drugged night after my last gladiatorial combat. Remembering those gentle but insistent touches as I protested that I loved another. Bile rose in my throat. "It is not the same."

The priestess responded to my protests. "Kyri, aggression, abuse, force, and rape, they are nothing more than attacks that take something from us we have no wish to give. There are many ways to violate a person. It doesn't always have to be violent, and it doesn't have to be sexual. Sometimes we accept the attack as the only option out of many that are worse. Sometimes we are not with our senses and are unable to say no. Your friend was attacked on that fateful day near your homestead and she suffered sorely for it. But Kyri, it was only that one time. How many times did you suffer as a slave? How many times were you forced to do a Roman's will? How much did they take from you?" I had been staring at my calloused hands, flexing long fingers and looking at my scars. She turned my face toward hers and I stared into eyes gone nearly gray. "Will you tell us your story, Kyri?"

Before I could respond, Ritsa had something to add. "We do know some of the tale. After all, we are one of the tribes nearest to your own. We heard that three people disappeared at the Preveza agora last spring. I was told that there was much heated debate as to what would happen. The ambassador wanted to send people to Roman lands in search of you. But just as with our sisters that were taken, it was decided that they could not risk the nation so foolishly for three people long gone."

I sorrowed but Iva and I had already assumed that would be the case. She glanced at Agafya before she started speaking again. "Telequire was still in mourning when the other Amazon nations began arriving for the Festival of Nations. Queen Orianna did not participate though she was supposed to. I spoke with her once while we were there and she seemed most distraught. No, that is not the right word. She seemed empty."

I closed my eyes to the pain and betrayal. "We—we were courting." I could not say anymore because it hurt too much.

"Ah." I glanced at Queen Agafya and she gave me a sympathetic look. "I noticed that she wore another's feather in her hair. And now that I think of it, the bead was the exact shade of blue as your eyes. You had exchanged, hadn't you?"

My answer was a whisper. "Yes."

"Will you tell us now?"

I nodded and took a few sips of my cooling chava. Where to begin? What words would make the most sense to them, would help them understand? I was not good with words and longed for Shana's silver tongue to honey-coat my thoughts and memories. Before I could stress more about it, I simply began my tale. I spoke of everything that had happened since that fateful day in the Preveza agora. Even as my throat grew parched and my heart weighed heavy in my chest, I never stopped the stream of words that told our story. I looked up when I was finished, feeling as though I had been in a trance the entire time. Even though it could not possibly have been more than late morning, exhaustion tugged at me.

I stood then, surprising the three women around me. I needed to wake up and I needed to wash the tears from my face. Almost as if she could read my mind, queen Agafya pointed to a table a little way from us. "There is an urn of water and a large bowl. You can refresh yourself there. We'll wait."

I nodded. "Thank you." It was only a few paces to the bowl and I only put a small amount in. The water was refreshing on my hot and swollen eyes and it did wake me up. There was no cloth to dry my face on so I simply lifted the bottom of my tunic to wipe the moisture away. I heard a gasp behind me and spun around.

The queen was the one who spoke after heartbeats of silence. "Your back, how many times were you put under the whip?"

I swallowed and tried not to remember the pain of the last time. "Just twice. The first time was on the slave boat after we were taken. The second time was by an overseer at Isidorus's villa, just before winter solstice."

"What did you do?"

My sigh was long and tired. "I did nothing. As gladiatrix, I was afforded better food and treatment than other slaves. Since Iva and I shared a cell, I also shared my fruit with her. The overseer thought that we were both liars or thieves and made to whip Iva. He had no idea I was Isidorus's prize filly. I threw myself over her and took the blows unto myself. He was eventually stopped by my doctore, my trainer. The captain of Isidorus's gladiators and guards whipped the overseer until he lost consciousness. That was the incident that led me to make the last bargain with Isidorus." Even though I tried to tell my tale with a bystander's distance, I still found my limbs shaking as I stood there. A candle drop went by before the priestess stood and approached me.

"Oh my child, Artemis has surely taken you down a long and rocky path. But be comforted that she will eventually lead you back home. I'm sorry for all the pain you received, Kyri, and I'm just as sorry for all the pain you were forced to give. But I'm grateful that you survived and brought our people back to us. Now we just need you to be whole again."

I truly looked at her then, gray eyes seeming to carry more wisdom that what she could hold in her middling age. "What if I am too broken? I—I cannot shut it off, that part of me that was a gladiatrix. And I have nightmares often." My voice broke further as I explained the pain I had given to Iva. "There are times that I—I hurt Iva in my sleep. I have choked her and hit her thinking she was naught more than an opponent. I almost killed Ritsa a short while ago. How can I be safe for anyone again? How can I get back to who I was?"

The queen and Ritsa stood and came over. Queen Agafya placed a warm hand on my arm. "You can never go back, Kyri. All you can do is move forward and try to be a better person tomorrow than you were today. As for the poison inside you, the nightmares, the killer instinct, you have to temper it and try to purge it all to be whole. When you get back to Telequire, find someone you can talk to, someone who you trust. Tell them your story, but also tell them about how you feel too. You learned to be a gladiator, now you have to unlearn. You will need help to heal those wounds you cannot see."

My bottom lip started to quiver and I could not stop it. "But what if they do not want me?"

The queen smiled kindly. "No one would turn away a sister in need. And if for some reason you find that you cannot stay there, so changed as you are, you will always be welcome here at Kombetar."

Chapter Four

Wounds That Do Not Bleed

THE FIVE DAYS south went by faster than I would have liked. Before we left Kombetar, Queen Agafya asked if we wanted her to send a messenger out in advance to let the nation know we were alive. I begged her not to. Iva acceded to my wishes with nothing more than a concerned look. Each step closer to Telequire brought more and more anxiety for me. Finally, after our evening meal on the fourth night, Iva felt the need to bring it up.

"Kyri, you know it's going to be okay, right? We've both been through a lot, but you especially have had it rough. And I will always be grateful for everything you've done to keep me safe." She drew in a deep breath and continued. "I see your struggles and I see your worry and so will the rest of them." She gazed at me in the firelight and for the first time since her declaration of love, it was not awkward between us. "Don't underestimate your friends and sisters in the tribe. No one will judge you for what happened, and no one will hate you for what you were forced to become."

I shook my head because while she was close, she still did not touch on the worst of my fears. "You do not understand. I am not worried so much about them hating. I am worried that they will not love me anymore."

"Ah, you're talking about the queen." I nodded. "Kyri, has she given you cause to believe her so fickle?"

I thought about Ori's singular lie to me and immediately discounted it. It was not a lie born of capriciousness, but rather fear. I knew she would not back down from a challenge, but I also thought it might be better for her if she did. "No, she has not. But I do not think I am safe to be around her anymore. You know how I am now. I am a risk to anyone I let close." My eyes slipped shut, hoping darkness would hold back the despair in my heart. "She is the queen and must be protected at all costs."

Her hand was soft on my arm but my lids stayed shut tight. "Trust in her love for you, and your love for her. Just don't run." Her hand was surprisingly strong as she squeezed hard, immediately garnering my attention. I looked at her and saw tears tracking down her cheeks. "Do you hear me, Kyri? Do not run from us or, by Artemis, I will track you down myself, as lame as I am, and drag you back by your feathers!" I cracked a smile as the image went through my head but was brought back to seriousness when she shook my arms good. "Promise me!"

Though my heart hammered in my chest at the thought of staying, I nodded. "I promise." Nightmares chased me until dawn.

I SLOWED AS we approached the Telequire nation boundary markers. It was dusk and darkness rapidly rose from the ground. Sensing my hesitation, Iva pulled her horse to a stop and turned around to look at me. "Are you coming, Kyri?" I nodded but did not move, could not move. A great gnawing fear had taken over my gut and my feet felt heavy as stone. Iva dismounted her horse and came over to me, and I swallowed the lump in my throat when she took me into her strong embrace. "Sister, it's going to be okay. Have faith in the nation, have faith in those you love."

I shook my head because her words were not the ones that could make it better. "I have never had faith. I do not know how to understand something I have never seen or felt. That is like you telling me to trust in my arms' ability to fly like birds. Do you not see, Iva?" I pulled out of her embrace and slapped a palm to the center of my own chest. "I am not *me* anymore! I am *not* that woman who became an Amazon. I am *not* the Kyri they know and love! I am stained with the blood of Romans. *I* am flawed." The anguish nearly brought me to my knees but I had to keep standing. I was afraid that if I fell to the ground I would never rise again.

My breath caught as Iva took a step toward me but knowing me as well as she did, she quickly stopped again. There were times I could be touched safely and times I could not. It sorrowed me that she had learned those lessons the hard way. I hated being so out of control and I hated not being me anymore.

"People change, Kyri, everyone does. Just as time wears our bodies into wrinkly old crones, so too does it wear our souls. The problem with tragedy and hardship is that it wears us disproportionally to our sun-cycles under the sun. People like us have had our souls aged faster and it leaves us out of balance. Where's your balance, Kyri? You can't find it alone."

Her words, those words, kept repeating in my head like an echo. *Where is your balance, Kyri?* Before I could answer her, I was thrown into the memory of a dream I once had. It was during the time I had traveled with Shana on her journey. I dreamed of my da sending me through the shooting trail back home and his countdown never changed from the number of men I had killed. He kept asking me where my balance was because I had been raised to always give back what we take from the world. And at the time, I did not understand that the balance of taking the lives of brigands was found in both the future and past. It was all the people that found justice in my arrows and all the people who were saved from the darkness of those men. "Kyri!" My head jerked up and I trembled as her loud call startled me. "I lost you for a candle drop. Are you okay?"

I gave her a jerky nod. "Yes.

She mounted her horse and looked me in the eye again. "Are you ready?"

"Yes." I was ready to heal wounds and find my balance.

We made it about ten candle drops into the forest proper before the perimeter scouts found us. I knew it would either be them or the interior scouts. Their rotation kept the Telequire land very well covered and ranging scouts usually picked up anyone that came through when the troop was not in the same general location. I saw them approaching in the trees and gave a low whistle to Iva. She immediately dropped her reins and clasped hands above her head. I hung my short bow over one shoulder and lifted mine as well. One masked woman flipped down from the lowest branch while the rest stayed perched above.

It was dark enough in the trees that I knew she would not recognize us right away but I recognized her. Certig was Second-Fourth when I left, my second in command of the perimeter scouts. I realized that she had probably been made scout leader after I was taken. I had always enjoyed her company when we were scheduled in the trees together. Her positive attitude made the onus of duty disappear more than once. The challenge in her voice was unfamiliar though, as was her wary stance. "You are trespassing on Amazon land. State your business or leave the way you came."

I let Iva answer for us. "We are two Telequire sisters returning home, that is our business. Will you welcome us?"

Certig immediately raised her mask and peered through the fading light toward our bookkeeper. "Iva?" At the speed of an arrow her gaze spun to me. "Goddess! Kyri!" The rest of the troop flew down from the trees at her words and Certig ran to me. I could not control my actions in the face of such a rush. Before thought or words could be applied, my bow was on the ground and I had my pugiones out. I dropped into a defensive stance waiting. Breaths came fast to my lungs, and I struggled to stay in the moment, to stay with them and not delve into my memories. Seeing my reaction, Certig stopped immediately and gave me a concerned look. "Kyri, it's me, Certig. I would not hurt you, sister!"

Iva pulled their attention to her. "Sisters, please. We have been through much since we left. Kyri has been through more. She needs space right now. If you approach her, do it slowly. Keep your words soft and try never to startle her. She lives on the edge all the time now and could easily do you harm without meaning it."

I swallowed hard at the resigned truth and experience in her words. I knew I had much to pay for.

Certig held her hand out then and spoke gently. "I'm sorry, I did not know. We were just so worried about you for so long, I let my emotion take control. Welcome back, Scout Leader."

With her words and the familiarity of the people around me, I finally relaxed. I sheathed my pugiones and reached out to clasp her forearm. I shook my head to deny the label she placed on me. "I am no one's leader now, and I have missed you all." They approached then, my scouts, my people. They wanted reassurance that I was well and that I was real. Then it came, the question I knew would break my heart all over again.

"Where is Pocori?"

I did not know who said it, only that my ears were left ringing in the silence that followed after. Perhaps it was the look on my face or the lack of answer, but they knew then that Pocori would never come home. Iva, always the soft one and always the buffer for me, finally said the words. "She is with Artemis now."

Scouts were a tough bunch, no doubt. And perimeter scouts faced danger much more frequently than any other. But the death of one of our own, the death of someone so young and pure, it was a blow. Certig covered her mouth and turned away where none could see her tears. I knew why. She was Scout Leader now and had to maintain some semblance of control. But the others were not so circumspect. They grieved openly and hard, if only for a short time. They were still protectors of the land and had a job to do. Iva turned to Certig. "We can find our own way to the village, but can you have a runner go ahead and explain the situation to the queen and ask them to meet us near the training master's hut? It should be empty after dark and the less crowd we have for now, the better it will be."

I thought about all Iva had done for me, had put up with from me, and I sorrowed for her. I knew her heart just as she knew mine. Even seeing our time together dwindle knowing that she would continue her days with unrequited love, she still sought to shield me. We had truly become friends. I met her eyes as she stared at me. "Thank you." She nodded, understanding more than what I could put into words.

"Degali, please run ahead and notify the queen. Be safe on the trails with the approaching darkness and meet us back at second night camp."

"Yes, Scout Leader!" The young woman who took third in the previous spring equinox spared a shy smile for me and took off toward the village.

Based on the moon distance traveled and knowing the trip as well as I did, I figured that we entered the outskirts of the village roughly a candle mark and a half after we left the perimeter scouts behind. There were torches lit around Kylani's hut but thankfully few people. Despite the cold air, I began to sweat as we drew closer to the handful of people that waited for us.

We were about forty paces out when I heard a noise that made my blood run cold. It was the sound of saw teeth on wood, the remembered sound of the leopards in the arena. My vision dimmed and in an instant I had an arrow knocked and aimed toward the approaching threat. My consciousness spiraled as I heard someone yell. "Gata, stay! Kyri, don't shoot!" As both cat and woman approached, I was thrown violently into the past. The gladiatrix continued to come at me as the leopard stalked her from behind. My arrow wavered between the two of them, unsure who was the bigger threat. Adrenaline surged through my veins as they chanted my name. "Ky-ri-us, Ky-ri-us—Kyri!" I was snapped back to reality as a body slammed into me from the side. Limbs entangled, they tried to pin me face down but I rolled out from under the body. I left my bow and arrow in the dirt and drew my pugiones to face the new threat.

"Kyri." Someone continued to call my name, but I did not take my eyes off the Roman. If I did I would die and we could never get home. "Kyri, we're home! They're friends! Please, Kyri, drop the knives!"

"My name is Kyrius! And all the Romans will die to my blade and fletch. I will lick their blood from my lips as their flesh sinks to the ground from which they came!" As if I were drenched in the coldest of streams, everything stopped. My eyes cleared for the first time, and I saw plainly the woman who crouched defensively waiting for me to attack.

Kylani watched me as I came back to myself, and I could see the wariness in her eyes. Sadness stole over me then because everything I had feared was true. I was not safe to be around. My first thought was to drop my blades to the dirt and my second was to sheathe them. Instead, I knelt in front of the cautious woman and held out the pugiones hilt first to the training master. "P—please. You have to disarm me." I felt broken and seared by my guilt and rage. In the darkness on our first night home, I was forced to admit to a wound I could not see. "I am—" I swallowed hard. "I am not safe to be around right now. I am not right." She watched me for heartbeats longer and then carefully took the blades. As their weight left, I brought my hands up to muffle the sobs that exploded out of me.

I had fractured into a thousand pieces and they could never understand. Even as I knelt on the ground in front of her, even as I trusted her and called her friend, I still did not trust her. I felt numb and angry, and I wanted to bleed so that people could see a reason for my pain. I wanted to bleed as I had made so many others bleed before. There was a constant terror in knowing that enemies were everywhere. Every time someone so much as looked at me, I wanted to run. And yet at the same time, I wanted to kill them. I was afraid to close my eyes because of the darkness that lived inside. How could they understand? The silence was deafening and Iva's voice was startling when she broke it.

"They trained and fought her as a sagittarius and a gladiatrix. She fought too soon and too often. They took someone with a tender soul and made her into a killer, and it broke something inside. She has nightmares and she rages. She doesn't trust or touch easily, and she needs our help."

Even after my tears had stopped, I kept my face covered. I did not want to see the revulsion or pity on their faces for the broken thing I had become, for the monster. Kneeling on the ground as I was, awash with my bloodless pain, I did not notice the subtle pressure at first. Someone or something leaned into my side and began to purr. When I moved my hands and opened my eyes, I felt a thrill of fear at first. It was a fear that melted away the instant Gata's head-butted against my tear-streaked face, scent marking me. Her familiar warm presence was like the lighting of a candle in a dark hut, and I cried out as my calloused fingers wove through her thick fur. She was like balm on a throbbing wound, and I had forgotten how much I missed my forest friend.

"Kyri?"

I looked up when I heard her, and the bottom dropped out of my stomach. Ori. Her very voice soothed me and conversely pulled my heart into despair. I was an oath-breaker and I could not bear to even look her in the eyes. I stayed kneeling and I aimed my gaze at the ground just as we had done as slaves. "Yes, my queen."

She continued to slowly step closer, but I did not move or raise my eyes. "I've told you before, it's Ori to you, always Ori."

I shook my head because she did not understand that the woman she uttered those words to was dead. "No, you told Kyri. And I am not that person any more. Kyri was good and honest, she was full of light and honor. I am none of those things. I have lost my honor and broken my oaths." I looked at her then in the light of the torches and moon and became frozen in her shadowed green gaze. It was not the eyes that held me, it was the feather in her hair. Kylani had moved away during my reunion with Gata and Ori had taken her place. To the watchers, it must have looked like I knelt at her feet in supplication and maybe I did. I held my hand out as if I could touch the feather from my place on the ground. "How?"

"I found it in an alley on the dock side of the agora." Shana's voice was another flame lit in my room. "I wanted to come after you. I wanted to tear that place apart, but— " She shook her head. "I knew we could not stay there any longer. We had to get back with the coffers and wagons. We had to let the queen know what happened. I failed you sister, and I've regretted it ever since."

Ori reached out slowly and lightly fingered the blue and green bead rite of caste feather that Iva had made for me. Her voice was hoarse when she spoke. "We all failed you."

I stood abruptly then and was sorrowed to see Ori step back warily. "No one failed me, I failed the nation! I failed to uphold my promises and my oaths and I continue to pay the price. Please, I know you want to speak with me but I am very tired. Things have been difficult for me since we came back to Greece and I just need a little time to accept that this is all real." I waved my hand to encompass all of them. "I need to see that my coming home is not another of my—is not just a dream." I did not want them to know about the nightmares. I was not ready to explain all my weaknesses and broken pieces. "I am officially requesting to give my reports tomorrow. I just need a bath and sleep right now." I glanced at Kylani and sighed. "I understand if you want to put a watcher on me for now, just in case I am outside myself again."

My queen, my beautiful Ori, lost her smile but she answered

me anyway. "I don't see the need for a guard, Kyri. Would you like someone to walk with you?"

Guilt and terror caused my legs to tremble. "I—I am not ready to talk yet."

"No talking, I promise. Please allow me to escort you to your hut." I nodded and she gave a discreet wave to the rest. Shana did not look like she wanted to leave until she was caught in Ori's gaze. After a few heartbeats of heavy silence, she moved away as well. I watched them walk out of sight until Ori startled me with her voice. "May I take your hand, Kyri?" I looked at the shadows around us and shivered. I wanted to keep my dominant hand free so I nodded and offered her my left. "Oh! What is this?" Ori turned my arm over to look at the tattoo of the sagittarius symbol that I received as a fighter. Easily a hand span long, it was stained black as coal could be.

"That is my brand. Many gladiators and gladiatrices are tattooed to discourage desertion. It is also a badge of honor to those who fight. But to the Romans, it is a way to permanently mark you as less. Even if a slave were to buy their freedom, no person with a tattoo can be a Roman citizen. My dominus allowed me this when I asked." Goose bumps raised up my arms as she traced the delicate skin of my inner forearm. Though the night air was cold, my body still felt hot when she stood so near. I clenched my teeth together with the strain of holding myself still.

"Did it hurt?"

I shrugged. "I have had worse with less of a result." We continued walking in silence until we reached my hut. Gata entered through the smaller door before I even got the main one open. The inside was clean, if cold. Clearly someone had been keeping my space tidied in my absence and I wondered why. I lit candles since there was no oil in my lamps. I looked around slowly, absorbing the remembrance of what home felt like to me. Ori did not come in behind me, as if unsure of her reception.

"I made certain someone came by each seven-day to keep it up while you were gone. I—I never lost hope that you'd return, no matter how hopeless it seemed."

I looked back at her over my shoulder and waved her inside. "Why?"

When she entered my living space, her eyes were clear as a cloudless sky and resolute as the sun in summer. "Because you made a promise."

I closed my eyes as a sigh escaped my lips. "Ori."

I trembled but did not otherwise react when her warm hand

closed over my wrist. "Kyri, whatever it is we will get through it. You have friends and family here who love you, and we will help you through this."

When I looked at her again, all I saw was a face full of love and faith. A very misplaced faith in me. "I have made many promises since you first met me. I have broken them all."

I waited as my heart and sadness spoke through my stormy blue eyes, and I saw the very moment that she knew. I saw the raw pain wash over her, and it cut my soul into pieces. Heartbeats went by as I watched her rebuild herself right in front of me. She answered when I expected her to leave. "Not all of them. You returned to me." Slowly, to give me time to pull away, she raised her hand to cup my cheek. "I've missed you so much!"

It was too much for me to process. I had lost too much to function in the face of such devout emotion. My lip quivered under her thumb as the first tear dropped from the confines of my lash. Another blinked free as my eyes fluttered shut. There was only one thing I asked for the entire time I was gone. There was only one thing that I wished upon the stars for all the nights I could see. That prayer came true because Orianna had never let me go. All that remained was for me to find a way back to who I was, or at least learn how to be a better version of who I had become. I turned my head to press lips to her palm and whispered the only truth I had left. "You were my only prayer."

She pulled her hand away from my cheek just as slowly as she had placed it there. "Then let that be our foundation. We have both changed since your absence, we have both been changed. From this moment forward let us see if we can remake something that was so precious before."

There was a lightness in my heart from her words, but I knew that healing was a long way down the trail for me. It would not be fair to her if she were forced to wait. "Ori, while it heals my heart just a little bit to hear those words from you, it would not be fair to expect you to wait for me. I am not good. I do not know if I will ever be me again. You deserve better."

She shook her head. "You are worth it to me, Kyri. Did you wait?"

Her words struck me, and I thought maybe she did not understand after all. "Ori, I—"

My queen interrupted with an impatient wave of her hand. "Not that, we'll talk about that when you're ready. I mean, did your heart wait for me?"

Through it all, my love for her was the only thing I could be sure of. "Always. My heart could never be with another."

In a move that surprised me with its memory as much as the action, Ori cupped my cheek and placed a tender kiss at the corner of my mouth. "You already know the way to my heart, Kyri Fletcher, we're halfway there." For the first time in moons I burst out into laughter and immediately pulled her to me. I needed her solidity, and I needed to know she was real. She eagerly welcomed my embrace and continued to hold me as the laughter turned to sobs. I pulled back slowly, grateful that she gave without expecting me to explain anything.

"Better?"

I nodded as I wiped my face with an old cloth on the table. "Yes, thank you."

When I turned back to her, Ori became serious. "I know someone who went to war sun-cycles ago and came back changed. You and he were broken in much the same way. What I'm trying to say is that while I haven't gone through what you have, while I'm not hurt in the same way, I do understand. Right now your body and your mind are disconnected. Fear will prevent intimacy and bonding with the people around you. I'll help you as much as I can but you have to be willing to help yourself too. Do you agree?"

"Yes, but how?"

She smiled at me. "We need to connect you again, and I need to touch you to know that you're real. I expect you to touch and to feel. Embrace your friends when you can, embrace me, learn to let people in. Can you do that for me?"

I nodded with some trepidation. "Yes, I think I can. But what about the times when I am outside myself? I gave my weapons to Kylani, but I am so afraid all of the time. And—and I rage." I looked down to admit the last part because it was the one thing that would not just hurt me. It had the potential to hurt those around me.

"Well we can't have you living in fear. I suspect the fear is often what leads to your rages and flashbacks, is it not?" I nodded and she continued. "You can stay armed in the village but you have to wear wood practice weapons. Okay?" I shivered at the thought of not having sharp blades at my side but nodded again. "As for the rest," She paused as if she were trying to find the best words. "The first step is for you to spend time with your friends. You have support here, Kyri, and you are loved. I'm also here for you any time you need to talk, but I won't push you. Iva can give the report of all that happened and you can just take the time you need. That will be my directive to the rest, okay?"

I smiled in gratitude. "Yes, and thank you. It is still so hard. I know it should not be but—"

She took my hand in hers and gave it a squeeze. "No, it is as hard as it is. There is no set of rules about how you should suffer or how long it takes to work your way through it. Never feel bad, just keep moving forward."

"I—I promise. I will not give up on this."

Ori kept hold of my hand while she continued. "You also need to get back into a routine here. Effective immediately, I'm putting you on restricted duty while you recover. The Goddess knows that having a wounded mind is no different than a wounded body. Spend time trying to understand the things that seem to trigger the flashbacks and rages. If you need space, take it. No one will touch you without your permission, and you need to work on techniques to help you through your feelings."

Ori continued to amaze me with the wide range of knowledge she possessed for someone so young. I was impressed and struck with a feeling of inadequacy. "How do you know all this?"

The darkness of unpleasant memory passed across her eyes and she did not answer right away. "My sister's husband, Gostig. He went away to fight with the Spartans at the time we had all just come to adulthood."

I looked at her in surprise. "I did not know Spartans let centaurs fight with them."

She gave me a strange look but continued. "He was only gone three summers but it changed him. He came back hard and angry, distrusting. It was quite a while before he could learn to love again. Despite the fact that he was no longer the man that Risiki fell in love with, she still loved him and stayed by his side. And eventually she fell in love with him again."

She swallowed and looked at me, and I was caught in the intensity of her gaze. "He broke her arm once while he was in the grip of one of his nightmares. It wasn't her only injury, nor was it his." Anxiety blossomed in the pit of my stomach at the thought of seriously injuring someone in my sleep, and I was taken back to the dream where I choked Ori to death. My face must have shown my terror and dismay because she rushed to continue. "Kyri, settle. There is a reason I'm telling you these things. He got through it and hasn't had a flashback or rage in sun-cycles. Risiki says he rarely even has nightmares any more. He healed, Kyri, and you will too."

It hardly seemed possible that I could eventually live in a

world that was not always on the edge. Hope was an emotion I had been long without and it filled my chest. I could not meet her eyes because I did not want to lose control again. But I said what was in my heart anyway. "Thank you, Ori."

She must have sensed the tenuous hold I had over my emotions because she let go of my hand and stepped back. "Will you be okay if I leave you here? Do you need anything, food or water?" My heart raced at the thought of leaving my hut, but I also resisted the thought of someone helping me. I shook my head but continued to stare at our feet. Unfortunately my traitorous stomach made me into a liar just as she turned to leave. My eyes filled with tears as Gata gave a small growl back. I could not help looking up as Ori gave a chuckle, and my heart soared at the beautiful face of my queen. "See, Kyri? Not all the paths have changed, you'll find your way back before you know it. I'll send someone around in a half candle mark with something for a late supper."

I nodded and walked her to the door. Before I opened it, I turned toward her and knew I had to make her understand what was inside me. "I—I really am thankful for everything. I know it is going to be difficult but I will do all that I can to be better for you."

"May I touch you?" Though nervous, I nodded to the woman that terrified me and held my heart. She slowly brought both hands up to cup my cheeks. Then, without losing eye contact she tilted her head and repeated the kiss from earlier. "Just be better for you. I'll love you either way." She left me standing there, fingertips pressed to the exact spot her lips had warmed moments before. My thoughts whirled and screeched like seagulls in a port city. I was home.

Chapter Five

Arrow of Artemis

IN LESS TIME than the queen had promised there came a knock on my door. I approached it with some trepidation and cracked it open. I was not terribly surprised to find Shana holding a tray with a cloth covering the dishes on it. "May I enter?" I nodded and stepped aside. When her hands were unencumbered, she turned to me with tears in her eyes. "Goddess, Kyri."

I stared into her watery amber depths and watched as my friend and near-sister covered her mouth in an attempt to stop the uprising of emotion. Her words were muffled around delicate fingers. "I should have followed, I should have come for you. We could have saved you—"

"No! You could not have saved me, no one could have saved me. Slavery is a sickness, a disease that affects the entire body of Rome. You would have gone in and ended up the same as us. I got lucky and circumstances allowed me to save myself but most do not get that chance." I shook my head at the thought of Shana at the hands of slavers. My sister was very attractive with her waves of dark curls and eyes of golden amber. I shuddered at the thought of her suffering in a Roman brothel. "It does not matter now because that is the past. Changed though I am, I have come home and this is the time that matters." I watched as she pulled herself together. "I have missed you, sister."

She took a step forward then hesitated. "I've missed you too. Can I hug you?" I remembered Ori's words and nodded my head at her despite the anxiety I felt. The very heartbeat that her arms came around me, my fear of her touch melted away. I felt a wash of love, acceptance, and family, and was nearly undone. I held myself together, albeit with difficulty. I did not want to break down again. I wanted to start building myself back up. Eventually I had to pull away because the smell of the food she brought overrode all my other senses.

I shrugged as my stomach gave a rumble. "Sorry, but we last stopped for rations at midday and my stomach is gnawing my backbone now." I sat down and waved at the tray I had uncovered. "Have you eaten, are you hungry?"

Shana shook her head. "I'm fine, thank you."

"Talk to me, sister."

She looked at me curiously as I stuffed a date in my mouth. "What do you want me to say?"

I chewed and swallowed as I looked back into her too-sad eyes. "I feel like I have been gone a lifetime. Tell me about what I have missed. Tell me the boring things and the normal things. Tell me of all your daily mundanity so that I can be convinced this is all real and not just another ni—" I stopped abruptly, nearly forgetting that there were some things I wanted to keep inside. I should have known she would not let the partial words lie.

"Not just another what, Kyri?"

I looked down as I swallowed a bite of soup. "Sometimes I have dreams. Nightmares." I looked up and she gave me an encouraging nod. "And daymares. There are times when it all feels so real that I cannot tell what is true and what is not. I have flashbacks when I least expect it and I—I have hurt people when I was not myself."

She covered my free hand with her own. "Tell me about your dreams." My entire body tensed with immediate panic and I started to sweat. Shana coolly brought me back to myself when she gave my fingers a strong squeeze. She kept her eyes solidly on mine. "No, I don't want you to talk about your ordeal, or your time away. Simply tell me about your dreams."

I swallowed thickly and stared at our joined hands. Hers was smaller than mine and less scarred. But I knew the strength was there from the long candle marks we sparred together with daggers in the practice ring. You have to have a good grip in order to fight knives against bigger weapons. You do not have momentum on your side as you would with a sword. All you have is quickness and the strength of your hands. "The fear and horror all feel so real, mostly because they are things I have experienced time and time again. Sometimes they are about fighting in the forums, sometimes they are about the people I knew before. But they always end up twisted and I rage in my sleep. I have hurt Iva too many times. I nearly killed her the last time and I had to leave our bed to sleep in the cold."

My eyes had cast down while I spoke and when I looked up again the surprise on her face quickly tempered to neutrality. "So you and Iva shared a bed?"

"Yes. We shared a cell and when winter came it was too cold with so few blankets so we shared a bed for warmth. Though with all the times I hurt her, she may have been better off cold."

The cause of her seeming worry quickly dawned on me when she let out the breath she had been holding. My face hardened as bile rose up my throat and I had to swallow it back. I pushed my tray aside. "Do not think so well of me, I do not deserve it. I am an oath-breaker."

Her indrawn breath was loud over the sound of the crackling fire in my hearth. My whispered name was louder yet. "Kyri."

I purposely ignored the direction the conversation was leading us. "You asked about my dreams. I will tell you about the one where I nearly killed Iva. I dreamed that I had come home, back to Telequire. Only the queen did not know me and told me to leave. When I looked into her eyes, she changed into one of the Romans on the slave ship, the one who first whipped me and tasted my blood. I tried to choke the life from him and only stopped when someone called my name. When I looked down it was Ori's lifeless face staring back at me. That is when I awoke and found Iva gasping in the moonlight as my hands stole her breath. She carried the bruises for more than a seven-day after that, but I will carry them forever."

"Oh, little one, what did they do to you?"

I watched for a few heartbeats as the tears tracked down her face and answered before I lost my nerve. "They broke me. I am not that girl who left her homestead so many moons ago. I am not the sister you lost. I have become a stranger in my own skin and I do not like her."

She did not say anything for a candle drop but merely wiped the wet from her cheeks. When she finally did speak she gave me a watery smile. "You will always be my sister, and Goddess willing, there are ways to fix just about anything.

I sighed and let her assurance bolster my thin layer of hope. Perhaps I could make it through with the help of those I left behind. While I had much to think on, I had very little to say after that. She helped me clean up then offered to take my tray back to the food lodge. I let her and, with another hug, I watched her walk away from my hut. After the door was shut, exhaustion seemed to grind my bones to dust and I decided to bathe in the morning. My only goal at that moment was to find my way into Morpheus's realm easy and come out again unscathed. I fell asleep to the feel of warm fur between my fingers and the comfort of an old friend.

THE NEXT MORNING I was in my bed contemplating the

emptiness of my belly when a knock at the door startled me. My first emotion was fear, but anger rode in swiftly behind it. The queen promised that people would leave me alone but I could not even get a morning to myself! Dressed in only a sleeping shift, I stalked to the door and jerked it open only to find another covered tray like the one Shana had brought the previous evening. I looked out my door but there was no one in sight to thank.

After my morning ablutions, I ate my meal and thought on what I could do with myself. The queen had left me very precise instructions for how she wanted me to start healing. I was to reestablish my old hobbies and patterns. I looked over at my fletching tools but felt no draw to that young girl's life. I did not want to spar because I thought it wise to stay away from fighting until I felt more settled and in control of myself. I decided against archery for the same reason.

The thought of shooting my bow caused me to wander over to where someone had hung my equipment after the ill-fated trade trip. Shana must have brought back my things that were left in the Telequire camp in Preveza. My Madagascar rosewood bow was unstrung and leaning against the wall next to the black oak bow that my da had made for me. Both were resting under my shelf of treasures.

One by one I picked up each displayed item. I had lost the arrow necklace from my da and the copper armband that Deata had given to me for saving her life. They were probably on some stinking Roman or sold to the highest bidder at a faraway market. I picked up the small carving of Gata and could not stay the smile that came over my face. After running my finger along the delicate lines of the miniature leopard I set it back on the shelf and picked up my first Artemis award. I traced the word written in the fired clay and thought about all that I had been through since leaving my homestead. What if my sisters-in-feather were right all along? What if my life had been guided by the goddess, Artemis? Despite the lack of belief in my heart, I was hard-pressed to deny the fact that I had returned safely to the Telequire village.

I was of two thoughts on the reason why. Either there was no goddess, so there was no one to care that I had broken the oaths I made in her name. Or there was a goddess and she allowed me to come home out of forgiveness. I set the clay statue next to the other two and let my mind wander. If Artemis was real, and she allowed me to come home despite being an oath breaker, then how was I to prove myself to her? And if the Goddess was nothing more than a common hope then how should I right my wrongs to the nation? Whether the broken honor was mine or belonging to Artemis, I had to redeem myself and my actions.

I scrubbed my face with both hands and cursed aloud my active mind and idle body. I needed to do something to clear my head. After dressing in the heavy tunic that I had brought with me across the sea, I set out for the training hut. I could not walk around weaponless and Ori had promised me wooden blades. Before leaving, I also donned the heavy hooded cloak that was purchased in Vlore. I did not want questions, so I kept the hood up to shadow my eyes as I returned the tray to the food hut and went to find Kylani.

As I drew near the practice ring, I could see her inside sparring with someone. It was fairly quiet because they were using wooden blades. I did not recognize the scout she fought but the woman looked younger. I assumed that was why they were using dulled wood instead of normal knives. I tried to stay in the shadows near the trees but I saw the training master flick her eyes my way and call an end to the session. She dismissed the other woman and waved me over as she picked up a water skin. I nodded at her in greeting. "Heyla, Kylani."

"Heyla, Kyri. What brings you over my way today?"

I suddenly became conscious of the fact that she stood in front of me armed with knives in each boot and two wood knives in one fist. I rubbed sweaty hands on my loose trousers. "In deference to safety concerns, Queen Orianna has asked me to carry wooden blades in the village in lieu of standard ones. I—I get worried if I am not armed, though it's probably best if my weapons are non-lethal."

She looked at me curiously for a moment before answering. "I think that can be arranged. Without poking your beast of memory too much, can you tell me about your training?" My gaze darted nervously between the daggers in her boots and the wooden knives in her hands. Almost as if she could read my mind she gave me a nod. "Give me a candle drop, I'll be right back." I watched her walk into the training hut and return unarmed. She then motioned toward a couple of tree stumps.

Relieved by her actions, I relaxed and took a seat next to her. My voice was quiet in a morning broken by wind through the trees and the sounds of a waking village. "Thank you. I—I can talk about my training, I think. What would you like to know?"

"Well I don't know much about gladiator training, mostly rumors from traders and such. What weapons did you train with? How were your opponents armed? When did you start training and how long did you train?"

Her questions were like a flood and it took me a heartbeat to pick them apart enough to answer. "I trained a lot as a sagittarius, which is a mounted archer. Shooting on horseback meant I had to learn to guide the beast with the pressure of my legs alone. And learn to stay on!" She chuckled at that and waved me to continue. "Captain Aureolus had me drill and go through an obstacle course that required tight turns, spins, and leaping charges. I also trained to fight as a regular gladiatrix."

"Where you a *rudiarius* then?" Kylani mentioned the carved wooden gladius gifted to those who had earned their way from slave to freedman status.

"No, I never earned my freedom in the arena. That was where gladiators received the *rudis*. My freedom was bought with an agreement made to my owner, the man whose son I saved."

Kylani apologized. "Sorry, I got us off track. Please continue telling me about your training."

I shut my eyes briefly, recalling the beginning. "At first we were given *rudus* only. The wooden training swords were non-lethal. Once I completed the training I was given the title of *Tiro*." I shook my head. "Sword training with the Romans was much different than ours. We used a *palus* to practice moves with the sword. The wooden pole was solid and easily withstood the strokes. We also used a shield and dummy, which were suspended from a swinging pole. Two swords were what my dominus preferred for me to carry though I was not very proficient with the gladii. That was why I was also allowed to wear a pair of pugiones at my waist. I learned to fight with and against all the gladiator weapons, whip, net, trident, swords, short spears, arrows, and pugiones. He also taught the art of unarmed combat, different from what I was learning as an Amazon. One of the most surprising parts of my training was being taught how to die."

"What?" Kylani's face showed clearly how perplexing she found my last few words.

"There are specific death rituals in the arenas of Rome. The spectators expected us to die bravely, to show no fear and offer ourselves willingly to cold-blooded murder by our opponents. In case our victory was not to be, we were taught how to die gracefully with honor."

Her eyes widened in surprise. "You learned all that while you were gone? By the Goddess, when did you start training?"

I nodded. "Yes. I started the day after my dominus brought me and Iva back to his villa. I trained from sun up to sun down, with only short breaks between. I would fall into my bed each night exhausted only to wake again the next day and do it all over."

"Rest days?"

I shook my head. "No matter how much gold I brought Isidorus in the arena, I was still a slave, his property. My rest days were no more than days I spent recovering from injury."

Kylani chuffed out a breath and I saw fear and respect warring on her face. "Goddess, Kyri! It's no wonder you live on the edge. Because of what you told me, I think it's probably best if you don't spar with weapons for a while yet. I think that the line between your reality and your training will blur and you may forget yourself. It would be too much like your life as a slave."

"Yes, I think you are right. But I am so..." I searched for the word. "Twitchy right now. I am not used to being idle and I have to get rid of all this energy. Can you think of anything for me to do?"

She scratched her temple as she thought then a smile broke over her face. "You could do rope checks? That will take you all over Telequire and reacquaint you with tree running again. How does that sound?"

I thought about all the ropes the Amazons used as easy ways down from the higher canopy in the forest. They could be found along the regular trails and around the village itself. None of the scouts cared for the duty. It was boring and it required carrying heavy lengths of rope to use in repairs should one be found that was damaged. "You know the scouts hate that job, right?" She nodded and grinned at me. Finally I gave in. "I will do it. I need more practice in the trees anyway. And when I feel comfortable with a bow again, I will bring game back each day."

"That sounds like a good idea, Kyri. Speaking of bows, I noticed that the one you came home with was different. When you're feeling up to it, would you care to give me a demonstration in that, and your unarmed combat sometime?"

I thought about her request, it seemed harmless enough. "Sure." Even as I answered I became conscious of the energy still coursing through me. "Though if you have time, I could show you the unarmed combat now."

She looked wary, but steady. "Do you think that will trigger any flashbacks?"

"No, I have not used that training in the arena as often as the rest. It was only for last resort if I were disarmed. It is the heavy fighting that—those are the memories that seem to come back when I do not want them to."

She nodded. "That is good. Now, explain to me how the Roman gladiator training is different from ours." She began a series of warm-ups and I quickly removed my cloak and did my own stretching, speaking as I went.

"Here in Telequire I was trained to use fists or to wrestle. But with the gladiators, everything they do is with the goal of winning, of entertaining the masses. I was taught the skills of entering, seizing, trapping, disarming, and tripping my opponents. I had to learn about human anatomy. We were taught all the parts of the body and their weaknesses. My doctore showed me how to break joints and bones at their weak spots, how to punch and kick correctly, and how to choke the air out of my enemies. While I only fought armed, I had to be prepared for any eventuality because losing was not an option."

"Fascinating! Okay, show me what you've learned." We entered the arena proper and began circling, both staying low on the balls of our feet. Kylani had her fingers curled into fists and I kept mine open. She came at me with a quick one two jab, both fists taking shots at my face. I ducked the first and spun around the second before landing a solid blow to her back, over the spot her *renibus* was located. I knew from experience she would feel numbness and pain from the hit, but I remained in control enough to make it lighter than normal. She gasped and spun around to face me, clearly feeling discomfort. Her caution grew as we began circling again. She telegraphed another hit and I reacted only to be surprised by a foot sweep that took us both to the ground. She tried to capitalize on the move by putting me into a choke hold but I dug my fingers into the nerves of her wrists and she quickly let me go.

Back on our feet again we traded blows for a few candle drops until I started blocking her fists. When I saw an opening I aimed a kick at her solid upper thigh muscle and while she was distracted by the pain I stepped close and grabbed her right arm in my left in a painful joint lock. Then before she could recover, I aimed a punch at the spot just below her *celiac plexus*. That was what the Romans called the place just below the bone between our breasts. She lost her breath immediately and I let her drop to the ground before stepping back.

There were other blows I could have used but all would have been more painful or caused more damage. I watched as Kylani lay on the ground, sweating and paralyzed with the inability to draw breath. The look in her eyes told me that she knew it would pass and my own experience told me that what she was going through was not pleasant.

Our match clearly done, I walked over and grabbed a skin of water. After drinking my fill I watched her stand and handed the skin to the training master. Kylani nodded and gave me a pained smile. "Thanks." After drinking down the rest of the skin she tossed it aside and turned back to me. "I knew I was in trouble as soon as you gave me that kidney punch." She shook her head. "Goddess, but you're so much faster than the last time I saw you. You were holding back, weren't you?"

I nodded. "While I could never match you for strength, I was taught many different weak points on the body, some more damaging than others. I did not want to seriously hurt you so I was limited in what I could use. Gladiators are taught to beat other gladiators. We do not fight fair,' we do not strive to incapacitate. We win. There are joint locks and moves that will easily break your elbow, your knee, or dislocated your shoulders. There are points on your body that will cause numbness, paralysis, or just extreme pain. I could break your nose and shove the bone up into your brain, crush your temple or your windpipe, gouge out your eyes, or break your neck. Most gladiators wore helmets so a lot of the head blows would do no good, with the exception of the nose and the throat."

Kylani rubbed the bruised area on her back where she took the punch and a thoughtful look came over her face. "Would you be able to show me what you learned? I could put a few candle marks every seven-day into my schedule if you're up to it. I'm curious about this style of fighting. As women, we often find ourselves up against larger and stronger opponents and I think that it would be good to fight on our terms instead of boxing or wrestling like the men."

I shrugged and gave her an honest smile. "I may as well. Due to the queen's directive, it seems like I have nothing but time. It will be nice to have something regular to look forward to."

After picking out my wooden daggers and saying goodbye I decided to grab a drying cloth from my hut and head to the small bathing chamber. Gata had taken to following me wherever I went but just as I remembered, she did not enter the hot cave. I watched her settle outside before dropping the animal hide back over the doorway. Each step into the hot water cleansed my spirit as much as my body. There was only one door into the cave and knowing that Gata watched over me, I relaxed for the first time since Preveza. The soak did wonders for my chilled and sore muscles, and while the water was hot enough to relax, it was not so hot that it would make me feel ill if I stayed in too long. At least not in the winter moons. Eventually I went all the way under to wet my hair and when I came up again there was a difference to the air, a feeling that caused me to tense. I glanced to the side and saw Ori standing in the low torchlight by the door.

Her voice was soft, tentative even. It was the same tone you would use to soothe a wounded animal or break in a new filly. "I don't want to intrude, but I came to ask if you would like some company."

I shivered in the hot water as I was torn between wanting her closer and pushing her farther away. "You are the queen, you can go where you will."

"Kyri." She drew my name out and I knew she waited for a real answer from me.

Pushing the fear aside and giving in to the hope within my heart, I let her have the words she wanted. "I would like it if you joined me." The smile almost made it worth my anxiety. I turned away to give her privacy as she stripped out of the cloak and cold weather gear she wore. It was dark near the pool since I had only lit the one torch by the door.

"Do you mind if I light an oil lamp?"

I picked up a nearby cake of soap and began lathering my arms. "No, go ahead." Foolishly, I gave no thought to the fact that more than just my mind and spirit had changed in my time away. I heard her go to the torch by the door to light a wick and was peripherally aware of the light bobbing back toward the pool once she had it lit. I sensed her come within a few paces of the water and then the light and footsteps stopped. My sigh escaped on its own and I rinsed my arm before turning around to look at her fully. Her eyes shone overly green with the lamp flame so near her face and her expression was a frozen rictus of sorrow. For a heartbeat I was confused, wondering what I had done to put that look there. Then I remembered the scars.

I wanted to turn away from her pain because it made me remember my own, but I did not. As I had been told, you cannot heal if you ignore your wound. "I have not seen them in full, only if I twist myself around can I glimpse the edge of them. I worried when I realized that the whip marks would scar. I feared that my skin would no longer please you, that my slavery had made me ugly inside and out. I was shamed and saw them as a penance of sorts, for failing to protect my sisters and for failing in my oaths."

As if my words had restarted her feet, Ori bent over to set the stone lamp on the floor next to the pool. Her breasts hung down casting shadows on the light skin of her belly. She did not speak until she descended the carved steps to enter the water in full. "You say *was*. Does that mean you no longer feel shamed, or that you are no longer afraid of how I feel?"

I shook my head. "I am always afraid. I cannot change the scars or your opinion of me. And I am working on the fear but it always swims below the surface. Much like the great toothed sea beasts that follow the fishing boats for their chum."

Her approach through the water was slow, excruciating. "And are they a penance?"

I shrugged, sloshing water across the top of my breasts. Her hot gaze did not go unnoticed. "Perhaps. Though who would be doling out such punishment I know not."

"Artemis, of course. The same being that guided you back to me, to us."

Anger was tight and I wore it like a cloak in the water. "The same being that allowed us to be taken in the first place? The same Artemis that allowed Pocori to—" My words cut off abruptly as I slapped my hand on the surface of the water in frustration. "Even if she were real, why would I want to follow one such as that?"

She interrupted me with a gentle touch to the back of my hand. I had not realized that she was so close. "Kyri, when you make arrows, do they all turn out exactly the same? Do they all fly the same path forever?"

I paid attention and thought hard on her answer. Ori was always one for talking about meaning within meaning and I knew she had something to say that was important. "No. I can only make the arrows, shape them, and put them in my quiver."

"What happens then?"

"I shoot them of course. Sometimes they hit their mark, sometimes they do not. Arrows can change with time, get damaged, become lost, and sometimes break altogether. What does this have to do with Artemis or my lack of belief?"

She gently laced her fingers through mine and stepped even closer. I could see her pale lashes in the lamplight and the way the heat had darkened her lips like wine. "We are nothing more than Artemis's arrows, Kyri. She shot you across the sea, and then the great huntress retrieved you again."

My response echoed in the small cave. "But why? She shot three arrows that day in Preveza, but only two came home!"

Her shout matched mine for intensity. "No, fourteen came

home! Perhaps it was the fates that allowed you to bring back our sisters of Kombetar and Ujanik, when they would have otherwise been lost until death in the fields of Rome. Perhaps it was nothing more than dumb luck that brought you to us, and took you from us. No one knows anything for certain, what it all means or how it works. Not until we die and our souls are released to the Golden Mountain. But Kyri, you are here with me right now after we were all certain you had been lost for good. Even as tragedy happened to you and around you, some good still came of the past moons. I have faith in my Goddess and faith that even while all of humanity has their free will, she still tries to guide us on our path through the forest. The world is full of evil intent, she cannot be everywhere. But know this, I am glad you returned to me above all the rest. And if that makes me a bad queen for placing my heart above the good of the nation, so be it."

I threaded the fingers of my free hand through hers so that we stood face-to-face with hands clasped. "You are an amazing queen and the nation is lucky to have you. And I am truly sorry for all that I have done and for all the pain that I continue to cause."

She pulled me slowly toward her like a *retiarius* would draw in his net. "And I am sorry for all the pain you have endured and continue to endure." The press of our skin, when it happened, was unexpected. One heartbeat water was between us and the next it was not. Her gaze was so loving and so serene that it broke my heart just a little but her request broke my heart even more. "Will you kiss me, Kyri?"

Her need and love were so much more than I deserved. My mind turned back to that hazy poppy dream night and I knew that my conscience would not allow the press of something so holy against my traitorous lips. As I looked into her shadowed eyes, my bottom lip quivered with the emotion of my loss. "I—I cannot. I am sorry."

She turned away then with a look of pain but did release me. "Then hold me like you never want to let me go." With a cry, I let go of her hands and crushed her to my chest. The water swirled around us and caught our tears together as our skins and souls became one. The passion was that of emotion alone, but it seemed all encompassing. Perhaps I could be reborn in the fires of her love. Perhaps we could be reborn together.

Chapter Six

Lifting the Veil of Memory

THE REST OF my day was spent with the queen. We did not speak of my time as a slave, nor did we speak of what she went through while I was gone. Instead we focused on learning to be friends again. She told me of all that had been done in the village and caught me up on what all those I loved had been doing in my absence. We took midday and evening meals together in her hut before she walked me back to my own. After a long embrace she gave me a delicate kiss to the corner of my mouth, just as she had done the night before. Throughout the day I caught her glancing at me with a conflicted look on her face. While I knew that she loved me and missed me in my absence, I also knew that we had both become different people. And I could tell that my unspoken betrayal was still very fresh in her mind.

After she departed to her own hut, I found myself alone with thoughts turned inside out. I could neither deny my longing for her smile and bright presence nor pretend like my physical attraction to her did not matter. But even as we embraced in the bathing pool, there was something stopping me from that physical manifestation of our love. The pain I could see just below her surface fueled my guilt, and I knew we would have to talk before letting the things between us go deeper.

Another issue was that I felt disconnected from my own body. Almost as if I floated outside of myself much of the time, and my emotions and feelings were somehow muted. I recalled Queen Agafya's words and knew I would need to ask for help, but I did not feel comfortable leaning on my friends for such a personal problem. I let my worries carry me into sleep, but I did not lose track of the way my lips tingled from Ori's sweet touch.

I woke early the next morning and decided to break my fast in the meal lodge, in search of the familiarity that the queen had spoken of. I wanted to get there before someone could be sent out with a food tray for me. I suspected that Ori had something to do with my morning meals. The lodge was not very busy since the sun was just barely over the horizon. I said hello to a few familiar faces and listened to the muted whispers of even more. It surprised me how little I cared what the others thought. It was a very different feeling from the time before I left.

I had been through an ordeal and witnessed things that humans should never have to watch. I found it hard to worry about the trivial as I did when I first came to Telequire. I had just begun eating my porridge when Coryn walked through the door. She spied me immediately and I watched as shocked surprised washed over her handsome face. "Kyri! Goddess, it is you! We heard rumors, but no one was sure." I stood and clasped her hand and was proud that I only gave a small tremor when she pulled me into a hug. The quiet voice in my ear sounded nothing like the confident scout leader that I remembered. "I'm so glad you're back."

"I am glad too. You have no idea how much I missed you all." She pulled back then and simply looked at me, taking in my scars and obvious wariness. As much as I had changed, I could see that she had changed as well. Coryn, First Scout Leader and stoic feather ruffler of the tribe, stood before me displaying barely controlled emotion. I refused to let her lose face in front of the people in the meal hut so I squeezed her shoulders and gently pushed her toward the food table. "Go get something to eat, we have plenty of time to talk."

Searching my face for another heartbeat, she nodded and displayed that famous Coryn grin. "How do you know I didn't eat already?" The wink sealed it and before I could stifle my reaction, laughter bubbled out. It was not her words so much as the realization that it truly was my friend who stood in front of me. No matter what we went through in life, there were anchor points we could always come back to.

Another shove. "Go!"

We ate in companionable silence for the first few candle drops. Abruptly she dropped her wooden spoon into her skyphoi of porridge and met my eyes unflinchingly. "Do you want to talk about it?" I felt warmed by her concern and her consideration. She understood that there were things I was probably not ready to speak of and showed patience. I shook my head and she nodded once. "I am here for you if or when you need an ear to listen or a shoulder to lean on, and you can trust me not to break confidence."

I knew I could trust her implicitly. Coryn was a much deeper person than a lot of people gave her credit for. While she was not normally one to discuss the depths of emotion and thought, she had always been there for me in the past, just as I had always done for her. "Thank you. I just need some time still." She gave me a smile and we chatted about various things while we ate.

After speaking with Coryn over breakfast my second morning back with Telequire, my days took on some semblance of a routine. I often spent my mornings doing drills and other exercises that I learned as a gladiatrix. On the days that Kylani was available I would work with her in unarmed sparring instead. Ori tried to make sure she had either midday or evening meal open for us to eat together. In the afternoon, I would run the trees and do essential rope repairs around the village and along the trails. Having responsibilities and a schedule of sorts made me feel a lot better, like I was contributing to the welfare of the nation. At the end of my first seven day I finally decided that I needed to talk about all the things I was feeling, and all the pain that I carried inside. I did not want to burden any of my friends so I asked the priestess if we could speak. Glyphera ushered me into a hut near the base of the great hill by the Telequire temple cave entrance.

"Good morning, Kyri. I've been wondering if you would come speak with me."

I nodded and took a seat where she indicated. "Queen Agafya and Priestess Kynthia from Kombetar mentioned that it would help with my healing if I could talk to someone about what I went through. And—and I remember Shana mentioning that she spoke with you after her attack."

"Yes, many come to me when they need to lighten the burdens of their heart and soul. While I cannot miraculously change things for you, it's often found that simply sharing your pain helps lessen the burden."

I looked down at my hands. The knuckles were nearly white and butterflies had taken over my stomach. "It is difficult for me to talk about that time. I think some of it was because of the trauma and loss. And some of it is because I became someone I did not like, someone without honor."

A gentle hand covered my rigid ones. While her skin was soft and devoid of callouses, I could see the subtle signs of aging. Shana told me that Glyphera had been priestess when she was born and I knew there would be a lot of knowledge and wisdom in her eyes if I were to only look up and see. "My child, the telling will get easier the more times you tell. Your heart and your mind have to get used to the way your past makes you feel, and eventually you will become familiar with it the same way you become familiar with a well-worn cloak. With each telling, you take away some of the power your trauma has over you."

I looked up curiously and became caught in her deep brown

eyes. I could sense that the older woman had her own power and I felt pulled into it. Perhaps it was Goddess given, or maybe it was her balance and charisma that put me so at ease, but either way she broke through my barrier of fear. I told her my story then, the entire tale. Every single candle drop from beginning to the end. I spoke of the way Pocori's death made me feel, and the death of all those I killed. I admitted to all the broken oaths and to the rage that lived inside of me all the time. I even told her some of what I remembered of the night after my last match as a gladiatrix.

She listened attentively and patiently, with very few questions. When my tale was complete, she poured us both tea and we sat in silence for a quarter candle mark. I needed that time of quiet because just the retelling of all I had done left me with a sick feeling inside. But as the oil lamp flickered, I grew calm again. Her voice startled me, despite the fact that she spoke softly. "How do you feel, Kyri? What emotion does your past as a slave spark within you?"

I did not have to think about it. "Rage."

"And who are you angry with?"

My gaze jerked up to hers. "The slavers and Romans, of course! I am mad at the men who took us from our homeland. I am angry with all the men in Rome who profit and deal with the slave trade, and I hate the Roman pig who bought Pocori for only the pleasure her body could bring! I have every reason to be angry, Priestess."

She nodded placidly. "I don't doubt that you have every right to your anger. But it seems like a lot of anger for someone who is away from all those people. You carry rage with you every heartbeat of the day. A fire needs fuel for it to keep burning. So what is your fuel, Kyri? Who else are you angry with?"

I stood so fast that my stool fell over behind me. My cheeks flamed with sudden heat. "Of course I am still angry with them, they are the reason I became a slave! I hate the slavers and the Romans for taking us away and bending us to their will!"

"Who else?"

I did not think, merely answered her. The words poured out of me and I could not stop them. "I hate Isidorus for fighting me over and over, and I hate Aureolus for training me to kill. I hate Aelia for t—taking something from me I did not want to give. And—and I hate myself for letting her." The sobs that came from me shook my body. Hot tears ran down my cheeks as I started facing all my truths.

"Kyri." Gasping for breath, I looked up at her and her face was solemn. "Who else?"

I screamed my answer and pounded fists into my thighs. "You! Okay? I hate all of you for letting us go, for not saving us! My friends, my love, the Amazons, I hate you all!" Almost as if I were a puppet at the agora whose strings had been cut, I dropped to the floor of her hut in defeat. Mumbled words tumbled from my mouth. "Why? Why? Why?"

"My child." Her voice was quiet and it slowly pulled me from my grief. I sat up and opened hot and tear-swollen eyes. "Hatred is a natural thing. It is a reaction to fear and sorrow, it can often be the consequence of loss. Even though Artemis guards our forests, our paths in life can often be difficult and dangerous. A happy life is not one that is free from obstacles, it is a life whose path takes you where you need to go."

"But Pocori—"

Glyphera shook her head. "Her path was not yours, Kyri. It's time you let her go and lay her to rest in your mind. You did not kill her, nor could you prevent her death. What you did do is give her a friend that she could see and hear all the way to her last breath. She did not die alone and that was all you or Iva could have done."

I understood what she was saying on some visceral level. "But why do I feel such anger with my sisters, my friends, and my love? Iva and I both spoke of the possibility that someone would come for us but we knew it would not happen. My anger makes no sense."

She laughed quietly but I felt no malice in it. "Oh, little one, when does anger ever make sense? Anger isn't rational, like the thoughts of the people that hold it. Anger is the fire that consumes rational thought and drives us to ruin. The question is, will you let it consume you or will you try to douse it?"

"I do not want to be consumed." My words reminded me of my very first talk with Shana about Coryn. I never realized there were many ways a person could be consumed. Passion, anger, love. Of them anger was the worst by far. "But how do I put out the fire of my rage?"

"Let's work backward and see who even deserves that anger, shall we?" I nodded, unsure what that would do. "Let's start with the Amazons. Could any of us have saved you and Iva once you were taken? Is there any way that a group of scouts or warriors could have come across the sea and rescued you, or bought you and stolen you away back to Greece?"

I thought on her question and considered all the factors of security and rules of Roman society. Finally I shook my head. "No, not without getting themselves killed, enslaved, or sparking a war. And we would not win such a war because their armies are vast and well-managed. It would be death to all the nations if Rome decided to invade and take over Greece. I—I think I can let that anger go."

She nodded her encouragement. "Okay, now let's talk about you and your self-hatred. Think about all the things you did as a slave, all the indiscretions and deaths that happened at your hands. What were your choices? Could you have refused to do any of those things without the punishment of death, which would eliminate Iva's chance to return?"

I thought on my actions and sighed. "I had to do whatever I was told or risk the whip or execution. I was actually quite lucky for the opportunity that Isidorus gave to me. The things I did as a slave, the killings, I had to do them in order to come back home. It was hard watching my fellow gladiatrix in the arena die to the leopard but she made her choice. It was harder still to kill the noble beast that reminded me so much of my Gata. The leopard had no choice, it was an animal subject to the whims of its master just the same as me."

Glyphera smiled. "Can you let that anger go as well?" I shook my head and swallowed down the familiar acid burn of dishonor. I did not have to say it aloud, she seemed to understand right away. "Ah, the night of your freedom with the other slave?"

"Yes." The word escaped as I forced it through my teeth with the tip of my tongue.

She cocked her head at me. "Tell me what happened."

I had been semi-vague with her when I told that part of my story, embarrassed and ashamed by my actions. "I do not remember much actually." She looked surprised. "I had been seriously injured by the leopard, with claw marks across my upper leg. I remember waking in the middle of the night feeling strange, like I was a little outside my body. I recognized the sensation from previous times I had been injured and given a drug made from the poppy flower. I always hated receiving the drug because it made me both euphoric and lethargic. My limbs would become heavy and it gave me stomach cramps. But it was what the *medici* administered to all the gladiators for injury because it was so potent." I took a deep breath to steady myself.

"One of my regular slave attendants, Aelia, gave me some water and told me that Isidorus had signed my papers of manumission. It was overwhelming to suddenly be faced with my freedom and I broke down. She soothed me even as I felt guilty that I was free when so many others were not, when people like her were still slaves." I took a sip of my tea, not wanting to relive that moment when I lost myself to the touch of another. "She told me that a slave's freedom could be found in many ways and that hers was to get what she most desired."

The priestess leaned forward slightly. "And what did she desire? Was she in love with you like Iva?"

I shook my head. "She did not love me at all. The tears of my breakdown were still wet on my face when she kissed me. I tried to pull back. I told her that I loved another and could not do such with her. But I was lost in a poppy haze. I had no strength in my limbs to push her away as her hands continued their ministrations upon my body." I covered my face, as if that alone could hide my shame. "I do not remember anything beyond that point. And what little I did remember I thought merely a dream when I woke the next morning. I raged at the world when I was able to puzzle out dream from reality. I feared the queen would never have me when she discovered how changed I was, or when she learned of my betrayal."

"Does she know?"

I nodded. "We have not spoken of my time away yet but I did tell her that all the pledges I made before I became a slave had been broken. And I could see in her eyes that my words were a dagger in her heart."

The priestess took a sip of her own tea, processing my words for a heartbeat. "And? Did she cast you out as you had feared?"

I looked down at the mug of nearly cool liquid in my hands. "No. She suggested that we start anew, that the two of us had been through changes and that we needed to rebuild what we once had. I told her that my heart could never love another." I stopped speaking then because words felt large and cumbersome in my mouth. Glyphera maintained the silence for a while, perhaps processing all that I had told her. Maybe understanding why I was so angry with myself, or being angry with me for my betrayal to our queen. The silence continued until the priestess ended it by setting her empty mug on the table.

"Kyri."

I looked up into her dark eyes, expecting to see judgement and silent rebuke but both were absent. "Yes?"

"Like you, I was not always an Amazon. My village was attacked many sun-cycles ago when I was just barely into my menses. The raiders came in looting the houses and burning many to the ground. My father and older brother went out to fight them with nothing more than farmer's tools and they found only vicious death at the end of a sword. My mother hid me and my younger brother in a storage bin with the hopes that they wouldn't find us. Four men entered our house and I was forced to listen as they brutalized our mother mere paces away from where we cowered.

Though I tried to keep him quiet, Stephan started to cry and we were found by the men. My first sight when they pulled us from the bin was that of my mother's bloody skirt and her open unseeing eyes. She had fought the men valiantly to the end, more than one having scratches and bite marks on him. One man held me down while another pushed a knife against Stephan's throat. He told me that if I didn't fight them, they'd let us both live."

My mouth opened at the horror of what she went through as a child but I stayed silent because she was not finished with her story. "They used me just as they had done to my mother, and I let them. But they did not honor their word. As the last man tied his trousers the first slit my brother's throat right in front of my eyes. He was only five summers old. They left me there with the corpses of my family, broken and battered but still alive. It took me a long time before I stopped wanting to die. It took me even longer to accept that I wasn't at fault for not fighting them like my mother had done, instead having gone along with the abuse."

I was shocked to hear her words. How could Glyphera possibly think that she had been at fault? "But you were nothing more than a child! They violated you!"

She gave me a sad smile. "Ah, but I gave myself to them, remember? They violated my mother. I simply let them have me how they wanted."

I shook my head adamantly. "No, you had no choice! You may not have been held down by the filthy hands of those men, but you were held just as tight by your own fear and fear for your brother. You did not consent to being used, you just had no other choice!" I was nearly shouting with my anger on her behalf.

"Ah, so are you trying to tell me that there are different kinds of violation, alternate types of force?"

I was pulled up short by the statement of the obvious. "Of course there are! It does not matter what prevents you from resisting, if you are taken against your will it is wrong! And it was not your fault. You do not still think it was your fault, do you?"

Glyphera gave me a strange smile and something scratched at the edge of my conscious thought. "No, I don't."

I was confused and I knew it showed plainly on my face. "Then why did you tell me all that?"

She stood and moved in front of me, taking my hands. "Because Kyri, you too were taken against your will. Aelia forced you."

"What?" I tried to pull my hands away but she was deceptively strong. "No! What I did, what she did, I remember that it felt good. She was not bringing me pain."

"Did you tell her to stop? Did you try to stop her?"

I looked into her eyes and held her gaze. "Yes."

"And did she listen to you?"

My sight grew watery as I admitted the words to myself and to another for the first time. "No, she did not stop." Suddenly I was thrown into a memory, one that I had not seen before. I remembered cresting beneath her hands. I remembered crying and trying to push her away with feeble arms. "No, no, please stop. Please—do not do this!"

"Kyri."

"I love another, please stop. Ori!"

"Kyri! You're right here, you're with me. Come back from your memory, Kyri, come back!" I opened my eyes and found myself swaying with her hands gripping my shoulders in a tight embrace. My stomach roiled at what had come back to me with the flashback. I felt light-headed and my mouth alternately grew dry and watered as I tried to keep from being sick. Glyphera quickly spun around to grab a pot near the hearth and thrust it under my chin and I lost the effort to keep my breakfast down. As my stomach emptied, I grew weak-legged and she had me sit back on the stool. I was handed a mug of water and a cool cloth for my face. Candle drops went by as I slowly got control of myself. The warmth of her hand on my arm brought me back. "Better?" I nodded. "And your anger?"

I shook my head and drew in a deep breath. "I—I never realized. I could not remember and I guess I thought that if I got pleasure from something, it could not possibly be against my will. I assumed that part of me must have wanted it."

"Kyri, your body will react the way it is made to react. You mustn't be ashamed of that and you shouldn't take credit for someone else's actions. As sure as Artemis is our witness, that slave took something from you that you did not wish to give, that you could not stop. You are not at fault and your self-anger is misdirected. Do you understand now?"

Our talk and my admissions left me shaky but feeling lighter of spirit. "Yes, I think I do." Perhaps sensing that I could not handle any more major revelations for the day, she stood and pulled me up into an embrace. I stiffened for a heartbeat then relaxed into her arms. She felt so strong and solid and I let her strength seep in to my heart.

She pulled back before the embrace grew awkward and gave me a smile. "I think that we should be done talking for the day so you can process your thoughts. But I want you to come back as much as you need, okay? Artemis will always hold her door open for you, and her priestess will always listen."

I walked to the door but before I pulled it opened, I turned back to face her dark eyes. "I will, and thank you. You have made me realize that maybe—maybe I am not as bad as I thought. That maybe healing is more than just an impossible dream."

She gave me another smile. "Live in the light, Kyri." I nodded and walked out into the sunshine with a head full of thoughts and a heart suddenly less crowded.

A FORTNIGHT BEFORE spring equinox I found myself once again breaking my fast with Coryn. "I heard the queen has you off regular duty until further notice. If I know you, you're probably bored already. Am I right?"

I laughed because she knew how much I hated to be idle. "As of a seven day ago. I already asked Kylani for a task and she gave me rope duty. I do that every afternoon."

Coryn pulled a face. "Broken branch! What did you do to make her mad?"

I put a hand on hers. "It is fine. I need to re-familiarize myself with tree running again, and spending time by myself keeps me from all those things that would trigger a flashback—"

"Flashback?"

My expression turned serious and she gave me serious consideration in return. "I—I was a gladiatrix and sagittarius, and my dominus fought me often. He fought me so much that I am having a hard time coming back from the edge. Sometimes I have flashbacks and I am not aware of what is real and what is not. The queen bade me wear wooden daggers and nothing else while in the village to help alleviate my anxiety and at the same time make me less dangerous."

Her stare was knowing and I wondered if she had ever been

stuck on the edge. "Does it help?" I shrugged because I did not know truthfully if it was helping. Other than the one with Glyphera, I had not experienced a flashback since the night we arrived in the village. But I had also been avoiding things that I thought might cause anxiety or take me back into my memories. My right hand started to shake and I quickly dropped my spoon into the bowl. Her fingers gently covered mine. "Are you less dangerous with the wooden blades?"

I swallowed and looked away from her piercing gaze. "Not as much as I would like."

"I'm not saying that I know anything about anything, Kyri, but perhaps avoiding that which we fear is not really the way to get past it."

"I am not afraid!" My anger was quick as it had been for the previous six moons and I regretted my words instantly.

She released my trembling hand and picked up her spoon again. "I'm not saying you are afraid, as such. What I'm saying is that when we avoid that which we fear, or that which takes control of us, we have no idea how to deal with it when we are confronted unexpectedly. Emotions will overpower thought and reason and hold us under their spell." She took another bite of her breakfast and swallowed. "Did I ever tell you that I was afraid of heights when I was younger?"

"But you are one of the best tree runners Telequire has!"

She quirked an eyebrow at me. "One of?"

I merely smirked at her. "Well I heard that Ori used to beat you regularly before she became queen."

"You woods weasel!"

I laughed quietly, reveling in the sheer joy of it as the long forgotten sound came from my lips.

I picked up a slightly wrinkled apple and took a bite. After a few heartbeats I spoke around the masticated food in my mouth. "I have missed this."

"Winter dried apples?"

I shook my head and smiled. "Friends." I waved my free hand at her. "Now please, continue your story.

"Anyway, as I was saying, I was very afraid of heights when I was younger. Every time I'd have to train in the trees as an initiate, I'd have an attack of panic. If I got more than ten paces off the ground I'd simply freeze and grow nauseous."

I looked at her curiously. "What did you do? Clearly you are over it because I have never seen you have an issue in the canopy."

She shook her head. "No, Kyri, I'm still afraid of heights."

"I do not understand."

Her eyes took on a faraway look and her food was forgotten. "I knew I couldn't simply avoid tree duty. I was an Amazon, the mere thought of it was ridiculous. Finally, I broke down and spoke with the previous training master, Kylani's predecessor. She took me to the tallest, straightest pine near the village and suggested I practice climbing it every day. Even if it was only five paces off the ground. She said that I should do it until I got used to the height then go a little higher. Eventually I came to understand that fear is not the thing that takes over our bodies, it is not the thing that prevents us from acting, or freezes our hands and mind when we most need them. It is our reaction to fear that does these things."

I tried to puzzle out her logic, to understand the point she was trying to make. "So what are you trying to tell me, Coryn? Do you think I should be sparring? Should I be doing all those things that remind me of my time as a gladiatrix?"

She shrugged. "I'm not saying you should do them necessarily. I'm saying maybe you shouldn't avoid them if you want to learn how to deal with and win through those flashbacks."

My head slowly moved back and forth, seemingly of its own volition. "I do not know if that is such a good idea. I nearly broke Kylani's arm when I first arrived in the village. I am not safe."

"Spar with me."

Anxiety bloomed in my gut. "No. While I am no master myself, you are not advanced enough in any of the weapons to keep me from killing you if I lose myself."

She looked at me for a heartbeat, thinking of other options. "The queen is."

"No!" Just the mere thought of facing my queen with the possibility that I would go into a rage squeezed the heart in my chest.

Her face was as a study of excitement then. "Wait, hear me out. It makes perfect sense, Kyri. Queen Orianna is better than anyone with the sword and she's also the one most likely to get through to you if things go poorly. Ask her."

"No, Coryn, just leave it be!" I could feel my face heat up as the familiar burn of anger made itself known. I stood abruptly and grabbed my meal dishes. Before leaving her at the table I wanted to make sure she truly understood the subject was closed. "I am not going to ask her and I will not discuss this with you again."

I turned to leave and came face-to-face with Ori. "Ask her what?"

Just as anger had caused my face to heat, dismay caused it to pale again. "Nothing, my queen." I made to leave but she stood her ground, not moving out of my way.

"Nothing, Kyri?

I did not meet her eyes, merely gritted my teeth to answer. "It is nothing of consequence."

She moved her hand to tilt my chin so she could look me in the eye. "Truth?" I did not want to answer so I stayed silent. "I can order Coryn to tell me, or I can ask you. I'd rather it came from you. What is it you're afraid to ask of me? I told you that I'm here for you in whatever way you need."

I could not keep the words in any longer. "Coryn's idea is too dangerous and she does not even know if it would help me work through the issues and the flashbacks. It has the potential to do you real harm and I cannot let that happen!"

She took a step back and held her hands with palms toward me. "Whoa, perhaps you should back up and tell me what you're talking about." She glanced at Coryn and the lead scout gave her a traitorous nod.

"My queen, perhaps we should take this discussion out of the meal hut."

Ori sighed but agreed. "Yes, let's take this to the council chamber. No one should be there right now." With a resigned slump of my shoulders I watched as she picked up a tree bar and an apple from the food table before leading us out of the lodge. It was a short walk to the council chamber but the queen had managed to eat her apple down to the core by the time we arrived. She started on the pressed bar of fruit, grain, and nuts once we got inside proper. "Talk to me, Kyri. What does Coryn want you to ask me that you're so afraid of?"

I sighed, still feeling the heat of my anger toward the scout leader. "She thinks that rather than hide from the things that remind me of my ordeal and send me into rages, that I should confront them instead. She thinks if I spar with one of my Amazon sisters that they can help keep me from going outside myself when the memories take over."

"I essentially told her that if she doesn't learn to control her fear, it will always control her."

Ori cocked her head for a few heartbeats, first looking at me, then turning her gaze to Coryn. "It's an interesting point and perhaps it has some merit. Think on this, Kyri. If an arrow becomes warped and stops flying straight, do you simply put it away and never use it again?"

I shook my head, starting to understand her words and thoughts. "No. I take it back and rework it until it is straight."

She nodded. "This could be considered 'reworking' you, or training you back to your original shape. Why does the idea bother you so much?"

"Because they did not train us to spar, Ori! They trained us to win, and to win by any means necessary. The bloodier and more exciting, the more they liked it. I have gutted a man and licked his blood from my blades. I cut another man's head from his body and threw it across the arena. I do not even know what I am doing when I go into my battle rages. Can you see how dangerous that is?"

Coryn answered. "So we make it less dangerous. We take away all other weapons but the one's you'd be sparring with. Make it a closed match, the less people the better. It will be up to your opponent to keep your feet firmly on the ground. What did you fight with the most?"

I looked at her, realizing that both seemed more and more convinced that Coryn's plan would succeed. "I mostly fought as a sagittarius, with bow and arrow. But I also fought with swords and pugiones."

Confusion washed across the attractive scout's face. "Pugiones?

"The Roman dagger. The pugio is wider at the base than Amazon blades. I always carried a pair of pugiones, one on each hip. Kylani has them now."

The scout leader shrugged. "How about daggers then? Either Shana or Deka can spar with you. They are both the best with daggers that we have."

"No." I was startled by the queen's voice and just as surprised that she disagreed with Coryn. "While they are very good, neither one is a hardened warrior. I don't think they would expect some of the things Kyri may try if she loses control. I will do it."

Tears filled my eyes and I suddenly felt as if they had backed me into a corner. "Please Ori, do not make me fight you. Nothing good can come of this!"

She took both my hands into hers. "Kyri, the more I think on this, the more I am convinced that it will help you. Trust me when I say that I won't let you hurt me, or yourself. We will take every precaution, love."

The problem was not my trust in her, it was that I did not trust myself. I sighed and shook my head. "I do not want to do this, but I cannot continue the way I am either. I am willing to try if you promise me one thing."

She gazed back at me curiously. "What is it?"

"That you will have archers around the sparring ring with arrows trained on me throughout. And if I break through your guard, if it becomes obvious that I am trapped into a battle rage, they will kill me." Ori sucked in a breath and Coryn murmured a curse. I moved my gaze from one to the other. "That is the only way I will try this." I stared into Ori's green eyes and could see the pain she held there. Finally she nodded and I let out the breath I had been holding. I had hoped that she would change her mind but she seemed resolute to their plan. "When?"

The queen shrugged. "I have no meetings this morning and I've already eaten. No time like the present I suppose." We walked out of the council chamber and she turned to Coryn. "Can you run and tell Kylani what we will need? I'll walk with Kyri to retrieve our swords." The scout leader nodded and took off at a fast lope toward the training grounds near the edge of the village.

We walked in silence for a short way but I could not stay silent. "Are you sure you want to do this, my queen?" She pinched my side, causing me to jump. I pulled her to a stop and ignored my loss of personal space as I cradled her face in the palms of my hands. "Are you sure you want to do this, Ori? I would rather die than see you hurt."

She reached her own hands up to circle my neck, pulling me down for a kiss. While it took me by surprise, it was the first time my traitorous heart had allowed such contact between us and it gave heavy racing thumps of joy. When we pulled back for air, she moved her hand to run the whorled pad of her fingertip over my bottom lip. I shivered at the long forgotten touch. "I too would rather die than see you hurt. And Kyri, I think you've been hurting long enough. I feel in my heart that this is the right thing for us to do, have faith." I opened my mouth to deny faith and she covered my lips, silencing my words before they could escape. "Have faith in me."

I searched her face for any reticence or fear and found neither. "I will."

Chapter Seven

Twist the Blade

THE PRACTICE AREA was cleared of anything I could use as a weapon by the time we retrieved each of our swords and arrived. There were four archers nearby, close enough to hit me with certainty if they all shot at once but far enough away to keep me from them. Kylani, Margoli, and Coryn were the only watchers besides the archers. Gata sat placidly off to the side. I felt a little surprised that more had not gathered until I saw Margoli glare sternly at a passerby that had slowed her step. There was a fear rising in me that I had no name for and I started to sweat with shear nervousness. I turned to Ori just before we greeted the others. "I am not the swordswoman that you are, nor your equal in any other weapon save the bow. But you must be wary. If I can take your weapon, I will. If I can overpower you, I will do that too. And most importantly, do not expect me to think like I always have before while we are sparring today."

She nodded and looked at me for a heartbeat longer before covering my hand with her own. "It's going to be okay, Kyri."

I frowned as my heart thudded away in my chest. "I pray you are right." We both shrugged into the harnesses that held our swords. Like most Amazons, I wore mine on my back. It was easiest because it did not interfere with tree running and I could fit my quiver over top if the need was there. The Amazon sword was shorter than some and surprisingly similar in balance to the gladius that I had grown used to across the sea. There was no word or action that told us when to start. We merely began circling each other after stepping into the scuffed area of the largest practice ring.

I watched Ori's eyes and was relieved to see the wariness I had requested. Her first strike was a thrusting feint that was quickly followed by a lazy swipe at my feet. I parried and did not come back slow. I pressed her quickly, setting off a rapid exchange that made us both sweat in the early morning air. I knew immediately that her skill was far and above anything I possessed. I tried to make up for the disparity by using brute strength and surprise. Ori did not fall into any of my traps and rolled out from under my hardest blows. The ringing of steel lulled me and when sweat dripped into my eye, the queen pressed the advantage and gave me a foot sweep. I fell to the ground and immediately rolled away.

Her long shadow caught my attention, as did the waiting leopard. I did not want my motions to be too fast because I was conscious of the beast sizing us both up. I looked up at the gladiatrix that wanted to take me down, that wanted to win my gold laurel and steal my future. I glanced over at the leopard again and considered making an offer for us to team up on the animal but I knew she would refuse. I did not know why the knowledge was so certain but it was there just the same.

Suddenly my opponent picked up the pace and her sword was only a blur as I tried to dodge and parry. She guided me around the open space, controlling my every move and I knew that my defeat was fast approaching. Losing was not an option. I was trying to keep up, occasionally scoring a few light cuts on her but she had me bleeding in multiple places with her well-placed strikes. Finally, out of shear desperation I tried to rush the other woman, to bring her in close where my strength would be an asset. I locked blades with her and pushed down, wary for the other woman to roll away and leave me off balance. That had been done to me before and I would not fall for the trick again. Rather than roll away, the blonde brought a knee up into my gut and a foot down to my instep. Before I could recover she kicked away from me and smoothly spun the blade from my hands with her sword.

I had only a heartbeat to determine my next action. Cutting my gaze to the right, I spied a tree I could use and bolted for it. I would let her think I was running away, just as I had done with the dimachaerus. As I had hoped, she bolted after me a few steps behind.

"Kyri! Kyri, wait!"

"Ky-ri-us, Ky-ri-us." I could hear the words but I did not have time to think about them. I had to win the laurel so I could go home. My heart was pounding as I ran and the battle lust sang through my blood. I knew the woman was close behind but for whatever reason, she did not swing at my back. My left foot hit the angled trunk of the large tree first, and I quickly ran up a few steps before flipping over the back of my pursuer. Before she could stop me I had my left arm locked around her throat and my right hand gripped fast in her short hair. She froze against me, understanding that I had taken control.

Despite my hold and upper hand, she still had the forethought to reverse her sword grip and had the blade facing behind her with its point digging lightly into my side. I had shifted my torso as far left as possible and locked my left leg around the front of hers to prevent escape and further movement on her part. Though we seemed at an impasse, she was in a much more dire position. I knew her blade would not kill me since it was too far to the side to hit anything lethal. "Kyri, wait! Talk to me."

I was surprised at my opponent's words but they would not affect the outcome. My voice was low and tinged with anger. "My name is Kyrius and your words mean nothing to me, Roman! You will not prevent me from the laurel, failure is not an option."

She was strong. I could feel it in the play of muscles along her shoulders and back but I knew I could still snap her neck. I thought perhaps I should let her live and knock her unconscious instead. I weighed my options. I could simply deprive her of air and when she passed out, wait to see if the kill sign was given. I tightened my grip and listened to the drone of her voice. "Kyri, don't make me do this!"

There would be no waiting. "It is already done." I tensed to twist the head in my grasp and pain exploded from my side. The blonde had pushed the blade through and stepped out of my grip. Agony flared up and down my right side as my dead hands dropped to the blade that was embedded in skin. My gaze went from the bloody blade of the sword to the eyes of the woman in front of me. My own laughter caused me to gasp and her eyes widened at the sound. "Foolish." I grasped the steel that had been sheathed into my body and slowly pulled it free.

"Goddess!" The voice had no meaning. Nothing had meaning but the pain that fueled my fire and the win that would see me home.

The heartbeats thundered by and still she watched until I had the sword unstuck and held in my hand. The grip and pommel were bloody from my fingers. "Nothing will keep me from my home." I took a step forward and she stepped back. Her eyes darted to the side and I saw her hand give a familiar signal of waiting but I ignored it. I pulled the blade back and stalked toward her quickly, intent on ending the match for the honor of my dominus and the purse that would finally take us back to Greece. There was a tension in the air but it meant nothing to me. I did find it strange that the familiar chants had stopped, leaving my blood bereft and empty. Who was I fighting for? I adjusted my grip and looked down at my enemy. Just as I made to swing, her voice cut through the cool air.

"Kyri Fletcher, your queen demands that you stop immediately!"

Words that had seared my soul a lifetime ago, came back to haunt me. The blade froze and dropped lifelessly from my hands. Ori—Ori was in front of me. Ori was the one I sought to kill. Nausea rose fast and I turned my head away as the burning sickness burst from my mouth. My convulsive vomiting sent a red-hot poker through the wound in my side and I cried out with the agony of it. I covered the bloody rent with my hand and painfully dropped to my knees in the dirt. Looking up at the woman that I lived for, the woman I had nearly killed, I could feel the tears run freely down my face. "I am sorry, my queen. I failed you." Strong hands grabbed me before I could fall all the way over and more came to take my feet. Restraint caused a surge of panic and I started to kick out.

"Kyri, it's okay. They are only trying to help you, let us carry you." I stilled immediately and gave a nod to the blonde at my side. I was taken to the healer's hut and placed on a too familiar pallet. A tutting sound caught my attention just before my tunic was lifted off me and Thera began tending my wound.

"Ah, this one was well placed at least. The blade wasn't even twisted, just straight in and out. It's gonna take some healing and time for you to remake a skin of blood but you should be well soon enough." She chuckled and I smiled at her surety, though I knew it would take more than blood to make me whole again.

"Kyri." I looked to the other side of the raised pallet where Ori stood.

I closed my eyes, the pain of my actions and my injury having made me weak. "I am sorry, my queen. I could not break free and I failed."

"No!" I looked to her then, wary of the angry outburst. "You did not fail. You were in the height of your battle lust with only the thought of winning. From the very center of your memory, you fought on and your only thought was in returning home. Even with a blade buried in your side you continued to battle toward your goal. But as soon as I said those words, every bit of you came back. I could see it in your eyes and the very stance of you." She placed a warm hand on my cheek. "You did not hurt me and you did not kill me. You came back."

I closed my eyes again. "But I still have a long road to travel."

Her voice was quiet, serious. "Yes, yes you do."

BECAUSE ORI WAS skilled enough to stab me so far to the side, the wound was not much different than the one made by an arrow the previous sun-cycle. While it was larger and consequently more painful, Thera remarked more than once over the following seven-day at how clean it was healing. No infection had set in, which was a miracle in and of itself. And at least one good thing had come of my time spent as a gladiatrix—pain did not affect me as much as it used to.

Iva came to see me the morning after I was injured. We talked for a while and she informed me of all that she had been doing since returning to the Telequire nation. She told me that she was seriously considering transferring to Kombetar tribe during the Festival of Nations at summer solstice. I asked her why and she said it was too difficult to see me around the village, feeling the way she did. She cried then and simply held my hand before placing the softest of kisses on my lips. I thought I saw a flash of blonde near the other doorway to the lodge but no one appeared after Iva left so I assumed it was one of the other healers.

There was a lot of anguish in my heart for Iva's pain but I knew that I was not really the cause. You cannot control who loves you and who does not. Because of my bed rest I also had a lot of time to think about the match with Ori and all the things we could have done to prevent my memories from taking over. I realized that she was right, her voice had brought me out of it when needed. Perhaps she should have been talking to me all the way through. I also realized that hearing my name repeated during the sparring session was one of the catalysts that caused me to be lost in my past. I wanted to spar again with the new insights but Thera said that even I needed more than a seven-day. I suspected that part of her was teasing me but the look in her eye convinced me to follow her instructions.

The seven-day of healing left me with only a seven-day until the spring equinox. After being gone so long, I wanted nothing more than to participate in the games. I needed to prove my worth to my sisters and friends, and to myself. Evening rolled around as I was trying to find a way to participate in the rapidly approaching event. Though I was sore with my healing injury, I had no problem moving around the village and my destination that evening was actually the food lodge. Before I could leave my hut, a knock sounded at my door. I thought maybe it was Shana.

She had been gone on a mission to the south performing her ambassador duties and promised to stop in and see me when she got back.

Instead I was nervously surprised to see Ori on the other side of the door. Seeing the tray loaded with food, I quickly hung the cloak that I was in the middle of donning and moved to clear a space at my table. She smiled at me as she set it down, but I sensed immediately that something was off about her demeanor. I smiled back though because I was genuinely glad to see her.

I had been in a good mood all day for a few reasons. First and foremost, I woke with the least amount of pain I had felt in days and it gave me hope about getting cleared for the archery contest. The previous two nights had also gone by with no nightmares plaguing my sleep. I had been speaking with the priestess every day since my breakdown. The subsequent talks were nothing like the first one. The blade of my anger seemed to have dulled after the initial purging of my memory. Though she had repeatedly suggested it to me, I had yet to speak with the queen about the more intimate details of my slavery. Perhaps that was why seeing her grace my doorway unexpectedly made me so nervous. "Good evening, Ori. You did not have to bring me dinner, we could have dined in the food hut."

She could not help smiling at my obvious good spirit and waved for me to sit. "You sound much better, how are you feeling?"

I met her sad eyes then and let my honesty shine through. "I am feeling well. My side is significantly better and I have slept sound for two nights in a row. I have not felt better since before I was taken." I paused, sensing that she was really interested in my welfare knowing that it directly related to her own. "Glyphera and I have been speaking every day about my ordeal and my feelings. She thinks I am finally making progress and I agree with her."

She nodded and gave me another strange smile before placing loaded food dishes in front of us and pouring water into our mugs. "Good, good, I'm really glad to hear that."

I didn't press her about the strangeness of her tone or looks. Instead I let her talk about her recent trip to the centaur village to see her sister, Risiki. She left the afternoon after our sparring session and was gone for a hand of days. Her words slowed to a stop as the food disappeared. Sensing she was at a loss, I placed my hand over hers. "Ori?" She turned those heartbreaking green eyes to me and I grew dismayed to see them full of tears. "What is wrong?"

"Iva is leaving the Telequire nation. She came to see me last night when I arrived back from my visit with Risiki." Her gaze never left mine and I was cast adrift on thought and emotion.

The news did not take me unawares because Iva had mentioned it to me. However, it was difficult because we shared the bond of slavery and I loved her as a friend still. "Di—did she say why?"

Ori looked down at our layered hands. "Did you know that she is in love with you?"

I sighed and followed her gaze to the table. "Yes."

Her response was quiet and sad, but there was a tinge of anger to it that I had rarely heard. "Why didn't you tell me?"

My gaze shot up to hers immediately, confusion roaring in my ears. "Tell you what, that she was in love with me?"

She stood then, abruptly dropping my hand from hers and knocking over the chair. "Why didn't you tell me she was the one, Kyri? Why did you let me continue to hope all the while she was pining for you?"

I was shocked. I could not have been shocked more if a tree fell from the sky onto my head in the middle of a field. Panic clawed at my throat that she would leave, that she would not hold on. I had to tell her, I had to explain. "The one? No! She—I know she loves me, is in love with me. She told me while we were still slaves. I told her that my heart belonged to another! I love you, Ori, and my heart has only ever belonged to you!"

The confusion swept from me to her and she trembled with it. "But our bond, your pledge, you said—"

My voice was nearly a whisper when I choked out the words. "It was not her." She was stunned and hurt, and yet I knew we needed to have the talk before another candle mark could pass us by. It was long overdue and the priestess insisted I open up to Ori before I could really start to forgive myself. I waved toward the bed that was against the opposite wall. "Please, can you sit? We—I need to tell you what happened."

She stood rigid and anger started to replace the shock. "I don't want to know that!"

"Ori, please!" I ran a hand through my loose hair, careful not to dislodge my restored rite of caste feather that Ori had given back to me. I knew my blue eyes would be dark and unhappy. Emotion always colored them their own way. "You promised you would listen when I needed to talk and I need you to listen now."

She did not reply. Instead she walked over and sat on my

bed, scooting backward until she could lean against the log wall, drawing her knees up to her chest. I put another large log on my fire and poured us each a mug of wine. Even if she did not need it, I wanted something that would help relax me. Despite her contrary words moments before, she sat patiently as I recited the entire tale of my slavery. I explained what happened the night I was freed and told her of my talks with Glyphera and the conclusions the older woman had come to. I looked to the mantle and noticed candle marks had mysteriously disappeared as I spoke. My mug was long empty and tears ran freely from our eyes by the time I was finished. Finally I looked up at her, pleadingly, and a sob escaped into the hand that covered her lips. My guilt flared at her upset. "I am sorry. I—I tried to stop her. I tried." I shook my head, unable to say any more.

When her green eyes met mine, I did not know how to interpret the look. "Kyri, surely from all you've said and from your talks with the priestess, you must know it wasn't your fault, right?"

I nodded. "I—I think I am starting to. But I did not think that way for a long time."

Confusion washed over her face. "Why? You had no control over what she did. She forced you, why would you feel like you had betrayed me?" Not able to stand still, I set my mug down and slowly paced the floor in front of her. I thought of my reasons why, and they still shamed me. How could I tell her? How could I admit to such a thing? "Kyri?"

The truth burst forth like water over a dam after spring rains. "Because it felt good! Even as I tried to fight it, even as I cried for my want of you, she brought me release and I liked it! If I really did not want her why would my body betray me in such a way? How could she bring me such pleasure when my heart was breaking? How can a woman be capable of such a thing?"

She leaned over and set her mug on the table next to the bed and moved to stand in front of me. Though my eyes were cast downward, unable to face the sure disappointment from my admission, I could see her in my peripheral vision. I was surprised but not startled when she turned my face toward hers. "First thing I want to tell you is that as much as it pains me to admit, a woman can be capable of all the same depravities as a man. While a woman is not normally strong enough to force someone to their will, make no mistake that they can be ten times more manipulative." She stared at me for a heartbeat, perhaps to see if her words had filled me with understanding. I had many discussions with Glyphera about what the queen was saying and it pained me to nod my head in admittance. After another heartbeat she continued. "Do you control the churning of your guts when faced with a fearful situation?"

Unsure where she was heading with her question, I answered truthfully. "No."

"Can you stop the bumps from rushing up and down your arms when you catch a chill?"

I shook my head. "No, but what does—"

She covered my lips with a finger. "Our bodies respond to stimulus and most of the time we cannot control that response. We are very physical creatures, Kyri. We get cold, we get hot, we feel pain and pleasure, and we cannot always say yay or nay on the what or when of it. You love me, right?"

Indignant, I gave her wide eyes. "Of course I do!" Suddenly her left hand squeezed tight against my healing wound and I cried out in pain.

She immediately let go and stared up into my eyes as her quiet voice continued. "And do you see how someone who loves you can cause you physical pain?" I sucked in a breath and nodded. "How is that different from someone who doesn't love you causing you physical pleasure? You cannot control how your body reacts. And while I hate the fact that she touched you, I am not upset with you. I do not feel betrayed by you." She sighed and ran a hand through her hair. "Yes, I am angry about the entire situation and it has been hard for me to get closer to you physically because of what I perceived as your betrayal. I have my own guilt that rides my back like a beast. But now that we both know the truth of it, perhaps we can really start to heal."

I looked at her curiously and paled at what she could be referring to. I knew that the queen had many lovers before me, though no love in her heart save for Artemis. Had she remained true in my long absence? "Your own guilt?"

She saw my look and immediately knew where my thoughts had gone. "No! No. Though it was hard and I wanted to forget my loss every day, I stayed true to you. Just as I said before, no one has ever held my heart before you and without that connection the act would be less. It would be emptier and not as fulfilling. But my guilt..." Her voice trailed off, perhaps searching for reluctant words.

"There was a big part of me that was still very angry when we sparred. I didn't want to hurt you, I never have. But I have to admit that there was a small part of me that took satisfaction in dealing you that injury. The thought of your betrayal, no matter what circumstances I could dream up in my nightmares, filled me with a deep anger. Even as my heart hated to see you in pain, I wanted to twist that blade in your side and hurt you the way you had hurt me with your words of admission. I'm sorry, but I didn't know the why of all that happened to you. When you told me that you had broken your pledges, I could see the guilt of it through your eyes and I assumed that you were at fault, that you willingly went back on your promise to me. And when I saw Iva with you in the healer's hut after, I ran. I took a trip to spend time with my sister and to get away. I promised you that we would work through things together and I would be here for you. But in that moment I was hurt and I'm sorry if I let you down."

Ducking my head, I felt both relief and sadness. "I wish I had been stronger."

She cupped my cheek in the palm of her right hand. "And I pray to Artemis every day, thanking her for your strength. Thanking her for you." There was a feeling inside me that seemed to erupt from her words. For the first time since I was taken, I saw the real potential of a future between us. Neither of us had let the other go. As my emotions threatened to overwhelm me, I did the only thing I could manage. Giving her time to pull away, I slowly moved my head toward hers. Though the mere thought of putting myself at another's mercy made me tremble, I pushed through my fear until our lips met with the barest of touches. Like the brush of fluttering butterfly wings we moved against each other, slow and sure. I did not escalate the kiss and neither did she. We were not ready for the drowning passion of our past. She pulled back with a sigh and looked into my eyes. I had no idea what she saw there but it brought her lips to me once again.

The second kiss was not a tentative exploration like the first. It was more of a persistent and sweet reminder of what we were capable of once the shackles of memory were finally cast aside. The delicate whisper of her lips against mine caressed something long forgotten in my soul and I smiled as she finally pulled away from me. My queen and love wore her own shy smile as she made her way to the door of the hut. Before pulling it open, she turned back to me one last time. "Would you like to breakfast with me tomorrow?"

I could not help the pure joy that quirked my lips and sent my heart fluttering. "I would like that very much."

"Until tomorrow then." With a nod, she was gone. I touched my lips and marveled at the tingling awareness that had spread throughout my body. It felt as if my limbs had all been asleep and were suddenly waking up. Perhaps they were. I knew for certain my heart had. The numbing ice that surrounded my beating organ for nearly a sun-cycle was finally thawing, and I welcomed more of Ori's fire.

I WAS DELIGHTED to see Shana in the meal hut the next morning when the queen and I arrived. Concern grew quickly though as I noted the dark circles beneath her eyes. Though my sister seemed genuinely happy to see me there with Ori, I could tell another sadness was lurking just under the surface. Then from one bite to the next a thought occurred to me and I nearly cried out with my own insensitivity. How had I forgotten so much about my previous life and the lives of my friends? I realized that I had not once asked her about how things had progressed with Coryn. I paused with eating knife in the air, trying to think of whether or not I had seen them together since coming back to the nation. I had not.

Feeling eyes on me, I continued with my previous motion and cut a bit of venison to eat with my morning bread. I rarely used to eat meat in the morning but since leaving Rome I had developed a craving for it. As a gladiatrix, I was not served a lot of meat. Most of my diet was made of fruits, vegetables, nuts, and beans. I was never lacking in what I needed, but there were many things that I sorely missed. Shana gave me a strange look and swallowed a bite of porridge to address the queen. "I heard that Iva and Kyri are being honored at the Equinox Eve ceremony."

I spun my head toward Ori, surprised at Shana's words. I assumed they would let our welcome pass by. I preferred it actually. Ori smiled at both of us. "Yes, the council and I decided we wanted to wait until both were healed and whole to celebrate their homecoming. We wanted to make it special because it's not every day that Telequire Amazons return from sure death or a lifetime of slavery in a foreign land."

I flushed at the thought of attention being put on me. I did not want to be honored for surviving a situation that was out of my control. I took a sip from my mug of water, mouth having gone dry at the thought of a nation of eyes on me. "Do—do you have to honor me? Can you not just honor Iva?"

Shana looked at me curiously. "Kyri?"

Ori gave me the answer I did not want. "You know we can't do that, just as you know that you deserve honor. What are you afraid of?"

My mind raced with the need for words to try and put my thoughts into something that could be understood by people who had not walked in my shoes. "I am afraid of the noise and the crowd, I am afraid to have so many faces turned toward me expecting an action, or reaction."

Understanding green eyes pierced me with their gaze. "Do you think it will trigger your memories?" I shrugged but she knew how I felt. She covered my hand with hers. "We'll keep you safe from your past, trust in us."

Shana reached across the table and covered my other hand. "We are here for you, Kyri."

I smiled at both of them, touched as their love enfolded me. "Thank you."

Ori broke the moment when she picked up her dishes in one hand and a wrinkled apple in the other. "As much as I hate to do it, I have to run. I have a council meeting soon and another meeting with Margoli and Steffi after that. Will you be okay?"

Shana smiled at our queen. "She'll be fine, I'm going to keep her company for a few candle marks. I had the scrolls from my trip sent to your council chamber and I'm due some downtime now."

Ori smiled at her fondly. "Yes, you certainly are. Thank you, Shana, for everything."

Once the queen was gone, Shana stacked her empty dishes and looked at me. "So what exactly are you doing today, besides letting your side heal?" Her look became stern. "I'm still angry as a wet pea-hen that you sparred with Ori. It was dangerous for both of you!"

I held up a hand to prevent her from winding further in the wind. "I know how you feel about it all, sister. But it was necessary, trust me." I stacked my own dishes and stood. "As for what I am doing today, well I need to see Thera about my wound and then I will figure it out from there."

She sighed. "Okay then, if you say so."

"I say so."

She laughed. "You're so stubborn!" With that she started walking toward the door, placing her dishes on the correct table on her way. "Well come on, to the healer hut we go!"

We were surprised to see Coryn inside the healer's hut being tended to by Thera upon our arrival. I noticed Shana give a start out of the corner of my eye when she first saw the scout leader but quickly schooled her face to neutrality. As we approached it became obvious why she was receiving attention. A large red area marred her left side over the rib cage, quickly turning into a bruise. She made a small sound of pain as the older healer poked and prodded at the spot, then sat calmly while her midsection was wrapped tightly with a wide bandage. Thera cackled at the scowl on her face. "Oh wipe off that frown, Scout Leader. Tis most likely just bruised, you'll be running the trees in time for equinox!"

Coryn continued scowling and turned her attention to us. "Heyla, what brings you two in so early in the morning?"

The healer turned her head and looked at me with concern. "Is your side bothering you, Kyri?"

I shook my head. "Actually no, I came in to see if you would clear me to shoot my bow."

Both Coryn and Thera's eyebrows went up but Shana's voice was the one that pierced the air. "*What*?"

"I'm ready to shoot and I have to shoot." I leveled a calm serious gaze at the old woman. "And honestly, if you do not clear me, I will take my bow out into the woods and shoot there out of sight from everyone."

"Kyri—"

I cut Shana off before she could mother me. "No! You do not understand this and I cannot explain it. But trust me when I tell you that this is something I have to do." I softened my voice and gaze when I looked at her. "Please, I need your support. Trust me to know my limitations." She did not answer, but she nodded.

Thera sighed and clucked her tongue before lifting my tunic to look at the wound. The red healing scar line stood pale on my skin but it was neither inflamed nor was it as tender as it could have been. Shana and Coryn moved off to give us some privacy and I stiffened when I heard a quiet comment. "Oh!" I turned my head as far as I was able in order to see my two friends. Coryn's face was stoic and Shana had a hand over her mouth and her eyes were wet with unshed tears.

I had told the story enough times at that point that the bits and pieces of it had become easy. "I was lucky in that I was only whipped twice. The first time happened while I was still aboard the slaver's ship. They did not like my defiant attitude so they tied me to the main mast and took the whip to me for insolence. I did not break any rules after that."

"Th—" Coryn had to clear her throat to ask the question. "Then how did you get whipped the second time?"

"One of the overseers at my owner's property thought Iva

was stealing fruit when in actuality it was mine. I tried to explain and he thought we were both lying. I could not harm him because it would have gone poorly for us do to so. Instead I threw my body over Iva's to take her beating."

Thera, who had already seen the whip marks, looked up at me. "What did they use to treat the wounds?"

The memory of the treatment was more painful than the wounds themselves. "I do not remember what was done the first time, I only remember waking in their healer building. The second time my wounds were scrubbed and treated with a salt brine. After that they let the wound dry and added a poultice a few times a day for the first couple days, then my back was left to heal in the open air." No one said anything but I could see it in their eyes. They all knew that despite the healing properties of the salt brine it would have been agony. And it was. Thera gave a shake and started poking at my injury to test it out. Unlike when Ori had grabbed my side I was prepared and only grunted lightly with the pain of it.

"How does it feel?"

My face felt tight with her ministrations but it was not debilitating, and it was not anything that I had failed to train through before. "It is fine, all things considering. I just need to know if it is healed enough that the wound will not split open again."

The old healer dropped my tunic and stepped back. Her eyes were sad but she smiled at me anyway. "Goddess knows you're bound and determined to turn me gray." We chuckled at the woman who had probably been completely gray for sun-cycles. "But your wound is healed enough for whatever it is you want to do. Well, with the exception of falling out of a tree that is." She looked pointedly at Coryn, who had the grace to blush. Getting the response she sought, Thera walked away chuckling.

I turned to my friend and laughed. "You fell out of a tree?"

She gave me an irritated look. "We were running in the southwest quadrant and one of the ropes broke as I was coming down out of the canopy."

I held my hands up. "Do not look at me that way. I have not made it to that section in my rope duty yet. And someone, who I shall not name, convinced me to spar and get injured before I could complete more."

The attractive woman gave a hearty laugh then promptly clutched her ribs. "I convinced you to spar, the queen's sword is what convinced you to get injured."

Shana watched us back and forth until she finally threw her

hands up in frustration. "You two are insane!" She looked at me. "You could have had a much more serious injury, you're lucky the queen is so skilled!" Coryn started to smirk at me until Shana leveled her honey-eyed gaze at the tall scout. "And you could have been killed as well! You shouldn't be so careless out there!"

Coryn raised an eyebrow at her, face suddenly serious. "Oh? And why is that?" Shana did not reply but merely leveled a furious gaze at her then turned and stomped out of the hut.

I cast a surprised look at the scout leader. "What was that all about?"

Coryn sighed. "I love her."

I had suspected as much the previous sun-cycle but her answer did not clear the water of my confusion. "Does she know that?"

My friend gave me a sad smile. "She knows. She just doesn't care."

Thoughts were dropping into place with Coryn's words. My eyes tracked to the door that Shana exited through. One thing I was certain of was that Shana was not as indifferent as Coryn seemed to think she was. I turned back to Coryn and nodded my head toward the door. "Since you are suddenly free of duty you can come keep me company on the archery range. We can see how much skill I have lost in the past few moons."

She groaned. "Oh please spare me from your false humility. I think you could out shoot most of us in your sleep no matter how out of practice you are!"

I grinned at her. "You, at least."

"Woods weasel! I'm not that bad a shot!" I laughed at the lightness and familiarity that I had sorely missed. Sometimes you do not realize you have an emptiness until someone comes along to fill it. Coryn's humor and friendship were balms to my soul and I smiled to realize that another candle had been lit in the dark room of my mind.

Chapter Eight

Reclaiming the Pieces

I RETRIEVED MY two most recently used bows and both quivers from my hut before we made our way to the training grounds at the edge of the village. I needed both quivers because the arrows for each were of differing lengths. I picked the target nearest to the tree line, hoping that I could avoid calling attention to myself. As I was stringing the first bow I glanced back at Coryn who was still wearing all her scout gear, having gone to the healer's hut straight from the trees. "Are you sure you do not wish to shoot?"

She looked at me as if I were crazy. "Did you not just see me in with Thera, clearly nursing bruised ribs?"

I glanced down at my own side then gave her a pointed look. "Did you not see me get stabbed a seven-day ago? You really should toughen up a little, First Scout Leader."

She growled in response then her face brightened noticeably. "Oh look, here comes Kylani!"

I turned my head as I finished stringing the second bow. "Heyla, Training Master."

She did not bother with pleasantries. "You're not supposed to be here."

My response came as I set down the Roman bow and donned my quiver. "Actually, Thera just cleared me to shoot. She said there was no danger to my wound as long as the pain was tolerable and I did not fall out of any trees." Coryn nodded to confirm my words but made a face at the last part.

"Well then, do you want the advanced target set up?"

"No, I have been away from the bow too long. I just want to shoot a few easy quivers first." My first handful from the multicolored bow were not ideal, but I slowly tightened my grouping as I finished out the twelve. The feel of the grip in my hands was both a long lost friend and that of a stranger. It had been nearly a sun-cycle since I last held the bow that I had purchased with my winnings from the archery tournament in Kozani. The way the arrow drew back with the knock sitting nicely at the corner of my mouth, the way the tension felt as I held the draw, brought memories of who I once was.

I switched bows and noticed immediately the difference in weight and balance. The grip was familiar yet strange on the short compact bow. Though I wanted to, I could not hate the weapon that saw me through the worst time of my life. The sagittarius bow did not change me, it was simply that I had been changed with that bow in hand. After I finished my second quiver I stood staring at the target in silence. My companions did not speak, they just let me absorb things on my own. It was then that I realized neither weapon belonged to me. The knowledge brought the familiar sadness of loss. I had owned three bows since I had been old enough to hunt on my own and each bow belonged to a different Kyri. I was no longer that naïve fletcher who left home so long ago, and I could never go back to that archer the nation once knew. I looked down at the short bow in my hand and decided then that I would never use it again. I refused to be the sagittarius amongst my family and friends. I turned to Kylani and I must have worn a strange expression because she shifted in concern. "I need a new bow."

Coryn looked confused. "I don't get it, your shots were all good. And you love your rosewood bow."

I did not answer her. The training master stared at me for a few heartbeats then nodded. I was relieved that she understood my need and motive. "I'm assuming you want something different, not the usual scout issue?" I nodded. "Goneah's bond mate is a bow maker in our sister village. I have some time today, would you like to go look at his wares?"

"I would like that, thank you." I looked down at the bows I held in each hand. "I will have to sell one or both of these to afford a new one—"

Coryn interrupted me with an uncharacteristically soft voice. "Kyri, you still have all of your money from your sales in Preveza. Steffi is holding it for you with the nation's coffers."

I looked at her in surprise and Kylani confirmed her words. "It's true. The queen was so convinced that you'd return that she ordered it there for safekeeping, the same way she ordered thorough cleanings of your hut every seven-day." The stoic training master ran a calloused hand through her short dark hair and sighed. "Despite the rest of us telling her to move on and let you go, she refused. She never lost her faith in you, Kyri."

I swallowed the lump in my throat. "I wish I could say the same but I did lose faith in me. I think that is when I became lost, when I became someone else. But now I am neither here nor there and I need to rediscover who I am all over again. This—" I held up both bows in front of me. "This is only one step of many."

Kylani smiled and I knew then that she truly understood. "Why don't you and Coryn go retrieve your money pouch and I'll saddle a couple horses for us. We can probably be there and back by midday then you can practice with your new bow. Are you coming with us, Coryn?"

The first scout leader shrugged. "I may as well. As long as you don't plan anything more than a brisk walk on the horses. I don't think my ribs can handle so much as a trot right now."

Laughter rang out over the empty field. "I'll have three ready and I promise to stay at a comfortable pace. Meet me at the stables when you're finished."

I brought my regular bow with me on the trip since it was foolish to travel without one. Even a journey to a town that was as close as the one that housed the boys and men related to the Telequire Amazons could bring danger. When we arrived I was pleased to find that Goneah's husband, Stephan, was a skilled bower indeed. The whip-thin man had shaggy brown hair that always seemed to fall in his dark eyes but his smile was easy and kind. His son Gonal was also his apprentice and could be seen though the doorway shaping a stave of bow wood. Kylani and Coryn both decided to go off and explore the market knowing I would be there a while trying to decide.

As I walked around the small shop I could see a variety of bows ranging from the short and powerful to the long and sleek. I picked up an unstrung short bow with curiously curved limbs. It was very similar to the bow I carried in Rome, but more bent and strangely wrapped. I liked the ease that I could slip my old bow across my shoulders but I had seen the benefits and maneuverability of the sagittarius weapon. My only problem with a shorter bow was that there was no place I could hang it while I ran the trees. I looked closer at the item I had picked up and could see that it was made from different materials bound together. Stephan noticed my interest and walked over. "Have you shot a short bow before?"

I nodded. "Yes, the ones used in the gladiator arena. But this one is different. What is it made from?"

"That there is a Scythian bow. It's made from layers of wood and horn, then wrapped and lacquered to keep it all together. The Scythian bow actually comes with a *gorytos*."

I raised an eyebrow at the unfamiliar word. "What is that, a quiver?"

He shook his head then opened a chest that sat along the wall below the section of short bows. He took out a leather item that looked like a large quiver with two compartments. "This is a gorytos. It is a holder for the bow and arrows all together."

I looked at the holder, then back at the twisted and bent bow. Looking at the knocks I could see that they were made from the horn core that Stephan spoke of and bound with sinew. The loops of the string were wrapped in soft chamois leather. It was a beautiful bow with primitive designs carved into the unwrapped portions of wood and stained dark. "How well does it stay together? I mean, with the wrap and the different materials, is it difficult to maintain?"

The bow maker grinned. "Not much different than a regular bow. It's pretty protected with two-thirds of it resting inside the case, and there is a soft leather cover that goes over the exposed end. As you can see, the quiver is attached to the outside to make it easy to get to your arrows."

I motioned toward the entire thing. "Can I try it on?"

"Sure." He handed it over after I had removed my own quiver and cloak and I slipped the gorytos over my head so that it lay diagonal across my back. The fit was good and both the bow and arrows were easy to remove with my right hand. He smiled, sensing that I was more than just casually interested. "The bow is traditionally used by cavalry and has a top distance of about three hundred paces. You'd have to be a good shot to hit your mark from that far though."

I mentally calculated each of my paces as about five hands long and whistled. "You are right, that is some distance. And all that from such a short bow, though I should not be surprised. It is just that the short bow training I received was mounted and much closer to my opponents."

He shrewdly took in the tattoo on my inner forearm. "Sagittarius?" I nodded and he did not question any more. "Why don't I take you out back to where I have some targets set up so you can try it out?"

I gripped the smooth wood in my hand and nodded, a little ball of excitement tumbling in my belly. When I followed him outside, I saw that there were targets set up at various distances. Some as close as twenty paces and others as far as fifty. I strung the bow and drew my first arrow, delighted to see that it was nearly the same exact length as what I had stocked for my Madagascar rosewood bow. The draw was one of the heaviest I had pulled but I knew that would give me the most distance and power. My first arrow landed within the circle of the forty pace target. Each arrow after pulled tighter and tighter in the formation until the last three split on each other in the center. I felt a bit of pride as it was Stephan's turn to whistle. I turned to him to begin the most difficult task. "How much?"

He named a price that was far above what I paid for my beloved rosewood. I haggled back and forth for a few candle drops until we finally met in the middle. It was slightly more than I gave to Torrel on my way to the Telequire nation. After paying him and collecting my cloak and weapons from inside, he grasped my forearm and we said our goodbyes. I found Kylani and Coryn at the blacksmith and told them I was all set. Kylani looked at my bow curiously and Coryn blurted out the first thing that came to mind. "That looks just like your other short bow." I pointed out that my sagittarius bow was made of a single piece of wood while the Scythian bow was made of multiple materials.

The training master ran her fingers over the string groove near the end. "What's the distance on this?"

"He said about three hundred paces." I also showed them the gorytos and how the bow was carried.

Kylani's look turned calculating. "How easy is it to remove from the holder and string?"

"It is fast. As is drawing my arrows." I tilted my head at her. "My reasoning for getting this is because I thought a smaller bow might be more efficient in the trees. My only concern was how to carry it while running the limbs but the gorytos solves that problem nicely."

"Hmm, I'd like your report on that after you've used it for a while. That might be a better bow for our scouts."

Coryn ran her hand along the unfamiliar curves and wrapped sections. "It seems strange, are you sure?"

Kylan shook her head. "You scouts are so set in your ways!"

I put my hand on Coryn's arm. "I will let you take a turn with it when we get home. I think you will like it." Just as I had predicted, both my companions liked the new bow, though Coryn swore at the way it pained her ribs to draw. Both also complained at the draw weight but I was used to it since I liked a harder string pull than most of the Amazons I had met. I easily stopped Kylani's pendulum target but only caught one ring on her new advanced target. It was a challenge that I wanted to meet in time for the Artemis games. Coryn wandered off to midday meal and I stayed a few candle drops after to speak with Kylani. She watched quietly as I awkwardly donned the two quivers and the gorytos and slung the three strung bows over my left shoulder. She walked with me as far as the training hut.

"What's on your mind, Kyri?"

I shifted one of bows higher onto my shoulder to keep it from slipping down my arm. "I have been thinking about my match with the queen last seven-day. Despite my lapse and injury it was the right thing to do, and I realized another trigger for my memories. I believe I would be fine to spar as long as someone kept talking to me, kept me grounded throughout. But Coryn was right in that I need to face a combat situation and learn how to live with it and deal with it like any other Amazon."

She stopped at the log structure that housed the training weapons and various scrolls about combat. "So what are you saying?"

"I would like to start sparring again. We can do it with me under the eye of archers if that makes everyone feel safest, but I really need this."

The training master looked at me closely, perhaps searching for the truth of my words and for the promise of safety to the other women of the tribe. She abruptly turned and walked into the hut, returning less than a candle drop later with my pugiones in hand. She held them out to me. "Here. I think it's time to return the wooden blades to the basket."

I tried to reject the offer. "But the queen said—"

She waved away my protests. "The queen and I have discussed this already and she gave me leave to decide when and if you get your weapons back. I think that time has come."

The daggers held a weight in my hands that I was unfamiliar with. I stared at them as heartbeats thumped by, trying to decide if they too should be retired like the sagittarius bow. No, I finally decided. They were utilitarian and served a purpose but were not my real passion. Bow and fletch had guided my life and would continue to guide it until I was nothing more than loam in the forest. I needed safety in the wood and string that cast my arrows aloft. I did not need such reassurance from my blades. Thoughts completed in a circle, I removed the wooden daggers from their ill-fitting pugio sheathes and replaced them with my Roman blades. "Thank you for your trust."

She grinned at me then and clasped my shoulder with a strong hand. "I'm glad you're back, Kyri. Now I must go but keep me posted on how effective the new bow is in the trees. I suspect it will go quite well."

I nodded. "That I can do." She went off to her duties, which left me to make my own way to midday meal.

THE DAYS THAT followed after my trip to Stephan's shop ran fast like water in a swollen stream. I continued to practice with the new bow, even making a few passes through the running course Kylani and I had set up the previous sun cycle. She also began sparring with me with a variety of weapons. Archers were present at first, but as I displayed no lapses into my past they eventually went away. The key was for us to keep talking as we circled with blades, staves, or chobos. I stayed grounded that way and much in the present. I met with the queen for various meals on all the days she was available and even found the time to hunt and make a pot of my rabbit stew for her.

Slowly, my life came back into focus and the routine that was so familiar to me had begun to return. One part of my new life that I dared not change was my daily visits with the priestess. We continued to talk through my memories and my emotions. Though the queen and I had been slowly but surely reestablishing the solid bond we had left the previous sun-cycle, I still felt reticence. I longed for her to touch me, but I was also terrified of what would happen after. Was she still upset that another had touched me in the most intimate and sacred places? Would she be repulsed by the crisscrossing scars on my back and the leopard claw scarring that now marred both legs and my shoulder? I had no answers, only fears and doubts. It made me uncomfortable to talk about such things, so the words that I felt deep within my soul were never said. The queen and I continued with only the smallest of kisses and touches but I sensed her frustration building and I did not know what would happen when she reached the end of her patience.

EQUINOX EVE DAWNED without the benefit of my waking eyes. I slept later than usual and woke feeling refreshed after another night of dreamless sleep. As I lay in bed listening to the village come to life, my thoughts turned toward the day ahead. Just as always, the temple ceremony would take place in the afternoon with the Ceremony of Light and feast following. There was nothing to be done about the unwanted honors being presented later so I needed to find something to keep my mind occupied elsewhere. Food was always welcome on solstice and equinox eve days so I figured I would practice a bit with my new bow after morning meal then go hunting to help keep the cooks supplied with meat. It would not go to waste. Whatever was not eaten off the spits would either be dried or cooked into stews.

Settled on a course of action for the day, I raised my arms above my head and gave a good stretch, glad for once that Gata had moved back to her bed on the floor. The nights were starting to warm up and with the big leopard fur cover and I did not need the added heat of an actual leopard. Wanting a change, I donned my girdle and long skirt made from leather strips, and put on my mottled green wrapped top. To avoid the chill morning I added my beloved green cloak on top of it all. Along with my knives and money, Shana had also brought the cloak back from Preveza. Because my mam had made it for me, it would have broken my heart to lose that too when I was taken by the slavers. It was tied loose to allow for the gorytos and bow that stuck above my right shoulder but otherwise left me feeling both free and warm.

Despite the fact that it was early morning, the village was noisy with the sound of so many people engaged in various activities. As I navigated the dirt paths on my way to the food lodge, my attention was caught over and over by women moving to and fro hanging garlands and other decorations. The hub of activity seemed greatest in the center of the village where the bonfire was being assembled. Multiple cook fires burned all around the open space, many with a variety of animals already roasting over the coals. In the large meal lodge I found an assembly of friends lined up on benches at the table farthest left of the door. Ori looked up as I crossed the threshold. The smile on her face was for me alone and a little more fear slipped away. It had been less than two moons since I arrived back on Greek soil but it felt as though a lifetime had gone by. Most of the dishes were taken by the time I went for food but I managed to find an old wooden platter left. The majority of Amazon plates were made from the abundant clay that was found near the river northeast of the village. I peered at the cracked wood and shrugged, figuring it was sound enough for a quick meal. Ori moved over on the bench to make room for me and I sat down to the smiles and laughter of my friends.

Over the seven-days since my return I had been growing more aware of the people around me. The tingling from Ori's kiss had set something much deeper in motion than just the awakening of my own body and self. Sitting at the table and talking among the people I cared for, I was ever aware of the feel of her thigh against mine. As I used my knife to place a tender slice of wood fowl in my mouth, a hand added to the pressure. I froze with the sharp tip clamped between my teeth, not daring to move. I trembled at her touch, both afraid she would take the delicate fingers away and afraid she would leave them. I startled as my thoughts were interrupted by Coryn.

"Heyla, Kyri! You're not supposed to eat the knife! Your arrows won't get any sharper that way." The table burst into laughter and I slowly removed the blade, grinning sheepishly.

"Ah, I uh, just paused for a thought." Hoping to redeem myself I called out to her in return. "Are you ready for the tree race tomorrow, Coryn? If you want I can sew some feathers into a cloak for you in case you should miss your step again. Maybe you will not hit the ground quite so hard." More laughter followed my taunt and even Shana snickered at that one. The attractive First Scout Leader sent a rude gesture my way and went back to her meal.

Ori squeezed my thigh to get my attention again. "Knife eating or not, I see your wit is as sharp as ever."

I narrowed my eyes at her playfully. "I would not have to defend myself if someone had not distracted me."

A delicately pale eyebrow rose over one of her green eyes. "Oh, is that so? Well it's not my fault you distract so easily..." Her words trailed off as her hand moved just a little higher. I had to set my knife down completely then as her fingers evoked the memory of our last time together and I was overcome with strong emotion. I could feel the heat as my face turned red with the resulting blush. I looked down at the table so the others could not see how much her touch affected me. Her hand immediately backed off then and concern laced her quiet voice. "Are you okay?"

Nearly against my will, my gaze slowly turned to meet hers. I knew the exact moment she became aware of my heightened state. Her lips parted ever so slightly and the pulse of her neck raced wildly, fast as my own hammering heart. "Oh." She looked at me with much thought then and cocked her head to the side. I knew she asked a question which until that moment I had no answer for. But the moment had come and gone and the answer sat surely in front of us. I smiled shyly at her and nodded. The fear was still there but over the course of multiple seven-days it had been deliberately moved to the side by love. The same love that stared at me through tear-shiny eyes. She wet her lips and spoke, if only to break the spell we had fallen under. "What do you have planned for the day?"

I swallowed thickly and it took two tries to answer. "Um, I thought I would do some target practice to prepare for the competition tomorrow then take Gata hunting for the feast. You are more than welcome to join me."

A smile curled her lips into something quite beautiful. "I have a surprising amount of free time today. I just have to be back a few candle drops before the temple ceremony. And I will need all the practice I can get if I'm to shoot against you again."

I saw that she wore her quiver and a quick glance near the doorway told me that she had left her bow there when she came in to eat. "We can shoot a few quivers after we finish eating and you can decide if you want to go hunting with me from there."

She placed her hand on mine and I grew warm inside my cloak. "I'd like that."

Other than Ori stopping briefly to speak with Glyphera and a runner, we went straight to the archery range after eating. There were quite a few people already practicing by the time we arrived. Finding an open target near the end, I removed my cloak and draped it over the rope that separated the range itself from our shooting positions. I grumbled as I strung my bow. "Why are there so many people here this morning? It has never been this busy."

The queen's light laughter brought my head up from the task at hand. "Kyri, you are the reason they are all here!" Confusion froze my limbs as my string slipped into place. She must have seen that understanding had not met me so she spoke more. "You're back with us and there is no one in Telequire that can give a greater challenge in the archery competition than you. The last Artemis games you participated in came just after the Western War when we had low turnout due to injuries. Now we have scores of scouts that want the chance to shoot against our greatest archer." I started my familiar protest but she stifled my words with a single finger to my lips. "You cannot argue that fact. Artemis knows you rival her with your skill."

I took the stifling digit between my teeth, causing her eyes to widen just before I released it again. "Artemis knows?"

"Of course."

I smiled at her and slipped into the once forgotten playful side of myself. "And how does her chosen feel about it?"

Ori's hands were free since her bow and quiver were still slung across her back. She used them to gently pull me down to her lips. I shuddered at the feel of something so soft against my newly sensitized skin. While the kiss was not deep or rushed it left me panting for air just the same. When she pulled away her words were slow like honey and sweet as the lips that had just caressed mine to fullness. "She finds your skill highly appealing."

She made to step backward and I drew her close again. "Perhaps we should skip target practice so you can continue with your show of appreciation."

The queen laughed at my words and I read the current of surprised delight underneath. It had been a long time since I felt so playful in both word and deed and the notion of it left me warm and happy. She must have sensed it and the light in her eyes told me I had done more than simply make her laugh. With a firm hand to the center of my chest, she pushed me back a step. "Oh no, you have to keep up your skills if you wish to earn more appreciation from the queen. Artemis's Chosen has very high demands."

I smiled. "And just what demand is the queen making from me?"

She removed her own bow and motioned to one of the Amazons down field, adjacent to our target. The woman jogged over and placed the pole with twirling wooden rings in the hole above our bullseye. "You have to beat me at the bow and fletch, of course."

I nodded at her with a mock-serious face. "Oh, of course." I motioned for her to shoot first. "By all means then after you, my queen!" The archers to either side had stopped and moved back to watch our friendly competition. Noting the assistant downfield from us, I called out before Ori could shoot. "One for one?"

The queen looked at me and nodded. "Sure." I watched as she drew and knocked an arrow then pulled it back until her fingers rested at the corner of those soft lips. A smirk played at the edges as she adjusted for the wind and twirling rings. She finally released before too many heartbeats thumped on. I was pleasantly surprised to see the arrow hit the center after it had pierced two of the three rings.

"You have been practicing!"

She laughed and stepped aside as more people came up behind us to watch. "I had to have something to do as I whiled away the candle marks waiting for your return. And strangely enough, the bow and fletch reminded me of you and gave me comfort."

In a voice that would not be heard by the gathered tribeswomen nearby, I recounted one of the things that I had learned in Kombetar. "They said you did not shoot at the Festival of Nations."

My simple observation was rewarded with a simple answer. "I couldn't. I was waiting for you."

I did not say anything because there was nothing to say. I merely waited for the assistant downfield to remove the queen's arrow so I could take my own shot. When the target was ready, I lined up my arrow. As the wind slowed I let go of the string, willing the arrow down its intended path. Murmurs went through the gathered Amazons as my arrow also caught two of the three rings. I turned to Ori. "Looks like we are tied. Should we shoot again?"

Ori's eyes narrowed and she looked carefully at my schooled face. "You're playing with me, aren't you?"

My smile was wide and innocent. "Oh, you mean because I have spent nearly the last ten moons with a bow in hand? I would never entertain such an idea."

She motioned for the assistant to remove my arrow and set up the target again. The suspicious blonde turned to me fully then, and her smile became decided mischievous. "Perhaps we should make this more interesting by adding to the challenge of it."

Curious I looked from her face down to the target then back to her face again. "That is the best target that Kylani has. How could we make it more challenging?"

"Simple. We are allowed to speak to the other while they shoot but no touching. The person farthest from the target after the next round is the loser."

With the words cast into the crowd from her mouth I began to sweat. She had to know what her voice alone could do to me. She had to be aware that mere words falling from her lips would leave me undone as sure as any mortal wound. I swallowed and nodded, acquiescing to her demand of both play and challenge. "Fine. But do not blame me if I miss the target completely and hit some unsuspecting scout in the backside!" Laughter rolled through the assembly of women as well as the queen.

"I might not blame you but I'm sure she would." Ori lined up to shoot with her left side facing the target and her back perpendicular to it. I stood behind her without touching or interfering with her shot, but close enough for her to hear.

She drew her arrow back and I carefully blew across the backside of her neck. Ori shuddered and closed her eyes for a heartbeat before opening them and re-focusing on the advanced target downfield. Just as I sensed her about to shoot I said the words that had been building for multiple seven-days. "My body misses your embrace..." My voice trailed off as her arrow sped away from us.

The head buried itself a hand span from the center and she turned to me with flushed cheeks. "That was cruel."

I laughed and held up my bow as I grabbed an arrow from my gorytos. "I followed all the rules. It is not *my* fault you are so easily distracted."

As I lined up I could hear her mumbling under her breath. A sound drew my eyes away from the task at hand. I let off my draw again and watched as the queen had found a small log to place behind my shooting position. She looked out at the crowd of watchers. "What? She's taller than I am!" They broke into laughter again as the queen bantered in a way that was familiar but had been long absent. Wanting to win our challenge, I drew again and sighted down the length of my arrow. The familiar blue and green of my fletching was a balm after so many moons without. I could sense the heat of her standing much too close behind me. "I dream of screaming my release to the Goddess, beneath you, the full moon, and the heavens above." Her words drew from me a tremendous shudder just as I released my string. The onlookers gasped in shock as my arrow nearly missed the target completely. Still too close, the queen chuckled behind me. "Who is easy now?" I missed the heat and scent of her when she stepped down off the log and away from me.

Laughter followed as she stepped away from me and a lone voice sounded from the crowd. "What did she say to you, Kyri? I want to repeat it tomorrow!" More laughter came after the brazen woman's words.

I did not repeat Ori's words but instead I knelt at her feet and kissed her draw hand. "I concede defeat to you, Queen Orianna. Your silver tongue has conquered me sure as the sun conquers the night sky each morn."

Another voice that sounded suspiciously like Shana called out from the crowd. "I bet her tongue conquers you again later!"

My face burned hotly but I took the jab in good nature. It had been much too long since I felt the laughter inside. It was as if something important had been returned to me. The archers dispersed back to their own targets after that and the queen and I had the pole removed and continued shooting until the quivers on our backs were empty. When we had shot our fill, Ori turned to me and took my hand. "I'd like to show you something." I nodded and she led me toward the opposite end of the village, near the temple.

I tugged her to a stop, nervously. "I am not sure if I am ready for you to do any screaming in the house of Artemis."

She laughed and tugged me forward again. "Fear not, love. We're not going to the temple."

My eyes narrowed as we made our way through the well-worn paths. "You did not answer the part about screaming."

Ori winked at me when she glanced back. "No, I didn't." My mind whirled at all the possible things she could want to show me. Was I ready for whatever she had planned? One foot trod in front of the other and I knew I would soon find out. I thought of her words to me just before my arrow went astray and I smiled.

Chapter Nine

The Fervent Rebirth of Passion

MY SURPRISE CONTINUED to grow as we neared the smallest bathing cave. Ori had not let go of my hand for the entire journey so I squeezed her fingers to garner her attention. "I thought we were going hunting? I was hoping to bathe after."

She stopped and her light-hearted expression turned more serious, but not solemn. "No hunting today, Kyri. I'd like the next few candle marks to be just for the two of us. Is that okay?"

I nodded and despite my resolve I felt very shy in that moment. Her presence, her smile, the queen exuded beauty in a multitude of ways. As we walked the last few paces to the heavy hide covering the door, I slipped into that old uncertainty. Despite all that I had been through and all that I had done, I was still fairly inexperienced with the ways of the heart and the passions of the flesh. My thoughts raced. Did she wish to be physical with me? Was she tired of waiting for us to connect on that most intimate plane? Perhaps I was letting my mind run too far away from my sense. After all, Ori did not say she wanted to be intimate, she said she wanted to show me something. "Kyri?"

I was startled by the sound of her voice. She had been speaking and was waiting for me, bent arrow and broken string! "Yes?"

She smiled as if she were aware of my internal conflict and doubts. "I asked if you were coming in with me."

Wide-eyed, I pulled myself taller and strode forward to the flap. "Yes." I pushed in ahead of her and the air rushed from my lungs all at once. Every torch was lit as well as more than a dozen oil lamps and a handful of flickering candles. The chamber glowed with an ethereal light. I had never noticed the sparkling bits of stone in the walls before. They were like the twinkling stars of the night sky. When I was able to draw breath again her name slipped out. "Ori, it is beautiful!" I could not contain the smile on my face as I turned back to her. "Is this what you wanted to show me?" She shook her head but did not say anything. Instead she removed her cloak in the hot cave and began unwrapping her shirt. I myself became overly warm. "I—ah—" By the time she got to her skirt, my face felt hot and I had to turn away from her.

My heart thumped as hands came around me from behind and removed my own cloak. She quickly started on my gorytos and I shrugged out of it to assist her efforts. "Won't you turn around, Kyri?" I shook my head and tried to swallow with a mouth gone dry. I shivered in the hot and humid air as she began unwrapping my top. When I was left standing in my boots, girdle, and strip skirt, she stepped close and pressed soft breasts to my scarred back. My shame spoke for me as I trembled at her touch.

"Please do not look at them."

She stepped away immediately and I was awash with relief and sadness. Calloused gentle hands began tracing the lines that crisscrossed my back and the first tear dripped onto my chest. She stepped close again until our skin slid smooth together and those same hands circled my waist. "Don't pull away. I think you're beautiful and no scar can convince me different. Every mark you bear is an obstacle you've overcome to make your way back to us, to come back to me."

I sucked in a shuddering breath as more tears fell. Her gentle touch, her words, they spoke of more than I thought possible. But it was not until I turned around within her grasp that I truly had an understanding of her thoughts and heart. Her eyes were shiny with unshed tears making the mossy green appear so much brighter in the intensely lit space. Her gaze was steady though, and the hands she clasped tight around my lower back were firm. She had not let me go. She would not let me go. Our flesh burned where we touched. As gently as I dared, I cradled her face between my hands and looked deep into those expressive eyes. "I love you, Orianna."

Ori gave me a squeeze and nuzzled my palm. "I love you too, Kyri Fletcher. Now, I still have something to show you."

"Something beyond the beauty of this chamber and the person who brought me here?" I looked around at the ceiling then back to the face of my queen.

She dropped her arms and stepped away. I watched to see what she would do. Ori walked across the cave to a small alcove that was carved into the far wall. When she returned, she carried a leather pouch about the size of two hands side by side. She spoke as she handed it to me. "Can you hold this for a candle drop?" I nodded and the pouch was placed in my palms. I was curious at the heavy feeling of it but I did not ask. Once again standing in front of me, Ori began to speak. "There was a night nearly a sun-cycle ago that a brave young scout traded feathers with an Amazon queen. That scout and queen had suffered from much miscommunication but they also carried a lot of love between them. Under the light of a three-quarter moon and in the watchful eye of Artemis herself, we pledged ourselves to the possibility of a future together." I swallowed thickly sensing the direction she was taking. As Ori reached up to untie her rite of caste feather, the tears threatened to return. When she finished, she held it out and met my eyes. "I have two questions to ask you. The first is, will you exchange feathers with me?"

I did not actually answer, but instead I tucked the pouch into the front of my girdle and untied my own feather. With shaking hands we reached out simultaneously and tied our feather into the other's hair. Happiness threatened to explode out of me but her voice brought me firmly back down to earth. She moved her finger back and forth to point at our two feathers. "This doesn't mean anything, you know."

"*What?* What do you mean this does not—"

I was surprised by the tender smile she aimed my way. "We've been pledged since that night. You only take back your pledge when you remove the other person's feather from your hair and when you remove them from your heart."

Hearing her say those words lit the last candle in the room of my soul. "Thank you for never giving up on me and thank you for loving me."

"Always." Her smile and eyes promised me more than the words and I knew she spoke truth. "There is one more thing, Kyri."

I wiped my damp eyes and laughed self-consciously. "I do not think I can handle more high emotion today."

She reached toward me and tugged the leather pouch from where I had stashed it. I watched as she slowly opened the ties that held the flaps closed and revealed what was inside. Two matching silver torcs rested on the leather. The ends where the metal nearly met with the other side featured stylized owls, animals sacred to Artemis. The center of each twisted stiff necklace displayed a turquoise bead of the deepest blue flanked by slightly smaller barrels of bright red coral. They looked like they were made for the Goddess herself, but there were two sitting in Ori's hands. I could only imagine at their worth and I assumed that they would be part of the costumes worn by the queen and the priestess during the temple ceremony. "Those are beautiful! What are they for?"

She tilted her head and gave me a strange look. "Do you not

know the meaning of matching torcs, Kyri?"

"I have seen plenty of torc necklaces, though none as magnificent as those. And I have never seen matching ones. Are they for you and the priestess?"

She shook her head and gave me a mischievous smile. "No, try again."

I closed my eyes for a heartbeat and it came to me. "They are a matched set for you and the regent!"

Before my head could race further down the trail she pulled me up short with her words. "They are for us, me and you."

My mind had gone blank and something, a small amount of realization, seeped in slow. "*Us?*" My voice was quiet but she heard me easily over the sound of the guttering torches and faintly trickling water. "Us." I repeated the word again, foolishly undone.

"With your permission, I'd like to announce our betrothal to the nation at the equinox ceremony."

I stepped back, dismay pulling my lips into a frown. "You cannot do that!"

Hurt flickered across Orianna's face but she continued to pursue the conversation. "Why can't I? Do you not love me? Do you not wish to join with me?"

"No!" The hurt look returned to her face and I rushed to explain. "I mean to say that no, that is not my protest. Of course I love you and I want to be with you. But you cannot join with me simply because I am not *me* yet! I am trying to unlearn all the things the Romans taught me. I have been trying to be the woman you exchanged feathers with last spring equinox. But I am not there yet. How can you wish to pledge yourself to someone neither of us truly knows?"

I watched as her face moved through a multitude of emotions and settled into one that was unfamiliar. "Kyri, you have always been you. Each one of us changes with the passing of time and experience and we can never truly go back. When you became the Fourth Scout Leader for our nation, it was impossible for you to go back to being that naïve girl from the homestead. And change has been wrought on you again making it impossible for you to go back to being that same archer that left us nearly a sun-cycle ago. The solution is not for you to become someone that no longer exists. It is for you to continue changing and evolving into someone you are proud to be. And even if you can't see it, you are on that path forward. I've been waiting for you, watching as you resolutely step further into the light each day. I don't need to see you reach the destination to know that I want to be there. When I say I love you, it means that I love all of you. Not just your best parts. And I would hope that you feel the same for me in return."

My hands trembled as her words sunk in. How could she love all of me? How could she love someone who had killed and took pleasure in the blood of her enemies? Did she really love those weak parts of me that wore the whip scars of a common slave? Had she truly forgiven my traitorous body for taking pleasure in another's touch? I had become a woman quick to anger at times, a woman who could be a danger to any future bedmate and she still loved that part of me? My lower lip quivered at the thought of her love and dedication and I tried to still it with shaking hands. As I brought fingers to my lips she stepped close again and my voice was a quiet whisper. "How could you love all those parts that cause me so much shame?"

She gently took my hands into her own, stilling the tremors. "Because those things are only a very small part of who you are. Because those things that you have done that shame you are in the past. They are not the woman in front of me and they are not part of your future. Look into my eyes, Kyri." She paused and I lifted my gaze to do as she asked. "I understand the blood lust all too well, I have also done things that I am ashamed of in my past. I have been ruthless, I have been vicious, and I have done things that hurt some while at the same time helped others. I have been quick to anger. I've had to make those difficult choices and I've lived through them and with them. As Orianna, I need someone by my side who has a strong heart and soul, but as queen I need someone who has a strong body and mind. Together we can help each other battle the daemons that drive us."

The last word she spoke echoed through my head again, as it had done just a short time before. "Us."

She nodded slowly. "Yes, us. That is, if you agree."

I did not answer, I could not. In that moment her nudity registered in my emotion fogged brain and I could only stare at the beauty that stood bathed in the candlelight. Instead of answering, I carefully took the torcs from her hands and set them on top of her clothes where they lay on the cave floor, then I unwrapped my own skirt. Once my skin was as bare as hers, I walked over to the carved steps leading into the small pool. I maintained eye contact with her as more and more of my skin was covered by the dark water. She looked as though she were holding her breath and when I finally broke the silence she sucked in an audible gasp. "Are you coming in? We cannot be an 'us' if we remain separated."

Her smile lit the chamber more than any burning flame and I knew that the path I marched was indeed my own. Agafya was right, I could never go back. But with each new day I could dedicate myself to becoming a better person than I was the day before. And my heart soared with the knowledge that Ori was not just waiting to love that better person, she loved all of me no matter where I was on the path to my future. She loved me completely and without doubt. I would dishonor us both if I did not love her the same in return.

Despite my resolution to move forward, to love her wholly and completely, my stomach was tight with nerves as she slowly entered the water. And slowly was exactly how she moved. It was like she knew that I was nervous and tried her hardest not to scare me. Not able to watch the gradual approach any longer I moved toward the side of the pool to grab a cake of lavender soap, then slid back to the center where she came to rest. She stood silently staring, perhaps waiting for me to make the first move. I held up the soap. "Would you like me to wash your hair?"

The woman who honored me with her heart nodded shyly and abruptly dropped below the surface of the water. When she rose again in the sparkling light, it was as if Aphrodite herself broke the inky surface in front of me. The short darkened blonde hair was slicked back from her face as rivulets of water ran from her skin. The muscles and breath in my body seized as one and all I could do was stare. She graced my mute wonder with a knowing smile but it quickly turned warm when my lips parted for desperate breath. I tried to focus but my body took on a life of its own as I stared dumbly at the queen of Telequire. Taking pity on me, or perhaps suspecting that I would not move until she broke us free of the spell, she turned her back to me. "I believe you promised something?"

My flesh tingled with sensation I had not felt so deeply in many moons. I had never been as affected as I was in her presence. While my heart and mind had been waking from the very moment I stepped foot on Greek soil, my body had not truly come out of its slumber until Ori's touch. Despite being wet, the strands of her hair felt light as I lathered them between my fingers with the hardened clump of soap. Moving beyond the cleanliness of her hair, I also massaged her scalp and eventually worked my strong hands down to the back of her neck and shoulders. I stopped and thought I heard a slight whimper, but I could not be sure. "You should rinse now so the soap does not burn your skin."

Even after she was rinsed I continued my ministrations on her shoulders, neck, and upper back. I received plenty of massages as a gladiatrix and knew just how good it could feel. Eventually my strokes slowed and I simply reveled in the feel of smooth skin beneath my fingers. One of the things I missed for so long was the intimacy that had developed between me and Ori. It was in the basic touch of another living, breathing person and the feel of a loved one being near. The sudden pang of longing moved me to wrap arms around the woman in front of me. As my breasts rubbed against her smooth back, she shuddered and let out a low moan. The Goddess herself would not have been able to resist such a sound had she been in my place.

My hands took on a life of their own and I traced her skin with more than just questing digits. I mapped her body with the entire length of me while standing behind her in the pool. My lips sought the back of her neck then traveled around the side to the spot just below her ear. I nibbled the lobe and moved down to taste the clean heat of her skin. Ori panted within the circle of my arms.

When my teeth nipped the jaw line near her mouth, I could not keep words in any longer. "My dream, my life, my goddess-made-flesh. My beautiful Ori, I have missed you. I spent moons missing the feel of you against my skin, on top of me, around me, and within me—" It was as if my voice alone were the catalyst she needed and she spun in my arms, taking my mouth with intensity. Her lips pressed tight against my own as her tongue mapped the space that had so recently been teasing her skin. Hands roamed under the water and out of the water, fanning the flames higher. It all came to an abrupt halt when I felt her hand brush against that place that had become the source of all my heat and fervor. I could not help flashing back to my night in Rome, nor could I prevent my reaction. I was unable to stop the fear and anxiety that washed across my features as I abruptly stepped away from her body. Tears pricked my eyes when I saw the hurt look on her face. I shook my head in apology. "I am sorry, so sorry."

"Kyri? What's wrong, love?"

I looked down, ashamed at my continued weakness in the face of such devotion. "I—it was a memory of—" I could not finish the words, all I could do was tell her how I felt. "When I felt you touch me I became afraid. The last time someone touched me

I—I had no control and—" Anger rose within me and I slapped the water in frustration. "*Futuo*!" Besides the frustration and fear within, my body still thrummed with arousal and I knew that Orianna must have felt the same.

Her touch came slow and soft but my eyes raised to hers anyway. "It's okay, I understand. Do you still want me, Kyri?"

I swallowed and nodded my head. I could feel the pulsing between my legs and my heart pounded in my chest from both fear and titillation. "Of course I do."

"Come here then." She pulled me to her and turned so her back was once again pressed firmly to my front. Before I could ask any questions she moved one of my hands under the water to cover her breast. As the point hardened beneath my palm, I caught on to her intent and reasoning. Bringing my other hand into the water I caressed both breasts at the same time, rolling hard nipples between my fingers. I brought my mouth down to her neck and Ori canted her head to the side as she gasped and moaned at my actions. The throbbing between my legs grew stronger as I snaked a hand down to skim across the center of her ardor.

While the water was warm, the place beneath my fingers grew even warmer when I stroked her. She turned her face up toward mine and I plundered her mouth with my tongue at the same time my fingers found the place that drew professions of love from her lips around the depths of our kiss. I could feel her skin and mons tighten against my fingers as her voice grew in volume and intensity. My free hand left the bounty of her breasts and I spread myself against the smooth skin of her gluteus. The strength of my fingers, arms, and hands pulled her against me and even as I stroked her to fulfillment I rubbed fervently against that firm muscle of her backside. While she climbed the heights toward that precious pinnacle, so too did I. As I grew closer to release I prayed that she would find hers as well because I knew my legs would fail to hold me when I fell over the edge. Perhaps there was someone watching over us answering prayers because between one breath and the next she cried out to her goddess and I followed immediately with the name of my own.

"Artemis!"

"Ori!" I lost track of how many heartbeats I bucked against her or she pulsed between my fingertips. All I knew was that in the moment of our release, all things that were made came undone. The light burst from my tightly closed eyes and in the darkness of its aftermath we were reborn together. I fell back into the water bringing her with me and when the tears came she was quick to pull me to the stone ledge beneath the water. I sobbed against her as she held me close and stroked my hair. Her words were quiet and I made no sense of them while I was so distraught but I was comforted nonetheless. When I finally found some semblance of control, I pulled away slightly and sat up next to her. Not able to bear judgement for my fears and weakness, I turned my eyes to the sparkling walls of the chamber. "I am sorry."

Slightly wrinkled fingers quickly turned my face toward the queen of my heart and nation. "Do not dare to apologize! That was beautiful and you are beautiful. I've missed you more than mere words can say."

"I am sorry for my fears then."

A concerned look crossed her face. "Were you still afraid when behind me?"

I shook my head. "No, it was perfect. I think I was afraid of the lack of control at first, afraid of someone taking, but when you moved me behind you I was no longer afraid." I sighed with contented pleasure. "Bow and fletch, but you continue to invade and overwhelm my senses when we are passionate together. I—I cry because I love you so much. I cry because sometimes when my body reaches that peak, so too does my soul and there is not enough of me to hold it all. It spills over and spills out of me, and my entire world is born again. Ori, your touch makes and remakes me every time we are together. You shoot me to the heavens where the stars explode behind my eyes and I do not know how to say all that when it is done."

She smiled up at me, and I could see that the passion was still there, though it was banked like a night fire. "My love, I think you just did. But now I'll know for next time."

I could not fight the need to touch her so I brought my palm to gently caress her cheek and jaw line. "So, us."

"Yes, us. There will be a ceremony, you know."

I sighed. "There always is."

She smiled as I covered her lips with my fingertips. I could feel the heat darkened skin turn upward. When she spoke again, it was slightly muffled so I moved my hand away to hear. "Everyone will be watching."

Another sigh escaped. "I know."

She brought her own hand up to delicately stroke my brow. "They will watch you pledge your future and undying love to their queen."

Tenderness took me as I smiled at her words. "She already

has that."

Ori continued. "They will watch you profess your eternal devotion and support."

She began tracing the shell of my ear as I answered again. "She has that too."

She cupped my cheek and looked straight into my eyes. "They will watch as the queen becomes betrothed to her future consort."

I blinked owlishly as the words settled in. "Oh." The sudden enormity of it all hit me as the word 'us' took on more meaning. Us was more than just Ori and I pledging to be together, it was more than promising to love each other until we died. Us for me and Ori meant that I would stand in front of the nation and represent the queen, I would stand in front of other nations and represent Telequire. Could I maintain a polite mien while all those eyes looked on expecting me to do—what exactly? My mind raced as I worried over the details of something I did not fully understand. What was the difference between a bond mate and a consort? What would be expected of me, and would I still be a scout? I had no frame of reference for such a thing nor did I have a love of attention. My breathing increased as panic crept in. But before I could spiral into a void of fear and self-doubt, she pulled me out.

"Kyri? Where did you go? You grew pale all of the sudden, is something wrong?"

I ran a hand through my wet hair and cursed when it tangled. It was then that I realized my failure to wash myself. I knew she was expecting an answer so I grabbed the cake of soap and lathered my hair. At the look in her eyes I thought she might join me to wash the dark strands herself, then I realized that she much preferred the view of my hands on my head and breasts lifted above the water.

I spoke in an attempt to explain my fear as much as distract myself from the heat that was rapidly rising again. "I only know of bond mates from my da and mam and I have no knowledge of consorts. What would I have to do? What would my duties be in the nation, would I have a job like scout still? Will I have to represent us to other tribes, would I have to take part in ceremonies like you and Basha? I do not think I can do that." Before she could answer the barrage of questions, I placed the soap back on the ledge and dropped my soapy head and body below the water to rinse. When I broke the surface again she was laughing.

"Goddess, Kyri, but you ask a lot of questions!"

I scowled at the fact that she found such humor in my worry.

"These are important questions!"

She moved toward me and placed a hand on my shoulder. "I know, love. Right this heartbeat though, I need to get out of this water. I don't know about you but my skin is starting to look like those dried dates you love so much." Ori made her way toward the drying cloths that were stacked in the large alcove and I followed her out of the pool. "We still have time, why don't we go back to my hut and I'll explain some of the details to you?"

After dressing and dowsing all the flames, we actually went separate ways from the smallest bathing chamber. Ori said the torcs had to remain with the priestess for a full season of blessing before we could be joined, another detail I did not know. I volunteered to get some food for a midday meal. The position of the sun and growling in our bellies told us that candle marks had burned down since we initially entered the cave. Because I made it back to the queen's hut before she did, I took the liberty of coaxing a small blaze from her banked coals with the intent of making some tea. Lunch was a light meal of olives, figs, cheese, and dried fish. It was as if the new intimacy between us had brought down another barrier. While we sat at the table eating, I listened as she spoke of what the future had in store for us. Ori told me that the Telequire nation had not seen a queen's consort in eighty cycles of the sun. Not only that but just as Ori was the youngest queen any Amazon nation had ever seen, I would be the youngest consort.

It was a lot of responsibility. The traditional consort role meant more than just bond mate of the queen. I was to be her champion, her representative, and her envoy, just as I had feared. My primary duty would be to guard the queen in all things, body, mind, and soul. Other than that, it would be up to me to find a contribution that fit with the nation's demands and my duties to the nation's queen. Since the torcs needed to be in a state of blessing for an entire season, we could not be bonded until summer solstice at the earliest. She laughed as I blew out a sigh of relief at that news. I had a lot to learn over the coming moons and I was glad to have time to adjust to it all.

She was getting ready to tell me about the betrothal part of the ceremony when we were interrupted by a knock on her door. Basha was on the other side and Ori waved her in. I gave her a slight wave before she turned her gaze back to Ori. "My queen, the priestess says to tell you that the preparations are complete for the added ceremony this afternoon, and that she will need to see you in about a candle mark and a half."

The queen quirked an eyebrow at her regent. "And she sent you instead of a runner with the news?"

Basha's face flushed. "Well, when I saw the preparations I was surprised. I mean we all knew that you had exchanged feathers before, um, before. I guess it's just surprising to hear that we will finally have a consort when nearly the entire Telequire nation has never known one. It was a shock."

With sudden realization I slapped the palm of my hand against my forehead. "Bent arrow and broken string, our friends are going to kill us for not telling them ahead of time! Shana will never let me live it down!" They both laughed at my words.

Ori placed a hand on the regent's arm. "I'm sorry that I didn't tell you, I know it is a surprise. While I've been planning it for a while, I only just asked Kyri today and I had no idea she would say yes."

I walked over to her and wrapped my arms around her from behind. "You knew I would."

She turned her face to mine and her look said it all. "I'd hoped, but fear was my daily companion for too long for that hope to be a certainty."

As we gazed into each other's eyes trying to read that hope and certainty, Basha's words cut through the silence with the gentleness of a feather. "I'm really glad you said yes, Kyri."

I looked back at her then and could not keep the stupid grin from my face. "I am too." After a few more words of well-wishing, she left us to the sound of crackling fire and a village preparing for revelry all around the queen's hut. Ori began cleaning up the detritus from our meal and I was left to stand in the middle of her open space wondering what I should do. I did not want to stay if she had things she needed to accomplish before the ceremony, but I could feel a nearly physical pain in my chest at the thought of leaving her presence. I did not want to seem needy with my affection. When she was finished I turned toward her and forced the words past my lips. "Well, I should probably go so you can finish preparing for later. I am sure you have plenty to do..." My words trailed off, perhaps because I was not feeling them in my heart.

When she laughed I pulled my gaze from the strong hands that rested on the back of her chair and met Ori's eyes. While I could read the mirth there, as evidence of her laughter, I also saw something more. "Well, I do have one thing left to do and I think we have just enough time before I need to meet with the priestess."

I watched with frozen breath as her eyes grew noticeably darker and her features were pulled into playful teasing. "Wh—what is that?"

"You." I swallowed hard, the butterflies returning with swooping and whirling flight in my stomach. I was unable to answer just then because my tongue felt thick but the look of worry on her face pierced me through the heart. "Unless you don't want to? I don't want to frighten you, Kyri."

Before she could worry more, I quickly closed the distance between us and took her into my arms. My mouth quieted her surprise as my fingers made short work of her clothes. Too much time had passed with us apart for me to waste another candle drop not showing the depth of my love. As long as I was in control, I remained unafraid and we could deal with the rest later. Goddess willing, the worst for us was over.

Chapter Ten

The Long Shadow of Rome

LOUD POUNDING BROUGHT me from a deep sleep. I felt Ori stir next to me as someone called out from the other side of her hut door. I recognized Basha's voice and thought for a heartbeat that we had overslept. "My queen, we have urgent news. There is a messenger here from Rome." My blood went cold at the regent's words and the queen stiffened next to me. Nearly in a panic, I scrambled out of bed and she followed. We quickly dressed and Ori threw the door open to an unpleasant surprise. There was a crowd of Amazon warriors outside with Basha, but the fear that coiled in my belly was due to the lone Roman. Basha glanced at the man to her left and quickly stepped forward. "I'm sorry, my queen, but we could not stop him. They have an army of at least two thousand strong positioned around the nation." The man was tall and well-muscled, dressed in traditional Roman battle armor. His hair was cropped short and he wore the sad look on his face nearly as well as he wore the swords strapped to his waist.

I was still in shock when Aureolus began to speak. "I'm sorry Kyri, but Isidorus has changed his mind and sent me to bring you back."

My mind whirled with confusion. "B—but you cannot do that! He signed papers and I am free!"

"I'm afraid he did not sign the papers and you remain nothing more than a slave. You can never be free. Kyrius will come back to fight for us once again."

Ori stepped in front of me with her palm out. "No! She will go nowhere with you, Roman! You have no authority here. I am Queen and I demand you leave our land and country immediately!"

He smirked at my fierce protector. "Ah, you must be her beloved, the one who let her spread her metaphorical legs for our pleasure. How nice of you to suddenly care, but I'm afraid your protests are for naught as my army will raze your village and set fire to the trees if you do not release her into my custody."

I began backing away slowly, shaking my head with denial. "No, no, no." I turned to the woman who held my heart. "Please,

Ori, do not let them take me away again. I will not survive!"

Sorrow washed over the queen's face as it finally registered what Aureolus had said. "Kyri, my love, they will kill everyone. I cannot in good conscience trade one person for the lives of our entire nation. I'm sorry, Kyri."

Terror froze me for heartbeats as I looked around at the gathered Amazons and the man who had trained me to be a gladiatrix. "Ori, no! Please, please, I will do anything if you let me stay!" Perhaps sensing that I was going to run, Aureolus strode forward and tried to grab me. At first I was able to knock his arms away but he quickly grabbed my wrists in his calloused hands. I struggled but the grip got tighter and Ori's voice broke through the frantic pounding of my heart.

"Kyri, what are you doing? Kyri, stop!"

I woke with a gasp, drenched in sweat. When I realized someone was holding me down, I bucked my lower body and twisted to the side to dislodge them trying to get away. The panic was still driving me to escape. With terror shaking my very limbs, I huddled in the corner, eyes shut tight. "Please, do not let them take me. Please, I cannot bear to go back!"

A light touch to my foot and a soothing voice broke through my desperate words. It was a calm voice and a worried one. "Kyri, no one is taking you anywhere. You're right here with me, love. I'm never letting you go." The hand moved slowly up my leg and I trembled. "Just open your eyes for me, let me see those pretty blues. I promise that no one is taking you back to Rome."

The words finally broke through my frenzied fear and I opened my eyes, surprised at what I found. I was crouched in the corner of the bed where the two walls of the hut met. The table next to her bed had been toppled and Ori was on her knees in the middle of the bed. Confusion washed through me. "Ori?"

All at once she seemed to sag with relief. "You've had a bad dream. A nightmare. But it's over now and there is no harm done. Are you okay, how do you feel?"

My eyes were drawn to her forearm where a large red mark was quickly darkening into a bruise. I reached out but stopped just shy of touching the injury. "I did this."

A smile reached her lips but I could not tell if it was for my benefit or hers. "It's fine, love, there was no harm done. Come, we should clean up and get dressed."

"No! It is not okay! I have hurt you simply by sleeping in the same bed. What if I choke you next time, like I have done so many times in the past with Iva? I could break your neck in my sleep and not even know 'til I woke! We cannot do this, you cannot do this. You deserve better!"

I think she tried to comfort me but when her hand grasped my arm I could not help cringing away. She pulled back but spoke anyway. "You listen to me, Kyri Fletcher! We can do this and we will. You have a piece of me for now and always, and I will not let you go again. Do you hear me? We are together until you say our love is done. Fear will not be our guide!"

Heartbeats bled into candle drops as both our breathing slowed. Gradually, my fear calmed as I took in her words. I was about to speak when a knock sounded loudly at the door. I could feel the blood rush from my face as I scrambled backward further into the corner. "No!" Ori looked at me curiously and I could no longer tell dream from reality. "That is how my dream started. Basha knocked on the door and told us she had urgent news."

She laughed quietly and I thought maybe she was the reality I searched for. "That was only a dream, I'm sure there is another reason for the—" Her words were interrupted in the worst way possible.

"My queen, we have urgent news. There is a messenger here from—" I did not hear the rest because nausea rose quickly into my throat and I bolted for the pot that sat in the opposite corner of Ori's hut. I convulsed with fear and sickness as I lost the small amount that remained in my stomach.

"Goddess, Kyri!" A shaking hand touched my shoulder then moved up to pull my hair away from my face. She held my long dark strands with one hand while the other soothed in circles on my back. She yelled out to the person waiting outside the hut. "Basha, take the messenger to the council chamber and I'll be there as soon as I can." She turned back to me as I miserably dry-heaved nothing but air and rancid bile. "Easy now, there is nothing to be afraid of. It's just us here and you're not going anywhere. There is nothing to fear."

My throat felt raw as I spoke. "But Basha, the messenger..." I trailed off, wanting the nightmare to end.

Ori reached over and grabbed a cloth from the nearby table. "Nothing is amiss, she's just letting me know that I have a messenger in from another tribe."

I looked at her then and sorrowed to see such concern in her eyes. "Not from Rome?"

She shook her head. "No, it was just a dream. You're here and you're safe, and I will not let anyone take you from me again."

In the blink of an eye I was overwhelmed by emotion and collapsed just as she pulled me against her. I could not be sure how long we sat on the floor while I sobbed on her shoulder, but my eyes felt hot and swollen when I was done. When the tears had run dry I pulled away from her and wrinkled my nose in disgust at the smell of sick so near. "I am sorry—"

"No, don't be sorry. You did nothing wrong, I'm just sad that you had such a terrible dream. I sorrow because you continue to battle your daemons of memory." She stood and offered a hand to help me up. "Come, I still have to find out what news has come from Shimax and we need to get cleaned up. I don't think it would be right to meet their messenger with your passion staining my chin."

I flashed back to the image of me sitting upright with her below. It was the only way I felt comfortable and in control. Heat suffused my face at her words but I accepted the hand up anyway. Despite my nightmare and all that had transpired prior to the knock on Ori's door, I found myself curious about the messenger. Similar to our own in size, Shimax was one of the largest Amazon nations and was roughly southeast of us. Its borders were closer to Telequire than all other nations, save Kombetar.

Ori poured water in her washbowl and found another rag so we could clean ourselves. As we dressed I thought about the other nations. "Why do you think they would send a messenger on the eve of equinox?" Ori froze and let out a sigh but she did not meet my eyes. "Ori? What is it?" I continued putting on my gear while I waited for her answer but she stopped me with a gentle hand on my arm.

"There has been much happening of late and I honestly forgot about Shimax." I gave her a curious look and she continued. "All of the other Amazon nations and their queens came here for last summer solstice, to celebrate the Festival of Nations. I was in mourning at the time because of losing you and the others but I still had to participate in the queen's council. It was there that I met Queen Alala and her daughter, Princess Alcina." When she stopped speaking we were both dressed and ready to head out the door but neither of us moved. Finally, Ori took a deep breath. "Queen Alala is of the same generation as Queen Myra, and Alcina is about twenty-one summers now, the same age as you." Ori stopped again to run a hand through her short hair, careful of the feathers tied in place. "Queen Alala was very encouraging of a match between myself and her daughter. I told her that I was in mourning and was not looking to bond with anyone and she seemed to accept my answer. However her daughter was not so easily dissuaded." I stayed silent even as anger colored my queen's features. "Alcina was borderline disrespectful in her pursuit of me, she refused to take no for an answer time and time again. She finally cornered me in the smallest bathing pool the evening before they were supposed to leave and it was there that she kissed me. I—"

I could no longer hold my tongue. "She what? That woman would dare touch you while you were in mourning and after you explicitly told her you were not interested in such a relationship?" I had no idea where the blossoming rage came from, only that it filled my belly like wine. A light caress to my cheek brought me back to the present.

"Peace, Kyri. I shoved her away from me and got my point across after that. I told her that I was still in mourning and could not think to love anyone else. I also said that even if I wasn't in mourning, that she was too young and I would never want more than friendship with her. She finally accepted my answer, though not gracefully."

I swallowed and nodded my head, anger easing away. "That is a good thing and there should be no more misunderstanding with her then."

Ori wobbled her hand back and forth in a sign of uncertainty. "Eh, as I said, I told her that she was too young. And now we get a messenger exactly nine moons after I told her I was in mourning, coincidentally the official Amazon mourning period. Which means I don't think we have heard the last from Princess Alcina. Despite the fact that you have returned to me, and despite the fact that we are to be betrothed." She paused and a breathtaking smile came over her face. "She didn't come across as someone who would let such things deter her. And if Alcina keeps inquiring after me she is sure to find out that you and she are the same age, thus invalidating my claim of her being too young."

It only took heartbeats for the anger to come rushing back and I gripped one of the pugiones at my side. "I have something that will deter her if she pursues such a suicidal course!"

"Kyri, no." Her hand covered mine and slowly pulled it away from my weapon. "This is a princess, therefore it is a delicate matter. I cannot risk offending the Shimax nation because they are the first line of defense on our southern border and they are a sister nation. If she continues to pursue me I will have to handle it diplomatically. Do you understand?" When she stepped close I had no choice but to return her embrace. She was warm in my arms and so very real. "Nothing and no one can tear us apart. Please trust me on this." I looked down into her eyes for a heartbeat then finally swallowed and nodded. Remembering the bruise on Ori's arm, I knew that I had already brought enough trouble into her life and did not want to be the cause of more. Ori grinned again as she felt me relax. "Besides, it is just a messenger that is waiting for me right now. I doubt very much she will just show up without cause and there is no reason for anyone from Shimax to travel north to Telequire."

We walked out the door and she went in the direction of the council chamber while I was left to wander with no real destination. I had been wanting to find a new outfit since I came back to Telequire. As comfortable as I was in my wrapped top with my girdle and strip skirt, I was ready for a change. I made my way to the supply hut where there was a variety of different clothes and sizes and I searched through the piles. I kept my girdle but picked out a new shorter skirt. It was about the same length as the tunic I used to wear in Rome. The skirt itself was made from overlapping mottled green panels cut in the shape of large pointed leaves, points facing down. It ended about mid-thigh and was very easy to move in. Wanting more freedom, I picked out a dark brown halter-style top, though I still kept the light green wrap that I wore. With a few extras of each in item, plus my original clothes, I made my way back to my hut to drop off my things. I still had my weapons on me when I wandered out the door again and eventually found my way to Shana's hut. I knocked before I was even fully aware of my actions.

"Kyri, look at you! I like your new clothes, sister." I had received a few appreciative glances on my way through the village and I knew that I had selected well. I only hoped that Ori would like them as much. I was only uncomfortable with the fact that they displayed my whip scars significantly more than the wrap, but it was a discomfort I would have to live with. The scars would always be there. "What brings you by, I thought you were spending time with Ori?" She opened the door to let me in and we both took a seat at her table.

I looked around, but did not see any dark-dyed skins nearby. "Do not you have any wine here?" Shana started laughing and I scowled at the response to my ordinary question. I waited, knowing I would get nothing of sense out of her until she had purged the humor. I did not have to wait long. "Goddess, I'm sorry. It's just that I said nearly those same words to you once in your hut, which means I know something is bothering you." She reached out and gently touched my cheek. "You look pale, are you and Ori okay?"

I scrubbed my hands across my face, trying to organize my thoughts and be objective about all that Ori had told me. Shana was our ambassador, so she would know more about the potential ramifications if Princess Alcina were to cause trouble. Meeting my sister's honey-brown eyes, I finally spoke. "Tell me about the princess of Shimax."

Shana sat back in her chair with a strange look on her face. "Oh. Well there is not much to tell. Alcina is Queen Alala's daughter and has been princess her entire life. As a result, she is..." I could see her searching for the right words to describe the woman I had suddenly discovered as my rival. "Let's just say, she expects to be treated as a princess by everyone. And I'll tell you that she has a very bloated sense of self-importance. She is conceited and is convinced that she is the Goddess's gift to women. Alcina also has a reputation as a feather ruffler in her own nation. I've visited there numerous times and she has never failed to proposition me." I raised an eyebrow at her, knowing that my sister had a friendly reputation in our own village. "I have always turned her down, much to the princess's displeasure. She is very attractive though and I suspect that she has rarely been denied. However, she hasn't asked since Basha and I physically removed her from Ori's presence last summer solstice."

"What?" While Basha was the regent of our nation, I had never seen her move a hand in anger or aggression. Was there more to the story than what Ori had told me?

Shana gave a self-depreciating smile. "Well 'removed her' is a strong phrase. We were supposed to meet Ori at the smallest bathing pool to wind down at the end of the day. The last of the visiting tribes, including Shimax, were scheduled to leave the next morning and many were either asleep or still enjoying the drum circle. We arrived in time to see Princess Alcina kiss Ori and watch Orianna shove the younger woman away in fury. When she didn't seem like she was ready to accede to the queen's wishes, Basha threatened to call the guards. Alcina stalked out of the water and dressed, unhappy with the fact that we were there to witness her rejection. She also got into Basha's face when she reached the door where we were standing. I grabbed her arm and she whirled on me, I think to strike. She never got the opportunity because Basha grabbed her other arm."

Shana stopped and went over to a chest where she retrieved a familiarly dyed skin of wine, the kind I had been searching for earlier. After we each drank some down, I tapped her with my foot under the table. "Continue, please."

"Anyway, I said she was very pretty but what I didn't say was that she is also very strong. She is the best in unarmed combat from her nation and she won the top prize last summer festival. Perhaps that was why Ori gave a trilling whistle. When Gata pushed through the cave flap, Alcina went a little pale and stopped struggling. We didn't see her again for the rest of the night, nor did she say anything when she departed the next morning with her mother and the rest of the Shimax competitors."

I sat there in silence as heartbeats thumped by. Ori had told me the truth but she had also downplayed it a bit to keep me calm. If I had learned anything as a slave and a gladiatrix, it was that some people did not understand the word "no" unless it was backed by more than words. "Am I required to show her the same obeisance that I would a queen? How do I refer to her and what happens if the princess continues to cause trouble?"

Shana's eyes narrowed as her brain tried to make sense of my words. "First of all, she is only a princess and not even of our tribe. So you can treat her with respect like anyone else, though it is customary to refer to a princess simply by their title. Customary but not a requirement. And second, why would she cause trouble? The queen told her she wasn't interested and princess Alcina went back south. We haven't heard anything from her since. It's not like they will be back to Telequire this sun-cycle because the Festival of Nations is never held in the same place twice." She paused and looked up at the thatched roof of her hut. "But, if she were to cause trouble wherever this sun-cycle's festival is held then we can lodge a complaint with the meeting Queens' Council. Why are you asking these questions, Kyri?"

"Ori told me about the princess, though she did not give as many details in her story. But she did say the princess had been pursuing her the entire time they were in Telequire despite repeated statements that Ori was not interested. And I am asking you now because the queen is meeting with a messenger from Shimax this very moment."

Anger washed over my friend's face. "That muck-sucking river snake! What is she playing at?"

I covered her hand with mine, much the way Ori had soothed me. "Peace, sister. I am sure Ori can handle it just fine. I just wanted to know what to expect, and to know what we could do if the princess foolishly pursues my betrothed."

"Wait, what?" Shana pushed back from the table and her

hand slid out from under mine. "What did you just say?"

I knew which words had caught her attention and feeling a bit of humor I chose to taunt her. "Ori would handle it?"

She slapped the table. "No, *betrothed*! You said betrothed! When did this happen?"

"Shana."

She huffed in displeasure. "Were you even going to tell me?"

I held my hands up to slow her down. "Whoa, whoa! Halt that horse of yours. It only just happened this morning after target practice. Ori asked me if I would go through the betrothal ceremony during the equinox celebration today and I said yes."

She stood in front of me shocked, though I was not sure why. After a candle drop went by she finally noticed my feather. "You've switched again."

I shrugged. "As Ori pointed out to me, we have been pledged since that first night. Despite all that we have been through, neither of us removed the other from our heart."

"This means you're going to be the queen's consort. How do you feel about that?"

I laughed because she above all others, save the queen, truly knew my heart with such matters. "How do you think I feel? I am terrified! I do not even know what I am supposed to do as a consort, or how I am supposed to act. Bow and fletch, some days I still feel like that kid that left the homestead and other days I feel older than the dirt beneath the trees."

She laughed with me. "Maybe I can help. While the queen's consort has no real political or war power, you will be an extension of the queen's word. You would be considered first consul, first of the queen's guard, first defender, and the person she would lean on during times of crisis."

A thought flitted through my mind. "I—I would never have to be queen, right? If something were to happen to Ori, I could never step into that role."

"No, that is why we have a regent. If the queen is seriously injured or she dies, the regent will rule until another queen can be selected. But that being said, if the queen and regent were killed or severely injured then you would become regent in the interim until another could be selected by the council. If the queen is challenged while still alive, the queen or consort can accept the challenge. However, if the queen is killed or incapacitated, the regent or the consort can accept the challenge. In either case the consort would not become queen with a win, she would merely preserve the status quo of rule."

It was a lot of information but I nodded my head with understanding, relieved I would never have to wear the monarch's mask. "Your words make me happy, now tell me what happened between you and Coryn?" My change in topics was abrupt but it was on my mind in that exact moment and I also suspected that I would have to catch her off guard to get an answer. Perhaps it was not the best time to bring up the subject but I had been putting it off far too long. And I felt as though the rift between them was somehow caused by my kidnapping and subsequent slavery.

Shana looked down at her worn tabletop. "It's my fault." Her voice was quiet but steady. "I didn't handle things well when you were taken in Preveza. I knew we needed to get the coffers back to Telequire and I had to tell the queen what had happened. But every step farther from where I last saw you was done in pain. And when we got back I had to be the one to tell Ori that you had been lost to us." She refilled her cup and took a few swallows before continuing. "She didn't say anything to me but I broke her heart that day. Goddess! Her eyes—" She looked up and I met her gaze steadily with my own heart breaking at her words. "Her eyes went dark and empty. I've always been able to read Ori but after that moment I no longer knew her thoughts. I just knew that without you she was incomplete. The only thing we managed to find out before leaving Preveza was that the city had sold a number of criminals to a slave ship that was bound for a city across the Ionian Sea. I begged the queen to let me follow to look for you and she refused. I then begged the council and they refused as well. I threatened to just leave on my own and they put me under guard for a fortnight." Shana pounded her fist on the scarred wood. "Goddess, Kyri! Losing you was like losing my own flesh and blood!"

She started to cry, silent tears tracked down her face at the remembered pain of loss. I moved around the table and crouched next to her chair. I knew that the guilt still weighed heavily on her shoulders. I had to make her see, make her understand that things worked out the best they possibly could have. "Shana, I understand your loss and I grieved with you as much as I was able." Her eyes were focused down at our joined hands and I needed her to see my truth. "Look at me." Her eyes tracked up to mine, red-rimmed and full of tears. "If there is one thing I want you to understand about my captivity, it is that there is nothing you or anyone else could have done to make it better. No one could have prevented the three of us from being taken. No one! And had you followed us to Roman lands, had you found us before we went up on that auction block, we would have all died." She looked startled by my words, nearly haunted.

"What do you mean? Why would we have died?"

My heart was heavy to speak of the event but she had to know what kind of people dealt in the slavery and servitude of others. "If you had been there, you would have joined us on the slave block. Sister, you are a beautiful woman and would have been bid on and won by the man who owned the *lupanare*. The same lupanare where he would have sent you and Pocori to join the rest of his concubinae. From the moment the first slave went up on the block, we knew what he was about. A lascivious pig of a Roman, he stalked around each pretty slave, taking his pleasure of them in his head while running greasy fat-fingered hands across their flesh. When he won the bid on our young sister, Pocori did what I had no nerve for. She fought for the right to die free."

I sucked in a breath at the painful memory of that day. "But for you, my sister, I would have fought. I would have fought them all even if it brought death down on the lot of us. We would have all fought and died." There was more truth beyond the words that had just squeezed my heart with memory. She had to know it all, to understand my whole motivation. "Beyond that and despite how hopeless and lonely I felt, I would not have wanted you there to see what I became." She started to protest but I silenced her with gentle fingers to her lips. "I was a slave and I chose to sacrifice myself over and over to protect my Amazon sister. I was whipped as a slave. I was beaten and pushed harder than most as a slave-warrior and I succumbed to the addiction of blood in the arena."

I watched her watching me and could see the thoughts tumbling through her eyes. "Did Iva ever see you fight?"

"No, and I am grateful. There was nothing of me in my many combats as the sagittarius, the gladiatrix, only the thought of winning a laurel. Nothing existed but the blood of my opponents and the chanting of the Roman crowds. Telequire, my friends, my love, none of them were real when I became Kyrius."

A candle drop went by as she appeared lost in thought. Finally Shana raised her eyes to mine again. "I understand, Kyri. I don't have to like all that happened but I'm glad that you are here with us now."

"And Coryn?"

She sighed and took another sip of wine while I rinsed and filled my own cup with water. "I pushed her away. After I lost you, I closed myself off because I was terrified of losing anyone else. I didn't want to let another close to my heart while it was still bleeding from the fact that my sister had been taken from me. Coryn offered me her love but I couldn't let her in, so I pushed her away and now she hates me."

I laughed and she looked at me as if I had gone mad. "I do not think hate is the word I would use to describe how Coryn feels about you. Perhaps you two need to have a talk, and soon."

Shana shook her head, curls bouncing with the abrupt motion. "I can't! Too much river has gone under the bridge. Perhaps it's best if we just left our history in the past where it belongs."

"Or maybe your future is waiting for you to step over that bridge."

She shot me an irritated gaze. "That makes no sense!"

I grabbed the wine skin and put it back in her storage chest. "Neither is denying yourself love and pleasure simply because you fear something that may never happen. Truly think about how you both feel because I can tell you right now that life is too short and too unsteady not to grab on with both hands when you find something or someone that makes you happy. Do not waste another day with uncertainty and trepidation."

"Who are you, Artemis's wise owl?" Before I could answer, horns sounded outside. She pointed at me when I made to open my mouth again. "I'll think on what you said if you promise to say no more. Now we must hurry. That is the call to temple and we certainly don't want to be late for your betrothal!"

A smile broke over my face as my heart lightened considerably. "No, we certainly do not."

WALKING INTO THE temple amid crowds of other Amazons felt like my very first time all over again. It had been exactly a sun-cycle since I last witnessed a ceremony within Artemis's sacred walls. The air was warm inside, since the temple was just a much larger version of the many caves that dotted the countryside around Telequire. They were the very same caves that contained our hot pools used for bathing. Torches flickered around the large chamber and up on the dais near the back. Shana and I pushed forward until we could get as close as possible. The sight of the priestess standing near the altar and the bleating of the goat nearby took me back and I reached up to itch my forehead where I remembered the dried blood to be. It seemed as if a lifetime had gone by since I had last received the mark of the goddess. When I glanced up at the great statue of Artemis I was startled to see that we were directly in line with her stony gaze. The beautifully carved goddess looked down on me and I wondered if she stood in judgement. The smaller stag and bear statues faced the altar, indifferent.

Per the usual, I found my head stuffed with too many thoughts and too little understanding. Debating my place in the grand scheme of things seemed a foolish waste of time. But so too did my continued puzzling of the religious thread that wove itself through the fabric of our world. Did I really choose my path in life, or was it as Ori said, I was nothing more than an arrow of Artemis that had been shot across the sea and fetched back? I looked up for answers but the goddess's gaze remained moored and impenetrable.

The crowd separated in a wave down the middle of the cavern and my breath caught as Artemis's Chosen walked through and up the stairs to the raised platform. Everything about her seemed to glow and for the first time in my life I felt in the presence of something holy. The nation of women warriors quieted all at once and a voice cut through the silence. "Hail to our goddess Artemis! She who is the hunter, she who is hunted. It is you who wields the bow bringing prey to their knees. You are also the doe fleeing certain death in the woods."

The words washed over me as past collided with present. Bits and pieces of the queen's opening speech had been seared into my brain because I had reached for them in a time of need, in a place of desperation. Feeling one gaze among hundreds, I saw the queen watching me and knew for certain that I had not been forsaken. I was aware that just as Ori was Artemis's Chosen, my heart and soul belonged to Ori. I was hers. My personal goddess was going to grace me with her future and I would do the same in return.

In the short time of recital and chanting, in the space of candle drops and sacrifice, I had lost track of what went on around me. There was too much in my mind to not be distracted by what was to come. I fully missed Glyphera's prayer to Artemis and the last woman walking in Artemis's footsteps was exiting the dais when I finally turned my eyes and thoughts back to the ritual. After the bowl was cleared away the priestess turned to the crowd as I had seen her do other times in the past. But that was where the familiar ended.

The priestess's voice called out again to the assembled

nation. "Goddess Artemis, nurturing mother, we ask of you one more boon today. It is for your chosen who walks the forest paths of this nation, your queen who guides our people to victory, prosperity, and solace. We ask you to bless a union between her and her future consort." The assembled women began to murmur around us and more than a few met my eyes in the crowd. "Kyri Fletcher, please come to the dais." The murmuring turned to a low rumble as I moved forward and up the steps to where I was directed, on the opposite side of the altar from the queen.

"To be the Chosen of Artemis is both an honor and lifetime of dedication, and to be an Amazon queen is a blessed burden to bear for the good of the people. While the queen of the Amazons belongs solely to the Goddess Artemis, she can also be touched by other gods who wish us well. Aphrodite graces the luckiest of us, allowing our hearts to open like a morning blossom where it can join in the light with another. Queen Orianna and Kyri Fletcher stand before you pledging their honor and hearts to the Goddess Artemis and the Goddess Aphrodite, to each other, and to the nation. Today we will seal that pledge and make ready for their bonding ceremony at summer solstice. The royal torcs will reside in a state of blessing for the next three moons until they can be exchanged under Artemis's watchful eyes."

Glyphera removed a razor sharp dagger from the sheath at her waist and turned toward me. I trembled and fought to remain still as old fears and anxieties raised their ghostly heads. The only thing that kept me from running was a pair of shining green eyes watching from the other side of the priestess. I need not have worried for she merely cut a lock of my hair and placed it reverently on the altar between us. Afterward she turned to Ori and did the same. Then in a moment that seemed anticlimactic, she reached down and tied the two locks of hair together. Strands both dark and light lay conjoined on the stone, tangled together like a strange and disjointed fuzzy caterpillar. I resisted the urge to laugh because it certainly was not a time for humor. My thoughts were brought to rein again by the traditional end of the ceremony.

"The sacrifice has been given, blessings have been made, and the pledge of the queen and her heart lay reverently upon your altar. Oh Artemis of the silver light, give us a sign that you have received our gifts and are pleased." Despite the monumental news of their queen's betrothal not candle drops before, the entire nation went silent. I expected Gata to run up the aisle and growl or interrupt in some other way. But she did not and I was startled to see her laying at the base of the statue of Artemis, serene as she had ever been. As the silence dragged out I began to worry. What if the goddess truly were real and she did not approve of our joining? Or what if there was no goddess, but the lack of sign meant the nation would not approve?

As my mind began to tumble into a panicked abyss, a feeling washed over me and marched up and down my spine. I glanced around expecting an enemy of some kind but saw nothing. Before I could guess another reason for my uneasy skin, tremors shook the ground lightly at my feet. Surprised gasps and exclamations came from the crowd that was spread out before us, and rocks began raining down onto the dais from above. The shaking ended nearly as quickly as it had begun. Tremors were common enough for our country so it was not unusual for one to happen and be felt. But I thought back to Shana's reasoning behind her belief in faith and goddess.

While tremors were common enough for the Greek people, the shaking of Telequire during spring equinox happened exactly when we were waiting for a sign from Artemis. I looked around the chamber and saw that no one appeared to be injured, including the three of us on the dais. What caught my attention though was the pattern of fallen stones. Rock, dirt, and stone littered the platform everywhere but where we were standing. The three of us stood within a circle of cleared wood that extended about ten paces out from the altar. Within that circle there were no rocks, no debris or dirt. We had been completely spared by the falling matter. Ori must have realized the strangeness of it at the same time because a small exclamation of surprise left her lips.

"Oh."

Seeing that not one person was injured and that the shaking was apparently finished for the time being, Glyphera finished the ceremony. "The sign has been received and Artemis's message of acceptance has spared us all from the tantrum of Poseidon's rage. Goddess of the hunt, Goddess of the wild animals, we thank you for your blessing today." Her words startled me for I had forgotten the old tale that tremors were caused by the god of the seas.

I chanted with the rest of the crowd to end the ceremony. "Shining moon and silvered brow, hear us Artemis!" And then it was done.

Glyphera began collecting her implements of ritual and Ori walked around behind her to embrace me fully. "You did well, love. You looked like you would run when the priestess pulled out her knife but overall you did quite well." She leaned back within the circle of my arms. "Do you feel any different?"

"I do not know, you are the one who has her hands on me. Do I feel any different to you?"

A few heartbeats went by before she understood my joke and slapped my arm. "Woods weasel!" Despite my teasing, we walked out of the cave into the bright sunlight shining down. My laughter stopped when I caught a glimpse of Shana and Coryn talking a little ways into the trees to the left of the great carved opening of the temple. "What is it?" Ori followed my gaze and sucked in a surprised breath. "They're talking."

I nodded and eventually turned my gaze from what I knew to be a private moment. "Yes."

Ori looked at me in wonder. "You?" I shrugged and gave her a little smile. A little mystery was good for the soul.

Chapter Eleven

The History of Us

THERE WAS ONLY a short break between the temple ceremony and the Ceremony of Light. My stomach had been tumbling since the arrival of the messenger, but it settled some after our temple announcement. I think I had feared the worst, whatever that could be, and when everything went as planned my nerves calmed. Unfortunately the other thing I feared was still to come and would require me standing in front of the assembled nation a second time in one day. Ori was called away for final preparations and neither Shana nor Coryn had reappeared since I saw them outside the temple. I fidgeted nervously, not looking forward to funerary or award portion of the ceremony.

"Heyla Kyri, you look like you're going to run off into the trees."

I jumped at the voice that sounded so near and cursed my lack of attention. I turned and smiled when I saw Iva. "When am I not? Are you ready to receive your honors?"

She looked down and I suspected what went through her head. "I don't want honor for what I went through. Pocori never made it home and I know I'm not a hero."

Neither of us acknowledged her shudder when I placed my hand on her shoulder. "I feel the same way and told the queen as much, but the council was not to be dissuaded. We just have to get through the next candle mark or so then we can enjoy the feast."

"Yeah."

The dark circles under her eyes were obvious and I wondered if Morpheus made her suffer as he had done with me. "I have been told that you are leaving Telequire after equinox."

She met my gaze and I easily read the hurt within. "I have to." It was then I truly understood the dark circles and weariness. I knew that being in the same village as me while feeling as she did caused her great pain. The announcement of my betrothal would only have intensified that pain

"I am sorry, Iva. You know I never meant to hurt you. I think my heart has always belonged to Ori, perhaps long before we even met. I know my words make no sense but I feel it deep inside."

Iva gave me a sad smile. "I know you didn't, but you hurt me just the same. Or maybe, it was me who hurt myself by yearning for that which I could never have. Despite my pain though, I can't help but wish you both happiness."

I looked away at her self-sacrificing words and felt a tear break free from my lash. When I was sure I had my emotions under control again, I turned back. "Where will you go?"

"Queen Agafya extended invitations to both of us, should we ever want to leave Telequire to avoid some of the more painful memories. It's not too far away,"

I finished her sentence, because I knew that she would not. "But still just far enough."

"Yes."

My guilt at her continued hurt would not leave any time soon, but I wanted her to be healthy and happy in her new nation. "Iva, when you go to Kombetar you should spend some time speaking with Kynthia."

Curious eyes looked back at me. "The priestess?"

"Yes. She and Queen Agafya were the ones who made me realize how hurt I could be on the inside and that I would need someone to help me heal. You know I suffered from nightmares and rages nearly every night, right?" Of course she knew, she had more knowledge than anyone else of such things. She nodded. "I have been speaking to Glyphera nearly every single day since my return and she is helping me work through the worst of it. With her I learned that sometimes we suffer from unseen injuries, injuries that our memory blocks completely, leaving only the symptoms and no understanding. Since my daily sessions with the priestess I have discovered things that my heart and mind had forgotten, that I did not want to remember. I am not telling you this because I want you to think more of what happened to me. I am telling you because you should think more about what happened to you. Speak to the Kombetar priestess, she can help you work through much of the pain. Sometimes it just helps to talk things through with someone. Though they are not gone yet, my own night terrors have faded in frequency and strength."

Both our heads jerked up at the sound of a hunting horn that told the nation that the Ceremony of Light was about to begin. Iva stepped close and enfolded me into an embrace. Our breaths were ragged with emotion as we relived the bond that our shared experience of pain and loss had forged. For a short while our paths had merged into one and we were able to lean on each other for support during the roughest part of the trail. But the future was a changing thing and so too had our journey. Her voice was a whisper but sounded loud against the softest part of my ear. "Thank you."

I nodded and swallowed back the lump of emotion. "Take care of yourself, Iva." I shut my eyes then to prevent losing control completely. When I opened them a few heartbeats later she was gone. Both Shana and Coryn found me near the front of the assembled nation and flanked my sides. When I saw the look in Shana's eyes, I knew they had come together there for me, to support me with something that had caused much pain.

Besides the normal bonfire, there was a smaller one set up closer to the dais to honor our fallen sister. Because there was no body to burn, the funeral pyre had not been set up at the outskirts of the village like normal. Voices gave a low thrum to the afternoon, and faint crying could be heard somewhere to the side of me. Pocori left behind a mother and younger sister and I was ashamed to realize that I had not even taken the time to speak with them since returning to Telequire. So tied up with my own pain, I had ignored my friends and responsibilities for too long. The young sister Pocori left behind could not have been more than twelve summers, the same age I had been when I lost my mam. I decided then that I would try to do something for the family. I was not sure what, but I owed them some of my time.

Everyone shuffled and the sound died down when the procession made its way up to the platform that rose above us. The queen and council, the regent, and the conference of elders were all present as the queen began to speak. Her words came slow and with much difficulty. I knew it had nothing to do with finding the right ones. Rather, it was hard to speak around teeth gnashed together in pain and sorrow for her nation and her fallen sister. While Ori was adept at wearing the mask of confidence and air of strength, I knew she felt things even deeper than most. It was one of the sacrifices she made to become queen. She took everyone's pain into her own heart and often bruised because of it.

"On this equinox eve, we come together as a nation to honor many things. We honor the Goddess Artemis for her continued support and guidance. We honor the light and dark of the world and the bounty our forests bring. It is also a time to honor and acknowledge those that have given more than expected, who have sacrificed themselves for the good of the nation. And it is a time to recognize those sisters who have fallen in their brave fight against the darkness that threatens each day. Theodosia and Panphilla Zevasdater, Kyri Fletcher, and Iva Biros, please come to the dais."

I allowed the others to go up the steps before me, watching to make sure none had difficulty. I purposely did not meet Ori's eyes because while she had a mask to hide emotion from the crowd, I did not. When we were in place, her voice carried easily across the quiet gathering. "Moons ago, during the Western War, twelve of our sisters were taken from Kombetar and Ujanik. We grieved for them and later sacrificed lives to help win their battle. But we were fortunate that Telequire had not lost any of our women to the slavers from across the sea. When our own sisters were taken from the trade city of Preveza to the south, we were forced to grieve for ourselves. We were angered and sorrowed, we cried that our own nation's lifeblood would be stolen from us and forced into servitude to the wicked nature of greedy men. We wanted miracles and restitution for having those loved ones ripped from us. I, your queen and strength, prayed to Artemis every day for their return. I shed my tears as an offering into the Goddess's plate, hoping that she would listen and heal my pain. Not only did two of our Telequire sisters return to us, but they also brought back those twelve women stolen from Kombetar and Ujanik as well. They suffered bravely through sacrifice and sorrow and stand before you today."

Basha stepped forward and handed the queen an eagle feather of bravery that had three beads on the thong. Two were white and one was black. "Iva Biros bravely gave counsel and comfort to her fellow sisters after they were taken by slavers. Even after she was bought by a Roman slave owner, she continued to give comfort not only to her Amazon sister, but all women she came into contact with each day. She treated with respect other female slaves and smuggled food to them whenever possible. For those reasons and many more, we honor her utmost bravery."

Ori tied the feather into Iva's hair and the entire nation watched as my fellow sister in slavery shed the tears of a hundred regrets. Ori's voice carried over the crowd once again. "This feather is different because it holds three beads of bravery. The two white beads symbolize the Amazon sisters who returned to us and the black bead symbolizes the one who was lost. Pocori has crossed over by will of the Goddess and we shall forever honor her memory." When Ori was finished, she placed her right fist over her heart in an Amazon salute. Iva merely nodded at her and stepped back, sensing her part in the ceremony was done.

Her tears ran freely for all that we had gone through and for the young scout we could not bring home.

When the queen turned to me I stepped forward as Iva had done. Basha came near again with another beaded eagle feather to match Iva's. Ori tied it into my hair next to her own rite of caste feather that she had exchanged with me just that morning. It was heavy with the added beads and I felt the pull of unfamiliar weight on my scalp. "On foreign shores and under siege by both men and darkness, Kyri Fletcher fought bravely each day. She sacrificed heart, mind, and body to see not just her own way home, but to bring all known Amazons surviving in Roman hands back to their land and tribes. A total of fifteen Amazon sisters were stolen from Greece and Kyri was responsible for bringing home all but one. For that dedication, strength, and sacrifice, we give her the eagle feather of bravery. It too is modified to show the three sisters who went into the land of Rome. While we mourn the loss of Pocori, a young soul cut down much too early, let us rejoice that Artemis's arrow was shot into the very heart of slavery and returned to us with more than we ever dreamed. Thank you for your sacrifice, Kyri."

Though her Monarch mask was firmly in place I could clearly see the tears shining in Ori's eyes. My voice came out as a whisper before I stepped back in line with Iva. "Thank you, my queen." I looked down to take a few deep breaths and when I looked up again the entire nation stood in salute. That was when the first tear tracked down my cheek.

The last two to be addressed were Pocori's family. Her mother, Theodosia, stood quietly crying with a hand over her mouth. The young sister had tears in her eyes but stood brave in front of queen and nation. "It is rare that the nation loses someone so young, and Pocori's death has certainly been a loss to this tribe. A fierce and brave scout, she won honors when the village was attacked during the Western War. While nothing can fill the hole you have in your hearts, we would like to present to you with a replica of her rite of caste feather, with blackened quill. With it you will also receive the same eagle feather of bravery as Iva and Kyri. Would either of you like to say something about Pocori?"

Theo stepped forward and addressed gathering. "After the death of my bond mate, Pocori and Pan were the lights of my life. I will miss her smiling face until the day I cross over to the Golden Mountain and join with Zeva in the afterlife. Thank you all for your support and respect." The tears intensified and she covered her eyes as she stepped back in place and I felt my heart squeeze in my chest when Panphilla stepped forward.

Her voice trembled but she stood firm in front of us all. "Pocori was the best sister I could have ever asked for. She taught me about the trees and animals when I was old enough to learn. She never once put me off or sent me away for being too young. She made a promise to me before she left on the trade trip to Preveza. She said that when she returned she would teach me to fly through the trees like a bird. Her passing has made me so sad I don't think I'll ever fly..." Pan's voice trailed off as her bottom lip started to quiver.

I could not have the loss be so acute for her, I would not allow it. I stepped forward again and murmuring started through the crowd. "My queen, if I may?" Ori nodded at me. I knelt down and met Pan's deep brown eyes with my own blue ones. "I know that nothing can ever replace what Pocori was to you. She has made a mark deep within all our hearts. But I also know what it is like to suffer loss of family and to feel alone. If you ever need a sister, I am here for you and I will teach you the trees if you let me. You deserve to fly, little one. I give my pledge of honor that you can call me your sister and I will always consider you such in return." I barely finished my words when I found myself with an armful of twelve-summer old girl and I wondered if I had ever been so young.

Pan pulled away after a candle drop and gave me a tremulous smile. "I would like that." The rest of the ceremony continued on as Ori presented the remaining feathers and the symbolic funeral pyre was lit. The great surprise of the afternoon was when she told us that the Festival of Nations was to take place in Telequire for a second sun-cycle in a row. Apparently Shimax was scheduled to host the Summer Solstice Festival but out of respect for all that the Telequire nation had been through and done for the other nations, they passed the honor back to us.

Shimax was a rich nation that was known for their clay, fish, and trade transport contacts with the rest of Greece. The Acheloos River cut through the eastern most portion of Shimax and they did very good river trade because of it. There was still much I did not know about the tribe because my teacher of such things, Steffi, really only cared about the economics of it all. The rational part of my head said that Shimax was a logical place to have such a large gathering because of their wealth and space, but my heart had other opinions. While it made sense to have the bigger, more bountiful, nation as a host, I was glad that we would be staying home. The most important reason was selfish. I wanted to be bonded with Ori in our home temple and in front of our entire gathered nation. But there was another, darker reason. While there was plenty that I did not know about Shimax, what I did know was that their princess was sure to cause trouble for me and I wanted to be among my own people when that trouble began.

The large bonfire in the center of the village was lit and the scouts were given first pass through the feast food so they could resume their duty in the trees. I knew from experience that second scouts would head out for afternoon duty and fourth scout troops would take off in the four directions so they can make it to the edge of Telequire before too much time passed with only rudimentary coverage by our allies. Because of the betrothal announcement, Ori and I were inundated by well wishes and blessings throughout our meal.

Eventually night fell and Ori left to prepare for her final role of the evening. I smiled as she walked away with Basha, remembering the Dance of Blessing from the previous spring equinox. I found a log that provided me an unobstructed view of the bonfire as the dancers were lining up, and Shana found me shortly after. Seeing her sitting there looking so pensive threw my thoughts into the past.

It was exactly four seasons previous that saw us sitting much the same way, waiting for the dance to begin. We were both surprised that night by the two people who sought to hold our hearts. I was not sure if such surprises would happen on the night of my betrothal. I wondered if the queen would carry my arrow again as she had done so many moons before. I also pondered the consequences between my closest friends if Coryn were to make another attempt at Shana's heart and the ramifications if she did not.

Like the memory of a forgotten dream, the distinctive drum pattern sounded throughout the center of the village as the cloaked dancers made their way around the fire circle, one by one. They lined up nearest to the fire and dropped their cloaks. Then Ori stepped closer to us, farther away from the center, to begin her dance. Once again, she carried one of my arrows in her hand to use as a focal point for her athletic display. The singing that accompanied the drums was not the traditional sort, rather more like a melodic chant. Every so often the queen would yell out to punctuate a spinning kick or a flip through the air. I followed her dance with keen eyes and realized that it was much like watching the mating dance of birds. Spin and dip, swirl and soar, all while crying to the heavens and the one they wish to court. If my parted lips and rapid heart had anything to say of it, I felt courted indeed. With a quiet voice I whispered my awe. "She is truly amazing!"

Shana glanced my way with an indulgent smile. "That she is. If I haven't said so before, I'm quite glad that you two have come together in this life. I have never seen her so full before." She paused with a thoughtful look on her face. "Ori has always been lit with some inner fire, but since meeting and falling for you, everyone has noticed a difference. I don't think she would survive if something were to happen to you again."

I sighed deeply as the woman we spoke of finished her dance with a yell. On one knee with both fists planted on the ground, she stared straight at me. I could not see much of her expression with the fire at her back but I felt it nonetheless. "Sometimes I feel as though we are two halves of the same person, that I never really lived until I found her. And when I was away this past suncycle I had become a shadow, a wraith. I survived off the strength of my conviction and the blood of my enemies, but not love. When I returned to Telequire I was nothing more than a starved thing, snipping and snapping at all who came near out of angry fear. But with the help of those who love me most, I have begun to heal." I turned fully to Shana as the next dancer started around the fire. "You have helped me heal and I thank you."

Her hand felt warm on my arm in the cooling night air. "You never have to thank me, we are family now. Speaking of family, it was a very nice thing you did for Pocori's sister. I don't know their family very well but Pan has always struck me as a good kid. I'm glad you're taking her under your wing."

"I was thinking, what if we started some sort of mentoring program here in Telequire? Pan is not the only one who has lost a sibling or parent. I am sure there are more here who could use a big sister." I looked at my own sister-friend expectantly, very interested in her thoughts.

Shana cocked her head as the second woman finished her version of the Dance of Blessing and the next started. "I think you have a good idea with that. I guess I've never really thought about what happens to the siblings of those who die young. We have really only focused on the parents or children. Let me speak with Basha about it, I think that might be something she would be interested in championing. Her own sister died when we were younglings together. Arethusa was about ten summers older than us and she died when the previous queen sent a band of young warriors on a foolish raid. Basha idolized Are, we all did. I like the thought that there would be someone who could step in as another sister of sorts." Both of us trailed off to silence to watch the next few dancers. As the fifth dancer started around the circle our quietude was interrupted by another.

"They are certainly something to watch, aren't they?"

I looked up to the woman who stood to the left of where Shana and I sat on the log. It was hard to judge her height, but she seemed stocky and well-muscled. Her hair was shoulder length with two feathers tied into the dark strands. I could hear Shana sigh next to me and realized that she did not care for the newcomer. "Yes, they are all very beautiful when they dance." As she peered down at me I grew leery of her dark gaze. I did not recognize her and something told me that I would not. Shana stood up next to me and I joined her, unsure why my sister had grown so tense.

"Kyri, I don't think you've met the messenger from Shimax yet." She waved toward the other woman. "This is Megara. She is the one who arrived today with word about Telequire hosting the next Festival of Nations."

I held out my arm to her. "It is a pleasure to meet you, Megara. I hear your river is as beautiful as it is bountiful."

She took my arm, perhaps squeezing a little harder than necessary. "You can call me Meg, and maybe you should come visit us sometime."

I laughed but smiled to show that it was not mocking. "Maybe someday, but for now I think I will stay close to home. I have had my share of travel for the time being." Her grasp lingered but she eventually let go of my arm and I resisted the urge to wipe my hand on my skirt. Something about her set me on edge.

"Oh? Why is that?"

Shana took a step closer. "You know why she doesn't wish to travel, Megara. Just as you know who she is. Kyri doesn't have to repeat her story for you."

Megara laughed and held her hands up, palm facing outward. "Peace, Ambassador. I must admit that I was surprised to hear Queen Orianna announce their betrothal today. I fear Princess Alcina will be most displeased when I return."

I looked at her curiously. "And why is that?"

"Because I was also here to announce her request for courtship."

Shana sneered next to me. "So sorry for the princess's luck

but I'm afraid she is too late."

The Shimax guard laughed again. "Oh, it's never too late. After all, no offense to Kyri here, but Alcina is a princess. I've been head of the Shimax Royal Guard longer than Kyri has been an Amazon. What could she have to offer the queen of a nation, over what a princess could bring? Shimax is wealthy and our princess is beautiful beyond compare."

The first emotion that passed through me with her words was shock. I could not believe she would stand in front of me thus and speak about me in such a way. Who was she to question my place, my dedication, and my emotion for Ori? Anger began to creep in as she described the beauty of her princess. I was about to respond when Shana stopped me with a simple touch to the wrist. "Kyri has many things that your princess could never aspire to grasp but first and foremost, she has Queen Orianna's heart."

Megara's hand traveled to the dagger at her waist as her brows lowered in anger. "Are you saying Princess Alcina is lacking in some way?"

"Well, if—"

I did not let Shana finish because I thought it might cause an incident that we did not want on such an auspicious day. "She is saying nothing of the sort. The truth is, Ori and I have belonged together for more than our lifetime. She is the sun to my moon, and I am the moon to her sun. There is no other bond possible for us. Our hearts and souls were sealed long before we ever met. Artemis knows there was a reason I came to this village and the Goddess knows there was a reason I was able to come back. There is no competition between your princess and I. Ori and I have proven that the bond between us is unbreakable, as is our dedication to each other. Alcina must find another path whether it is love or power she seeks."

"The princess makes her path where she will and no one will keep her from what she wants!" With teeth bared, Megara spun on her heal and stalked away. I thought I heard her mutter a word once her back was to me but the chanting was too loud. I sighed and moved to sit down again but stopped at the look on Shana's face. It was one I had never seen before in all the time we had known each other. She was furious.

"Did you hear what she called you?" She took a step to follow the other woman but I grabbed her arm to keep her with me.

"No. What did she say?"

"She called you *doulé*!"

I looked at her, trying to judge her level of affront. "So? I was a slave once."

Shana sighed and made to sit down again so I let go of her. "You are not a slave now! And she didn't mean it as an observation, she was passing judgement on you."

I sat with her and took a breath to let the sounds of the drum chorus filter through me. "Again, so? I am neither bound by her judgement, nor does it alter the path of my future. Neither Megara's nor Alcina's thoughts matter to the bond between Ori and I. Do not let her words bother you so." When I turned back to the fire I saw another familiar face start around. She was the last dancer and wore the large amber necklace that I remembered from before. I sucked in a breath wondering what Shana's reaction would be. Her exclamation made me glance to my right.

"Oh!"

I took my eyes from the glistening nude body of the Telequire First Scout Leader. "Did you know she would dance?"

My sister answered without moving her eyes from the acrobatic woman that danced for her. "She said she was."

"Did you think she would not?"

Shana cleared her throat and finally glanced at me. "I think I hoped that she wouldn't."

Her eyes once again moved to Coryn and I studied my friend. Her face was a carved statue of pain and longing. "Why do you fight your heart so?"

"I don't know." Her voice caught on the last word and I knew she would have tears in her eyes.

I tried again. "You know, the Romans had a saying."

She looked at me. "What is that?"

"Sometimes the pebbles in your hand are outweighed by the stream slipping through your fingers."

Shana cocked her head in confusion, then turned her head back toward the fire. She watched until Coryn had danced around to the other side of the flames before speaking. "What does that even mean?"

I stood when I saw Coryn end her dance, knowing the queen was done with her duty for the night. "I told you that Coryn is a deeper pool than you give her credit for. Has she waited for you the entire time that I have been gone?"

"Yes."

I watched Ori approaching and prodded Shana for one more answer. "And have you waited for her?"

She sighed. "Yes."

I put my hand on her shoulder and smiled. "Then I think you

know what it means. I will see you tomorrow, sister. Peace to your dreams."

She responded in kind. "Yours as well." But I was already moving toward my heart.

ORI AND I walked back to my hut to put my arrow away. As I was placing it in my quiver she came up behind me and wrapped her arms around my waist. "What's wrong?"

I turned around when I was finished but did not step away. Instead I graced her with a smile and the briefest of kisses. "Nothing is wrong, I promise."

She looked up at me with curious eyes in the candlelight. "Why did you and Shana seem so tense? Was it because Coryn danced the fire again?"

My hands reveled in the fine hairs on the back of Ori's neck and I thought of how to answer her question. "That was a small part of it. She is struggling with the present and past right now. My disappearance really affected her and in turn she has become afraid."

"She is afraid to let another into her heart. I have known Shana nearly my whole life and she has always had a tendency to be defined by loss rather than by what she herself has gained. It started with the death of Basha's sister, but it has only developed over the seasons with each person she loses who had a part of her heart. Both her mothers are gone, killed in the same battle a handful of sun-cycles ago. Combe and Sikara are actually the reason that we do not allow both mothers to go off to battle together now."

I nodded. "She told me about her mothers. When I first met her she spoke of her second mother's rabbit stew."

Ori laughed. "Oh yes, it was amazing. But not nearly as tasty as yours!"

I laughed with her. "Good answer, my queen."

She looked up at me then and caressed my bottom lip with her forefinger. "I like it now. Before I hated it when you would say that." I gave her a questioning look, knowing I would not have to ask. "I like it when you call me your queen. Before I didn't want to be your queen. I wanted to be your lover, I wanted to be your love. But now that we are betrothed..."

I smiled and kissed her fingertip. "Yes. And I am proud to call you my queen, just as I am proud to call you my love." I gazed into her eyes in the dimly lit hut and let the feeling wash over me before switching thoughts. "Should I bring the things I will need for tomorrow back to your hut? I'm assuming you will want to sleep there tonight?"

Ori grinned and it promised mischief. "Who said anything about sleeping?" Heat suffused my body with her words. I tried valiantly to cool the fire that had begun to rise.

"It is still early, my queen. We should probably rejoin the festivities."

She sighed. "I suppose we must. We can stop at my hut to leave your things before going back to the drum circle. Would you care to do a little dancing with me?"

"Always."

With arms loaded down we made our way to the queen's hut. When we were finished there and heading back to the center of the village she brought up our earlier conversation. "You said that Coryn's dance was only a small part of the tension earlier. What was the larger?"

It was my turn to blow out a breath while I gathered my thoughts. "I met Megara while Shana and I were watching the Dance of Blessing."

A blonde head turned toward me in the light of the torches along our path. "Oh? And what did she have to say?"

"She informed me that her princess would be disappointed to see that you were now betrothed. She said that besides informing you of Shimax giving Telequire the honor of hosting the Festival of Nations again, that she was also bringing a request from Alcina to seek courtship with you."

Ori nodded. "She did. And I informed her that Alcina's request came a few lifetimes too late."

"Shana said as much but in a less friendly way."

"Our Shana? The silver-tongued woman whom I made ambassador for Telequire?" Though her words pretended shock, I knew she was implying otherwise.

"Yes, she is very protective of us. After I informed Megara that our bond was unbreakable she went away on her own, spewing threats and insults under her breath."

Ori's face darkened. "If she insulted you then she is breaking courtesy and I will demand she leave tonight!"

I put my hand on her wrist, much as I had done for Shana. "Peace, Ori. All is well now, she is simply loyal to her own princess the way Shana is loyal to you. Besides," I raised an eyebrow at her so she could see I had thoughts that were not innocent. "I have better things for you to do with your mouth than to tell some royal guard where to go."

The queen burst out laughing. "Oh Goddess, you really have changed!"

Concern flitted through my belly, disturbing my nerves and surety. "As you said, I find that I am constantly changing. Do you like who I am becoming?"

Ori pulled me to a stop just before we reached the circle of dancers. "I love who you're becoming, just as I love who you are right this very heartbeat." As we kissed slow and sensual amid the chanting rhythm, the drummers gave a flourish as the dancers yipped and ki-yayed at us. Though I could feel my face heat up in the fire lit darkness, I was lost to the taste of her lips and caressing tongue. After their teasing we danced until we were both drenched in sweat, then we gathered a few different skins and some food to take back to the smallest bathing pool. I expected to see Gata lying outside the heavy flap that covered the door and was surprised to see two young scouts instead.

They both saluted with fist to chest. "My queen, Scout Leader!"

I laughed at them but they knew I was not making fun. "I am no scout leader, merely a stinking and sweaty slave to the queen's desires."

Both mouths dropped open as they struggled for the words to respond to the seeming irreverence I had to my own past. Ori saved the poor women from terminal embarrassment and relieved them of duty. "You can both be excused now. Why don't you go join your friends at the fire?"

The darker skinned woman spoke for both of them. "If that is what you wish."

Ori waved them both off. "Yes, Saba, and thank you again for your duty in watching the cave for us tonight. Now take Trina and go enjoy the rest of your night." Once they were gone we entered the cave. I lit the torches by the door with the provided flint and striker and Ori brought a wick over to light on a torch. It was easy enough after that to use the wick to light the olive oil lamps that sat on the floor near the water's edge. We made sure the food and drink skins were within reach before walking down into the pool. "Ah, this feels divine after dancing for so long."

I watched as she shut her eyes and floated on her back in the warm water. I tore my gaze away with difficulty and grabbed a nearby cake of soap. "Yes, it does." She continued to float with a peaceful look on her face as I lathered my skin and rinsed, then ducked down to wet my hair. When I came back up she was very close to me.

"So, a slave to your queen's desires?"

I slicked the hair back out of my eyes and she followed the rise of my breasts out of the water. "Always and forever."

She watched me watch her nervously. "And if I demand you let me touch you?"

The breath hitched in my chest at the thought of not being in control. I had hoped that the fear and panic would go away after we had successfully breached the barrier to our passion. The rapid beating of my heart told me that it had not. I cast my eyes down to the water with equal parts sorrow and shame. "I will try, my queen."

"Hey." I looked up when her gentle fingers touched my chin. "We will go at your pace. As long as we are both getting pleasure there is no rush for else. Eventually we can conquer your fear and in the meantime we will take things slow." She popped a date in her mouth then grabbed her own cake of soap. "Now let's get clean, I have a surprise for you."

Curious about what she could have set up in the short time that we were away from each other, I began washing my hair. "What is the surprise?"

She pointed toward the back of the small cave, below the alcove where she had hidden the torcs earlier in the day. A mound of comfortable looking furs was piled up on the stone floor, with a few decorative jars near one end. I turned to her, delighted. "That is for us? How did you—"

She interrupted me with long missed laughter of the lightest kind. "Does it matter how I did it? What matters is that we have comfortable furs to lie upon. We have jars of olive oil mixed with fir and lavender to massage our bodies with. Would you like a massage, love?"

I thought about it and decided I would be able to submit to such. I had received massages many times as a gladiator for Isidorus. It was only when the touching turned intimate that the panic started to rise. "I would love a massage, only if you let me return the favor." My body warmed even further with the thought of putting my hands all over her body, digging my fingers into well-oiled skin. I ducked down to rinse my hair and feeling playful, tugged her feet out from underneath her. We came up out of the water at the same time only she was sputtering and wiping short strands of hair from her eyes.

"Woods weasel! You are going to pay for that, Kyri Fletcher!" She dove at me while I was still laughing and we went under again. We came up entwined and suddenly were not laughing any longer.

I looked deep into her eyes while she waited. "Today has been the best day of my life." Then, because it seemed to be the only thing left for us to do, I kissed her. I could still taste the sweet date on her tongue, with just a hint of the wine from the dark skin we brought. If I thought the skin beneath my fingertips was soft then I had no words for the lips that caressed my own. They alternated between firm and inviting. And when her questing tongue sought entry between my teeth, I let her in. The kiss continued while each heartbeat merged with the next. It deepened as olive oil lamps sputtered and danced to cast shadows upon the floor. The tiny flames flickered and popped with each caress and moan. Forced apart by the necessity to breathe with more than desperate gasps, I pulled her closer to me. Ori rested her head on my hammering chest and sucked in her own needed air.

When I felt us calm again she pulled back to see my face. "We will have many more days in the history of us. I hope that all will be as sweet as this one."

I smiled at the word that had become so familiar and enchanting to my ears. "Us."

Ori nodded her head. "Yes, us. Always us."

With the pricking of tears in my eyes I swallowed the lump in my throat to speak. "If I were left with only one word for the rest of my life, I would pick just that one. It holds more meaning for me, more love, than the entire history of that which we speak."

The queen looked down for a heartbeat, then returned her gaze to my eyes. She backed away from me in the water toward the stone steps and held out a hand. I took it gratefully and waited for what she had to say. "You honor me with your perfect words and honest eyes. Come, let me honor you in return." Together we walked out of the pool and completed the dance we had begun candle marks before. We may not have called the Goddess's name to the heavens above, or lay upon the altar of her divinity, but we worshiped the promise that we made to each other while standing in her temple. We honored our past, our present, and our future. The stars themselves could not have told our tale more perfectly than the questing fingers of our hands. I had given up everything and received the most precious gift of all.

Chapter Twelve

The Tremors of Rage Left Cold

IT WAS QUITE late by the time we returned from the bathing pool. Dawn must have found us dreaming in exhausted sleep because it was a candle mark or so after that I woke to feel a gentle caress on my cheek. I opened my eyes and squinted at the bright light that filtered through the gaps in the closed shutters covering the window. Dust motes floated in the air along the length of the sunbeam and I smiled at the way I felt warm inside and out. My queen's voice was quiet and rough still from our night of celebration. "Good morning, love." Ori was leaning on an elbow, propped above me. She moved her head into my view and suddenly blocked the sunlight, which in turn formed a halo around her golden hair. As I looked into her eyes I could see exactly what prompted her to wake against the drag of much needed sleep. Unable to resist the lure of her expression I pulled us into a frenzied and carnal kiss.

We continued as such for longer than I thought possible, with blood pounding in our veins and sweat slicking the length of our nude skin. I shivered at the first touch of her hand to my breast but did not stop my exploration of her lips with my mouth. My hands mapped her back and moved up to the hair at the nape of her neck. Gripping the fine strands I found there tight in my fist elicited a whimper and she moved even closer. So caught up in the fury of our passion, I missed feeling her hand slide its way down my abdomen. The first touch of her fingers caused me to tense with fear and start to shake. With eyes tightly shut, I had nothing in my mind's eye but the memories of a night stolen from me in a faraway place. Ori's hand froze while her words drew me back slowly. "Shh, it's just me. I'm right here, love. This is me loving you. Open your eyes, Kyri."

Very aware of the way she rested atop my mound, I opened blue eyes to peer up at her. "Ori." Her name whispered between my lips as her gaze locked with mine and her hand started to move once again.

"Just keep looking at me. Feel me and know that it is my love you are receiving and no one else. Can you feel me?" I swallowed thickly and nodded my head as the pleasure started building with her touch. She continued to talk as she took me higher. "I am your queen and your lover. It is my hands that claim you and worship you."

She moved her lips to my breast while slick fingers continued to caress and slide against my most sacred offering. Heat built low in my body at its very core and I moaned at the onslaught of feeling and emotion. I pulled her from my chest where both nipples stood at rigid attention and brought our mouths together into a clashing battle of lips and teeth. Pleasure had my eyes open barely a slit, but I still felt her and knew it was her who spiraled me higher and higher toward the sun. When at last the light broke over the horizon of my fear, I screamed through the tatters of my soul. As I lay in her arms, I sobbed like a broken thing. Or perhaps I sobbed as woman who was broken no more. When I was able to look into Ori's eyes, I grew dismayed to see them full of tears as well.

With two shaking fingers I gently wiped the tears from her cheeks. "Why do you cry?"

"Because I have been lucky enough to receive two of your most sacred of gifts and I thank the Goddess every day for the treasure that is you."

"I am no gold crown nor necklace of fine gems, my queen."

"No, you are infinitely more valuable." Her words of sheer honesty prompted me to roll us both onto our sides and show her exactly how much I appreciated her love. Despite all that we felt and yearned, we did not linger in our love as we would have liked. There were games to be held and another feast to be had after all.

The morning was a new beginning of sorts. We were newly betrothed, we had finally broken through some of the remaining fear I held between us, and it was the day of equinox. We washed each other playfully from the basin and pitcher of water kept on one of the tables in her hut. As we dressed we spoke of the day to come. "Which events are you going to enter today? I assume the usual, with archery and perhaps skill."

"Yes, I would like to repeat last spring's skill demonstration, with your help of course."

"I can do that."

I continued with a more wistful tone. "I wanted to enter all the events because I have missed it all so much but I am aware of how foolish that is."

Ori gave me a concerned look as she settled her sword harness onto her back and slung the quiver over that. "How is your side?" A look of guilt flickered across her features and I knew her injury to me still caused her pain.

A sigh escaped before I could check it. "I will admit, it is better but not well enough to enter all the events. I will do archery, skill, and tree running."

She reached out to caress the scar that was visible below my new halter top. "Given the way we had to split up most of the events this time, it probably would not be possible to do everything. Are you sure about the tree race though?"

Laughing, I grabbed her hand and kissed the fingertips. "If Coryn can compete with nearly broken ribs then I can surely compete with a half-healed little poke! Besides, this may be my best chance to beat her." Ori joined my laughter as we left her hut to start the day. Once we ate our first meal and the opening ceremony was complete I left to gather the items I would need for the skill demonstration since that event was always first. Kylani had anticipated my needs and already had the standard archery target placed by the tree line. When my turn arrived it was exactly like it had been a sun cycle previous. Ori shot two arrows at me. The only thing I changed was that I dashed away the first and caught the second since I knew she would be shooting two. Immediately after shooting at me she turned and aimed at the target down field. Just as intended, I shot the arrow I caught and easily dashed hers away before it could reach their goal. My next three landed in the red painted circle, ending my demonstration. The assembled Amazons erupted in cheers and hooting. I was eventually awarded the Artemis statue for first place after all other competitors had finished with their own demonstrations.

I worried at first that the crowd and conference of elders were showing favoritism to me in light of all that I had gone through and the fact that the queen and I were newly betrothed, but Coryn that reassured me they were not. Being the last to congratulate me on my success, she must have seen the doubt in my eyes because she did not let go of my arm after our embrace. "Kyri, no one came close to what you did today, your statue was well-earned." She shook her head and smiled. "You and I are so different sometimes. It is as hard for you to admit success as it is for me to admit failure. Accept the elders' judgement on this."

I glanced at the statue of Artemis with the word "SKILL" carved into the base. "I will, and thank you for showing me your confident face."

Coryn laughed as she released my arm and slapped me on

the shoulder. "Well don't get used to the view because all you'll see during the tree race is my backside!"

I made like I was going to poke her in the ribs of her injured side and she stepped away fast. Giving my own laugh I smiled back at her. "I am not so sure about that."

Coryn carelessly ran a hand through her hair and snagged her First Scout Leader feather. "Hades! With both of us on the mend it may be that neither will win!"

"What are you two hoot owls laughing about over here?" Shana looked back and forth between us curiously.

"Just my humility and Coryn's lack of."

Shana's laughter was a relief as was the absence of circles under her eyes. While I did not know what had been said between them the previous day, I was hoping that she had at least found some peace. "That is certainly the truth. Now, are you two ready to watch the sword matches?" She turned to me. "Ori said to let you know that she had to resolve an issue with the council and she would meet us over there."

By the time we arrived, the first round of sword bouts had already begun. Numerous pairs were spread out in the practice rings on the outskirts of the village. Because there were an odd number of participants, Ori actually had a pass and would not fight until the second round. She smiled and embraced me when we arrived. I was not sure if she felt the same way, but since our betrothal I had a hard time not touching her in some fashion whenever we were together. Whether it was an embrace or just simply leaning together at the shoulders, something about her touch and her presence soothed me. She made me feel real and grounded. "What took you so long?"

I kissed the top of her head and pointed a thumb at Coryn. "That one wanted a tighter wrap for her ribs because she seems to think it will help her win the tree race later."

The scout in question made a rude gesture and gave her own explanation. "Your newly betrothed also walked us halfway across the village so we could put her precious statue in her hut. Let's not forget about that."

The queen laughed at our antics. "Well you two are certainly in fine form, aren't you?"

"Always!" We both answered at the same time, which elicited laughter from Basha and Shana, who were also standing near.

Ori gave me a mischievous grin. "Maybe I should enter the tree race and show you both how it's done!"

The First Scout Leader smirked. "I think you may be a little out of practice, my queen."

"Who says I haven't been practicing?" She finished the statement with a wink and walked over to the ring where they called her for her first match.

Coryn groaned and the other two laughed.

"Is she really so skilled at tree running?"

Basha answered my question. "She was the youngest First Scout Leader Telequire has ever seen and she always took first in tree running."

"Broken string and bent fletch! Is there anything the queen cannot do?"

The ever put-upon First Scout Leader raised her hand high. "Reach tall branches?" We all burst into laughter at her joke about the queen's height, then turned to watch her match.

The two people I rooted for in swords both won their matches handily. After the third round the sword contestants took a break and both chobo and staff began. A few of my fourth scouts had entered the two wood events so I watched for a short while. Kylani and Ori went in search of some tree bars, looking for a little extra energy for the remaining rounds, and I wandered over to where the story telling event was about to begin. Shana came with me since she wanted to enter the contest as she had done many other times before.

An idea had been tickling my thoughts since Ori asked which events I wanted to enter. I spoke with the priestess nearly every single day since returning to Telequire, but I had yet to tell my full story to anyone else. Shana, Ori, Kylani, they all got bits and pieces of it. While I was not ready to disclose my entire tale, I thought maybe it was time for Pocori's story to be heard. I followed Shana to the table and grabbed an arm tie for myself. Shana turned to me with a startled look on her face. "What are you doing?"

I made eye contact with the councilwoman who was taking down names, indicating that I wished to participate as well. "What does it look like, sister?"

She punched my arm. "I know exactly what it looks like but you hate being in front of people and you hate speaking. What are you up to?"

My eyes felt sad when I looked at her but my heart was bolstered by courage. "Maybe today I have something to say."

Heartbeats went by while we stared into each other's eyes and the moment was only broken when Ori interrupted the tableau. "What is this?" She tugged the red competition tie knotted snugly around my arm. "Since when did you become a story-teller?"

I embraced my queen and pulled her close. Maybe it was so she could not see my eyes when I admitted the reason for my sudden need to speak. "Since a brave young scout died for the sins of slavery. Since the sorrow of her death has been outweighed by the joy of my return. I want the tribe to understand the young woman that I knew as her scout leader and as her friend."

Ori sucked in a breath and pulled back in my arms to look me in the eyes, but I closed them tight before she could read my emotion. I could not bear to see doubt or sadness shining back at me. "Kyri." She gently cradled my head in both hands, thumbs lightly caressing my closed lids. "Look at me, please." After only a heartbeat longer I obeyed her wishes. What I saw took my breath away. It was love, not doubt, that pierced me clean through. "I am proud of you." I did not answer, I could not. I merely nodded and swallowed the tidal wave of emotion that threatened to crash upon my shore.

Because we were the last two people to sign up, Shana and I were the last ones to tell our stories. Shana's was full of humor and revelry, something that had been much needed in my day of heavy thoughts. I laughed along with the rest of the crowd at her hilarious antics and witty dialogue. The nerves began as she wrapped up her speech and my stomach threatened to rebel when I replaced her on the small stage that had been built. Looking out over the crowd, I saw a surprising number of people walking up to watch. And I nearly lost my nerve completely when Glyphera joined the spectators with Pocori's mother and sister close behind. Without another thought I cleared my mind to all but the person I wished to honor and began.

"I sing a song of a young scout whose heroism was as clear as a cloudless sky. While not overly fond of the smell of fish, she was both kind and kindhearted. As a junior scout she displayed courage beyond expectation when she fought wounded against a superior force—" I spoke of the girl I knew who had been so brave at such a young age. I told the story of a young woman who fought with everything she had to break free of her captors and sacrificed that fight in order to warn me of danger. And finally, in a voice rife with heartbreak, I put into words all that she had given up in that hot Roman agora. Her bravery allowed her to die a free woman, unbroken and with the spirit of Artemis coursing through her veins. "—because of her sacrifice, we did not have to fight a hopeless battle only to die in the hot sun. Because of her gift, Iva and I lived to see another day and eventually return home. She was brave in a time that I could not afford to be and my heart will always grieve for such a senseless life lost. Wind to thy wings, sister, and Goddess speed you to your heart's reward." The crowd was silent as I finished and I took the opportunity to discretely wipe the tears that had gathered in my eyelashes.

Before I could make my way from the stage a voice started off to the side of the crowd. It was Glyphera and she sang the same song fourteen Amazons intoned their first night on Amazon soil. "As long as you live, shine. Let nothing grieve you beyond measure. For your life is short, and time will claim its toll." Women, watchers, contestants, and spectators all joined in, lifting the message to the heavens as they sang the round over and over the traditional four times through. No voice was left out of the people gathered near the stage, though some sang with more tears than others. It was a moment that none of us in the small gathering would ever forget. I made it down the steps and found Theo staring up at me with red-rimmed eyes.

"Thank you for honoring my family, and for continuing to think of us." I kept my emotions under control throughout her embrace. It was only after she wandered back through the crowd that Ori pulled me aside and I allowed myself to break down. When they announced winners, I was not surprised to hear that Shana had garnered the first place spot. But I was taken aback to hear my own name mentioned third. Knowing that the top three would compete at the Festival of Nations, I withdrew my name. No one questioned my decision and it would not have done any good if they did. I had no other stories to tell.

Eventually we found our way back to the second half of the sword competition and in the end it was Ori who beat out Kylani for the Artemis statue. I noticed Megara watching while the weapons master and my queen battled. To an outsider it probably looked a little one-sided. Our small and trim queen faced off against a woman who was about my height and more solidly muscled. But Ori's muscle was there if one chose to look beyond her quick humor and smiling face. And her humor was not the only thing that was quick. She veritably danced around the larger woman in the sparring ring.

One thing I noticed about Ori in all the times I had seen her with a sword in hand, she always appeared to be only a little more skilled than those she fought against. It was as if she did the bare minimum she needed to win. A careless opponent would assume she was only slightly better but they would be wrong. Her skill within the Telequire nation was unsurpassed and much talked about. But without her competing in the previous sun-cycle's solstice games, no other tribes would know of that skill with the exception of those Amazons who had seen her battling in the Western War. I watched the Shimax royal guard captain and had a feeling her interest in the battle for first place was more than just a passing fancy. I shrugged it off though because the world could not stop on the wonderings of "what if."

Unfortunately I could not shrug off her voice as she came to stand by me halfway through the match. "Your little queen is quite good with the sword." I did not bother to answer since her words seemed more of an observation than anything else. Or perhaps they were more of a goad. Either way, I did not rise to her bait. "I hear she even stabbed you once when you tried to kill her. And look at you now, betrothed!"

I clenched my teeth to avoid lashing out at her true words. I waited a few heartbeats before answering. "Yes, it is quite amazing how things worked out." She irritated me with her chatter while I tried to watch the sword contest between my two friends.

Apparently my indifference irritated her as well. She turned to me full and took on a challenging stance and I assumed correctly that her next words would be fit to insult. "Tell me, Kyri Fletcher, does nothing bother you? I have called you out for the doulé that you are, I have belittled your queen and informed you that you are worth nothing compared to my princess, yet you take it all with unflappable acceptance. Do you care so little at that which goes on around you or was all the fire beaten out of you as a slave? I am very curious to know."

I controlled my breathing and with difficulty controlled my temper as well. I knew without a doubt that Megara sought to elicit a reaction from me. For whatever reason, I sensed that she wanted a measure of my temperament and physicality. One of the first things I learned training as a gladiatrix was that your enemy will taunt you, will try to push you into anger. The angry warrior became sloppy and made mistakes. The enraged warrior became easier to read. I would not be so easily read by the likes of her. I also knew that I would do nothing to interrupt our festival, nor would I cause difficulty for those that worked so hard to forge allegiances between the tribes. Megara was a troublemaker and I would not provoke her bad humor.

I did not even give her my full face when I responded, merely cutting my glance her way. "It is not that I do not care but that I have learned many hard lessons in the short amount of time I have been under the stars above. One of the greatest things I have learned is that life is too short to care about that which matters not." I watched as Ori finished with a flourish, disarming Kylani and eliciting a surrender. Then I turned to stare directly into her eyes. "You matter not. Now if you will excuse me, I have to congratulate my *little queen*." I left her standing with face red and fists clenched tight.

The knife event immediately followed sword, and the unarmed combat was to begin when the knife fighters took their break. After the second half of the knife event, the unarmed would finish their rounds and the tree race would begin. The first place matches for chobo and staff would not be held until the tree race was finished. The last two events of the day were always archery and long distance running.

It was the first sun-cycle that most of the events had to be broken into halves, similar to what was done during the Festival of Nations, and some of those events even overlapped slightly. Competition for the summer solstice events were spread out over five days because of slight changes with the contests. Telequire was a rapidly growing nation and many wanted to represent us at the summer solstice so there were a lot of women wishing to compete on my first festival since returning home. Because of the greater number of participants in the regular competitions, all practiced single elimination. That meant the rounds ended much faster than they would at summer solstice. At least, that was how Shana explained it to me.

When the knife event got underway, Shana was paired with a fairly easy opponent. Ori decided to take her Artemis statue to her hut and search for more tree bars. I kissed her soundly and sent her on her way then turned back to watch my sister-friend. While Shana and the other woman circled each other in the ring, Basha moved closer to me and quietly spoke from my right side. "I heard what she said to you. Why didn't you tell Ori after she was finished with the match? You should not have to put up with such disrespect, Kyri. It was almost as if she was purposely trying to provoke you."

I kept my voice low because I did not want Kylani to hear, mere paces away from us. "She is a troublemaker and I think she expected me to say something, or at the very least to confront her directly. She was trying to incite me for whatever reason and I have always found it better to do what is not expected."

"But—"

I interrupted her so that her raised voice would not call attention to us. "No, trust me on this. It is enough that I know the measure of her person and I will be prepared when she causes trouble again at summer solstice."

Basha's look turned contemplative. "You think she will then?"

"Do you not?"

The regent sighed. "No, unfortunately I think you're right. I too will be wary when Shimax returns to Telequire."

I recognized quite a few fighters that were still in the running for the statue after the first half of competition. Shana and Deka were the two most obvious ones, being the best at knives in the tribe. But I also recognized Maeza, Mitsah, Gerlani, and Certig. I was proud to see that at least two of the fourth scouts that I knew better than most had done so well. Kylani approached me before the unarmed event was supposed to start. Ori had returned from her errand and we watched as the contestants were picking up their red ties from the correct area. Kylani herself sported a red wrap. "Are you going to compete in this one too, Kyri?"

Megara had found her way back and stood close enough to hear our conversation but not so close that she could be included in it. Rather than answer for myself, Shana laughed and spoke for me. "Kyri, fight in the unarmed combat? Surely you must be joking!" Kylani looked like she was going to dispute my sister's statement but closed her mouth when she caught my slight head shake. Other than the training master, no one else was aware of the fighting techniques I had learned as a gladiatrix. The knowledge was not something I wanted to share and certainly not with Megara listening so intently. It was also not a casual practice to be used in sparring. I had been teaching Kylani because she specifically asked me and I knew that she was a student of all forms of combat.

I smiled at the training master. "She is certainly right, I am not one for competing in such an event. I will leave the throwing of people on the ground to you!" As I had mentioned to Kylani before, most Amazons, or even Greeks in general, used the standard forms of unarmed fighting. It was a mixture of straight forward blows done with fists and wrestling. There was nothing of what I learned from Aureolus. Hand-to-hand fighting for a gladiator or gladiatrix was done as a last resort only if you were disarmed. We were not taught to disable when fighting against opponents wielding swords, pugiones, spears, and nets. We were taught to cripple and to kill. It was a technique that had no place in the Amazon games.

Many people who were not competing, or were between events, wandered across the length and breadth of the village and large field set aside for the competition. After watching Kylani win her first event, Ori and I did our own wandering. I had grown hungry so we went by one of the cook fires for a few slices of venison. Gata found us shortly after and managed to beg a good-sized piece from me. She kept putting a large paw on my thigh while we sat on a log talking. I had a skyphoi loaded with the savory meat and had no qualms about stuffing it into my mouth as fast as I could chew. Ori laughed. "You spoil that cat! And look at you, I think she eats cleaner!"

"Ha-ha, your humor is astounding!" I bumped her shoulder with my own and threw the nearly grown leopard another piece of meat. "I did not realize how hungry I was until the unarmed event started. And I need my strength if I am to beat Coryn in the tree race."

The queen gave me a mischievous look. "And who is going to beat me?"

I blinked at her, shocked by her words. "I had not realized you were serious earlier."

"What's wrong with me entering the tree race?"

What was wrong with it, indeed? I took a drink from my water skin and thought about how to answer. "Well, you are the queen—"

She interrupted me before I could attempt to put my tumbling thoughts in order. "Not this again! I'm starting to feel you think I have no skills at all. You prick my pride, Kyri Fletcher!"

I quickly set my skyphoi on the ground and wiped my hands on the scrap of cloth I kept on my belt for drying the sweat when tree running. When I turned to her fully, she wore the impish smile that had become so familiar to me. "On the contrary, I often wonder if there is anything that you cannot do well. It is very intimidating. You are so accomplished and skilled and I feel so mortal living in your shadow."

She covered my mouth with her fingers. "Please stop or I will get a swollen head and my monarch's mask will no longer fit!" Unable to hold it in any longer, we both broke into fits of laughter.

When we regained control of ourselves I cocked my head at her. "It is true though, I have often felt inadequate in the light of your sun."

Ori took my hands in both of hers. "But don't you see? You

are more than just a sun to me. You are my moon and stars, you are the whole of the heavens above. Without you my light would have no balance."

I smiled with humbled affection. "Such pretty words my queen speaks."

She shook her head and smiled back. "Truer words were never spoken."

Lifting her hand to my lips, I kissed each fingertip in turn. "I can think of three."

"Oh?"

"I love you."

We were frozen in the warm haze of truth spoken and continued to share the moment for a handful of candle drops. With a sigh I turned back to retrieve my late lunch and only found an empty bowl. Gata was nowhere to be seen. "Woods weasel!"

Ori moved her head to look around me. "What's wrong?"

"Do you notice something missing?"

She peered closer. "Gata?"

"And?" When she spied the empty skyphoi, she let loose peals of laughter. Even after nights of passion and the moment of our very betrothal, her voice alone could still stop the breath in my chest.

She politely ignored my look of wondrous befuddlement and pulled me to my feet. "Come along, beloved. You've had enough to eat for now, we wouldn't want you to be slow in the trees!"

The finish for knives was nearly identical to what I remembered from the sun cycle before. Shana took second just behind Deka. Shana told me once that while their rivalry had been going on since they first learned which end of the knife to hold, it was all with good nature. Shana had won out over the Second Scout Leader just as often as not. Kylani won the statue in unarmed fighting and I was surprised to see Coryn's friend Sheila take second with my gossip-prone fourth scout, Geeta, take third. All three of them would be representing Telequire in the coming summer festival. When the time came for the tree race I was definitely not slow. As soon as the call to start went out Coryn and I took off through the canopy. I lost sight of Ori right away and only felt marginally bad that she fell behind so fast.

The trees surrounding the village were very large which made running the branches easy enough. The trick was to pick your way through without touching or interfering with the other tree runners. Occasionally a gap would be too large and we would make use of the ropes hanging down to swing across. We ran for nearly three quarters of a candle mark around the village outskirts until I could see the rope hanging down that was the finish. While we were nearly tied as we ran, the nearest competitor was still a handful of trees behind us. When I glanced up at the First Scout Leader, I saw a familiar look of stubborn determination wash over her face and she gave a great leap forward. Despite the twinging in my side as I twisted and ran through the branches, I too dug deep into my reserves.

As we approached the end and the rope that hung placidly down to the ground, the crowd of watchers began hooting and cheering. I could tell by the set of her shoulders that Coryn was preparing herself for the final push and leap but at the last possible heartbeat we were both surprised by a trilling cry from higher above us. I watched as Ori delivered a brilliant flip over our heads and grabbed onto the rope at the last possible moment. Coryn swore and seeing that she was distracted by the queen's win, I dove for the rope next. The race ended fast after that. I teased my friend mercilessly for finishing behind me, and Ori teased us both. Coryn made a face at her. "I can't believe I was beaten by you, yet again!"

Ori scoffed. "Should I be worried that two of our top tree runners couldn't even keep up with one sedentary queen? Maybe our scouts have grown soft."

The First Scout Leader started laughing. "Sedentary? Never in my life have I see you as such!"

"Oh, well, I have been spending a lot of time on my back lately..." Ori trailed off and smirked at us while my face blazed bright red. I could feel the heat of it and knew my blush would not subside any time soon.

I whispered to her fiercely. "I cannot believe you just said that!"

She patted my cheek lovingly. "My hut is near the center of the village. If you think they haven't heard us by now you are sadly mistaken." I had no answer other than for my face to continue its burn. We had a break before the archery event was to start. It was due to the fact that chobo and staff still had to complete their first place matches. Ori and I used the opportunity to cool down and catch our breaths. We watched as one of the chobo fighters took a hard knock to the head and still come back to take the win. Afterward, the first place stave fighter broke two fingers on the left hand of her opponent. None of the injuries were severe enough to prevent them from competing in three moons.

When the archery competition was ready to begin, Kylani

explained all the changes that had been made. It was different from the previous sun-cycle I had competed. Because of the sheer number of contestants, she had to weed more out sooner. The first round consisted of everyone shooting at a standard target with twenty arrows. All twenty needed to go into the hand-size red circle to move on. Quite a few people were still left after that. On one hand I was proud at the skill of our nation's archers, on the other I was worried for my chances to win. Kylani had all the remaining shooters gather in a group and the assistants set up the pendulum targets while she explained the next challenge. "Because we have such a large group, you must all either hit the pendulum, or stop the pendulum with a center shot.

Malva, my veteran fourth scout, called out from the middle of the group. "Well we all know one person who will be moving on to the next round!" Everyone laughed at her jibe and I simply took it in stride. After all, I was the only one who had made the impossible shot so her comment was both accurate and funny. Soon after her words, we all lined up and aimed at the pendulum targets. Ori's arrow caught the pendulum, very near to the hole in its center and I raised an eyebrow at her increased skill. With only a finger to the right, she would have stopped it with a center shot. When it was my turn I made my shot easily, almost too easily. The pendulum stopped with my blue and green forest fletch arrow buried with the red circle behind it.

While I was watching the last few competitors to my left, a gasp went through the crowd to my right. I turned to see the training master's second, Cyerma, had made the impossible shot. Whoops and shouts went up throughout the area. I knew she was good after competing against her the previous spring equinox, but she too had gotten even better in the time I was gone. When the new targets were set up, I think we were all surprised to see four rings swinging along the length of the stick that faced us. I had never done more than two and I wondered why Kylani had added the fourth ring. Then a thought came to me in a rush. Had Cyerma gotten so good that the training master thought it necessary to added more difficulty?

Feeling a sudden bout of nerves, I took a deep breath to ground myself and thought of my da. A fletcher and an archer, he was the man who first made me. He was also the man who continued to make me with every new thing he taught. His life's work and passion were both my creed and calling and his love of bow and fletch had become my own.

As six of us approached the final round, I continued my deep breathing and tuned out the sounds around me. I focused on the ground beneath my feet, on the air in my lungs, and the sound of the wind rustling the trees. Gone were the voices of bravado and wagers. The human press of watchers had faded into the background with everyone else. There was a slight breeze that twirled the rings capriciously. The first two archers split their success. Malva caught one ring but the other woman did not catch any. Ori shot third and also caught one ring. The crowd's tension escalated with each new person. Cyerma shot fourth and much to my dismay she caught two of the rings with her arrow. The crowd began to murmur and when I glanced around I saw more bets being made behind us. The fifth woman I recognized as Dina's second but her name eluded me. She also failed to catch a ring, though she had a nice center shot on the target.

The wind was an impish sprite who toyed with our emotions mercilessly. By the mirth and grace of the fates, I had the last turn and felt the pressure immensely. When the fifth archer's arrow was cleared away, I lined up for my own shot. The breeze occasionally caused my feathers to dance though my braided hair stayed in place well enough. The voices had begun to rise behind me where the crowd continued to grow. But all went silent when I drew my arrow and nocked it. Sighting down the length of my shaft I watched the line of rings and waited while feathers caressed my cheek. The wind continued to puff little gusts and my draw grew heavy as I waited for it to die down. Just as the first tremor threatened my grip I got the break I was looking for and sent my arrow on its way. I released my breath in a chuff when I saw the first two and last rings trapped securely by the arrow in the center of the target. A great cheer went up over the crowd and Ori grabbed me around the waist.

"You did it! Congratulations, love."

I looked down into her green eyes and felt as though I had won more than a mere contest. "Thank you."

After I received my statue, Ori and Malva had to shoot again to see who would take third place and represent the nation at summer solstice. On their second round, Ori caught two rings as Cyerma had, but Malva still only stopped one. As we waited near the training hut for the distance runners to come in I tickled Ori playfully. "You are just breaking hearts all over the village today!"

She shot me a curious look. "What do you mean?"

I ticked off the items on the fingers of one hand. "First in sword, first in tree running, and you stole the third place from poor Malva. Not to mention the fact that you are newly betrothed, which I am sure has caused many eligible Amazons to shed tears of sadness." I pointed a finger at her and smiled. "Heartbreaker!"

Ori's curious look turned to one of concern. "Do you think I should not compete with everyone else because I'm the queen?"

"No!" I shook my head vehemently to show how much I disagreed with her words. "On the contrary, I think it is amazing that you do not just lead us well, you lead us by example. Every nation would be lucky to have a queen who is as beautiful and talented as you."

Laughter followed my gushing words. "I think you may be a little partial, love."

Shaking my head, I pulled her close to me. "Do not mock my truth simply because it makes you uncomfortable to hear it."

"You're right, I shall accept your intimate wisdom on the matter. Now, since we were just informed that the runners are still more than a quarter candle mark out, I'm going to relieve myself and refill my water skin."

I sighed dramatically. "'Tis the circle of life the way we constantly take in and release the waters of our world. I shall wait in darkness for my sun to return. Come soon sweet light and take away this dark night!"

She laughed delightedly. "What was that from? Is that a play?"

I nodded. "One of the senators who hosted a funeral with gladiator combats hired actors to perform after the evening convivium. I do not know what it was they performed, I found the drama a little too high for my tastes."

I got a lingering kiss in response. "Well I happen to like your sweet words and I'll expect more from you later." She went off toward the village well and I stood lost in my thoughts. I should have known, I should have expected the interruption. A handful of candle drops later my peace was once again interrupted by the irritating Shimax royal guard. There was no other person near me when she came to take up the space at my left side. We stood at the corner of the main training hut, looking out into the surrounding forest.

"I've been asking around about you."

I did not feel like verbally sparring with her. "I did not realized you were so interested. Fortunately for me, I am already spoken for.

She did not acknowledge my rejoinder. "You should be proud to be so popular among the Telequire Amazons, especially for someone so young and new to the tribe."

My feathers bounced when I shook my head at her observation. "I am merely another sister in a tribe of sisters. There is nothing I would not do, or have not already done, to protect my tribe and nation. If you have a point then make it because I am starting to lose patience with you."

"What's the matter, doulé, does it prick your pride to be so easily beat by your little queen? Perhaps that is why she likes you so much, because you let her beat you in private too like the slave that you are."

I took a deep breath and let it out slow. I would not give her my anger, nor would I fuel her fire of provocation. "What the queen and I do in public is respect each other. What we do in private is none of your concern but rest assured it is as beautiful as only Artemis would allow." I turned to her then and could feel that my face had gone hard. Easily as stone as it had been so many times in the past when faced with Roman gladiators. "While I will let you disparage and insult me, because ultimately your words do not matter to my life's path, I will not let you speak poorly of my queen. She has earned her place with every battle she wins, treaty she writes, and life she saves. Her beauty surpasses all but our most esteemed Goddess and her words as Artemis's Chosen have more meaning than a lifetime of your illiterate bile." My voice was quiet but harsh and I took a step toward her with my last words. "Now move your body away from my presence or I will remove it for you!"

Megara's hand dropped to the dagger she wore at her waist. Her intended threat was obvious. "You think you frighten me, doulé? I am a warrior, not some slave you can cry and compare whip marks with. I'd wager you are nothing at all unless you have a bow in hand. Isn't that right, Kyri Fletcher?"

I looked at her and recognized the anger in her eyes. However it was nothing compared to the rage that filled me and sent twitching tremors through my muscles. I shook my head at her, sadly. "I wish I could say that were true." Aware of the rising tide that threatened to swamp my senses, I ground out the only words I had left to speak. "You need to leave."

She smirked at me and I closed my eyes to the sight. "What's the matter, doulé? I see you shaking, are you so afraid of a few harsh words? I will leave when I'm ready, I am a guest here—"

"Your status as guest has been rescinded!" I recognized Ori's voice but I could not open my eyes. Rigid with fury I was afraid to move, afraid that my anger would find targets other than which I intended. It was not a time to kill and that was all my rage knew how to do. Many footsteps sounded around me and I assumed that people had come over to see what the queen was yelling about. But those same footsteps moved away quickly. "Kyri? Please open your eyes."

A hand closed over the top of mine and I fought the urge to throw it off. When I was finally able to obey, I found the area around us conspicuously cleared. She tugged my hand and looked down to see I had a white-knuckled grip on the handle of my pugio. I released the blade and she swiftly pulled me into the training hut then shut and barred the door. I could not stop the shaking and my breath came in panting gasps. The anger inside was roiling like a sickness with no way out. Her voice was gentle, coaxing. "Let it go, Kyri. You need to let it out."

I shook my head and closed my eyes in the darkened space. "I cannot."

She stepped close again but did not touch. I could feel the heat of her and her breath rustled the feathers that hung down from my left temple. "How can I help you?"

While rage burned hot through a person's body, it was a cold emotion. I tried to hold onto Ori's words, to bask in the warmth of her love through the sound of her voice. But it slipped desperately through my fingers. "I do not know." My muscles tensed and dread came over me because I knew what was to come. I could not control the rages and in turn the shame always controlled me after. Perhaps sensing the change in my demeanor, Ori stepped back. The only sound in the dark was of my ragged breathing. Finally, the queen's voice tried again.

"Scream."

My breath caught and I tried to see her through the dim light. "What?"

She took another step back. "I said scream. Your fury wants you to lash out, to release all the built up anger that is crashing inside of you. Get it out, scream." Still I hesitated and she pushed harder. "What are you afraid of?"

Ori's words broke the dam that held back the rolling waters of my emotion. "I am not afraid! I am furious!" I screamed even louder then, an unintelligible howl of primal anger and rage. When it was done, I dropped to my knees on the floor as if I were a puppet with my strings cut. I twitched and trembled still but it was no longer that of building rage, but rather a sudden relief. She knelt down to me and I reached for her impossibly fast. While the rage was gone it had been replaced by something equally as strong. There was no thought to our actions and I did not fight when she grabbed the back of my braided hair and pulled our mouths together with desperate intent.

She pushed me onto my back and I was forced to unfold my knees that were beneath me. I would have protested the position but for the placement of her firm thigh pressed between my own. I lost track of time while our lips fought for dominance and our fingers urgently sought the other to bring about our release. It could not have been very long though because the fires within burned so fast and out of control. Her hand had shoved its way inside my girdle to aid the strong muscles of her leg. When I crested beneath her she swallowed my hoarse cry with her mouth and when she came apart above me I did the same for her in return. All strength left our muscles in the aching heartbeats as we lay on the floor after. Both of us panted as we tried to catch our breath. I continued to twitch with her fingers still pressed tight against me.

"Goddess!"

I could not control the laughter that bubbled up at her satisfied exclamation. And before more than two heartbeats had gone by, she joined me in that laughter. We did not speak of the incident after. Instead we lay there for a few more candle drops while we collected our stamina and thoughts. It was the first yells and cheers that prompted us to scramble up from our recumbent positions on the floor and straighten our clothes. I shielded my eyes as we exited the hut, the sun bright after a double hand of candle drops in the dark. And as the first place runner crossed the finish line, I gave a trilling scout call to celebrate Degali winning the Artemis statue. My speedy fourth scout was no longer third best.

So much had happened while I was gone and I was starting to realize that not all the changes had been bad. If our moment in the hut had taught me one thing, it was that I was no longer too broken to function in Ori's world. It showed me that no matter what emotion raged and clawed within my chest, Ori understood me and would help me deal with it. She was my anchor and with her I would face each day with reassurance that we would make it through together.

Megara was allowed to pack then she was escorted to the edge of Telequire lands. The Shimax royal guard was also warned that if she ever caused trouble again she would be exiled permanently and no queen or princess could change Ori's decree. It was no small coincidence that the majority of scouts that escorted her to the border were none other than my fourth scouts. It was a declaration to Megara and in turn to the princess, that all of Telequire honored one another and that through blood and tears I had earned their fierce loyalty.

Chapter Thirteen

Blood by the Same Brush

IT DID NOT take long for the bliss of post-festival to wear off. Once it became apparent that I was healed again, I found myself busy with weapons training, hunting, replacing tree ropes, and learning the new information that I would need to know as the queen's consort. Truthfully I was not required to take care of the old ropes but it gave me the opportunity to run the trees and be free for a few candle marks each day. A fortnight had passed since our betrothal and the bond between us strengthened with every touch and conversation. I continued attending sessions with the priestess and had even begun to speak more about my experiences with Ori.

The first interruption to our peace came when I was checking ropes in the southeast quadrant. It was midday and I had just finished a light meal in the trees. The trilling call of scouts went out through the canopy and I jumped up with the message. The whistles of "urgent," "attack," and "friend" echoed around me. I quickly draped the spare coil of rope across my chest and took off in the direction of the scout calls with worry speeding my heels.

I arrived to see fourth scouts on the ground with—I blinked twice to clear my eyes and realized it was no man-beast with them but rather a simple mounted rider. What confused me was the fact that the man wore fur leggings that exactly matched the coat of his mount, making his legs invisible. At least until he turned slightly and I saw the horse's head on the other side of the man's torso. "Centaur." The word breathed from my lips in a whisper. I dropped down from the canopy above, startling two of the nearest scouts. I recognized Maeza, Geeta, and Shelti but did not see any veterans, nor did I see Certig or Deima.

Maeza looked away from the mounted man as I approached. I could see he sported an arrow in his left shoulder. The arm hung limp to his side while the blood oozed sluggishly. "Scout Leader!"

The rider sported thick, unkempt hair and the beginnings of a dark beard. He turned to me and narrowed his eyes. "Ai, so are you one who can get yer queen soz ta com help us? Tis urgent that I speaks ta her!"

I sighed and spared a glance at the entirety of the fourth troop quadrant that had come into the forest. "I am not their scout leader but if I were I would ask why they have left the Telequire border unguarded!"

Maeza gave me a shame-faced look. "We weren't sure what to do, Sco—Kyri. Malva was our only veteran this rotation and she fell sick yesterday and had to return to the village."

I clenched my teeth in frustration, not wanting the responsibility that had suddenly fallen into my hands. "Okay. First I want all of you to go back to patrol with the exception of Maeza and," I looked around and spied my speedy fourth scout, "Degali." The nine unnamed scouts took off for the perimeter at a fast lope and I turned to the stranger. "Who are you and why have you come to Telequire?"

"I be Gostig Stonehoof and I'm here ta call ona treaty 'tween yer Amazons and us centaurs. We be under siege by a force that came ta shore last night. I slipped out ta bring help back."

Protocol said I was supposed to request permission from the queen for men to enter the village, but I knew that mounted he could reach the village faster than even Degali. "Have you been followed here?"

He shrugged his good shoulder and winced. "Dunno, 'tis mebbee."

I closed my eyes, thinking furiously. If he were followed then the border patrol I just sent back would be in danger. I turned to Degali and Maeza. "Think, who would be closer right now, fourth scouts to the northwest or to the southeast?"

"Northwest." Maeza's voice was certain.

I looked at her closer. "You are sure?"

"Yes, Scout—Kyri."

I nodded. "I want you to run for the closer patrol, and I want Degali to go for the one that is farther out. But first, do either of you have a west whistler?" After the Western War, one of the more enterprising young scouts came up with a blunt-tipped arrow with a small wood whistle attached to the side. There were four arrows with four different whistles for each cardinal direction. One or two are shot, depending on the direction from village center that you need help. When shot into the air above the trees they would fly surprisingly far and created a screech like no other thing in the forest. Maeza nodded and handed me hers. I immediately drew and strung my bow and found a break in the leaves above us. Then I positioned myself so I could shoot the arrow in the direction that I had last seen the interior scouts. The screeching cut through the silence of the trees and a flock of birds took flight from the canopy nearby. I turned back to the two women. "Now go, we have no time to waste!"

Degali pointed at the centaur. "What about him?"

I looked up at Gostig. "Can your horse carry double?"

He grimaced with distaste. "If'n it must."

I addressed the two scouts that were waiting for my response. "I will personally take him to the queen. Now go!" As soon as they took off, I backed away from the horse then gave a little running leap onto its back, behind the inhospitable man. He smelled like sweat and his horse but I ignored that fact to focus on what was in the forefront of my mind's eye. Ori's sister lived in the village that was under siege, as did her nieces and bond-brother. Despite the fact that his mount must have been exhausted, we galloped into the village a little over half a candle mark later. We had entered on the trail nearest the training grounds and Amazons immediately surrounded us in alarm, with all manner of sparring weapons drawn. Kylani was the first to speak.

"What is going on, Kyri?"

I dismounted and immediately began shouting at the people around us. "We need a healer, Margoli, and the queen!" I looked at Kylani. "Centaurs have been attacked and their village is under siege. Gostig made it out to request help but he is clearly injured. Can we also get someone here to rub down his horse? I am afraid the beast is done in."

She called out to a couple more watching women. One ran off toward the center of the village and the other came over to take the centaur's horse. "Filipina will take the mount, she's one of our hostlers."

Gostig slid off his horse with difficulty and I helped steady him when he hit the ground. Before releasing the reins to the young woman he gave her a stern look. "He needs a'coolin and only feed him wheat, not yers barley."

Filipina gave him an incredulous look and Kylani waved her forward. "Just do it!"

She led the horse away just as Ori and Margoli approached us at a dead run. Semina, our second level healer from the trade trip, was fast behind them. "Gostig! What has happened?"

I was shocked as any to see the rough man drop to a knee and show proper obeisance to our queen. "Queen Ori, raiders gots te village surrounded. We's had enough warning from ta towers to pull the near horses inside the walls and blew the horn ta scatter te rest. We has te well and arrows enough but if'n they build a ram or fire us out, we's won't last."

Worry clouded my betrothed's features. "And Risiki?"

"Not ta worry, Ori. She and te little ones are safe in our lodge for te time bein'." Shock piled on top of my surprise when I realized the gruff, angry man I had shared a horse with was none other than the queen's bond-brother.

Ori blew out a breath and ran a hand through her short hair, careful of the feathers tied in that must have weighed on her like stones at that very moment. She waved the healer forward and together with Kylani, they led the man into Kylani's main training hut where there was a cot and basic medical supplies. Ori exited again after a candle drop and everyone but Kylani and the healer remained outside. Margoli spoke first. "My queen?"

Ori remained unfocused for a heartbeat longer then turned and began dictating to her Right Hand all things that needed to be done. "Call an immediate council meeting. Ready as many warriors as you can for immediate travel and the rest can follow later. Send our fastest messenger to Kombetar with spare mounts. We need her there yesterday!"

Margoli paused with a concerned look on her face. "Are you sure, my queen?"

It was in that moment that I saw a bit of the queen's own rage as Ori's temper manifested itself. Her face became a dark mask and her personality multiplied by two until she appeared larger than anyone standing near. "Am I sure? Am I sure that we should waste no time in aiding the centaur nation who gave us unquestioned and invaluable aid during the Western War? The very same Centaur nation who watches our western border every solstice and equinox, and is the first line of defense against raiders coming in from the sea? We have a treaty and I will fall upon my own sword before I go against that and tarnish the honor of this nation! We are allies, friends, and family with them. Am I sure? I refuse to turn my back on their need!" With every word, every single breath, her voice grew louder and more strident. Her declaration ended with a hoarse yell and Margoli wisely did not question her any more. She merely took off in a fast lope toward the village center to do as commanded.

"Ori." I called soft to get her attention without garnering any of her wrath.

She gave me a look that was hard and I read the fear beneath. "Are you going to offer me your doubt as well, Kyri?"

Instead of answering right away, I drew my sword and knelt

at her feet. "I would never offer you doubt. Instead I offer you my sword and arm to wield it. I give you my bow and fletch to aim as you see fit. And my pugiones are yours to command."

When I lifted my gaze to hers she gave me a piercing look. "Can you do this?"

I knew what she was asking. Could I go into combat on horseback with the darkness at our heels and not lose myself to the chanting and the blood? That was what she wanted to know, and it was a valid concern. I let a little of Kyrius out, not a lot but just enough for her to see. And I knew that she saw who I was deep inside because her eyes widened a bit and her breathing increased just so slightly. I thought back to the lines I had spoken a lifetime ago. "If the nation is threatened, let me be your shield, and if the nation seeks retribution for a wrong done, you will find no other arrows as true as mine." I stood in front of her and held my sword between us. "They will regret setting foot on Greek soil!"

DESPITE HAVING NO time to properly prepare, within three candle marks we had a force one hundred strong heading past the boundaries of Telequire. More warriors, supplies, and support personnel would follow a few candle marks behind us. We carried the bare minimum needed to make it there and fight. Rations, weapons, bedrolls, and mules for horse fodder. We rode in silence down the road to centaur lands and I could see that Ori's mind was turning in circles of anger and fearful desperation. She never mentioned her parents but Shana told me that they were both dead, killed by raiders similar to the ones that were currently laying siege to the centaur village of Sagiada. The sisters were taken in and raised by the Amazons but Risiki eventually left when she fell in love with a young man from the neighboring centaur nation.

Wanting to break her from those dark thoughts, I spoke just loud enough for her to hear. "I know you wanted me to meet your sister but this seems like a bit large of an escort for so simple a greeting." Gostig snorted where he rode off to my right and I realized that he heard me despite my low voice.

Ori cracked a smile and shook her head and the dark horseman finally spoke to me willingly. "So yer her beloved, na?"

The queen spoke up. "Betrothed now, Gostig. We are to be joined at summer solstice."

He nodded at her. "Glad ta see things worked out fer ya." He turned back to me. "Te Romans beat ya some bloody I see. Train ya some good, na?"

His speech was hard to follow but I caught the gist of what he was asking.

"Goss." Ori's voice was low, a warning.

I met her concerned eyes. "All is well, Ori." I turned back toward the man riding next to me. "I took two whippings while a slave. The first was to cow the rest of the slaves on the ship as much as to punish me. The second was a mistake and my doctore whipped the overseer into unconsciousness for it. I was trained as a sagittarius and a gladiatrix. I fought many times and earned money for my freedom."

His dark brow went up. "Oh? Sagittarii some fine arches. 'Tis na gone fer long, na? Done more'n te fightin', na?"

Anger washed fast through me at his implication. "I was only a gladiatrix! I fought often and I fought well, nothing more than that."

Gostig snorted. "Matter naught if'n yer fuckin' er fightin', still a whorin' fer Rome."

"Goss!" Ori's yell was abrupt and loud and a few other heads turned our way along the column of riders. "That's enough!"

He shrugged his good shoulder and sniffed loudly. "Dinna mean nuthin' but te obvious." His looked turned dark. "Don' matter if'n we fight fer er against te Romans, we's were all whores ta them. Ya did good some ta come back ta our Ori. Welcome ter te family, as such." I took his jumble of words as a tacit approval for our joining and let the rest go. There was more to worry about than the thoughts of one man who had been broken and embittered by a bloody war. However, I did not forget the fact that he had made it through.

That evening we camped in a clearing halfway between Telequire and Centaur land. We eventually made it to a place about a candle mark outside Sagiada, a day and a half after we left our own village. I could see throughout the trip that Ori wanted nothing more than to ride ahead, to run our beasts into the ground and cut a swath through the raiders. But she was wise and kept a level head about her. Margoli sent out scouts to see exactly what the status of the village was and to count how many enemies we would face. When the scouts returned, the three of them took a knee in front of Ori. "My queen, it looks like about two hundred fighters camped all around Sagiada, down in the valley. They have not breeched the walls, nor have they attempted fire."

She nodded. "They probably don't want to chance harming

the horse stock, nor the people. My guess is they are looking for bodies for a quick sale. I'm sure they assumed that it wouldn't take more than a few days to break through and they could be gone from Greek soil within a seven day."

"Ori." Gostig's rough voice seemed loud in the early morning. "If'n we's circle farther south through te foothills, we's ken come up through te valley and cut off te way ta ter ships."

Margoli grunted. "We are sorely outnumbered."

"Der Centaurs some smart, Right Hand. We's will only defend te village but if'n help comes dey will attack. Te village be holdin' another fifty strong warriors and te fletch never fails us!"

Ori smiled grimly. "We are going to have to count on that because I'm not sure when the rest of our warriors will arrive."

"If I may?" Eyes turned to me and I grew uncomfortable under the scrutiny. "Is there another way back to the harbor?"

Gostig scratched his stubbled chin. "'Tis mebbee one dey'd know of. Runs west a te village and circles back down ta te harbor from der."

"And how wide is it, would it be easily defended?"

The horseman cocked his head a little in thought. "Been suncycles since I seen te trail, but 'tis narrow with high walls. If'n you were up top te walls, be easy ta shoot down. What ya thinkin' Sagittarii?"

"Yes, Kyri, what are you thinking?" The curiosity in Ori's voice was tinged by an emotion I could not figure out. Worry, fear, skepticism? I was not sure.

Rather than dwell on insecurity and fears I described the idea that had been going through my head. "What I am thinking is that if you circle the main force to the south end of the valley where Gostig says, we can block their retreat. If you send a messenger out to the other part of our force and have them circle around to the north side of the valley then we will have them pinned down. They will have no choice but to escape through the narrow trail where a score of archers can easily pick them off."

I could see exactly when the queen understood my intention. Milani, Margoli's second and current branch leader, spoke up. "And who will lead these archers?"

"I will."

Despite seeing the understanding in her eyes moments before, Ori still startled at my answer. "No!"

I looked her straight in the eye. "I am your best archer and I am experienced at leading others. I just need the twenty best shots of those that can do some light climbing. The raiders will take the pinch, I guarantee it. Slavers are cowards and will not risk their lives if things turn poor for them. When they rush to escape, the combined forces can run them down from behind while we pick them off from the front."

Ori looked ready to protest again until Margoli leaned over and whispered in her ear. With an angry set to her shoulders, she looked resigned. "Fine." She glanced back and forth between me and Margoli's second. "Go with Milani and pick out your archers. Be ready to leave in a quarter candle mark. You will have to ride hard to make it around the valley and get into place before we reach the south end and attack."

"Yes, my queen." Our voices were near identical in pitch and demeanor as we spoke at the same time. Then both of us turned and took off at a fast lope toward our waiting army.

When we reached the line of mounted women, Milani turned to me. "Who do you want?"

I glanced toward the column that wound a little ways down the Centaur road. Horses were positioned four abreast and twenty-five rows long. I spied fifteen of my fourth scouts and named them off. I also named Cyerma when I saw her and told Milani to choose the last four since I had no knowledge of their shooting skill. The twenty riders were slightly confused but followed me forward to the point where the road went either north or south. "Where are we going, Scout Leader?" Maeza was the first to ask the question that had been itching at all of them. Lucky for the group she was due to rotate off duty just before Gostig came riding into Telequire, and she volunteered to go with the warriors rather than back to the village. Every person we had available to fight was essential.

"Call me Kyri, please."

Milani shook her head and interrupted. "No, today you are the Scout Leader they need you to be." She narrowed her eyes at me, perhaps not trusting in my experience or plan. "Do not fail them."

Deima bristled at her words of warning. "She has never failed us!"

"She failed one of you."

I could see most of the group swell with anger and I needed to stop things before they escalated further. I did not know Milani nor did she really know me. Perhaps she was a friend of Pocori and still pained with her loss. Perhaps she saw me as the reason. I could not help such things. But we had to focus on the moment and not things that had already gone by. "Enough!" A few scouts startled, never having heard me yell in anger. But I had to assert my leadership to the new team. I had to show them that I was strong and someone worth following, someone they could trust. I turned to the branch leader with a face wiped of emotion. "You can go back to the lines now, I have all that I need here." She looked angry but stalked off, rudely brushing past Gostig on her way back to the line.

"Huzzah, Sagittarii! Gonna tell's ya, if'n ya keep ta speeds that na be hurtin' yer horses, be less than a candle mark around. There be a mess a trees at te west end of te pass, you's can picket yer horses ter."

I thought for a heartbeat. "How long until you reach the south end?"

"'Bout half a candle mark."

We could only hurry so much around the north end. "Can you delay leaving for a quarter candle mark?"

His eyes darkened with anger. "With'n m'wife and babes inside?"

I looked hard at him and tried to make him see. "Do you want these men?"

Gostig's hand tightened on the makhaira he wore at his waist. His voice growled out through gritted teeth. "Yes."

He left me with a jerky nod and I quickly explained our mission to the gathered scouts. Then we took off at a canter down the north road. I wanted to go to Ori before we left, to hold her and tell her it would be okay but I could not. I knew that having her sister inside was hard enough but seeing me riding into danger would leave her undone. I would not let my queen be seen as weak in front of our nation. Just before spinning my own mount and following the line up the road, I met her haunted eyes. All I could do was mouth three short words to her, letting her see them on my lips and hope it would ease her worry. "I will return."

I caught up to the score of warriors a candle drop later. The valley where the village was settled was surrounded by a mix of tall hills and low rolling mountains. The north road was in very good shape, a testament to the skill and prosperity of the centaurs. We had no view into the valley below but I kept scouts ahead and behind us just in case the raiders had people in the area. As Gostig had promised, it took less than a candle mark to circle the north end of the valley and find the point where the canyon walls sloped down to meet the trail. We picketed the horses in the trees and I split the force into two groups, one for each side. As we climbed up each side and made our way down closer to where the canyon met the valley, I was pleased to note the large rocks and boulders that would not only provide us cover but could also be used as weapons.

The small canyon was only about fifty paces wide. I sent Deima and ten others up the far side while I took Cyerma and the remaining eight with me. We all carried rations, double water skins, and backup scout quivers. We were as ready as we would ever get, the hardest part would be waiting. A candle mark went by as the sun made its way across the sky. Some scouts grumbled about missing the action but I reassured them that we would see plenty once the second half of our force arrived to the north. I had grown so weary of the heat that I was surprised by the sound of a screeching arrow echoing through the pass. I jumped up and shouted across the way. "They come! Be ready to fire on my mark, not until." Deima nodded from the other side and we watched as the first raiders started rushing into the canyon.

We were spread out along the top on each side, and I had positioned myself toward the end farthest from the centaur valley. Scouts shifted nervously as raiders passed them by, with more and more rushing into the pass from behind. I waited, watching both the raiders in the lead and the ones that continued to pour in. Some were on horseback and others on foot. Finally, when the first man was nearly below my position I took him with an arrow to the chest. The raiders in front immediately pulled to a stop and glanced up in fright, effectively bunching the entire group below us. "Now! Make all your shots count!" Part of me felt sickened by the slaughter we perpetrated on the raiders below.

As the arrows and rocks rained down from above, many of the horses got spooked and threw their riders. Despite the chaos on the trail, eventually the fleeing men starting thinking through their dilemma. The raiders that had shields held them overhead and bolted for the open end of the pass just as both Amazons and Centaurs filed in from the valley. Seeing that some might escape, I took off running along the top hoping to head them off where the sides dropped down level with the trail near the trees. A few of my scouts followed my lead on both sides. When I was near enough to jump down without killing myself, I discarded my bow and drew the pugiones at my side then dove for the man running at the front. We crashed to the ground and tripped up half a dozen other men around us. The other Amazons that followed me drew swords and engaged the fleeing men. The man below me was dead with a blade to the chest and one to the neck so I hauled myself off him and took on another. The copper smell of blood was overwhelming as I blocked his sword with one blade and slashed at him with the other. I watched as the blood began to flow where the boiled leather chest plate did not protect. Someone yelled behind me and it ran together into a cacophony of echoing sound.

"Kyri, look out!"

As Kyrius, the blooded whore of Isidorus and bitch gladiatrix, I fought on. I spun in place and dropped into a crouch as the sword swung overhead. Right hand blade angled up into his gut, below the chest plate, the left took him in the artery of his groin. I pushed him over and attacked another that was fighting against one of my scouts. She was young and would not have lasted as he beat down on her with an overhand swing. She cried out as I slashed at his hamstring from behind and drove a pugio into his neck as he fell.

On and on it continued as I dispatched one after another. Blood and bodies grew thick as the mounted warriors pushed the raiders farther down the trail toward us. A blade drew a line of fire along the right side of my back and hand span above my waist. I kicked the man in front of me straight into the knee joint eliciting a scream of agony as he crumpled to the ground. Sensing another blow coming, I dodged to the left and spun around to face him. He was big and easily twice my mass in muscle. The man gave me a wicked grin and spat blood to the ground at my feet.

"Futuo! But yer gonna die slow with me!" Despite the immense size of his blade, he was fast. My back burned and I could feel the wearying wetness seeping into the girdle above my skirt. A bleeding cut above my right eye threatened my vision and for the first time since riding away from Ori earlier in the day, I worried about keeping my promise. He came at me from above and it took both blades just to block his one. His weight bore down on me and I was fast running out of stamina. A boot caught me in the upper thigh and I went down hard, rolling away at the last instant when he tried to stab me.

Panting, I tried to catch my breath as the behemoth charged again. He was readying to take another swing when I dove between his legs and rolled up behind him. Before he could spin around I leaped onto his back and brought my pugiones around to his throat, crisscrossing along the tender flesh. The heavy sword dropped first then I rode his body to the ground screaming in triumph.

Sensing no more fighters, I knew I had won the gold laurel. With eyes shut listening to the quiet around me, I brought the blades to my lips as I had done so many times before. I opened them again to find my dominus in the crowd, to see recognition for my win. Instead of my master, I was faced with the darkest of my dreams.

Ori stared at me with an unreadable look on her face. I became aware of my body, feeling the blood and the gore as it dried on my skin and the throb of my lower back. "No." My voice was a whisper as I shook my head to deny what I was seeing, what she had seen. "No!" Tears pricked my eyes and I turned away from her. I looked down at the blood coating my hands and every crevice of my weapons.

"Kyri." I cringed and tried to block out the judgement and pity. I wanted to run but something held me there, a voice froze me in place. A hand. She called again. "Kyri, look at me." I looked down to see her bloody hand on my wrist. Our skin had been painted by the same brush. Heartbeats flowed like honey as I slowly drew my gaze up to hers. "I love you."

I trembled and sounds came back to me in a rush. Chuffing horses, creaking leather, voices, cries of pain, and the moaning of dying men. The onslaught pressed down on me. "Ori? I—" Pain stopped my words as the fire in my back made itself known again. I dropped my pugiones as a cry left my lips and I reached around to touch that which hurt. She caught me in her arms and carefully lowered me to the ground, turning me onto my left side so she could see my wound.

"Goddess!" Through my haze of pain I could see her look around. Spying someone nearby, she yelled out again. "Semina!" I groaned as the healer began cleaning the wound on my back just below the bottom of my halter. I could feel my teeth grind together as I tried not to cry out. "Don't you have anything for her pain?"

Ori's voice snapped through my haze. When I saw a vial come near my face I weakly pushed away the hand that held it. "No! No poppy!" I glanced up as a helpless look washed over the queen's face. She quickly removed one of my leather bracers and bid me to bite down, just as Semina's needle pierced flesh. I had received many stitches as a sagittarius, mostly along my legs and torso. You never quite forget the pain of tying your flesh back together with threads of flax and linen. By the time she was finished, sweat beaded my forehead and I felt as though the leather would shred apart from the strength of my aching jaw. My hair had come loose from its braid and lay matted and stuck to the light wound above my eye. I knew the cut was not bad, heads just bled a lot.

With shaking fingers, Ori pushed the hair away from my face. I looked up at her and voiced my fears. "Did you see her?" She looked confused for a heartbeat then slowly nodded. I swallowed and went on, needing to know how far my shame was known. "Did they all see her?"

Her mouth held sadness to her lips, as if she had just drunk from a mug of tears. "Yes." My breath caught in my chest and I could not control the sob that came out after. She did not say anything, merely pulled me to her breast and held tight. At least a candle mark passed with us sitting on the rocky ground. Occasionally someone would come ask the queen a question but she never let me go. I suspected those who were not wounded were busy sorting the injured from the dead, and friends from foes. When I saw people go into the woods and come back with cut poles I glanced up at Ori.

"Were many of ours injured?"

She sighed. "About a score, though most can ride." I looked at her and did not need to ask the rest. "Three Amazons and two Centaurs lost their lives."

I shifted painfully. "And your sister? Gostig? My scouts?"

The queen smiled but did not meet my eyes. "They're fine. One of the younger women with you, Taren, broke her arm but of everyone that held the canyon you were the worst hurt. You're lucky the cut wasn't deeper or the blow didn't break your ribs. Can you ride?" I was still lying half in her lap on the ground, my wound sewn and bandaged in a wine soaked wrap.

"Help me up." She got out from under me and together we got to our feet. I swayed for a heartbeat but eventually stood steady.

She repeated her question with uncertainty in her eyes. "Can you ride?"

I took stock of myself and nodded. "I will."

"That's not what I asked."

Ori handed me one of my pugiones and I cleaned it with the rag I wore in my belt pouch while she cleaned the other one. "I still need to go up and retrieve my bow. I left it at the top of the canyon before we ran down to head them off." When she handed me the cleaned pugio I sheathed them both.

With her rag, Ori reached over and wiped the blood from my lips where it had dried. I had forgotten about it. "Margoli came by just a little while ago and told me that one of your scouts brought it down earlier." I nodded and swallowed nervously at the look on her face. Her thumb followed the path of the rag as she stepped nearer to me. "I was worried from the moment you left my sight."

Sorrow followed her words because I knew my actions could not have assuaged her fears. "I am sorry. What you saw probably did not make you feel any better about me. I would understand if you want to break our betrothal— "

"No!" I was startled by her outburst but she quickly continued. "While I may worry for your sanity much the same as I worry for my own, I no longer worry that you can keep yourself safe."

"But what you saw..." I could not finish, I could not put voice to who I had become.

Ori's eyes gentled as she gazed back at me. "What I saw was a fierce warrior who was taken by the battle. I saw a woman who saved her sisters over and over and in the end vanquished her enemy. I saw my lover, Kyri Fletcher."

I shook my head. "You saw Kyrius."

"You are Kyrius, and Kyrius is you. When will you accept that fact?"

Breath froze in my chest as her words grew and built upon themselves in my mind. I was Kyrius? No, the sagittarius was a killer. The gladiatrix was a slave to a Roman man. "I— " Voice failed as my thoughts grew tangled.

Ori cradled my face in her hands. "Kyri, you act as though you have no more depth than a piece of blank parchment. But you are a flower, with many petals and colors. You can be both Kyri and Kyrius. You are a fletcher and an archer, a lover and a warrior. We are all a sum of our past experiences and we carry that with us for the rest of our lives. Do not fight who you are, accept it. And if there are parts that you do not like, only then strive for change." I must not have looked convinced because she kissed me. It was a soft press of lips, sweet amidst the ruins of life all around us. When she pulled back again her lips curved into a smile. "My hands too were bathed in the blood of our enemies, do you judge me so harshly?"

Judge her? "Never! You are the queen and a warrior."

"We are both warriors. And I am reassured to know that my consort will be strong in heart and in battle. Come now, we must get back to the Sagiada. Are you sure you can ride?"

I searched her eyes for any sign that she was speaking false, for an indication that watching me in battle had disturbed her in some way. I did not find it but she shifted her eyes away before I could search long. "Yes, I can ride." Moving was painful and mounting was agony. I panted with the effort but eventually I made it to the back of my horse. It was not my gentle Soara, she had remained at the Telequire village with a new foal. Instead I rode a young gelding named Ánemos. He had a lot of energy but seemed solid enough. Ori rode back to Sagiada with me while others stayed behind to set up pyres to burn the bodies of the enemies and wrap the bodies of our own. Gostig determined that since the canyon was nothing more than rock with a few sparse growths of brush it would be fine to set up the fires there. And luck had found the wind blowing strangely out to sea, so the smoke would not follow us into the centaur village.

When we arrived, the gates stood open to a wide packed-dirt street and we rode only a few candle drops before stopping in front of a stone house. A woman with dark blonde hair came outside to greet us. She bore a strong resemblance to my Amazon queen but she had neither Ori's presence nor conditioning about her. She wore a long chiton which was partially covered by a cloak and her feet were bare.

"Ori!" She looked around frantically. "Where is Gos?"

The queen smiled down at her. "He's fine, Risi. He just stayed behind to oversee the cleanup and fire for the raiders' bodies. He should be along in a while." She dismounted and came around to help me down. If anything, it was harder for me to dismount than it was to haul myself into the saddle. "I would like to introduce you to my betrothed, Kyri Fletcher. Kyri, this is my sister, Risiki."

Ori's sister wore a look of barely veiled curiosity when she first saw me but as my stiff movements and wrapped torso became obvious it turned to a look of concern. "You're injured, come inside." Their stone house was well made, if small. It appeared to be two rooms with a loft above. There was a little girl playing quietly with a hand-sewn stuffed horse while a baby slept in a bassinet near a cushioned chair. Risiki lead me over to a *kline* where she bid me to lie down. I had seen the piece of furniture as a slave but I had never sat upon one of the high couches.

I tried to catch Ori's eye but she looked away. Instead, I looked down at myself to take in the blood and filth and tried to protest. "I do not want to dirty your fine bed, I am not fit for such things."

"Nonsense. It is not our bed, merely used for our occasional royal guest and a place to sit while eating."

Ori raised an eyebrow at that. "You didn't tell me that Gos made that with me in mind!"

Risiki shook her head and laughed. "Well we couldn't have the Queen of the Amazons sleeping on the ground atop skins and dried herbs!"

"I am your sister before I am a queen."

The queen's sister wagged her finger at her. "Ah yes, but you are a still a queen and thusly will not sleep on the ground like the huddled masses of Larissa." She mentioned a great city that was on the other side of the country, roughly southeast of Telequire. It was known for the great prosperity of its wealthiest citizens and for the sheer poverty that allowed the less fortunate to sleep in the streets or thieve for their very food.

Ori sighed and helped me to lie down onto my stomach. "Who am I to argue with a mother twice over?"

"So, betrothed? And this is how you tell me?" Risiki turned her attention back to me when Ori merely shrugged. "We have heard so much about you, Kyri. I feel like you're already family. And I am heartened to hear that you came back from so evil a place. Orianna mentioned you were poorly done over there. How do you find things now? Do you need something for your wound? Wine, spirits?"

Risiki's words were rapid and her questions unceasing. I felt the day start to drag me under and answered as best I could. "I, uh, things are well now. I am fine, my wound is fine." I do not remember anything after that. Exhaustion claimed me and I sped off to meet Morpheus before I could wish for no dreams.

Chapter Fourteen

Without It We Fall

WE STAYED TWO days with Ori's sister and bond-brother to allow for the worst injured of us to heal a bit before traveling again. Even though it was nice to meet and get to know Ori's family, we both knew that we had to get back to Telequire with our fallen sisters. Despite having a few days to recover, the return was painful. I tore the stitches dismounting on the first night that we made camp. Ori fretted but I knew she understood more than some that healing took time.

One thing that sorrowed me was the fact that Ori had avoided meeting my eyes again since that defining moment at the end of the battle. Perhaps she no longer saw me but rather saw the slave I had been. Maybe the image of Kyrius had burned itself into her mind's eye at the sight of my murderous rage. By the time we rode into Telequire, I wanted to drink a skin of wine to numb the pain of my back and my heart, then sleep for a sevenday. Looking at my wound with objectivity, it was not much worse that the deepest of my whip marks. I was lucky that the raider had not been closer, or a few fingers farther to the left. I would have been rendered paralyzed or dead from the blow.

Given the way the queen continued to deflect her glances, I wondered if that would have been best. I had not spoken much since the battle of Sagiada. My heart was heavy with the realization that Kyrius was still inside me. I had done so much work trying to purge the sagittarius from my psyche and it felt like all that work was for naught. What was the point of speaking with Glyphera each day? What was the point of trying to change at all if every single direction I stepped just circled back around to the beginning? I knew the gladiatrix well, the details of my past as a slave could never be forgotten. So how then could Ori truly ever love me knowing that Kyrius and I were one and the same? My queen was a warrior and she said she understood the bloodlust and pounding in your veins. But she could never truly understand what it was like fighting in front of thousands, all of them calling for you to betray yourself, to kill and be someone else. Every chant felt like a wound to my soul and I bled for them in so many ways.

Gostig was also right. While I did not spread my legs for them, the Roman people violated something much more sacred, my heart. The blood and rage soaked into me like linen drinks of spilled wine. But how was I to remove that stain? Ori assumed my solemn mood was due to my injury and I let her. I did not want to burden my queen with worries and doubts when her mind was heavy with the loss of three of our people. There would be another ceremony, funeral pyres, and recognitions of bravery. The thought of standing on the dais again for whatever reason left me feeling sick. Why would anyone want acknowledgement for the acts committed while in the red haze?

When we entered the village the wounded, including myself, were taken straightaway to the healer's lodge. Ori apologized and left me in the company of a tutting Thera. It was the queen's duty to inform the families of those we had lost and speak with the council about the events that had taken place in Sagiada. Thera's long graying hair was pulled back into a braid to keep it out of her way. Though signs of age were obvious in the lines of her face and hands, she was quick and gentle when she checked my injury and changed the wrap.

"Always in trouble eh, little one?"

I sighed. "I never search for trouble, you know that."

She chuckled. "'Tis true, you're never lookin' for it. But just the same, I'd rather it finds you than most anyone else I know." I turned my head to her as the hurt blossomed in my chest. Why would she wish me harm over others? When Thera saw the hurt on my face she gave my shoulder a gentle pat. "I would never wish you harm, love. But I wouldn't wish a sewing job on a tanner, nor a healing job on a cook. I simply trust you to handle trouble more than most. You're a very talented and capable young woman."

I could not stop the shy smile from gracing my lips. I had liked Thera from the moment I first came to the village, injured and cradling a tiny leopard cub. "Thank you." It did not seem enough for the trust she placed in me but it was all I had. Later in my hut, Gata joined me on the bed. She had started the trip to the Centaur village with us but Ori was the one who suggested we order her to stay behind. She said that the Centaurs prized their horses above all else and she did not want to cause an incident if Gata were to attack one. The big cat had never displayed any inclination toward a mount before but I agreed anyway. After all, I did not want to take my furred companion into battle. I would have been distracted with worry for her.

I dozed on my stomach for a candle mark or so before a knock roused me fully. It was late afternoon and warm in my hut but I had no interest in moving enough to open my shutters. I had even less interest in opening my door after such a fitful nap. After all, I had not even bothered to remove my boots when I returned from the healer. I scowled as I acknowledged the person at my door. "Come."

I was shocked to see both Shana and Coryn walk in. Shana carried a red dyed wine skin and the scout leader held a small wrapped bundle in her hands. "Heyla, sister! We come bearing gifts for the wounded warrior." She paused. "Deh, but it's warm in here!" Shana placed the skin on the table and immediately opened my shutters as wide as they could go.

Coryn grinned. "Honey cakes for the hero?"

"Do not call me that!" Startled by the sound of my own rough voice I apologized. "I am sorry. I did not mean to take my temper out on you two, please forgive me."

While Coryn looked surprised by my outburst and apology, Shana wore a knowing look. "What's the matter, Kyri?"

I did not wish to speak of the desolate feeling that turned my heart to lead. The only thing that the battle of Sagiada had convinced me of was the hopelessness of change. "It is nothing."

"I know you and I know when something is wrong."

"There is nothing wrong other than I am weary of lying abed!"

My sister in all things but blood, my patient friend, looked at me with patience lost and I closed my eyes to it. "Kyri Fletcher! Untruth spills from your mouth like water from a tipped jug. I am your sister and worth more than your lies. Look at me and speak plain!"

When I opened my eyes again, there was frustration evident on her face and Coryn's hand circling softly around her arm. Shana's anger was uncharacteristic and I knew that I had pushed her too far away. Though I did not want to admit to weakness, I knew she would not leave without some type of explanation. "The battle at the Centaur village has left me empty inside. My thoughts are jumbled and my memory of it is spotted like Gata. I remember the men coming down the bed of the ravine. I remember running to cut them off and fighting. But I cannot even recall much of the fighting to be honest." I moved to sit up and both rushed over to help me then took chairs nearby.

Coryn's voice was quiet in the fading light. "You were in high enough spirits before the battle, what happened to tip you back into the darkness?"

"I fought."

The First Scout Leader cocked her head. "I don't understand. You knew you were going to fight, you've fought many times before."

I shook my head slowly, trying to deny my actions by movement alone. "No, no. I fought as her, the gladiatrix. The woman I was as a slave."

Shana's voice was also low, as if I were a wild animal to be startled and provoked by sound. "I spoke with Deima. She said you were amazing, that she had never seen you move in such a way. She said you were like A—"

Bitter words spewed like bile from my lips. "A vicious beast with no thought or sanity? An animal who snaps and slobbers over the blood of fallen men? Yes, I was all those things and more. But then, what would you expect from Kyrius, the gladiatrix slave? I was her that day, and she was me. I thought I had purged her, I thought I was better!" I slapped the fur on my bed as angry tears dotted my dark lashes. I blinked them away and Gata moved off to lay on her own bed, not appreciating my angry outburst.

"That is not what she said! She said you were like Artemis herself come down from the heavens, delivering retribution upon the raiders. She said you stood in the face of a hundred fleeing men as they rushed down the canyon from the Centaur valley, and you didn't even flinch." She stood and loomed over me then. "You are not even sure of what happened that day yet you sit here wrapped in a cloak of fallibility and sip from your cup of self-pity Every day you mourn all that you've gone through and what you've lost, forgetting all that you still have. You are betrothed to a queen who loves you, we love you and want you to be happy. All this high emotion for your loss but you should be glad that you have survived it all!"

"Shana." Coryn's voice was panicked, nervous.

She was right and the words came from someplace deep inside me. "I wish I had not!" Just as her temper had broken, so too had mine. "Ori has not even looked me in the eye since the battle. If she, a warrior, cannot even bear to look at me then what remains that is good? If all that is left of me is this broken, murderous thing then I wish I had simply died fighting in that Roman agora!" The slap was loud and stinging and it rocked me. I did not remember getting to my feet and when the silent echoes followed the sound of Shana's hand to my face, another presence became obvious.

"Kyri?" Ori stood in the doorway wearing a look I had never seen. Her face was pale and eyes shiny in the afternoon sun that came through the doorway around her. I had become nothing more than a wounded animal so I reverted to what I had always done before. In a span of heartbeats I became that naïve girl who left her da so long ago. Just that fast I bolted out the door into the sunshine with a heart blacker than night.

My trip into the canopy was swift and accompanied by a burning wet pain in my back. I ran until I could find a place that would hold my tears then I settled in. Thoughts spun in circles and my wound throbbed with the agonizing rhythm of each heartbeat. I knew that my skin had torn open again but I did not have long to ponder the drops of blood as they seeped into the bark behind me. Quiet footsteps tracked through the branches until I felt the barest of tremors on my own. "I'm sorry."

I wondered if her words were just another manifestation of the cycle that I seemed to be trapped in. I always ran and she always found me, sorry. Only I knew that she had nothing to be sorry for, it was my own failing that saw me sitting in the tree like a broken-winged bird. "Do not apologize for something that is my sickness alone. You are not at fault." I stared at the hands in my lap and could not get the image of blood out of my head.

"There is no sickness in anything other than your view. And once again we suffer from miscommunication and wounding silence. I have felt guilt every day since the battle and that is why I could not meet your gaze."

I looked up at her sharply, surprised by her words. "Why would you feel guilty?"

Ori sighed and took my hands into hers. For the first time since the battle our eyes met across the expanse of our arms. "As the queen I take personal responsibility for every single person I send into battle. My heart bruises with each new injury or death, and more so when it is my beloved getting injured. I feel personally responsible for your pain and I haven't dealt with it well." She pulled a hand away from mine and ran fingers through her short hair. "I guess I didn't think about how you would view my actions. I feel as though I've failed you, Kyri."

Failed me? How could she ever think that? I was the one who lost control, who flung blood all around me in a frenzy. "No! You could never fail me. You are my Goddess, my sun, and when you turned away I felt the darkness creep in, like you too believed that there was nothing good left in me."

Sad green eyes stared into mine so hard it was as if she were reading my thoughts. She was Artemis's Chosen so perhaps she was. "You put me on a pedestal that will only hurt us both when I fall. I am no Goddess, just a woman with determination who loves Telequire and Artemis with all my heart. And I love you too. I think the problem is not that you have no good inside, it is that you have lost sight of your goodness."

She finally understood. I nodded at her words. "Yes, because I have changed so much."

Ori shook her head to deny me and I grew confused. "You have not changed so much, Kyri. When I say you've lost your sight, it means your perspective is all wrong. Look here." She pulled something out of her belt pouch. It was small but I could not see what the object was because it was wrapped in a scrap of dirty cloth. She held it clenched in her fist like the grip of a bladeless sword. The only thing showing was a block of hardened clay, rough and slightly uneven. "Can you see the beauty in this?"

I thought her mad, like maybe she had lost track of our conversation. "No."

"Do you recognize it, does it hold any sentimental value to you?"

"No, of course not."

"So you wouldn't care if I threw it to the ground and destroyed it?

"Why would I care? I do not know what it is, I have no sentimental value for it. I would care only if it belonged to someone I loved and they held it in high regard. Why do you ask?"

She unclenched her fist and began unwrapping the item in her fist. The breath left my lungs with what she unveiled. Our eyes met again over top the Artemis statue she held up between us. Carved into the base on the side where I could not see was the word "SKILL." It was my Artemis award! "Do you understand now, love? You have been looking at the roughest part of yourself, mistaking it for the whole. But that is not who you are."

Understanding dawned then but also illuminated something else to me. "So that means I am flawed since that part of me is bad. Kyrius serves no purpose in my home here, the sagittarius merely makes me unstable and unsafe for the people I love most."

"Kyri." She tipped the statue so I was left staring at the bottom again. "Does the ugliest part of the Artemis statue serve a purpose? Would you remove it to leave Artemis in all her perfection?"

What foolishness was her suggestion? "Of course not! That is the base, without it the statue would fall and break. Its purpose is to display the pride of a skill hard-earned. The base itself is part of the award, with the name of the skill carved in. Why would you remove it?"

"Why indeed?" She smiled at me and a shaft of light broke through the canopy just then. A fist-size sunbeam streamed down to kiss her shoulder and continue its way to the ground below us. "Did your training as gladiatrix not come in handy on that battlefield? Did your actions, albeit bloody, not save countless lives of the Amazons under your command? Kyrius is that rough part of you that serves a purpose when you need her. Your task has been wrong all these moons. You have sought to purge her from your system when you only ever needed to understand that part of yourself and learn to control it. And you have learned to control it."

My back was starting to throb deeper but I was on the breakthrough of understanding. I clutched her shoulders with anxiety. "But I have not! In Sagiada—"

She interrupted quickly. "In Sagiada you were ferocious in battle and never harmed another but those that came to the Centaurs seeking to do harm. Think, Kyri. You had rage boiling inside of you the day of equinox and yet you did not let any of it out. You could have killed Megara but you did not. You spoke calmly and rationally at all times to her. You have no idea how much respect you gained from the council that day after they heard the story of what Basha and I were both witness to. You earned even more respect from me as well."

"But that means..." Words failed me as my entire worldview changed in a span of heartbeats. Again.

"You've been so busy trying to bury the past, trying to cut it out of you like an unwanted splinter, that you had missed the entire point of change and betterment that Glyphera has been preaching."

I looked at her suspiciously. "How did you know what counsel the priestess has been giving me?"

She smiled. "I know because I had similar self-doubts after I made my first kill and she guided me much the same way." The idea that my queen, my Goddess-made-flesh could suffer the same fears and doubts as me was inconceivable. I knew she suffered the pains of loss and consequences of her decisions because Ori ran deep with empathy. But I could not picture her crippled by uncertainty as I had been. Someone so beautiful inside and out was not one to be rife with self-loathing. Her eyes searched me again, seared me with their vision and insight.

"I see you questioning my words, not believing that I could be so human. I was eight summers old when I came to live with the Amazons after having watched my parents die a brutal death and—killing a man myself. Anger was my constant companion for many sun-cycles. The only ones that kept me sane were my friends, Basha and Shana, Risiki, and the priestess. Glyphera got me to open up and talk about all that had happened. She made me accept my anger and understand my actions. The difference between us is that I came into my rage earlier than most, while you came into yours later."

I gasped to learn she was so young to kill another, eleven sun-cycles younger than my own dealings with death. But her words were a thorn punching through the thick skin that had grown over my understanding. I had come into my rage. Anger was easy, I had been managing it and letting it go for many sun-cycles since my mam had died. But the rage was new and unfamiliar. It was a dark and slithering thing that crept up like a snake when I least expected it. And the poison from such anger left me weak and disoriented, distrusting of all my other senses. But Ori understood all that, she had experience managing the rage and that was how she knew what to do to calm me the day of equinox.

My lips parted as awareness continued to blossom inside my chest. All at once I understood another part of her reticence when we first began the dance between us. She was not merely afraid that I did not know my own heart. She feared that I did not know hers fully, that I would be afraid or repulsed by the rage that had become a part of her. The changes wrought unto me as a sagittarius did not take me further from her heart and mind, it brought me closer. I could not put my sudden understanding into words so I just spoke what was in my heart instead. "You are the sun and I am the moon. We will continue to spin around each other until the very end of time itself. My heart knows no other."

She nodded and graced me with a knowing smile. "We are as one and we have always been as one. The Goddess herself has written our history in the stars. She has drawn our future in the rings of every tree and veins of each leaf."

"Yes."

Our lips met in a brief declaration of love and recognition. We could not make it more because of our position in the tree. After a short span we pulled apart and Ori stood to balance on the limb in front of me. "Come, we should return. I'm sure Shana and Coryn are beside themselves with worry by now." She pulled me up and I swayed slightly, head dizzier than I would have liked while so high up in the canopy. She looked at me in concern. "Are you okay?"

I shook my head slowly. "It is my back, I tore it open again."

Her laugh took me by surprise. "Goddess, Kyri! What am I going to do with you?"

Laughing with her, I shrugged lightly. "You can start by helping me down so that I may go visit Thera for a scolding."

THE VILLAGE HAD their ceremonies for the fallen sisters, and others of us received awards of bravery. I did not want such things but I knew it was pointless to protest. I apologized to both Shana and Coryn for my bad temper and poor attitude since I had returned to Telequire, and both said there was nothing to forgive. Within a moon after the Battle of Sagiada I was only speaking with the priestess twice a seven day. But to replace those times of counsel I began learning calming exercises from Ori. They were working well for me. My irritability and impatience had greatly diminished. While I still felt the occasional rage, I no longer feared losing control to that battle-bloodied beast inside.

We had a little over a moon to finish preparing the village for the Festival of Nations. The first tribes were to arrive a seven-day before summer solstice. Most of the infrastructure was still in place from the cycle before, but a few things needed to be repaired and updated. I helped often since I was in hale health and possessed a strong pair of hands. And with Certig having officially replaced me as the Fourth Scout Leader, I had more free time than most. My deeper studies of tribal ethics and roles were near completion and I had gained a full understanding of what the title of Consort would entail. Once the queen and I were joined, I had the option to create a troop of royal guards and oversee them if I so chose. But that was a decision I would have to make with Ori. Some consorts were known to champion causes or push for innovation within the tribe. At first I worried that I would have no free time left but Basha assured me that I would not be working every candle mark of every day.

Ori spent the occasional night in my hut but most times we shared her bed. She told me in no uncertain terms that I would be living with her after the joining but I was still reluctant to move my things beforehand. The queen's living space was more than twice the size of the average hut and sparsely populated. There would be no problem fitting all of our things together, I simply did not feel right doing so until we officially became bond mates.

It was a sunny warm morning that found us at breakfast together with a group of our closest friends. Shana and Coryn had been growing noticeably closer as each seven-day passed by. Ori and I discussed their progressing relationship a few times and both agreed we were happy for the scout leader and ambassador. The rest of our friends also noticed based on the knowing looks that circled the breakfast bench but none had brought it up. It was unusual for things to be left so unsaid. But I think we all sensed that what was developing between them was a delicate thing to be nurtured as long as possible. They were happy and we let it go. My mind was glutted with thought as I worked my way through a bowl of porridge, at least until Ori jogged my arm. "So what are you going to do with yourself on such a beautiful day while your poor queen is cooped up inside the council chamber?"

Shana laughed and mocked her childhood friend. "Poor Queen Orianna!"

"I know!" Ori pouted playfully and popped a date in her mouth. Because the festival was growing so near, the queen and council had received numerous scrolls pertaining to special requests and questions from the other Amazon nations. I sat in on one such meeting a fortnight before and did not enjoy it. It was an all-day process and sadly kept me from the sun and trees.

I squeezed Ori's knee under the table. "I can tell it will be a traumatic day for you. I can kiss all of your hurts away tonight if you wish."

Coryn rolled her eyes and the queen smirked at my comment. "Well I'm going to be sitting on my royal backside all day. What do you think you'll be kissing?"

The First Scout Leader burst out laughing. "She's already kissed that plenty!"

I could not help the lecherous smile that crossed my lips. "I have kissed every finger's width of her body, some places more than others. It sounds like a perfect evening to me!"

Shana shook her head. "You two are nothing more than a couple of dizzy goats!"

"So says the woman with sucking bruises all over her own body!" Basha may have been the quietest one of the group but she certainly knew what to say and when to say it. Shana blushed deep red at her words and Coryn's face flushed as well. They studiously ignored each other and the entire table burst out in laughter.

I grew distracted when I saw Panphilla walk into the meal lodge. "Pan!" I called out to her because we had not spoken since the equinox. Too many things had happened and I regretted losing track of her and my promise.

She walked over and eyed my tablemates shyly, especially the queen. She saluted Ori before addressing me. "Queen Orianna, good morning. You wish to speak with me, Consort?"

I sighed. "It is Kyri, please just call me by my name." I grinned and lightly clapped her on the shoulder. "After all, we are sisters!"

Her smile spoke clearly of how she felt about my words. I took a heartbeat to look at the girl I had declared as family. Her eyes and hair were a match of lustrous brown, and she sported dimples in chin and cheeks whenever she smiled. "Yes, Kyri."

"How are your studies progressing?" She made to answer and I held up a finger. "Wait, before you speak why not get your own morning meal and join me here?"

She held up her hands palms out, with a look of alarm on her face. "Oh, but I couldn't!"

Ori smiled at her and directed everyone to move down on the bench, thus creating space at the end next to me. "Of course you can. Go on now, get yourself a hearty bowl of porridge, it's great with goat's milk and dates!"

"Yes, my queen." The young girl blushed and nodded before heading to the food table.

"You never told me what you have planned, does it have something to do with young Pan?" Ori's questions and observations were usually astute.

I nodded and swallowed a bite of apple. "Yes, actually. I promised to start showing her the trees as a sister would, it is time I kept that promise to her." When Pan returned I engaged her in conversation as did the others around us. She was quiet and very shy at first but she was chatty enough once we got her going. She had a zest for life that I admired and I had a good feeling about the young charge I had taken on.

With the training master's permission, we spent the day running the trees. Gata even joined us for a good portion of it which thrilled my young sister. Pan picked up the basics quickly and had a talent for balance and nimbleness in the canopy. She was small and still growing but after working with her for just a handful of candle marks I was certain that she would become a fine scout with a few more sun-cycles of training. It was later that afternoon when I finally got to know her even better while we were both sitting on a tall branch sharing some dried venison. "So what kind of training are you doing now?"

Pan looked at me curiously. "Well it's just the usual stuff. I've finished with all my primary education and now I'm full time with the secondary skills."

I knew the basics of Amazon education, but did not know the details of each level. "What is the difference between primary and secondary?"

She grew confused. "But Cons—" I held up a finger in warning and she amended her words. "Kyri, it's what all Amazons go through before they move into their tribal duty."

I laughed lightly. "Ah, but you forget that I did not grow up as an Amazon. I had my own schooling from my mam before she died, then I got my skill training from my da. I was just wondering how different it was from what I grew up with."

She made a silent "oh" face and nodded in understanding. "We learn the basics from about six to twelve summers. We have different teachers for each prime subject. A *grammatistes* for reading, writing, and arithmetics. *Grammata* is one of the most important parts of our education."

The last bit sounded a lot like she was mimicking her teacher and I could not help the smile that formed on my lips at her words. "I think I heard those very same words from my mam, many sun-cycles ago. Go on."

"We have some Greek and Latin scrolls on the great poets and such, and we practice on wax boards. Besides Grammata, we learn music, ethics, and religion. We also have a *paidotribes* that teaches us physical education. We learned to wrestle, throw javelins and discus, and we practiced running."

Her words shocked me a bit. "That seems like a lot for children so young."

Pan's face was a study of seriousness. "But that is the way it has to be for women to thrive and remain strong in the world of men."

"Did your instructors teach you that as well?"

She nodded. "Yes."

"I think I understand then, and perhaps they have the right of it. And after twelve summers?"

Pan continued with a little more excitement indicating that she preferred the next level of education more. "That is when we start secondary training, which teaches us a little bit about all the Telequire trade skills. Things like cooking, sewing, tanning, building, weaving, farming, and many other things. We also start learning scout stuff and basic weapons like chobo, staff, and archery. But no bladed weapons until our second sun-cycle of secondary."

I grinned because she had made a face when she mentioned archery. "Not a fan of the bow and fletch?"

"I'm terrible! I have a hard time seeing so far and it's just blurry enough that I never make a center shot." She shrugged and gave me that dimpled smile again. As if to say "what can I do."

"So what is your favorite subject?"

She thought for a heartbeat. "I like to sew and create stuff with my hands." Her face lit up then and she practically gushed out her words. "I love your cloaks, especially the white one you made for Ambassador Shana!"

I chuckled at her enthusiasm and an idea blossomed with her words. "Pan, would you be interested in learning how to create such cloaks?"

Her face transformed with each heartbeat that thumped by. It started as curious then moved on to shock. Her final face was one of ecstatic pleasure. "Oh my Goddess! Would you really teach me?"

"Of course I would. I have no family left and if it is something you are interested in, I would be honored to pass on my mam's craft to you. But—" I held up a finger. "While I can teach you tree running during the time that you would normally be scheduled with the training master, we will probably need to meet in the late afternoon or evening for cloak making. Will your mother mind?"

Pan thought for a heartbeat. "She cooks in the lodge, mornings and noons mostly. But one night a seven-day she has to do evening meal. Maybe you could show me then?"

"Which day?"

She scrunched her nose. "*Hermoũ*."

Ah, the middle of the seven day. It was a free evening for me so it would be perfect to show her my mam's craft. "That would be fine, I have no obligations then. Why the bad face?"

My young sister sighed dramatically and I was certain I had never done such at her age. "Because it is in the middle of the seven day and it takes forever to get to *Krónou*! That is now my favorite instruction day!" I blushed because the training master said I would be instructing her in tree running on the last day of the seven-day, but only the mornings. According to Kylani, Pan would still have staff, chobo, and archery in the afternoons.

Despite my embarrassment I managed a grin for her enthusiasm and stood on my branch. "Well today is Krónou and Kylani has graciously given us the entire day for our first meeting so we should not waste another candle drop. Would you like to finish out the day by hunting for some rabbit furs to start your very own cloak?" Her face brightened, then fell again.

"But I don't have my bow with me and even if I did..." I understood her intent and knew that her aim would not be true for such things yet, or would never be true if her distance eyesight was so bad.

"Well, it is a good thing we have a friend with us then! Gata will do the hunting for us." She looked at me as if I had spoken a sacred incantation. But after whistling for Gata, the leopard and I proved out her skill to my charge. We ended up with three skins good enough to tan the fur and we donated the meat to the cooks in the meal lodge. While we were there, I made sure our new training schedule was acceptable with Pan's mother. Afterward Pan went off to tell her friends and I was left with the furs in hand. To avoid doing all the messy work I decided that her next lesson would be in treating the skins of that which we killed. Before I could wander off with the furs, Theo took a break from kneading bread and called out to me.

"Kyri?"

I was nearly to the door but came back to the kitchen with rapid steps. "Yes?"

She swallowed hard and wrung her hands together near her waist. "I just wanted to thank you for everything you're doing for Pan. I know it means the world to her that she has a big sister again. It means a lot to me too."

Sorrow still clung to me at the reason that Pan would need another sister. "I have a duty and obligation to the tribe for not bringing Pocori home. I grieve for that fact alone. I would have given my life for her to return to you safe but that was never an option where we were and I am sorry. But besides all that, I enjoy Pan's company and look forward to teaching her what things I can."

Theo looked down and took in a deep breath. "I sorrow as well, but I would never blame you. You did all you could and now you've given Pan a little joy again."

I looked at Thedosia and wondered what joy she had left. After losing her bond mate sun-cycles before and also losing a daughter, it was a miracle she held up under the weight of her sadness. "Have you spoke with anyone since the pyres?" She shook her head. "I know from experience that just talking about your feelings sometimes helps. I have been speaking with the priestess since I returned to Telequire and it has helped me immensely. While it cannot bring back that which we have lost, sometimes it is nice to know that someone cares and maybe they know what you're going through. It is just a thought."

She looked curious and introspective with my words. "Perhaps I will. Thank you, Kyri. Now if you'll excuse me, I must get back to my baking so we have bread for evening meal."

When I returned to the queen's hut she was already there and I was unable to keep the smile from my lips. "You are finished already!"

"Yes, I'm finished. Thank the Goddess! Did you have fun with Pan today?"

I nodded. "I did actually. We were mostly tree running and I got a chance to talk later in the afternoon. I even learned what her favorite instruction is!"

Ori smiled. "Let me guess, archery?"

I laughed loudly. "No, quite the contrary she hates the bow and fletch. Her eyes are not very strong at distance. No, she loves to sew and expressed interests in my cloaks."

"Oh, so you are going to make her one?"

Shaking my head, I smiled broadly. "No, I am going to show her how to make her own. Once a seven-day while her mother is cooking evening meal I will give her instruction in my mam's craft. She is very excited to learn."

A knowing smile graced the queen's lips. "As excited as you are to teach?"

I blushed and met her eyes. "Maybe. I am just glad that I can pass on the skills I learned from my own mam." Ori did not answer immediately, instead we stood there in silence for a candle drop or two. She looked at me curiously and I could not help responding in kind. "What is that expression on your face?"

Ori stepped closer and wrapped her arms around my waist. "You look very happy, Kyri. It makes me very happy to see such joy on your face."

"I—" The words froze in my mouth while my head grew understanding of them. They were surprising and unfamiliar after so long on the edge of sadness. "I *am* happy. I forgot how much I loved my life here in Telequire and I let my grief overwhelm me for much too long. And you, two limbs to my four, one head to my two, you are my completion and reason for fighting through it all. I love you."

She closed her eyes to my words and it took a heartbeat to

realize that it was not out of rejection. She looked as though she were savoring them the way you would close your eyes to take in all the beauty and complexity of a good wine. And the smile that graced her face after my clumsy words tumbled out, the simple curve of her lips was a thing of beauty and holiness. Before she could respond to my declaration I covered those sacrosanct lips with my own. It was one of many we shared in the space between our love and evening meal. After all, I had a promise to keep from earlier in the day and I was loath to let her down.

Chapter Fifteen

No Love before You

A SEVEN-DAY before summer solstice found everyone in the village in high spirits. Ori and I were eating breakfast when we were interrupted by a messenger with news that two different tribes would arrive later in the day. One was Tanta tribe and I wondered if I would know any of the Amazons coming for the festival or if they would remember me. Much to my displeasure, the other tribe set to arrive was Shimax. I learned from Basha that the tribes that were closer and did not need a large window of travel time usually arrived last. I had been hoping not to deal with the princess and her royal guard until a day or two before solstice eve. When the messenger left, Ori discreetly squeezed my leg below the table and kept her voice low. "I know you do not wish to see them but things will work out. You will see."

My voice was a whisper as well. "You and I both know they will cause problems."

She leaned closer and gave me an intent stare. "Do you trust me?"

"Of course!" My trust in her was absolute as she well knew.

"Then unless you need to physically defend yourself or someone else from malfeasance, let me handle Shimax. Agreed?" I nodded and she changed the subject to something just as distressing. "We are now a seven-day away from our joining, are you nervous?"

Shana started laughing and pointed at me, which in turn garnered the attention of people around us. "Look how pale she is! Good Goddess, Kyri! Don't vomit on the table, we are eating here!"

I directed an insulting hand gesture her way, which only made her laugh more. Since it was later than we normally ate morning meal, Coryn was not with us. I looked at Shana with mischief and pointed right back at her. "Oh, and you would not be nervous if you were joining with someone in a seven-day? A certain tall, attractive, scout leader perhaps?"

Since I had so succinctly brought it out into the open, Ori had no problem picking up where I left off. "Yes, Shana, how is the romance fairing between the two biggest owls in the Telequire forest?"

Her pale face grew red as she sputtered a response. "You—she—"

"Oh, Artemis! Has our esteemed ambassador run out of words? Perhaps a squirrel has gotten her tongue." Basha enjoyed teasing her childhood friend as much as Ori.

Someone else called out from another table. "I don't think it was a squirrel. Not from what I saw when I walked into the bathing pool last night!"

Shana groaned and scrubbed her red face with delicate fingers. As the laughter finally died down she ran a hand through her riotous mass of dark curls, further mussing them. "I have no idea what to say to you all right now!"

When her hand dropped back to the table I covered it with my own. "We mean no harm, you know that." She nodded so I continued. "Has she finally earned forgiveness?"

Shana nodded and smiled. "We both have."

"And you are happy."

Her smile grew wider and I could see the joy in her eyes. "Yes."

"Then that is all that matters."

With each nation bringing about three score of competitors and support staff, we had to allot the entire southeast clearing for the tribal camps. Ori told me there were unused tribal and guest huts for all the royalty, so they would be staying in the village. The festival events themselves would take place in the training grounds and fallow field on the outskirts of the village to the south.

The temple was located along the hilly west side, just before the forest began again. Unfortunately, it was not large enough to hold all the assembled nations. The cavern could hold perhaps a few hundred more than the Telequire population but that was it. Because of the size limitation, the previous Festival of Nations solstice ceremony was held in the clearing that sat at the bottom of the hill, near the west-facing temple. The fresco of stone columns outside the entrance was grand but a new statue had been added outside just the previous sun-cycle. A team of carvers worked for moons to create a stone sculpture of Artemis at the top of the hill. It was easily seen by people gathered in the small valley below. When I first saw it upon my return I thought the marble likeness beautiful and even sterner than the one inside. The Goddess was the height of three tall women and stood on a low pedestal. Kerdina, our master carver, had truly outdone herself with the design.

Artemis stood braced and leaning back with a drawn bow facing toward the sky. She wore a chiton and light armor and had a magnificent headdress that featured stag's antlers. I could not believe such beauty could come from human hands until I remembered the small carving of Gata that Maeza had given me. Perhaps we were all capable of greatness in our own way.

Both the solstice ceremony and our joining would take place outside in front of all the gathered Amazons. The sheer magnitude of it swirled butterflies through my stomach and threatened me with sickness again. While I was learning about all the duties and expectations of being consort to the queen, I was also learning about the summer solstice celebration. There were elements of it that I had never seen before because they only took place once a sun-cycle.

Summer solstice was the height of all celebrations that occurred and life's milestones were recognized then. The Blessing of Births, the Rite of *Arkteia*, and the *Ilio Choroú* would all happen before our joining ceremony and after the opening invocation to Artemis. While I was excited to see the new components, I was not so excited to be part of them.

Between that and the news of the arriving guests my nerves ran high. I knew the cooks would appreciate extra meat on the spits so I decided to take Gata hunting while Ori was checking on final preparations for the incoming queens and nations. I missed noon meal, having gone out twice to bring back a roe deer each time. I let Gata have the first rabbit and brought more of those back as well. I had time to tan the skins for Pan's cloak and clean up before scouts reported the first group of visitors was a quarter candle mark out. Wearing my new outfit I stood next to the queen, Basha, the council, our ambassador, and conference of elders while we awaited Shimax's arrival. My stomach had long turned to stone and sweat formed persistently under my arms and along my brow. The day was not overly warm but my anxiety had heated my skin beyond comfort.

When we saw the beginning of the procession come through the trees on the southernmost trail, Ori took my hand and gave it a squeeze. "Relax, love. Things will work out fine. Just smile and be respectful, that is all you need to do."

I snorted at her words. "That is easy for you to say! You have been a queen for cycles now and are well practiced at the art of diplomacy. While I am rough and uncomfortable on the smoothest of days."

She laughed delightedly at my self-deprecating words. "You have more sleekness than you will admit. You'll make a fine consort and representative for me and the Telequire nation. It's time to start now." It became immediately obvious who was queen and princess as they approached. Both were tall in the saddle with nearly black curly hair. While the queen wore hers short, the princes had long hair that cascaded down her back. I briefly wondered how she did not cut it all off when re-sheathing her sword. I kept my own hair braided for a reason. The visiting Amazons all wore their masks but had them pushed up to the top of their heads so faces could be seen. I noticed only a handful actually rode mounts, probably to save space once they arrived. Shimax was not so far away that the journey would be a hardship on foot. The nations that came from farther would need their horses for the trip and would require a place to picket the animals once they arrived.

While old enough to be my mam, Queen Alala was a very beautiful woman. I could also see that Princess Alcina took after her in fairness of face if not perhaps temperament. Megara rode just behind and to the side of the princess, performing her duty as royal guard. The two royals dismounted and approached after the rest of their people came to a stop. My queen saluted them and bid them welcome, as protocol dictated. "Welcome to Telequire, Queen Alala and Princess Alcina. I hope your journey was light of foot and your sunshine plenty."

The visiting queen and princess saluted Ori in return, but there was a certain look in Alcina's eye I did not care for. "Goddess bless you for your welcome and hospitality, Queen Orianna. May the leaf and loam grace your feet each day and the game always be plentiful in your forest." After the greeting was complete, the two queens embraced and the rest of the mounted Shimax Amazons dismounted.

Ori turned with a smile on her face and introduced the rest of us. "Queen Alala and Princess Alcina, you have not yet met my betrothed, Kyri Fletcher. She has recently returned to us from across the sea where we had thought her gone forever."

Queen Alala saluted me and gave a nod of her head. "Greetings Kyri and congratulations to you both. It is good to see you whole and hale after your queen was so lost in mourning last suncycle."

I saluted her in return. "Thank you, Queen Alala. It is good to be home and back with my love's light. Welcome to Telequire, to you and your warriors."

Ori continued her introductions. "Of course you remember my regent, Basha, our ambassador, Shana, the council, and conference of elders. Now I'm sure you wish to get settled after your trip here. My regent can take your Amazons to the southeast field where they can set up camp and picket the horses. Kyri and I will personally take you and the princess to your huts." Someone brought a pack mule forward that must have held the royal saddlebags and gave the lead to Megara. Others led their horses away with the rest of the procession. While we walked toward the section of the village that held the guest huts, the queens engaged in conversation. I was slightly behind Ori, while Alcina was behind her mother. I did not know what to say so I was content to merely follow and listen to their conversation. Suddenly, Megara called out from behind us.

"Princess, I need to tighten the girth strap on the mule, can we pause for a heartbeat?"

Ori and Queen Alala turned around at her words but Alcina waved them off. "We can wait for her, Mother. You two go on ahead. I'm sure Kyri can show us to the huts if we lose sight of you." Ori raised an eyebrow at me and I gave a small shake of my head indicating that I could handle the princess and her guard. I had a feeling that they wished to speak with me and had schemed to cause a short delay to make private conversation possible. I waited as Megara fussed with the mule and candle drops passed by. Finally she finished what she was doing and nodded toward us. It only took steps into our walk for the princess to initiate conversation. "So, *you* are Orianna's betrothed?" As a princess herself, she was not required to use Ori's title if they were acquainted but I knew they were not. However it was not her words that caused my ire to rise, it was the tone in which she spoke.

"Yes, Queen Orianna and I are betrothed and set to be joined on solstice eve."

Her steps grew slower as she turned to look at me. The princess of Shimax was a few fingers taller than I was. But while I ran more toward lean muscle, Alcina beat out even our training master in toned bulk. Judging by pure physicality alone, I figured that the princess's reputation in unarmed combat was well-earned. Her eyes narrowed as she spoke again. "Your return has been most inconvenient to my future with Orianna. I can't figure out what she sees in you." She looked me up and down with disdain. "Average in looks, gangly, and your only skill seems to be with a bow. Any Amazon worth their feather can shoot a bow. But you—" She came to an abrupt stop and spat on the ground at my feet. "I see the whip marks on your back, you are nothing more than a doulé. A queen deserves better than some Roman whore, some slave! You are not worthy of even her glance yet you dare to sully her bed and her very future with your presence?"

I did not let her anger fuel my own, instead I thought of the possible reasons and motivations. "Tell me, Alcina, why are you so interested in a woman you only just met a sun-cycle ago? She has never once expressed interest in you, and you know nothing about our queen. Why are you so persistent, could it be that you are interested in becoming more than consort of Telequire?" I did not know what her motivations were, but I had seen similar to what I implied many times while in the company of the Roman nobles and plebeians alike. Queen Alala was well-liked and in her prime. If Alcina were power hungry, she would either have to challenge her mother or search for it outside their tribe. I could think of no other reason she would be so invested in a joining between her and my queen when Ori had made her lack of interest clear.

Alcina's face turned hard and Megara put a hand on the dagger at her waist. "You know nothing, doulé! Your queen deserves another royal as her consort, and she will get it or someone will pay!"

I could see a few off-duty fourth scouts coming from the training grounds so I smiled and gave a slight nod to the princess. "Queen Orianna deserves exactly what she wants, and what she wants is me. Now I think the matter is closed, do you agree?" My fourth scouts were not lacking in intelligence and they noticed two tense newcomers as well as Megara's hand on her weapon, so they stopped when they reached us, thus interrupting whatever Alcina was about to say.

Malva, a veteran who was ten cycles my senior, addressed me but took us all in with her gaze. "Is everything well, Scout Leader?"

"Everything is fine, Malva. I was just escorting the princess and Megara to the guest huts and we stopped to discuss the merits of having well-trained archers on the border. Would you like to walk with us and join the discussion?"

My scouts knew that my words were either an untruth or an over-exaggeration. I had never lied well in the past and Megara's hand on her dagger was too obvious. Which meant they knew that I wanted them to help me escort the two contentious visitors.

"We would be happy to." They walked along with us and within a handful of candle drops we arrived at the assigned hut and left the princess and her guard to settle in. After we left, Malva pulled me aside. "I do not trust her or her guard. Some of the things that Megara said when we escorted her from Telequire a few moons back..." She left her statement open but I had an inkling of what she implied.

I nodded in understanding. "Ah, so you were one of her escorts? I was told it was mostly fourth scouts but I did not know who. Well anyway, thank you for the escort. While I am not afraid of them, it was two against one had they chosen to spar with more than words. I also wanted to effectively discourage them from breaking the peace and causing an incident that would negatively affect our two nations. You did me a service today and I will not forget it." I held out my arm for a warrior grip and she obliged me.

Malva frowned as she spoke. "You owe no service, Kyri. You have done more for us and sacrificed more for us than we can ever repay. I will never forget that. Peace, sister."

I watched as she walked away. "Peace." The trouble had begun.

TANTA WAS THE second tribe to arrive that day and I was overjoyed to see familiar faces with them. Queen Myra led the procession, but Deata and Baeza were also with the group. I found out that Deata was to compete in the unarmed, archery, and stave contests. Baeza said she was competing in tree running, storytelling, chobo, and skill. The rest of the tribes began trickling in over the next five days. The Varvara tribe from the Chalkidiki peninsula, the island nation of Dasi, and the Koupaki and Oros tribes from south of Shimax all fell into the two days following Shimax and Tanta. The last few days before solstice eve saw the arrival of the Tsemperou tribe from the northern part of the Peloponnesus peninsula, and the Dasos Kato tribe from the east along the shores of the Aegean Sea. And lastly, the northern tribes of Shebenik, Ujanik, and Kombetar.

We had to go through the same greeting for each that we did with Shimax. Luckily, there were no more disgruntled princesses or ill-tempered royal guards to contend with. Throughout the lead up to the Festival of Nations, the training grounds, archery field, and any other suitable open spaces were full of Amazons practicing their crafts and skills. I took archery practice with Ori and Deata a number of times and continued to run the trees on rope duty whenever I could find the time. Evenings were taken up by dinners with the queens and other important persons within each visiting nation. As future consort, or maybe as a friendly companion, Ori bid me to sit through the meals by her side. Even though I lived to be near my queen, I would have traded those nights to eat a quiet meal in my hut with Gata or at the meal lodge with friends. At least there I would not have had to contend with pointed looks and barely veiled disrespect whenever the queens were not looking. I had heard rumors about altercations between Telequire scouts and Shimax royal guards, but it was being brushed off as simple pre-festival rivalry. I knew better and so did Basha, who brought the rumors up to me two days before solstice eve.

I had been to the temple to speak with the priestess and was just making my way down the path toward the village when Basha met me. "Kyri, I'm glad I caught you!"

She seemed agitated, which was uncharacteristic for the mild-mannered regent. "Is something wrong?"

Basha nodded and I followed where she directed off the main trail. "It looks like your prediction of trouble has come to pass. I'm starting to hear rumors of arguments and small fights between some of our scouts and members of Princess Alcina's royal guards."

I nodded. "Yes, I too have heard about the altercations.

She frowned. "I also spoke with Malva about what happened the day Shimax arrived. Why have you not said anything about this?"

"I did not want to burden Ori when she is so busy in meetings with the visiting queens. Are you the one handling the day-to-day issues while they are in conference?"

Basha nodded. "Yes, and I intend to put an end to the rows and bickering. Do you know what they are fighting about?"

Grimacing, I recounted what I had heard from Coryn and Certig. "Yes. They are fighting about me. Alcina is more determined than ever that I am not worthy of joining with the queen. They have been speaking ill of me to our scouts and calling the scouts themselves weak for following a beaten and broken slave of Rome."

Her brows drew down in anger and lips became tight. "They said that? Exactly?" I nodded. "By Artemis, they will not get away with that! Today is the first day that all the queens are here for session and I don't want to interrupt, so I'm going to just speak with the princess myself. Would you like to go with me?"

I thought for a heartbeat and shook my head. "No, I do not think that would be a good idea. It would just provoke them, and in turn provoke you. However, I do think you should take a handful of warriors with you as a show of power. From what I have seen, the princess and her royal guards are nothing more than bullies. Be wary of them, Basha."

Her look was stern but resolute. "I will. And thank you."

I knew her words would not do any good. Ori told me that Alcina continued to approach her whenever they were alone, which thankfully was not often. And Ori continued to rebuff her. The only thing that would end the advances was our joining ceremony. The next day followed my usual routine of breakfast with my queen and friends, then archery practice, and finally running the trees repairing ropes. Gata had followed me for a while but eventually wandered off to do her own thing. I was about a half candle mark out from the village when I sensed company in the trees. "What is this, the slave is not even good enough to be a scout? They have you out stringing rope rather than protecting the nation like a real Amazon." Megara's voice was grating to my nerves but I continued tying the knot I was working on rather than answer her mocking observation.

"Is she right, doulé? Are you nothing more than a servant of the nation now that you have whip marks on your back?" Alcina's voice was just as unwelcome but I did not wish to engage them. Rather than answer, I finished my rope and made to continue on with my duty, only to find two of Alcina's royal guard blocking my path.

I looked around and saw that there were five in total. Alcina, Megara, and three of the guards. They could kill me without anyone else around to know. I had very few options without engaging in a fight if that was their intention. I tried to be political and non-provocative with my words. "We are all servants of our nations, Princess. Our sisters deserve the best of us at all times. As soon-to-be consort I have no current duty within the tribe so I choose to donate my time making the scout's lives easier by fixing ropes that are in disrepair."

One of the guards on a branch a few trees from me laughed mockingly. "Perhaps she doesn't know how to fight, my princess. None of us would be so weak as to allow a whipping by a man's hands."

Another laughed and spat out her words. "I would have died rather than become a slave!"

Megara joined the taunting. "I hear that one of the Amazons with her did. Apparently the young scout was the only true Amazon with them. Of the three, the other two were nothing more than a cripple and a coward."

More laughter followed her words and I felt myself grow cold at the memory of that day in the Roman agora. Knowing that things were bound to escalate, I had two options. I could stay and fight and either lose badly or die. Or I could run the trees back to the village. While safer because I doubted that any of them could keep up with me, it could certainly be seen as the coward's way. There was really no decision to make because I would do nothing to jeopardize my future with Ori. I laughed with them but it was not a laugh of either humor or mocking. It was a dark and broken sound that put an uneasy look on their faces. "Pray to Artemis that you are never given the opportunity to prove your words. Now if you will excuse me, I am meeting my queen in the bathing pool and I do not wish to be late!"

I turned my head and winked at Alcina then with no warning I took off and sprinted down my branch and leaped for another, past the second laughing guard. They startled at first but soon gave chase. As I felt the leaves and breeze rush by me I could not help laughing out loud. The Telequire trees were my home and no one came into my home to do me harm. Rather than take a straight path back to the village, I led them around it slightly and came down out of the trees near Kylani's training hut. They did not follow me, rather I saw them melt back into the branches and go off in a different direction.

The training master looked up from where she was inspecting knife blades. Her eyebrows rose when she saw me drop into her area, breathing hard and with a flushed face. "Oh ho, have the races started already?"

I shook my head and caught my breath for a candle drop. "No, I was merely losing a few starlings in the trees." I could see the thoughts roll across her face. Starlings were the bullies of the bird world, chasing other birds out of their nests. They were loud and annoying as well.

"Problems?"

I shook my head and smiled. "None I could not handle." She nodded and let it go so I walked away toward the council chamber to deliver an invitation. After speaking the idea aloud earlier, I was going to make my statement a reality by finding Ori and making sure my queen was as clean as she could be for the solstice eve ceremony the next afternoon. I sucked in a breath as the realization of time came to me. Time, sun-cycles, moons, seven-days, candle drops. I was to be bonded in less than a day's time with my queen and my heart. Under the sky in a nation I loved, in front of friends and near-family, I would be joined with sun to my moon. We would become as one. A feeling burst from my chest and worked its way up to my lips as a smile, and I sped up my steps. I could not wait.

I woke alone the next morning in my own hut. After a pleasurable candle mark of bathing when she finished with meetings the previous afternoon, Ori suggested we go our separate ways for dinner and sleep. I grew concerned at first but was quickly reassured by my queen. She said it was tradition to spend the evening before joining in solitary meditation. While I was not sure if I would do any praying to Artemis, I used the time to think and contemplate my future with Telequire. After all, Ori and I would have plenty of nights together once we were bonded.

The sun was up but I could tell by the angle which it shone through my shutters that it was not long past the horizon. I contemplated lying abed longer but knew that I would never get back to sleep. I could feel my muscles and limbs practically vibrating with nervous energy. Instead I rose and got dressed then put away the fletching materials I had left out the night before. Even with all the changes that had been wrought on my heart and mind, there were still things in the world which could sooth me like no other. I turned to fletching arrows rather than prayer, but the result had been the same.

I smiled into the early golden light at the memory of a sleep free from nightmares. I donned all my gear and decided to get some archery practice in before meeting the queen to break my fast. The field had been very busy with all the added Amazons around the village so I was glad to see it nearly empty so early in the morning. I was only slightly surprised to see Deata there. She was just coming back after retrieving her arrows from the target when I walked up. "Heyla, Kyri Fletcher! I see you're up with the birds this morning, eh?"

I shrugged and returned her smile. "I am not normally one to be up this early, but I could not sleep."

She gave me a knowing look. "Nerves, huh?" I nodded and she clapped me on the shoulder. "Not to worry, it's nothing a quiver or two of arrows won't cure!" We both took our places to shoot at neighboring targets. We made a few shots downfield before she spoke again. "I know I said it when we arrived a few days ago, but I'm really glad to see you so well and happy. Especially after the news we received last time we were in Telequire. My heart sorrowed for you, friend. You did a great service to bring home not only yourself, but our other Amazon sisters as well."

I shook my head, never liking such praise. "I was lucky, nothing more. I had the opportunity to bring them back with me so I did. Not everyone had such luck."

"Kyri." I looked up at the somber tone in her voice. "I don't believe in luck, you know that. You fought your way back against greater odds than I could imagine. No matter how much it pains us to admit it, battles will always have casualties and yours was in the life of that young scout. But in return, you brought back sisters that would have died in the hands of Romans had you never gone across the sea."

Her eyes were intense and I could not maintain eye contact. "Some have said that I was merely an arrow fired by Artemis specifically to bring them home."

"Heyla," I raised my eyes again and she rested a hand back on my shoulder. "Even the best archer knows that there are a lot of factors that go into an arrow's true flight. And the farther we shoot, the more chance we have of not hitting our mark, or even finding our fletch again. You may have been Artemis's arrow, but the flight and return was all you. Kyri, you burn with a fire of determination that I've not seen in any other. I truly believe that there is little you cannot accomplish if you set your mind to it. I still owe you a debt of life."

"No—" I tried to protest but she waived my words away.

"Yes, I still owe you a debt of life. I've seen your scars and I've seen the darkness just behind your eyes. And I have some advice for you. Always walk toward the sun."

I looked at her confused. Her advice was impossible. "Training Master, I do not understand."

Her intense eyes pierced me. "Think, Kyri, the words are not literal. I mean that you should not let your past darken your path forward. Do not forget what happened to you, but always remember what is important. Keep in mind all those people and things that you love."

The words whispered from my lips with wonder, but she still heard them. "Ori is my sun."

Deata laughed and released me. "Well then it is a good thing you two are becoming bond mates today, Consort."

She startled me for a heartbeat with the title she bestowed upon me. I often forgot that I would be gaining more than a bond mate with our joining ceremony. I would be gaining a title and immense responsibility to my queen and nation. It was a daunting thought. When I saw her smirk at me, I let out the breath I had been holding. "Sometimes I forget that there will be a title and responsibility coming to me along with my queen's hand." I shook my head. "I will always think of myself as just Kyri."

She pulled me into a one-armed hug and laughed. "Don't worry, you'll always be 'the kid' to me!"

We shot for another half candle mark until I had to leave and officially begin my day. I went to the food lodge next where I saw Shana, Coryn, Basha, Deima, and a handful of other acquaintances sitting at one of the long tables. "Kyri!" Shana waved me over when she saw me enter. As soon as I made it to the table they all broke into a bawdy rendition of a well-known scout song. It was about a woman joining with her veiled bride and only when the ceremony was complete did the woman realize that her bride had run off and left a trussed and propped up sheep in her place. Because of that song, it was a common joke among the Amazons to never trust a bride in white.

My face turned red at their teasing but I had no opportunity to voice a complaint because in that moment, Ori appeared in the doorway. The breath caught in my throat and I remained immobile in the sheer beauty of her presence. It had been a double handful of candle marks since we last laid eyes on each other, yet my heart throbbed with the ache of missing her. Each step closer was a balm to that lonely pain and her smile clearly spelled out our future together. I lost track of all those around us as conversation fell to a low buzz. All I was aware of was the shape of her lips and the green of her eyes. She was happy, and speaking. Awareness of her lips moving brought me back to the present.

"...said breathe, Kyri." Words, syllables, and sounds finally broke through to my hazy brain and I drew in a great and gasping breath. Just the sight of her had stolen the very sense from my body. My heart raced as she placed a palm lightly against my cheek. "Are you well?" I nodded. "Are you hungry?" I nodded again. Her laugh was delicate and caressed all the parts of me that yearned to hold love. "Well then, I think we should go select some food to break our fast. After you, my love." She held a hand out for me to go first so I turned toward the long table along the back wall of the lodge. I took maybe one step when I felt a tap on my back and turned around again. "Aren't you forgetting something?"

The twinkle in her eye was obvious and I found my voice at

last. "No, I have not." Sweet and slow like bee's nectar running from the comb, I moved toward her lips. I caressed them with my own and coaxed them open. She was soft inside and out, and I moaned lightly at the feel of her tongue against mine. The kiss was unhurried and it ended of its own accord. Our languid release from each other did nothing but leave me wanting more. "I missed you last night." The first whistle pierced the air around us, which only served to set off the rest of the featherheads in the lodge. While Ori did not seem affected, I regained my earlier blush. She waved them all off with a smirk and threaded an arm through mine to steer us toward the food.

Over the next few candle marks, we laughed and chatted with friends, and took a long walk around the far edge of the village. We strolled hand in hand and I could not imagine a more perfect moment in time. For midday meal, the two of us took a picnic near one of the many streams that ran through the trees around the heart of Telequire. It was idyllic and serene, and much needed to calm my nerves for the afternoon to come. After we had finished eating we sat in silence, watching the water move the lilies back and forth. Ori turned to me with a curious expression on her face. "Are you happy, Kyri?"

A ripple of shock went through me, much the way a thrown stone would cause the surface of a pond to transform. Had I done so poor a job of showing my emotions to the people closest to my heart? I sputtered for a heartbeat before finding the words to answer. "O—of course! How could you ask me that?"

She smiled and took my hand in hers, tracing the lines of my palm with her fingers. "Tell me about your childhood dreams." Like other things between us, my childhood dreams seemed to be a discussion that would happen over and over.

I sighed and closed my eyes, wanting to look back into my past so I could give her the best answer possible. "I have had many dreams and wishes. The strongest was for my mam to stay with me, then it changed to wishing she could come back to us. After that, my only dream in life was to be a master fletcher like my da and run the trees. What of you?"

Ori was silent for a nearly a candle drop but eventually answered. "I don't remember a lot before I came to the Amazons."

I prompted quietly, because she rarely spoke of her childhood. "But after? Though Shana does not often like to speak of her lost mothers, she told me once that you and Risiki came to live with them when you were brought to Telequire. What were your dreams then?"

"After we came here, my only dream was to create a safe and happy place for me and my sister. I knew it would be difficult so I worked every single day to be better, stronger, and quicker than anyone in my path. Some would say I was overly ambitious at such a young age but I knew what I wanted and knew what I had to do to achieve my dreams."

I smiled at her. "And you have."

Her eyes were clear and shining in the midday sun. "I have everything I've always wanted in the palm of my hand." I blushed at the implication but understood that she also meant it on more than one level. When the silence stretched again she traced the center line of my palm, eliciting a ticklish twitch in my fingers. "And with your dreams, what of love?"

My thoughts dove and folded over on themselves, searching for an answer to her question in my previous life. I found no response there. Instead, it was in the future that spread before me. "I had no dreams of love before you."

Ori sucked in a breath as her hand closed tight over my fingers in surprise. Before another heartbeat could tremble by, we came together with a kiss that transcended the passion that either of us had dreamed of. We were more than two souls brought together by fate or divine circumstance. We were one soul that had been broken long ago, and only together were we truly whole. Sun and Moon, I planned to ride the sky with her for as long as the world would hold us. We dallied by the stream on a soft bed of moss, lighthearted as we had ever been. It was only when the sun had traveled well past the zenith that we finally left. We had a ceremony to see to. We were to be joined, and in front of the eyes of all we would become that which we had both yearned for. We would become "us."

HORNS SOUNDED AS we walked through the edge of the village and Ori turned to me in a panic. "Goddess, we're late! I cannot believe I lost track of time like that!" We both ran to her hut to change for the ceremony and grab any items that would be needed. When we got to back to the crowd amassed outside the temple, Ori left me to find Glyphera and I stood in awe of the gathered Amazons. I had never seen so many women in one place. Once I got over the shock, I moved near the open space below the dais that had been erected outside the temple opening. The large carved columns of the fresco around the doorway seemed quite grand while staring up at them. But it was the statue of Artemis at the top of the hill that made the event come to life.

Looking at her likeness that was poised to shoot somewhere in the heavens, I pondered whether it was really her that shot me across the sea. Perhaps she had, but I flew true to my own fletch and came back of my own accord. My strength of will was mine alone. Perhaps that was the key after all. Maybe the Goddess Artemis was not a flesh and blood being of supreme capability, perhaps she was only thought and idea that lived in the heads of her followers. She was a notion of community and service, protection, and sacrifice that shaped the Amazon nations. The Goddess was a myth but her idea of love and family was a legacy that held together the very fabric of our lives. It was then that I decided I could live with such a notion, with such a legacy. I knew that I could take Artemis into my heart and still be true to myself.

I was startled from my revelry by the second sounding of horns. When I looked around, Shana and Coryn stood to my right engaged in conversation with Kylani. Certig and Maeza stood to my left with big smiles on their faces. Panphilla and her mother were nearby on the other side of the platform and my young sister turned my way with a smile. I waved until our gazes were distracted by the priestess ascending to the dais. All the nations were on hand, each grouped with their own people in the valley behind the tribe of Telequire. It was our temple, after all. Another low horn sounded and the gathered crowd split down the middle as our queen approached.

Ori was resplendent in an outfit that matched my own. They had been given to us by Basha, who had them special made for the occasion. My gaze was momentarily caught by the sun shining on the bright marble surface of the statue high above us and my mouth dropped open. It was exactly then that I realized our outfits matched the one worn by the Goddess in her eternal pose of protection. Stylized armor with the draping of a light chiton. The difference being that ours were colored in Artemis's sacred shade of red. Ori even wore the stag antler headdress. Her ceremonial sword gleamed from her back as she walked up the steps to join Glyphera and the gently bleating goat.

The sky had been off and on overcast throughout the morning and it continued to be so for the start of our solstice eve ceremony. The clouds above us chased each other and played across the surface of the sun, light-hearted looking as I felt. The priestess raised her hands for silence and Ori started the Invocation of

Artemis. Her words took me back to the day of my twentieth birthday. "Hail to our Goddess Artemis! She who is the hunter, she who is hunted. It is you who wields the bow bringing prey to their knees. You are also the doe fleeing certain death in the woods."

With sword raised high, Ori held the entire assembly of Amazons focused on its very tip. Voices thundered from behind me as we all answered her call. "Shining moon and silvered brow, hear us Artemis!" I had never before heard such amassed vocal power and my skin broke out in chill bumps. The ritual continued as the priestess received the sacred sword and took over. The clouds rolled above us as time swept past on the delicate wings of wind. The goat was sacrificed and the line of those walking in Artemis's footsteps seemed endless with women coming up from every nation. I smiled as I watched Pan receive the blood mark upon her forehead that I remembered all too well.

When that part of the ceremony was finished, the bowl of blood was cleared to make room for the initiations. The queen moved forward and announced the Blessing of Births. All those with babes born since the previous summer solstice moved up to the dais so their children could receive Artemis's blessing and their rite of caste feather. The priestess blessed each child brought forward while the queen presented the feather to the mothers. In addition, each child received the sacred mark of the Goddess upon their forehead, written with a stick of ochre.

At the end of the blessing of the wee babes, the Rite of Arkteia began. Flute players stood around the bases of the dais while a line of young girls dressed in saffron robes climbed the stairs. Music played while they ran around the stage yipping and growling in a display of frantic wildness. The dance was to symbolize their maturation, but I remembered the myth's deeper meaning. The story stated that there once was a she-bear that lived in a sanctuary of Artemis. The bear scratched out the eyes of a little girl who was playing with it and her brothers killed the bear in their grief. Famine befell the people and when they inquired about the cause, Apollo told them it was punishment for killing Artemis's bear. Hence forth all girls were required to "play the bear" before they could pass through puberty and be married.

For the Amazons, the dance had become a symbol of girls transitioning into young adulthood and readying their bodies for their menses and greater physical demands. Just when it seemed the girls were on the verge of insanity, their spinning and scrabbling suddenly formed into a line behind the queen and priestess.

With one final yell, they stood tall and threw their robes to the ground and just as quickly they knelt down to prostrate themselves near the back of the dais. Folded over as they were, only the barest line of their nude backs were visible to the assembled nations. They were quiet, they were seeds. The girls had become buds, waiting to blossom. Everyone around me and behind me began yipping and clapping to celebrate their transition.

The girls stayed on the stage but the musicians changed to drummers as the flute players walked back into the crowd. The next element was the Ilio Choroú, where young women were passed into adulthood and deemed ready to begin their duty to the nation. Their dance was more militaristic and each one carried a pair of wood chobos. The forearm's length sticks beat a complicated pattern as they false fought against each other in pairs. The rhythm sped faster and faster in unison and as a counterpoint to the drum pattern being played below the dais. As the beat neared a crescendo, the stomping women split and moved in two lines behind the younger girls, finishing with chobos crossed in front of them and with a glorious yell. "Hail Artemis!" The last beat of the drum ended on the last syllable of the Goddess's name.

Another roar went up among the assembled Amazons as young women were passed into adulthood. Drummers below the dais started another slower rhythm and singers began to chant. The young girls donned their robes again and followed the newly-anointed adults from the dais. The queen and priestess gathered items and set them on the altar in the interim. My breathing took on the form of heaving gasps as I realized that my time had come. My heart raced with panic as Shana turned to me mouthing words. I could not hear, nor could I see as vision tunneled into the spot right in front of me. I felt hands grab my arms from either side as my sister's voice broke through. "Oh Goddess, she's going to pass out! Kyri, Kyri!"

I turned my head toward her as if I were moving in thick sap. "Yes?"

"Look at me sister and slow down your breathing." She took exaggerated slow breaths and bid me to copy her. In less than a candle drop I began to feel better and my vision returned to normal. "Are you okay now?"

Shana's face was a study of concern while Coryn wore a smirk. "It seems my fearless friend has finally found something that affects her."

"Coryn! You're not helping."

I steadied myself and looked from one to the other, finally

focusing on the First Scout Leader. "I am okay now. And do not worry my friend, your time will come soon enough." My legs had stopped shaking so I dared another look at the people amassed behind us. "You look out over that crowd and tell me *your* legs would not wobble a bit at the thought of joining with the one you love in front of such a gathering." With just a look behind us, Coryn swallowed and paled slightly. I had no idea why I could face down beasts and strange men in a combat arena but the mere thought of professing my love in front of thousands left me weak.

Both singers and drums cut off abruptly and the priestess's voice washed across the Amazons below. She called out to all the nations present. "On this solstice eve in the moon of *Ioúnios* we celebrate times of change. We come together beneath Artemis's knowing gaze to consecrate new beginnings and rites of passage. Because this day holds special meaning in the Goddess's heart, it is considered auspicious indeed for two people to unite in a bond of love. Kyri Fletcher, please come to the dais."

The drums began their beat again and I could not prevent my feet from stepping to the same rhythm. When I reached the altar, the drums stopped and I stood in the exact same position as I had for our betrothal. The queen and I were on either side of the priestess, facing each other. Glyphera's strident voice cut through the air and I was startled by the strength of it as the sound echoed through the rocky valley below. She held out a hand to receive Ori's left arm. The priestess drew the same sharp dagger I remembered from before and poised it just to the bottom of the queen's inner forearm, above her wrist. "Chosen of Artemis, child of divinity and truth, you are here to give sacrifice to our Goddess and ask for a blessing on this day." She pressed the blade into the skin and a bright bead of red welled up to run and drip onto the altar below. It was not a deep cut, just enough to bleed. Ori had turned to face the people below, holding her arm over the sacred stone table of her Goddess.

The priestess turned to me and I held my left arm out when asked. It was the one with the sagittarius tattoo but her knife was poised lower than the image. "Arrow of Artemis, child of love and surrender, you are here to give sacrifice to our Goddess and ask for a blessing on this day." With a quick flash of pain my own blood ran onto the table below. Next, Glyphera stepped back so there was nothing left between me and the queen. "Now I ask our queen and her chosen consort to turn and offer their sacrifice to each other." We turned and pressed our outstretched forearms together, merging my blood with hers, our heartbeats, and our very souls.

With left arms clasped tight in the reverse of the warrior grip, it had a meaning of love. Glyphera wound a cord around our arms to bind them together for the rest of the ceremony. I was hesitant at the thought of being tied in some way but the smile on Ori's face quickly calmed me. I had tensed and she knew of my fears in such things. The drums started again, along with the chanting women who sung of eternity and Artemis's love. The priestess lifted one of the wrapped bundles from the altar and slowly unwound the white linen. When it was bare, she let the linen fall back to the altar in a non-bloodied place. Torc in hand, she gently placed it around Ori's neck. I stood in awe as the woman I loved looked at me, an image of beauty and splendor in my mind's eye.

Glyphera repeated the step for me and the cool metal warmed quickly against my own skin. With necklaces placed, she bid us to pull our arms apart and spent a candle drop wrapping each wound with one of the discarded clothes. The three of us turned as one back toward the assembled nations and when the priestess raised her hands high above, the chanting and drums stopped. In that abrupt silence the priestess once again petitioned our Goddess for approval. "Artemis, Goddess of the hunt, protector of the wilderness, hear your priestess! We have sacrificed to you, given both blessings and rites, and we have joined together the Telequire queen and her consort as their blood lays drying upon your altar. Oh Artemis of the silver light, give us a sign that you have received our gifts and are pleased. Mother of our hearts and protector of our sacred pools, please acknowledge our love to you and the union of two you love."

We waited for a candle drop with no sign, then the candle drop stretched for two. I hated waiting, hated wondering what was real and what was true. But before I could stress over some imagined disapproval, gasps whispered across the crowd below like leaves rustling in the wind. We turned to follow the pointing hands and saw a large sunbeam had broken from the clouds, greater than the one I had seen before the ceremony began. That ray just happened to be striking the great statue of Artemis at the top of the hill, perfectly illuminating the leopard that lounged on top of its base. Gata, again.

Ori's lips curved into a smile and a single quiet word escaped from her. "Goddess."

I smiled too because I knew we had been received and accepted by all gathered below. The torc was an unfamiliar weight around my neck but staring into the eyes of my beloved, my sun and personal goddess, I was lighter than anything I had ever known. When she pulled her gaze from the effigy above and turned her eyes to me I smiled back at her. In the scheme of all that had happened and all that was left to occur in our lifetime, my whispered word held more meaning. "Us." I had never seen my queen look more radiant than in that moment.

Chapter Sixteen

The Blind Challenge for a Nation

AS WAS THE usual custom, there was a short break before the Ceremony of Light. When I exited the dais with Ori, we both got caught up in a long line of well-wishers. She had to excuse herself to return the ceremonial sword and I was carried away in a sea of hugs and slapping hands. My bandaged arm throbbed lightly and the day had turned warm but nothing could sully my good mood. Over and over again the word that had stressed me for so long was uttered repeatedly from the lips of my Telequire sisters. Consort. I tried to look everywhere and smile but it soon became overwhelming and the panic began to set in. Before I could start pushing myself out of the demanding press of people, I felt the solid reassurance of my two closest friends at each side of me.

"All right everyone, you'll have your chance to give your compliments at the feast, but for now the Consort needs to make her way to the dais." Shana had a way of speaking that made people listen. It was a boon that she was held in high regard as our ambassador. The imposing presence of the First Scout Leader at her back also helped. A path opened up in front of us and my breathing began to ease.

When we broke free from the main crowd and went down the wide path to the village, I slowed and looked at my escorts. "You two have excellent timing! I was starting to feel..." I trailed off, unable to find a word for the tight chest and trapped feeling that the large crowd had given me. I turned around to look behind us, hoping to catch a glimpse of my queen. "Where is Ori?"

Coryn grinned and clapped me on the back of my shoulder where my gorytos did not cover. "She is actually the one who sent us to rescue you. She was caught in a discussion with the priestess and Basha and knew you would not do well in such a large crowd."

I swallowed thickly at the thought that my friends made no mention of my weakness, merely sought to help me in whatever way they could. "Thank you."

Ori caught up with us when we got to the center of the village. Her face was flushed in the heat from jogging all the way from the temple. When I saw her, my heart raced and I drew her into a great embrace. With her feet lifted off the ground I spun her around out of sheer ebullience. My queen laughed and let out a gentle sigh as I set her on the ground again. Cupping my face in both her hands, she stared up at me. "You really have found it, haven't you?"

I knew exactly the thing she referred to, it was my joy. "Yes." My face hurt from smiling. Before we could speak more, another horn sounded, calling everyone to the large village center. It would be a tight fit but there would be plenty of room for the immense crowd. While I was not terribly hungry because of our light picnic at the water's edge, my stomach still growled at the smell of roasting meat that wafted through the air around us.

"Come, we must go up." Ori tugged my hand and I looked at her in alarm, then glanced at my friends who were gathered near the dais.

"But—"

Ori smiled at my confusion and explained. "Consort, it is your duty to be by my side in all things now. The tribe is ours together."

I truly had not realized the responsibility would be so complete or would encompass so much. "Oh." Shocked, I let her lead me up the steps to the raised platform. Besides our usual representatives of the regent, council members and conference of elders, we were joined by all the queens and their own consorts. Not all were bonded though. Of the eleven other tribes, only six had consorts. Two of the tribal rulers were old and Shana told me that their mates had died many cycles before. The other three, one of which was Queen Alala, were simply un-partnered.

While there were not a lot of announcements for our queen to make before the lighting of the great fire, the other queens all took turns naming their nation's competitors for the festival events. The Festival of Nations and other competitions had an event for every nation, twelve in total. All of them represented necessary parts of our life and society. The events that displayed our skills of battle were sword, knife, chobo, staff, and unarmed combat. Woods craft and hunting were represented by archery and tree running. Individual aptitudes manifested themselves in shows of skill, strength, speed, and distance running. And lastly, the importance of oral tradition and memories were carried on by the best storytellers of any tribe.

I liked that the Amazons made that a priority just as much as battle. I paid close attention to the events that Alcina and Megara were entering, as well as the other Shimax guards whose names I recognized. I felt a brief twinge of concern for my queen when I heard that Megara would be competing in swords, but I quickly brushed it away. I was confident that Ori's skill was far above all the rest. Predictably the princess entered the unarmed combat, chobos, and strength events.

After a lengthy Ceremony of Light, the great bonfire was lit and all the duty scouts made their way through the feast lines. Scouts always had to select which events they wanted to compete in ahead of time so that new schedules could be made that accommodated them being off duty for their preferred competitions. Even though the Festival of Nations competitors had been determined at spring equinox, their absence still needed to be planned in the scout rotations. There were rewards for those scouts that did not compete at all and spent all the festival days on duty. They got an extra rest day each seven-day for a moon, plus a silver coin each. When more people wanted to enter than could safely be spared from patrol, the decision came down to rank and seniority.

The feast itself was kept casual, mostly because there would never be enough tables to accommodate everyone in the village. Some chose to take food back to their huts or camps, others just sat in large circles on the ground to facilitate conversation. The tables we did have were reserved for queens and their bond mates, council members, elders, and other respected women in the tribes. It was a way to show honor for those that continue to lead us into the light. Despite my discomfort during the meal, afterward turned quite pleasant. Ori and I walked around the gathering, accepting more embraces and blessings. We danced, played, laughed, and conversed with people from every tribe. The only time I saw the princess was during the feast itself but I never saw her after. Though a part of me remained on guard throughout the night.

Later in the evening the two of us sat on a log by the great fire, resting from what felt like candle marks of dancing. There were plenty of others around us, making conversation and passing skins of wine. I saw one of the familiar skins of Tanta spirits make its way around the fire and smiled. When it found its way to my hand I calmly uncorked it and took the tiniest of sips then handed it nonchalantly to my left. Ori took it willingly, thinking it was our standard wine. I knew it was a cruel joke but I managed to keep a straight face as I watched her upend the skin and take a gulping swallow. Just as fast she brought the skin back down, coughing and sputtering.

When she finally caught her breath again, she voiced her displeasure. "Goddess on high! What in the world is that, poison?" The look on her face was too much and I was unable to hold in my laughter. Seeing that she had clearly been tricked, Ori swatted my arm. "Woods weasel! You knew what that skin was, didn't you?"

I tried to play innocent but failed miserably at wiping the smile from my lips. "Oh, you did not like it? That is an alcohol that Tanta refers to as spirits. I believe they call it brandy after the Amazon sister who created it."

She scowled and gave me a look of distaste. "And you like that?"

I shook my head. "Goddess no, it is terrible!" We stared at each other before breaking into laughter again.

When we calmed down again, I turned to gaze at my queen in the firelight, aware of the sound of drums and chanting all around. Even as shadows danced across us with each Amazon who circled the fire, contentment rested comfortably upon her beautiful face. Dark lips were slightly parted as she watched the revelry and they parted even more when she turned to me and smiled. "What is it?" I shook my head, self-conscious at having been caught staring. Ori took my hand into hers and gave it a little tug. "Could I interest you in a soak before we retire to our hut?"

Her words startled me for a heartbeat. I had forgotten that it would become our hut after the joining. I imagined that I would have to move my things once the festival ended. "I would love that. Should we bring something to eat?"

Ori's eyes took on that familiar glint and her teeth gleamed white in the firelight. "I'm bringing you."

Even with our history and all that I had experienced, her words still caused my cheeks to burn hot. I wanted to make sure of her intentions once I pulled us both up from the log. "So you do not want to join a group in the large pool?"

"Kyri, we are newly bonded. There is only one person I wish to be with right now." Her words held sudden intensity, an urgency that had not been there a candle drop before. With breaths coming faster I looked down at her with new understanding. Quickly grabbing the water skin from the ground, we made our way hand in hand to the smallest pool. We were both surprised by a large rock in front of the door to the minor cave. Leaning against the rock was a piece of wood with words written in charcoal. "Queen and Consort only." Ori's voice seemed loud in the echoing silence by the cave entrance.

I smiled. "That was very kind. Do you know who did it?"

She shrugged. "It could have been anyone. I don't have a guess as to whom but I'm going to take advantage of it. I didn't relish begging anyone to leave and exercising my rank as queen."

I looked at her curiously, never having seen her take advantage of her position before. "Would you really have done that?"

Ori shook her head. "No. I would have suggested we soak in the larger pool for a short time, then go back to our hut." Torches were lit inside nearest to the door. We could not tell before entering because the large leather hide that covered the door let out no light. No one wanted a drafty bathing chamber. There were a few natural cracks near the ceiling of the small cave that the torch smoke found an exit through, but for the most part it was pretty warm inside. I was not sure how long we could stand the heat of the pool since it was high summer but I was glad to wash off the day's sweat and grime.

We undressed and entered the water, one right behind the other. Ori went under the surface completely as I moved to fetch a cake of soap from the edge. When I turned back she broke the surface again, water streaming in dark rivulets from her hair. It cascaded over her shoulders and breasts to join the inky pool below. Breath caught in my throat as I gazed at the sight that I considered the first true beauty. Perhaps it was only in my perception, but her smile left me awestruck on a regular basis. In that moment, with her clearly in my view, I sent a prayer to whatever force or deity was real in our place in time. As I watched, her features took on a look of concern. "What's wrong?"

I smiled and drew in my first deep breath since entering the pool. "Nothing is wrong, I was simply saying a prayer in my head, a wish."

"What did you wish for?"

"That I would never lose you again." I looked down because the mere thought of us being driven apart again by the wills and whims of man pitched me to the edge of despair. I did not understand why I was feeling such high emotion, but tears pricked my eyes with my admission.

She moved quickly in the water, wrapping me in an embrace before a single tear could fall. "Oh, love, I would move the heavens themselves to make sure you stay with me. I would resign my monarch's mask if need be just to search for you and bring you home."

Shock stole my words for a heartbeat. "But you cannot do

that. You are the queen! The nation needs a strong leader, they need you."

Ori covered my lips with a single finger. "Shh, I need you more than the nation needs me. I would not survive without you again, the blackness of loss did not sit well with my heart." When she pulled her finger away, I kissed her with every scrap of joy and sadness contained within me. We clung to each other in the hot pool, wet skin sliding against each other with delicious friction. There were no words we could say to each other that would convey more meaning than the desperation and longing of that single kiss. Time passed in a cluster of caresses, soft sighs, and trickling water. We washed each other and rinsed with the slowness of wax dripping from a fat candle. I pulled back when my knees grew weak and I became lightheaded. "Are you too warm?" I nodded. "Well, we can leave now that we are both clean and refreshed."

I sighed, saddened by the thought of leaving her embrace. "But I do not think I can leave your arms."

Ori laughed and stepped back anyway. "It is a short walk to a sturdy bed."

In a moment's decision of daring, we raced back to our hut wearing only soft boots and carrying the rest of our clothing. She arrived first and quickly closed and locked the door in front of me. I knocked quietly, hoping no one would hear or see me in my uninhibited and undressed state. "Ori." She did not answer but I could hear giggling from the other side of the door. Looking around once again in the darkness, I spied Gata's door. Hearing soft footsteps approaching from the opposite direction, I wasted no time scrambling through the swinging flap to the safety of our hut. I dropped my clothes and pointed my finger at her when I stood upright. "Woods weasel! Someone was coming!"

She laughed even harder at my revelation. "Oh, Goddess! What I wouldn't give to have seen your face, or your backside as you crawled through that door!"

My ire was up but so was my humor when I stalked toward here. "You think that is funny?"

Her smile did not abate with my aggressive approach, almost as if she were looking forward to being caught. "Yes!"

I charged her and lifted us both to the bed, pinning her beneath me. Her struggle left us both breathless, from arousal as much as exertion. Being larger and stronger than the woman below me, I had no problems holding her immobile. I grew warm where our skin slid and pressed together, breast rubbing against breast. Leaning down, I moved my lips closer to her ear and watched as my panting breath moved the small golden hairs. "That was very cruel, my queen." My voice was a wet whisper and when I took her ear lobe between my teeth she shuddered below.

"Oh? Is there a punishment, my consort?"

I reluctantly pulled my mouth away from its travels down her neck to gaze into her eyes. "That depends. Are you going to do that again?"

The smile she gave me in return was pure mischief. "As often as it suits me." In the face of such defiance I had no choice but kiss her. I released her wrists as my mouth swallowed the moan that issued forth from her lips. As I settled myself firmly between her legs, Ori moved her questing hands along my back and backside, gripping and pulling. I acquiesced to her needs and my own by pushing against her in a rhythm that was older than time. Without warning, I moved away from her mouth and she gasped my name as I took a hard nipple between my teeth. She lost her grip on me when I slid down so she moved her hands up to grip my head instead. She grew wet with the ministrations of my teeth and tongue and my stomach became wet with her.

The next time she spoke my name, it was less a plea and more of a demand, and I knew she waited for my touch. My love and my life, she had shown me so many things. Ori had opened the sky to me and allowed the stars to shine down. I would have done anything if it guaranteed her happiness. Moving down the expanse of skin, I took her into my mouth as I let her very flesh draw me in. She had taught me everything but I still had much to learn. Both of us burned hot and sweat ran freely down my temples and spine but I would never stop in the face of our conflagration. Her fire was the thing that made me new, made me clean. In what seemed like no time at all, Ori grew hard against my tongue and lips, and her muscles stiffened below me. Then with a great clutching cry, she burst forth and stole the heart from my very chest. I clenched and shook with her but remained tightly on edge. When I met her gaze along the smooth length of her body, she tapped my shoulder lightly.

"Come here." No sooner had I moved up to her side then her hands were on me, in me, spreading the fire of her passion. I thought certain that the very same heart she had stolen would explode into a sky full of bright and sparkling lights. In a heartbeat, or a thousand cycles, a harsh voice burst from my chest and fell off the softness of my lips. I cried out for her and with her, then I just cried. There was no worship beyond her touch, no magic without her eyes looking down at me. And with her soft caress and reassuring murmurs, I knew that I had come home. With her strength and my heart, I reveled in the solidity of us.

THE FESTIVAL OF Nations was very different from all other competitions I had seen before. Because there were twelve different events with people participating from each tribe, officiating had to be altered and everything was spread out over a five day period. The most popular events were split into rounds, similar to what we had done at the spring equinox. The Festival of Nations differed from the seasonal festivals in that you had to lose two times to be disqualified in sword and knife events. Sword and knife also needed the most time so were spread into sessions to be held on the first, third, and fifth days of competition. Archery, staff, chobo, unarmed combat, and tree running were two days each. The rest were all finished in the same day.

After the opening ceremony, the distance runners were released and the skill competition began. At Kylani's suggestion, I did not change anything of my skill demonstration. She assured me that no one had ever done what I had with both shooting and catching arrows. Another difference from the competitions I was used to was that instead of the conference of elders judging the event, it was a selection of one woman from each tribe. The training master proved right and I handily won the Artemis statue.

Immediately following Skill was the beginning matches of sword fighting, and after that, the first round of knives. I was happy to see that Ori and Kylani had moved on to the next round of swords but uneasy to note that Megara had as well. The thought of her going against Ori left me with a strange sense of foreboding. When I asked Shana about her at the end of the first sword round, my friend just said she was good but not on the same level as our queen.

Our best Telequire Amazons moved on after the first day. Ori came to find me as we watched Shana fight her second round. Deka had her match prior and was already moved up to fight in the knife final rounds. Both Ori and Kylani had moved up but Kasichi, one of the branch leaders during the Western War and third place in archery during equinox, had suffered one of her two losses to Megara. She would move on but only to the loser's rounds. Near the end of the first competition day, the distance runners came in. We all clapped and cheered as the first few crossed the finish line. I nearly burst with pride to see Degali, my light-footed fourth scout cross in front of everyone else. Women from Kombetar and Oros tribes took second and third place. The top three finishers for every event received Artemis statues but they had numbers on them, so you could tell which place was which.

The day ended with food, friends, and laughter. Since some of the queens competed during the daytime, each evening they spent a candle mark in the council chamber meeting on a variety of subjects. Even though I was a newly-made consort, I did not have to participate in such meetings. I knew most of what was said from Ori, who would fill me in afterward. They discussed trade, learning, politics of the regions surrounding each nation, and much more. The Amazon nations were spread out enough that we encompassed a wide variety of cultures and traditions. Basha mentioned that the heads of the other disciplines held meetings as well. Inter-tribe learning for things like education, weapons training, healing, and military tactics were very valuable when conflicts were always cropping up around Greece.

The second day started with the foot races. The rounds went fairly fast so statues were handed out by midmorning. Ori, Coryn, and I participated in the first round of tree races and all three of us moved on. Chobo was next and I saw a few of our scouts continue as well as Baeza of Tanta tribe, Alcina, and two of her guards. Archery encompassed a number of challenges that were standard for any Festival of Nations, no matter who hosted. There was a round of basic target shooting, with all twelve arrows having to hit the center section. The second saw all targets moved back to twice the distance from the shooters and eight of the twelve had to hit the red eye. By the end of the first portion of archery competition, half of us remained to compete in the final rounds that would occur the day before festival closing. Staff fighting closed out the second festival day and the only faces I recognized that were moving on to the final round were two fourth scouts, Maeza and Geeta, the Tanta training master, and Megara.

After the meeting of queens and our meal, Ori suggested we find a quiet place to watch the sunset. When she started off down the temple trail, I shot her a surprised look. "I thought we were going to watch the sunset? Where are we heading?" The place I had in mind was the one where we had taken a picnic on solstice eve.

She looked back at me and smiled. "You'll see." She carried

both water and wine skins slung over one shoulder and I had the soft fur cover that I had made from Gata's mam. The leopard herself was pacing us off to the side of the trail. I suspected she did not enjoy the larger number of people that had come into the village for the festival but we had yet to see any issues from the great cat. Instead of continuing down the path to the temple cave entrance, Ori led me down a less followed one that continued up a steep incline and eventually brought us to the base of the new Artemis statue.

The view of the surrounding land and forest was amazing and the sky had already started turning pink when I arranged the fur onto the ground. She sat with legs bent and folded over each other while I stretched mine out in front of me. Ori's voice was quiet in the fading light. "Look how the Hesperides' apples glow for us." It was said that the goddess-nymphs were the guardians of the tree of golden apples, as well as the keepers of the other gods' treasures. Maybe the sky glowed in the light of such, or maybe it was a passing storm on the horizon. I had seen the coming clouds change and melt blue sky to red when I lived near the sea as a slave. I had yet so see any fantastical events that could only be explained by the actions of our gods. I did not contest Ori's description, merely enjoyed the beauty of it. After a candle drop I turned my gaze from the ever-changing kaleidoscope of color to that of my queen's face.

"It is beautiful, though not nearly as lovely as you."

It was unusual to see her blush, but she managed in the fleeing light. Ori turned her head away slightly. "How much wine have you had? I am not fairer than anyone else, Kyri. I meant what I said about you putting me on a pedestal."

I laughed and reached across with my left hand to turn her face my way. Her cheek was soft beneath my palm. "I am not placing you anywhere, I merely describe what I see. I have eyes like anyone else. And while it is true that a person's beauty may be subjective, that does not make you less beautiful to my love-colored gaze. It is not merely your face that I find fair, it is your mind and your heart that draw me just as sure. Do you find me less attractive with the scars on my back that no one else in our tribe seems to possess?"

Her eyes widened. "Of course not! I have always thought you beautiful, why would you ask such a thing?"

"Now you understand what I am saying. I have always loved you and I would have loved you even if you were not a queen. I know the difference now between observation and expectation.

We are both fallible with our flaws, and yet we both swim in deep tides of emotion for the other. It is exactly as it should be."

Ori smiled and bumped her shoulder into mine. "How did you get so wise, love?"

Instead of bumping her back I wrapped my right arm around her and pulled her close. Helios was nearly lost to sight as I rejoiced the feel of her in my embrace. "I have learned a surprising amount about life and the people around me from my sister, our esteemed Ambassador of Nations. But do not tell her that."

Under a sky of fading red turned purple, Ori laughed and pushed me back onto the fur. "It can be our secret. Now, I see a full moon rising and I believe we have a dream to fulfill."

She straddled my hips and I looked up at her curiously. "A dream?"

Rather than speak aloud, she leaned down and whispered the same words she had on the eve of equinox. "I dream of screaming your name to the Goddess, beneath the full moon and heavens above." I thought for certain that screaming my name at the feet of her goddess was bound to get someone's attention but once my queen placed her lips against me I no longer cared.

DAY THREE BEGAN with the second session of sword and knife matches. The unarmed rounds started and the last portion of the day was finished with storytelling. The same faces I recognized that won their matches on day one, also won their matches on the third day. Others were eliminated or dropped to the losing rounds. Shana took second place in the storytelling event, just behind Queen Agafya in first place and ahead of Baeza in third. When I congratulated Queen Agafya after her win, she pulled me into a strong embrace. I knew she was happy to see me doing well and I accepted her comfort for what it was.

With so much activity going on each day, the festival felt as though it were rushing by. I met many women from the visiting tribes. More than a few tried to get me to tell my tale but I always declined. I heard many whispers in my vicinity about things that had been gossiped about but I tried to ignore them as much as possible. I was not a hero, I was not a slave. I was only Kyri. A fletcher, an archer, and a sagittarius, I had been many things before becoming Consort to the Queen of Telequire. All were a part of me as sure as any limb of flesh and blood.

The fourth day was when things began to get interesting. The day led off with the contest of strength. A selection of logs was set up for each competitor to carry. As they progressed through the rounds, they had to lift heavier and heavier logs and carry them for a distance of ten steps. Ori and I both watched the event, curious about the princess of Shimax and her renowned physical prowess. She was indeed impressive with the log that she successfully handled, and she easily won the event. The tree running final race was the next one after strength. We had a quarter candle mark between the two events and Coryn used it to rib and cajole me. The rest of our friends stood by waiting to watch. "Are you ready to lose, Consort?"

I grinned at her. "I think that by your own words I have already won."

"I don't get it."

Shana elbowed her in the side. "You just called her Consort and being with Ori has always been her heart's desire."

The First Scout Leader laughed. "Well consort or no, you're going to be eating leaves and feathers as you race to catch up with me in the trees!"

"Are you fighting over second and third place again? That's quite cute." Ori walked up just in time to add her opinion to the rest. Coryn glowered at her and I took the jibe with a smile. While I was competitive and did not like losing to my friend, I knew I was outclassed when it came to our queen. And she always made up for my losing later. Before I knew it, the race had begun and the whittled-down group of eighteen of us took to the trees. As with before, I lost sight of Ori early on and Coryn and I quickly moved ahead. But before a quarter candle mark had gone by, the other tribeswomen were catching up to flank us.

I lost precious heartbeats searching for a close limb and was passed by a lanky scout with long red hair. We were half way around the village when I was passed by Deesha of Ujanik. Cursing, I pushed myself and started to close in again when I noticed someone pacing me one tree over. Within a heartbeat she leaped onto the same limb I was running and gave me a solid elbow to the side. Luckily I was near a down rope and grabbed on to break my fall but I also scraped the palms of my hands in the process. Someone yelled out from the ground as I landed on my feet.

"You may enter the trees and continue, Telequire runner! Shimax runner, you are disqualified!" I did not look to see who had shoved me, I quickly ran up a slanted trunk and took to the canopy again. It was illegal to touch the ground during the race but it was also illegal to engage another runner. The race watcher must have seen what happened and let me continue, not that I had a chance of winning once I was shoved out of the trees. I was dismayed to realize I had lost too much time. In the end, Ori took first place and Coryn took second. And while I was sad to miss out on winning a statue, it did my heart good to see Deesha take third. From what I had heard, her young sister was doing well since returning with us to Greece. Slavery had scarred her in every way but she was not as broken as many feared.

After they received statues my friends came to find me. Coryn wasted no time teasing me for coming in so far back in the group since I had finished eighth overall. "What happened to you out there? Did your feet turn to stone and your feathers forget to fly?"

I shrugged and grimaced, for indeed they had. "It is true, the trees were not with me today and I would not have placed. But I was also purposely shoved from the trees about half way around."

"Are you okay? Who did it?" Ori's face turned from mirth to concern in a heartbeat.

Holding up my hands I made a face. "I caught myself on a rope on the way down so just my palms and my pride were scuffed. And I do not know who it was, just that she was from Shimax. The observer saw it and disqualified her as she let me go ahead."

Coryn swore. "Cheats! What is the deal with Shimax this suncycle?"

I shook my head. "I do not believe she was trying to cheat because I was too far back to benefit the Shimax runner. No, I believe it was personal. I would wager that she is either a royal guard or one of Alcina's friends."

Ori frowned. "That is a very serious charge, Kyri. Are you sure?"

I nodded. "I am serious, but I will not lodge a formal complaint or issue any accusations. I am doing as you requested and handling these things quietly and peaceably."

Ori looked surprised at my words. "These things? You mean more has been happening with Shimax? Why didn't you tell me?"

Basha was standing with us and she cleared her throat to speak. "I made the decision, my queen. You have been in meetings with the other queens and we did not wish to disturb you for such minor skirmishes. They were small ones between the Shimax royal guards and some of our scouts. I spoke with the princess personally the day before solstice eve. Things have gotten better."

"It's true, my scouts have not reported any new issues since she spoke with Princess Alcina." Coryn was quick to back up the regent's words.

Ori looked irritated and little lines appeared between her eyes as she frowned. "And what were these skirmishes about?"

"Me." They all turned to look at me at the same time. "The princess is angry that you refused her, and angrier yet that I became your consort. I have had encounters with them many times since they arrived, once even in the trees when I was running ropes."

My queen's face became a hard mask. "And what did they do?"

I shook my head. "Nothing. I did not give them the chance, I ran and outpaced them back to the village. They took off as I landed near the training master's hut. But I cannot say yay or nay as to whether they would have done me harm. I felt in danger at the time so I ran, though they probably thought me a coward after."

Knowing Ori perhaps better than I, the others wandered away sensing temper to come. "Kyri."

I looked down, not liking the anger or disappointment in her voice. "I am sorry, my queen. I did not mean to displease you or bring shame to the tribe."

"Heyla, you did neither of those things. Look at me, please?" I met her expressive green eyes and grew lost in her emotion. "It is not you I am upset with, it is the princess and her guards. You have done nothing wrong. Actually, you have shown remarkable restraint, all things considered." She sighed and ran a hand through her hair. "We have one more day of competition after today and I can only hope that their actions do not escalate to the point where someone gets seriously hurt." Ori cocked her head at me. "I'm surprised you are not angrier with all of this going on."

My face felt drawn tight as I tried to control the sudden emotion that pulsed in waves toward the surface. Perhaps the rest of my friends assumed that I was the same Kyri inside because the outside remained tractable and complaisant. But I thought for sure Ori would know what was hidden below. "Just because I am equable in the face of all the events inspired by my Shimax rival, do not assume that I am not incensed at those events. The anger eats at me below the surface but I know that it would do no one good to let it out. You and I both know the consequences of such an action. Never fear, my queen, I will remain in control."

"I disagree." My eyes widened at Ori's words. Had she so little faith in my strength and will? Shaking her head, she smiled at me. "She was never your rival, love. There has only been one woman for my heart and she is you. She has always been you." My heart and soul warmed with her love.

The remaining rounds for Chobos and Staves had already begun by the time we made our way back to our friends. We went back and forth watching Amazons from our own tribe and other women we were familiar with. Deata and Malva were doing quite well and I predicted they would both win Artemis statues with their staves. Alcina was also cutting a swath through the competition with Chobos. She was faced off against Baeza, the scout leader from Tanta tribe, when I grew concerned. Baeza was significantly smaller than the brawny princess, but she was very fast. However, Alcina was fast too and I knew it was only a matter of time before one of her heavy-handed hits did real damage to my Tanta friend. After a handful of candle drops into their fight that moment came. The princess did a fast disarm move and sent one of Baeza's chobos spinning away. Before the smaller woman could recover, Alcina brought a length of wood down on Baeza's left collarbone. The Tanta woman cried out in pain and her arm instantly fell to her side.

The match observer yelled out to stop the fight. "Hold!" But Alcina ignored her and brought the chobo around again and delivered a solid hit to Baeza's upper arm on the same injured side. The loud cracking sound was obvious to the gathered crowd. "Hold, hold, HOLD!" The observer ran into the sparring circle to make sure her words were obeyed the second time.

Alcina was smooth with her reaction and stepped back immediately with an apology. "I am sorry, Watcher. I got caught up in the moment and did not hear you the first time."

A nearby healer quickly led Baeza out of the sparring ring and began tending to her injuries. Based on the breaks, I knew that she would be healing for moons at the very least. I also knew that the scout leader would not be happy to be grounded from the trees. It was just another thing that added to my fury toward the Shimax princess and I hoped that her time to pay restitution for her dishonorable actions would soon come. I turned to Ori, who wore a strange expression on her face. "She did that on purpose."

Ori nodded. "I believe so, yes."

I turned and pulled her into my arms. With my mouth so near, I spoke just low enough for her to hear alone. "I do not trust her or her guard captain. Please use caution in the ring with Megara tomorrow. My gut is telling me that they have more planned."

She tightened her embrace at my words. "Don't worry, my

love. She will not beat me tomorrow." Alcina advanced and eventually beat a warrior from Varvara tribe for first place. Because both opponents for third were from Tanta, Baeza's competitor conceded the match to the injured scout leader, thus letting poor Baeza receive the statue for third. With any luck, she would not suffer any permanent damage from Alcina's malfeasance. The Tanta training master was victorious in the Staff competition. Deata took first and our veteran fourth scout, Malva, took second. A warrior from Shimax took third. Their competition did not seem to suffer the brutality that Chobos had though.

The last event of the day was Archery and I was ready. I had practiced nearly every day since the spring equinox and I knew that my arrows flew more accurate than they ever had before. More than half the competition had been eliminated on the first day, which left only sixteen for the final rounds. Our first shot was to be at the advanced pendulum target and many of the faces I recognized down the line from me looked determined. Ori and Cyerma had advanced to the final rounds with me after the first day. The only ones I recognized from the other tribes were Deesha, and Deata. It did not surprise me that the Tanta training master had advanced. She was one of the best archers I ever met besides my da.

The first round required us to either hit the pendulum or hit the center to stop the pendulum. Simply hitting the target without getting your arrow dashed away was not good enough to move you forward. Many people from Telequire were surprised when at the end of the round, three people had hit the pendulum to move on to the rings target, one of which was Deesha. Not only that, but three people besides me had stopped the pendulum with a center shot. Ori, Deata, and Cyerma were also moving on to the rings.

Because it was the end of the day after all the other events were finished, and because archery was a very popular competition in the Amazon nations, we had a very large crowd of spectators. Women were gathered behind the archers and many stood on logs or rocks and even perched in trees and on top of nearby huts to get a better view. To decide the shooting order, we all drew colored stones from a pouch. Once we had our color, the stones were drawn out one by one at random and that order determined who would shoot. Red, yellow, orange, black, green, brown, and blue were the words we all had in our heads. I had drawn out black so I found myself in the middle of the shooting order. Ori had drawn blue and would shoot at the end.

If any of the top three tied, they would shoot again to determine places. An archer from Dasi shot first and caught one ring with her arrow, and the next archer from Shimax did the same. Cyerma was third and did not disappoint when she caught three rings on her first shot. The crowd cheered and yelled at what seemed like an impossible feat and I began to sweat. After all, I had only ever caught three rings myself. As they removed her arrow I took my place and began my calming exercise. The crowd quieted as I drew one of my forest fletch arrows and took aim down field. I thought of all the things I had accomplished and all those things I had yet to prove. I glanced to my left to see Ori's face and my heart was left aflutter. Her eyes radiated the purest of love for me and I understood my da's words from so long ago. Those very words echoed in my head as I zeroed in on the rings dancing downfield.

"Kyri, your emotions will always control how you fly. Sadness will make you slow and imprecise. Anger will make you fast and careless. Never aim an arrow when you do not have complete control."

I let go of my sadness and my anger.

"Passion, love, and loyalty will give you the truest shots of all."

I closed my eyes and said a prayer to someone that existed only in my mind, then re-sighted my arrow. Before I could think more of the past, I released with a quiet thrum. The crowd exploded into a cacophony of noise all around me as my arrow caught all four rings with its solid length. It was not perfectly in the center but still within the red painted circle. While the win was not a guarantee with three more archers to follow, I was still proud of my shot. And I was even more proud of the legacy my da had left me. He was a good man who deserved every honor that I could give from my heart.

I stepped back so the next woman could come forward. She was another Amazon from Tanta tribe and she shot two rings which put her in third place at that point. After her, Deata stepped up to the shooting line. The Tanta training master also shot three rings and the crowd roared their approval. Ori was last to go and the crowd quickly quieted again as she drew and nocked her arrow. I was surprised to see that she used one of mine. I had not realized that she filled her quiver with my very own forest fletch arrows. In another surprise for the tournament, she too shot three rings which tied her with Deata and Cyerma. I had been assured my first place position but the other three would have to all shoot again to determine second and third.

On the second round, the spread was easily determined. I was saddened to see that Ori only caught one ring on her second shot, while Deata caught three and Cyerma caught two. I was awarded the first place Artemis statue and quickly made it to the side of my queen as her arrows were returned to her. "You had some very good shots today, I am sorry to see you did not win a statue for them."

She leaned up and gave me a tender kiss on the lips. "But I am not sorry to see you take first place, nor am I sorry to lose to the better archers. It tells me that the Amazon nations are well defended by bow and fletch."

The celebration that evening was rowdier than the days leading up to it. But the representatives of the various nations did not let loose of their inhibitions completely. There was still one more day of competition, with some of the most popular contests yet to be decided. The next morning dawned hotter than all the other festival days. Ori, Shana, Coryn, Basha, Steffi, Margoli, Kasichi, and Gerta all gathered in a group to watch Kylani in her bid for the first place statue in unarmed fighting. Even Dina, the Third Scout Leader, stayed up after her shift in the trees to see how our training master faired. It came down to two matches to determine who would fight for first. Kylani and Alcina both moved on to the final round. The third place match was won by a tough warrior from the Dasi tribe. As I stood shoulder to shoulder with my queen, awaiting the final match, I could feel my entire body tremble with tension. Ori jogged me with her elbow and I glanced away from the approaching unarmed combatants to see what she wanted. "Are you okay?"

I knew exactly what she was asking and I gave a short nod. "I am just nervous for her."

"Kylani?"

"Yes. I do not trust Alcina, especially after what she did yesterday with chobos. I do not trust her or any of her closest people not to use dirty tactics."

Ori grimaced. "Yes, I know what you mean. But Kylani is very good, she almost always wins the unarmed competitions within Telequire. While last sun-cycle was our first time competing in the Festival of Nations after so many seasons being held back by Lydella, she still took third place then." Alcina and Kylani entered the sparring ring and Ori glanced at me sideways. "I also know you've been teaching her some of the fighting techniques that you learned as a gladiatrix. I am sure she will be well able to defend herself."

I was startled by her quiet words. "How did you know?" Before she could answer, it came to me all on its own. "Kylani had to tell you as part of my reintegration, right?" Ori nodded. While I was not nearly as well trained as the gladiators that had spent sun-cycles battling in the arenas and forums, what little I had learned was deadly. When I told Kylani that I had trained from sun up to sun down, I was not exaggerating. I was nothing more than property, a beast of burden. I was worked as Isidorus and Aureolus saw fit, which was often. I probably could have requested a small amount of personal time but I did not for a few reasons. I had no want to sit with nothing to do other than lament my lack of freedom or the things that I had lost when I was stolen across the sea. I also wanted to become the best fighter that I was able so I could win our manumission papers to come home.

So while I trained in a majority of the gladiatorial fighting practices, there were only a few that I spent a significant amount of time on and excelled at. My riding and archery skills were first and foremost. I had also gotten quite good with a knife. My sword fighting was average at best and I was well aware of that fact. But the one thing that Aureolus wanted to be certain of was that I could still defend and kill should I be disarmed. The amount of time I spent studying the weakest parts of the human body was double to that that I spent learning sword technique.

Not only had I learned all the deadly Roman techniques, but I had cause to use them on too many occasions. I had not told Ori about my training in unarmed combat because it was another part of me that I tried to forget, that I did not want her to know about.

My attention was drawn outward again when the observer began speaking to the two woman in front of her. "I want you to fight clean, fight like Artemis is gazing down on you expecting honor. I do not want to see anything like what happened yesterday, is that clear, Princess Alcina?"

The princess gave a mock bow. "Yes, Watcher. Though it truly was an accident." The observer nodded and stepped back out of the ring. I wondered how many people actually believed that her actions the previous day were accidental or simply happened in the heat of the moment.

"Contestants, begin!" The official event observer called out the start of the match and Kylani and Alcina began circling each other warily. Alcina was a finger or two taller and broader than our own training master. She was also about eight cycles younger and her endurance would play a factor in their match. Alcina made the first move with double punches at the older woman's head. Kylani refused to be baited and dodged both. She was not fast enough to avoid the kick that followed the punches but she recovered quickly. A quarter candle mark went by as they traded blows back and forth. I was surprised to see that Kylani was not really using what I had taught her, but then again they were not moves for a competition of sport either. They were meant to disable and seriously harm your opponent.

Another handful of candle drops went by and I could see that Kylani was starting to tire against the strength and barrage of Alcina's blows. The end came fast as the princess followed up a long grappling session with a foot sweep that took Kylani to the ground. She quickly scrambled behind the training master to administer a nearly unbreakable headlock. Kylani slapped the ground in defeat and the Watcher entered the ring to declare Alcina winner. However, the princess had not let go of Kylani and she was fast losing consciousness. Luckily for my friend, Queen Alala was also watching the match.

"Alcina, release her now!" The queen's voice was not the higher pitched yell that many had but more of a loud bellow and easily garnered the princess's attention. Alcina quickly let Kylani go after that and the training master spent a few candle drops light-headed and drawing in rasping breaths of air. It was not only me that breathed a sigh of relief when Kylani proved fine, just winded. She graciously accepted the second place statue but I could see that anger had colored her features. The princess's actions had won her another potential enemy.

After the unarmed event was finished, there was a short break and the Knife matches started. The knives did not feature the level of violent drama that some of the Shimax driven events did and for that I was glad. I would have worried for my sister the entire time. In a surprising occurrence, Deka was out early with a knife wound to the shoulder. With Shana's biggest rival out of the action due to her injury, that left a slightly easier field for our ambassador. In the end it was Shana who took the first place statue, followed by Deesha and a warrior from Shebenik. I was pleasantly surprised at how well the Ujanik lead scout was doing in the competition. My only interaction with her had been during that time we dropped off the rescued women when we returned to Greece. But I had heard plenty of stories from her tribeswomen and knew she was a very capable and skilled First Scout Leader. Her actions at the Festival of Nations had certainly proved such declarations on the breadth of her skill.

There was a slightly longer break between the Knife final rounds and the beginning of the Sword. I walked with Ori back to our hut to retrieve her sword and on the way we stopped for a few tree bars in the food lodge. I fussed over her, worried about what Megara might do during the matches. "You should eat one more so you have plenty of strength for fighting. And drink some water too!"

Ori laughed and pushed the third bar away. "Kyri, love, enough already! I've had two and I'm plenty full. If I eat any more I'll feel slow in the ring. And everyone knows you don't win a sword fight by vomiting on your opponent."

I held my hands up in defeat. "Fine, if that is your last word I will heed it. But I am bringing two full water skins just so you can stay well hydrated!" She laughed but threaded her arm through mine as we walked. She knew why I was worried, and I knew she would be as safe as possible. She was no babe in the woods when it came to combat. She was my queen and I was certain that she was the best swordswoman the twelve nations would ever see.

Since the sword fighting was the last event of the festival and it was the most popular, everyone wanted to watch the matches. Because of that, they were moved to an open area that was in the southeast temple valley. Since the swordswomen fought in rings at the bottom of a natural bowl shaped by the land, it was easy for people to gather on the surrounding hillside and see the action. I was lucky enough to have a spot right near the front by all my closest friends. All but two of the healers were also standing at the ready since the sword matches usually resulted in the most injuries.

Dirt had been hauled to the area in carts to help level and pack down the ground where the rings were marked. Shana stood to my left, and Coryn was just on the other side of her. Certig and Basha stood to my right. As the rounds got started, I was happy to see that all of Ori's matches were quick and decisive. While she did not look as if her skill far surpassed her opponents, only a true master could control the fights so thoroughly. She elicited yields with neither injury to herself nor with a significant amount of time passing by. Every candle drop she saved herself from fighting would be a boon in energy when it came to the final match.

Despite what must have been a painful and exhausting final match in unarmed combat that morning, Kylani was back to finish the sword rounds as well. Eventually the third place round came down to Kylani facing off against a scarred Dasos Kato warrior who looked to be about the same age. Whether it was the other warrior's skill, or Kylani's waned stamina from her morning matches, I did not know, but she eventually fell to the Dasos Kato woman and missed out on a statue with her fourth place finish. There was a very short break after and I used it to give Ori one last embrace and a kiss for luck. Megara had of course made it to the final round and worry was like a heavy stone in my gut. My breathing had started to increase in anticipation and I purposely tried to calm down. "Kyri." My gaze was drawn to the left and I found Shana watching me intently.

"Yes?" She flicked her gaze down to where my hand was tightly clenched around the grip of my pugio. I released the blade abruptly with a curse. When her look turned to that of a question I had to speak my fears. "I worry for her and I do not trust Megara."

She nodded. "None of us trust her, including Ori. And that is why our queen will prevail. Relax." I nodded and tried to follow her example. Shana was not worried and she had seen Ori fight in more circumstances than I, so she would know best what she spoke of.

The fight began and I could tell that Megara was indeed good with a sword but I could also tell that Ori was holding back. To the average observer they looked well matched, and to perhaps Megara herself. But I knew Ori and had sparred against her many times. She began to pick up the pace and started driving the Shimax royal guard around the ring. Megara began to tire and make mistakes but Ori did not take advantage of them. Instead, she drew out the match even longer. Then in an instant rattling display of swordsmanship, she made a series of moves that left Megara disarmed and panting, her sword sitting in the dirt behind my queen. I thought for sure the match was done but there was a look in Megara's eye that I did not care for. "Do you yield?" Ori's voice was loud but that was not what I focused on.

Instead I watched Megara's gaze cut to Alcina and the princess gave a subtle nod. Megara's hand inched to a pouch on her side and fear coiled within my chest. I could not keep silent when I saw the hand dip below the flap. "Beware!" My warning came too late as a fine white powder flew into Ori's face. She immediately brought a hand to her eyes as she started choking on what she had inhaled. I moved to enter the ring and I was grabbed by both Coryn and Shana. "Let me go!" My voice was rough with distress. Before I could struggle within their grasp, Megara had rolled to the side and dove behind Ori for her sword. Then thinking my queen distracted with pain, she made to strike her from behind. Her sword never pierced flesh though. Just as she had done in the fight against me when my gladiatrix had taken control, Ori reversed her grip and drove her sword behind her. However, her thrust into Megara was no harmless strike intended to disarm her opponent. Ori had angled the blade up, thus piercing the Shimax guard's gut and further into her chest. Megara was dead before she hit the ground.

The crowd was left in shock but I quickly broke free from the hands that held me and rushed to Ori's side. "Healer!" I yelled in desperation, my heart racing with panic as Ori struggled for breath in my arms. It was like a nightmare come true. Her eyes were red and streaming with tears, already starting to swell. Semina was first to arrive and she bid me lay the queen on the ground so she could look at her. After setting her down I spun around and pounced on the first Shimax royal guard I saw, recognizing her from the trees the day they confronted me. "What powder was that?" I screamed in her face, spittle flying and flecking on her cheek and I did not care. My rage was rising as fast as my fear and they would all pay before the day was done. She looked afraid but did not answer so I drew my pugio with one hand and held it to her throat. "Tell me what it was!"

As a thin trickle of blood made its way down her neck her courage broke. Perhaps she thought me insane or saw that indeed I would take her life, but she started speaking, nothing like the voice of the braggadocio scout that had made fun of the pain we suffered in that Roman agora. "I—it is powder from the burning rock! She—she t—told us not to tell! I swear, Consort!"

I threw her down to the ground in disgust and ran back to where Thera was kneeling next to my love. "Did you hear?"

Thera nodded grimly. "Yes, she used lime powder, or quicklime. It is made from grinding limestone into dust."

I swallowed and asked the obvious as I watched Semina crush a mixture of herbs and garlic with a mortar and pedestal. "Is she blind then?"

The old healer patted my hand. "Fear not, young Kyri. She will be fine. Semina is making something that will help with her breathing and we have already flushed her eyes well with fresh water. We should keep them covered for a few days while they heal but she will not be blind. We will need to monitor the queen for the next moon to make sure she does not build up fluid in her chest and get the coughing sickness from the powder she inhaled."

I breathed in a sigh of relief and suddenly took in the rest of the gathered nations that stood around. None of them had heard Thera's words and all worried about our queen. I was uncomfortable with the thought of being the voice of information but knew that something had to be said. I stood and spun in a circle to take in the large crowd that surrounded the sparring ring and moved my gaze to look at the ones up on the hillside. I used the same voice that had once belonged to a sagittarius in the lands of Rome, a voice that was pitched to be heard by the spectators all around me. "Queen Orianna has been temporarily blinded by the dishonorable act of the Shimax royal guard. However, she will heal and be better within a few days."

My gaze landed on Basha's pale face and Shana's grip upon Coryn's forearm. A cheer went up as I noticed Ori getting to her feet behind me. Stomping and clapping greeted my warrior queen as she proved that she could not be kept down by the likes of Megara, blind or no. Her eyes had a cloth tied around them and her lips seemed a little blue, but her breathing looked much easier after the garlic. I had no idea that it could help with breathing in such a way. I had not learned about those types of remedies in my training with Thera, just emergency treatments. My blood had started to calm with the realization that Ori was safe and the Shimax drama was over. The festival events were finished and all that was left was the closing ceremony and the feast. After that I would have been happy to never lay eyes on another Shimax Amazon again. My calm proved short-lived.

"Queen Orianna, I issue a challenge for your mask!"

The murmuring of a few thousand Amazons broke over those of us in the center like a tidal wave. Sweet old Thera surprised me with her shout back. "She cannot fight now, you vile bitch!"

Alcina pushed her way through the crowd until she reached the sparring ring then turned to face Basha. "I know that, crone. I guess her regent will have to defend the mask for her."

Basha blanched and her face was a study of fear and panic. She was no match for the brute princess and she well knew it. Queen Alala also pushed her way through the crowd. "Daughter, do not do this. You and your guards have brought dishonor on our entire nation with your actions. Do not make things worse for you!"

The princess sneered. "What could be worse than waiting for you to die so that I could become queen? I deserve the monarch's mask and I will wait no longer! You should be happy that I'm not challenging you, old woman!" I knew why she did not challenge her own mother. There were rules that made it difficult to become queen in such a way. With any other challenger, you simply had to win to become queen. But if you were challenging your own family member, the council had to approve with a majority vote or you would not wear the mask even if you won. The nation would turn against you. And I doubted their council would approve such a thing, Alcina was rotten to the core. Gasps echoed through the crowd at her disrespectful words and Queen Alala's response was swift and harsh.

"Banishment."

Alcina laughed and turned back to Basha. "I'll take my chances. Step forward now and defend your queen's mask!" Megara's body had been taken away right after Ori fell so the ring was empty.

I heard a soft sound behind me, quiet and pleading. When I turned to look, I saw Ori standing next to Thera, holding the old woman's hand with a white-knuckled grip. "Kyri." She said nothing more than my name but I remembered the rules and knew what she was asking of me.

"No!"

The princess turned to me with a look of surprise. "You cannot stop a challenge that is legally given, *Consort*." She said my title with scorn, with a sneer, indicating just how she felt about my place within the tribe.

I smiled at her as Kyrius plunged to the surface. My sagittarius, my gladiatrix, she had been called to serve and obeyed with relish. "No, I cannot stop a challenge. But as Consort to the queen I can accept the challenge in her place. Name your weapon, Alcina." I did not even bother with a title for her. She deserved nothing from me but pain.

Alcina laughed again but it seemed empty and I wondered how much of an effect her mother's words actually had on her. "Chobos. Let's see how the doulé does with a real Amazon weapon!"

By Amazon law her challenge was allowed and had to be seen through. Kylani sent a runner for the official challenge weapons and we waited. In the interim, the training master brought me a skin of water. She offered words of advice as well. "Do not let her draw you into close contact with those chobos. I know you are not well practiced at that weapon and it would surely mean your loss. If you can, get her to fight unarmed and do not hold back on her!" I looked up at the venom in her voice. Calm, stern, unflappable Kylani had never used such a tone in my presence. "Do you hear me, Kyri? She had her woman blind our queen, your bond mate!"

Anger filled me, bloated me full and I nodded. I pushed the emotion down to leave a cold emptiness behind. Rage could not be my guide for such a fight because I needed to keep my wits about me. I glanced over to Ori's unseeing face and knew what my guide was to be. I would use anger as my fuel instead. When the runner returned with the weapons, Kylani inspected them to make sure they had not been tampered with, as had happened with the previous queen. Alcina and I were each handed a pair and left by ourselves in the ring. There was no call to start, we merely began circling.

I had a plan and for it to succeed I had to make her think she had the upper hand. Alcina was a bully and reveled in physically dominating those she saw as weak. While weapons were required in a royal challenge, any fighting was allowed after the match had begun. Faster than her bulk implied, she came at me striking high and low at the same time. The wood made loud clacks with each hit I defended and I danced back out of her reach. More and more I had to resort to my quick feet to avoid her hits or turn them away, but I was not skilled enough in chobos to do any damage in return. In one particular exchange, she caught a glancing blow just above my left eyebrow, opening a gash that dripped blood. It felt hotter than sweat and twice as thick as it trickled around my brow and down my temple. I quickly wiped it with my forearm and circled back out of the way.

Her eyes narrowed and nostrils flared as she watched the red essence of life drip from my face and I knew it was time. Alcina was a beast, an animal that wanted to see a slow progression of physical injury so I offered myself up to her. During another rapid rattling of chobo on chobo action, I let my grip loosen and both weapons went flying out of my hands. I did a tumbling roll to come up behind her and gave the bigger woman a kick to the backside. The crowd gasped as she came up furious, face red and contorted with rage. I added to it with my words. "What's the matter *princess*, do you not like being kicked around by a slave? You think you are a good fighter? You would have been nothing more than a slow moving beast in the arena!" She screamed and dropped the chobos, charging me with both hands balled into fists. I waited until the last possible heartbeat then grabbed her wrists in my hands and dropped to my back. She flipped over the top of my prone body and landed hard on her own back, the breath momentarily knocked from her chest. I quickly rushed over to her chobos and threw them from the ring out of her reach. If I was going to fight her, it would be on my terms.

She rolled to her feet, unwilling to give up so easy. "You think you can defeat me with your fancy tricks, doulé? I'm going to break you slow, like the Romans failed to do!"

Alcina came at me again with a flurry of punches. I swept away most and blocked the rest, then gave her a solid knee to the abdomen. She quickly recovered and moved in to grapple, assuming her greater size would win against me. She got hold of both my wrists but I foot swept her again and dumped her to the ground. Angrier than before, she threw a wild punch with her left hand but I caught her fist and gave the entire arm a great twist behind her. I knew from experience that the pain was excruciating but she continued to fight me. "Yield, Alcina! You are no match for me and I am trying very hard not to hurt you."

She laughed and her face took on a zealous expression very similar to the last gladiatrix I fought for the gold laurel. I faltered at the look and she twisted away. "I'll tell you what is to happen today, doulé. I am going to kill you, then I will sentence your queen to a slow torturous death and both your bodies will be left to feast the crows!" My face must have finally shown the internal fury that seethed within me. "Oh, is that not a fitting end for the sagittarius they called 'Kyrius?' Do you miss them calling the name of their favorite slave, the whore of Roman noblemen?"

Her words seared me and burned me into a cold madness. The memory came back of the taunting under the hot sun, of the blood and sweat of the other gladiators, of my pain. Thinking me distracted, she swung again and I caught her hand. Just as fast I used my palm to punch the side of her elbow and snap the joint. She howled in pain and tried to kick me away. I blocked it and delivered a hard blow to her kneecap with my heel. The leg joint was no match for such an assault and it broke, leaving bone sticking out of the skin. She dropped to the ground in agony and I flew at her, straddling her waist. She screamed again as I drew my right hand back to deliver a killing blow. The crowds were chanting around me and all I knew was the glory of a battle won. My fingers were curled to lead the blow with the base of my palm but I remained frozen. Gradually the crowd quieted and my arm started to tremble. Alcina looked up at me with hatred in her eyes and spat blood in my face. "What's the matter, slave? Are you afraid to kill me with honor? You are nothing, you will always be nothing! A doulé could never be a true Amazon."

I was snapped out of my daze by the sound of a scratchy roar.

Gata had somehow found her way through the crowd and stood at the edge of the circle. As my gaze wandered to the cat that I had saved two sun cycles prior, I felt Alcina shift beneath me. I looked back just in time to catch her knife hand before the blade could pierce my gut. It took all my weight upon her remaining good arm but I pointed the blade toward her own chest and drove it home. Death was never a pretty thing, nor was it clean. She gasped a few times while I held the dagger in place, then finally the light left her eyes. They remained sightless and staring as her bodily functions were released with her passing, and I quickly rolled off her to the side. I had never watched someone's eyes from so close as the life left their body and it was an experience I never wanted to go through again. A shadow fell over me as Queen Alala came near and dropped to the dirt on her knees. She slowly reached a hand down to close her daughter's eyelids then took in my battered and bloody face. I knew her heart felt the pain of Alcina's passing just as surely as she knew that I would do it all over again if given the chance. There was no other option where the princess was concerned. I gave her the only words I had left after such a violent and pointless death. "I am sorry."

She gave her daughter one last glance then stood and looked down on me. "I am too." She walked away from the sparring ring then and the crowd opened up to let her pass.

Shana and Coryn came running over, followed closely by Ori who was led by Basha. "Kyri?"

I pulled myself into a standing position and moved to take Ori into my arms. She clung to me tightly and I let her presence soothe my racing heart. "I tried not to kill her."

Kylani had walked up with the rest and looked over as a group of Shimax scouts came to collect Alcina's body. "She gave you no choice."

I did not release my queen, but I followed the direction of the princess's body with my eyes. "No, I suppose she did not.

Epilogue

THE CLOSING CEREMONY of the Festival of Nations felt subdued for all. Deesha was voted as top all around warrior of the tournament and I was happy to see such an honor go to one of the smallest tribes. I had been given to understand that the feast on the last night of competition was normally one of much gaiety and celebration. But death and dishonor cast a pall over all twelve assembled nations. The very next day Ori and Queen Alala spent nearly two candle marks in conference together before Queen Alala led her people home. Over the following days the rest of the nations also took their leave, each queen stopping in to give condolences and prayers for quick healing to my queen. By the time all our visitors had left Telequire, Ori's sight was well enough to remove the bandage. Her eyes were still irritated but her eyesight, for the most part, had returned to normal.

It took another moon before her breathing and strength returned though. The entire time I never left her side for longer than a candle mark. We took walks together, we bathed together, and we ate our meals in the quiet of our hut. Despite the fact that killing Alcina had given over just a little bit more of me to Kyrius, I could not help but feel as though the events that happened during the festival had brought the queen and I closer together. There were no more obstacles, there were no more enemies, just the two of us.

Once Ori began attending sessions with the council again, I started working with Kylani to look for ways to improve and expand our training. It was a warm day that found me at the archery range while my queen was in another long meeting with the council members, Basha, Margoli, and Steffi. She warned me that they would be late and asked if I would wait for her to eat evening meal. So instead of making my way to the meal lodge I decided to spend time at the archery range. Shana found me as I was finishing off the last quiver I wanted to shoot. "Kylani is going to have to come up with a greater challenge for you, Consort."

I made a face at her and shrugged. "I will do my best no matter what she thinks up, you know that. And since when did you start calling me Consort?"

She grinned. "Since just now when I realized it would irritate you." Shana laughed and I gave her a punch to the arm. She walked with me downfield to retrieve my arrows and we walked back together in silence until we once again reached the shooting line.

"So what brings you out here, just the will and want to torment me?"

She sighed and took a seat on a nearby log. Sensing a serious discussion I put my bow back into my gorytos and sat down next to her. "I actually had something to tell you."

I felt a little concern because I could think of no reason for my sister to be so serious. "What is wrong?" A quick thought flashed through my head and I turned to her in dismay. "There are no problems between you and Coryn, are there?"

Shana shook her head quickly, causing a mass of curls to bounce with her rite of caste feather and her jade green ambassador feather. "Goddess no, but it does have to do with her."

I looked at her close with curiosity crawling up my spine. "Oh?"

"Did you know that it has been almost exactly two sun cycles since you first came to Telequire?"

I blinked at her abrupt change of topic. "I had not really thought about it but I suppose you are right." I looked toward the trees, thinking back to my arrival to the village. Injured and with a leopard cub in my care, I felt very inadequate in the face of so much change. "It seems like a lifetime ago." I turned my gaze back to Shana's intense eyes, noticing a different look than what I had seen before. "What does that have to do with you and Coryn?"

"I have known you less than twenty-five moons, yet you are blood to me. You are my only family I have left. I have known Coryn my entire life and she continues to surprise me."

I took in her distressed features and haunted eyes. "Has she done something to upset you?"

"Yes. No. I—I don't know."

My arm felt natural around her slim shoulders as I pulled her close. "Tell me what is wrong, sister."

She shook her head. "It's not wrong exactly, I think it's supposed to be all right."

"You are confusing me."

She laughed and it sounded strange. "I'm confusing myself." I waited for her to continue, knowing that she had to work things around in her mind before she could let the thoughts out. "She offered me her feather today."

Her words left me momentarily mute though I should have figured Coryn for the braver of the two of them. Finally, I found voice to speak. "And? Will you accept?"

Shana sighed. "I wanted to speak with you first. You have none of my fears or history coloring your views. What do you think of Coryn, honestly? Do you see a future between us?"

I thought for a heartbeat then took her nearest hand between both of mine. There was a fine tremble hidden within her fingertips and I tried my best to soothe her fear. "Coryn is a good woman, one of my very best friends and I do not say that lightly. I trust her with my life and with the heart of my very dearest sister and friend. But there can only be a future between you if that is what you wish for." I shook her hand to draw her gaze up to mine. "Is that what you want?" As if our thoughts of her alone had drawn the First Scout Leader from the ether, she appeared around the corner of the scout hut and began walking in our direction. Her gaze never even strayed to me, it stayed firmly planted on Shana. And Coryn's look said everything that was in her heart. I repeated my question while Shana watched her lover approach. "Do you want her future?"

Shana looked over at me and smiled and I had never seen her so happy. The strength of that one look alone caught the breath in my throat. "Yes." Then as Coryn walked up she stood and repeated that single word, only the second time it had significantly more meaning. "Yes."

I also stood and walked away. With one last backward glance, I left my friend and sister to their embrace. As I came around the corner of our hut, I nearly ran into Ori as she was exiting. She carried a fur over one shoulder, a wine skin over the other, and a basket in her hand. I stepped back in surprise so as to not knock her to the ground. "Are you going somewhere, my queen?"

She smiled at me mischievously. "That is a very astute observation, Consort. I am heading up to the top of temple hill to take evening meal with our Goddess. Would you care to join me?"

I laughed and took the basket into my own hand to carry. "How could I turn down the company of such a beautiful woman, and you too of course."

"Woods weasel!" Ori bumped me with her shoulder as we made our way down the path that followed the setting sun. A quarter candle mark later we were seated on the fur that had been laid out at the base of the great statue of Artemis. Ori rested between my legs with her back a solid warmth against my chest. I sat with my own back propped by the base that held our Goddess. The sun had turned the sky deep red and stars were in clear view on the opposite horizon. I did not retrieve the food right away because the view was much too pretty to interrupt with such things as physical sustenance. Instead, we spent precious candle drops filling our souls. "Have you ever wished upon the setting sun or the rising stars?" Ori's voice sounded young and wistful, like the world had never once crashed down upon her shoulders.

I thought about her question for nearly a candle drop. My own voice grew quiet and young too as words began to fall from my lips. "I have wished upon many things. Spring rains and a well-made arrow. The weeping willow where my mam was buried and on all the celestial bodies in the heavens. I learned long ago that it is on the back side of need that we discover want."

She turned her head to look up at me. "But what does that mean?"

I sighed and held her tighter. "It means that I have never once wished for something I needed. My wishes were saved for my heart's desires alone. I wished many times for the lives of my mam and my da, though the loss of neither put me in peril."

"What else?"

I placed a reverent kiss on the top of her head as the ball of hot light sank below the horizon. "I wished for you every single day that you were not in my life."

Ori turned to look at me with humored astonishment. "Surely not before we met!"

I nodded and smiled at her, my heart aching with all that I had been gifted with in life. "Especially before we met. I wished every day for a home and a heart full of love. My life with you has at last given me my heart's desire."

My queen graced me with a shy smile. "I don't know what to say."

I grinned and stole one of Shana's lines. "Say thank you, Kyri."

"Just what am I thanking you for?"

"This!" I rolled her back and to the side and began kissing every inch of her skin that I could reach.

Ori giggled at the onslaught and tried to be the voice of reason between us. "But what about our plans to share a meal with the Goddess?"

I glanced up at the stone huntress, whose gaze peered into the heavens above as she sighted her great bow. Ori looked at me curiously as I gave her a wicked smile. "The Goddess already knows what I am hungry for." I was happy. While Artemis was not real to me the way she was to the rest of the Amazons, to my queen, I loved the notion of her. In the rising darkness, with stars twinkling overhead and blazing sky slowly dying like cold embers, I worshipped Artemis's Chosen, my goddess-made-flesh. With every kiss and every single touch, I showed her my heart and received hers in return. The history of us had become our future.

About the Author

Born and raised in Michigan, Kelly is a latecomer to the writing scene. She works in the automotive industry coding in Visual basic and Excel. Her avid reading and writing provide a nice balance to the daily order of data, allowing her to juggle passion and responsibility. Her writing style is as varied as her reading taste and it shows as she tackles each new genre with glee. But beneath it all, no matter the subject or setting, Kelly carries a core belief that good should triumph. She's not afraid of pain or adversity, but loves a happy ending. She's been pouring words into novels since 2015 and probably won't run out of things to say any time soon.

OTHER YELLOW ROSE PUBLICATIONS

Brenda Adcock	Soiled Dove	978-1-935053-35-4
Brenda Adcock	The Sea Hawk	978-1-935053-10-1
Brenda Adcock	The Other Mrs. Champion	978-1-935053-46-0
Brenda Adcock	Picking Up the Pieces	978-1-61929-120-1
Brenda Adcock	The Game of Denial	978-1-61929-130-0
Brenda Adcock	In the Midnight Hour	978-1-61929-188-1
Brenda Adcock	Untouchable	978-1-61929-210-9
Brenda Adcock	The Heart of the Mountain	978-1-61929-330-4
K. Aten	The Fletcher	978-1-61929-356-4
K. Aten	Rules of the Road	978-1-61919-366-3
K. Aten	The Archer	978-1-61929-370-0
K. Aten	The Sagittarius	978-1-61929-386-1
Georgia Beers	Thy Neighbor's Wife	1-932300-15-5
Georgia Beers	Turning the Page	978-1-932300-71-0
Lynnette Beers	Just Beyond the Shining River	978-1-61929-352-6
Carrie Carr	Faith's Crossing	1-932300-12-0
Carrie Carr	Love's Journey	978-1-932300-65-9
Carrie Carr	Trust Our Tomorrows	978-1-61929-011-2
Carrie Carr	Heart's Resolve	978-1-61929-051-8
Carrie Carr	Beyond Always	978-1-61929-160-7
Sharon G. Clark	A Majestic Affair	978-1-61929-177-5
Tonie Chacon	Struck! A Titanic Love Story	978-1-61929-226-0
Cooper and Novan	Madam President	978-1-61929-316-8
Cooper and Novan	First Lady	978-1-61929-318-2
Sky Croft	Amazonia	978-1-61929-067-9
Sky Croft	Amazonia: An Impossible Choice	978-1-61929-179-9
Sky Croft	Mountain Rescue: The Ascent	978-1-61929-099-0
Sky Croft	Mountain Rescue: On the Edge	978-1-61929-205-5
Cronin and Foster	Blue Collar Lesbian Erotica	978-1-935053-01-9
Cronin and Foster	Women in Uniform	978-1-935053-31-6
Cronin and Foster	Women in Sports	978-1-61929-278-9
Jane DiLucchio	A Change of Heart	978-1-61929-324-3
A. L. Duncan	The Gardener of Aria Manor	978-1-61929-159-1
A.L. Duncan	Secrets of Angels	978-1-61929-227-7
Anna Furtado	The Heart's Desire	978-1-935053-81-1
Anna Furtado	The Heart's Strength	978-1-935053-82-8
Anna Furtado	The Heart's Longing	978-1-935053-83-5
Anna Furtado	Tremble and Burn	978-1-61929-354-0
Pauline George	Jess	978-1-61929-139-3
Pauline George	199 Steps To Love	978-1-61929-213-0
Pauline George	The Actress and the Scrapyard Girl	978-1-61929-336-6
Melissa Good	Eye of the Storm	1-932300-13-9
Melissa Good	Hurricane Watch	978-1-935053-00-2
Melissa Good	Moving Target	978-1-61929-150-8
Melissa Good	Red Sky At Morning	978-1-932300-80-2
Melissa Good	Storm Surge: Book One	978-1-935053-28-6

Melissa Good	Storm Surge: Book Two	978-1-935053-39-2
Melissa Good	Stormy Waters	978-1-61929-082-2
Melissa Good	Thicker Than Water	1-932300-24-4
Melissa Good	Terrors of the High Seas	1-932300-45-7
Melissa Good	Tropical Storm	978-1-932300-60-4
Melissa Good	Tropical Convergence	978-1-935053-18-7
Melissa Good	Winds of Change Book One	978-1-61929-194-2
Melissa Good	Winds of Change Book Two	978-1-61929-232-1
Melissa Good	Southern Stars	978-1-61929-348-9
Regina A. Hanel	Love Another Day	978-1-61929-033-4
Regina A. Hanel	WhiteDragon	978-1-61929-143-0
Regina A. Hanel	A Deeper Blue	978-1-61929-258-1
Jeanine Hoffman	Lights & Sirens	978-1-61929-115-7
Jeanine Hoffman	Strength in Numbers	978-1-61929-109-6
Jeanine Hoffman	Back Swing	978-1-61929-137-9
Jennifer Jackson	It's Elementary	978-1-61929-085-3
Jennifer Jackson	It's Elementary, Too	978-1-61929-217-8
Jennifer Jackson	Memory Hunters	978-1-61929-294-9
K. E. Lane	And, Playing the Role of Herself	978-1-932300-72-7
Kate McLachlan	Christmas Crush	978-1-61929-195-9
Lynne Norris	One Promise	978-1-932300-92-5
Lynne Norris	Sanctuary	978-1-61929-248-2
Lynne Norris	Second Chances (E)	978-1-61929-172-0
Lynne Norris	The Light of Day	978-1-61929-338-0
Paula Offutt	Butch Girls Can Fix Anything	978-1-932300-74-1
Schramm and Dunne	Love Is In the Air	978-1-61929-362-8
Patty Schramm	Because of Katie	978-1-61929-380-9
Surtees and Dunne	True Colours	978-1-61929-021-1
Surtees and Dunne	Many Roads to Travel	978-1-61929-022-8
Barbara Valletto	Diver Blues	978-1-61929-384-7

Be sure to check out our other imprints,
Blue Beacon Books, Mystic Books, Quest Books,
Silver Dragon Books, Troubadour Books, and Young Adult Books.

VISIT US ONLINE AT
www.regalcrest.biz

At the Regal Crest Website You'll Find

- The latest news about forthcoming titles and new releases
- Our complete backlist of romance, mystery, thriller and adventure titles
- Information about your favorite authors
- Media tearsheets to print and take with you when you shop
- Which books are also available as eBooks.

Regal Crest print titles are available from all progressive booksellers including numerous sources online. Our distributors are Bella Distribution and Ingram.

CPSIA information can be obtained
at www.ICGtesting.com
Printed in the USA
FFHW02n0409210818
47834417-51519FF